TRAIL TO DESTINY

TRAIL TO DESTINY

A Novel

Cheri Kay Clifton

iUniverse, Inc.
New York Lincoln Shanghai

Trail To Destiny
A Novel

Copyright © 2007 by Cheri Kay Clifton

iUniverse books may be ordered through booksellers or by contacting:

iUniverse
2021 Pine Lake Road, Suite 100
Lincoln, NE 68512
www.iuniverse.com
1-800-Authors (1-800-288-4677)

Because of the dynamic nature of the Internet, any Web addresses or links contained in this book may have changed since publication and may no longer be valid.

This is a work of fiction. All of the characters, names, incidents, organizations, and dialogue in this novel are either the products of the author's imagination or are used fictitiously.

ISBN: 978-0-595-46934-5 (pbk)
ISBN: 978-0-595-91218-6 (ebk)

Printed in the United States of America

For my loving husband, Mel
And son, Chad

And in memory of Mom

Do not go where the path may lead.
Go instead where there is no path
and leave a trail …

Ralph Waldo Emerson
(1803–1882)

ACKNOWLEDGMENTS

My heartfelt appreciation to the following people for
their help with this book: Pat Sciranko and Sharon Scherdin
for their thoughtful critiques; Martin Little and Buffy Flowers
who closely resembled my main characters and posed for the
book cover; and Karol Clifton to whom I'm grateful for her
friendship and support.

Prologue

Indian Country, 1845

Ten-year-old David walked along the creek bed, proudly gripping the bow and arrow he'd made himself. He'd tied turkey feathers to each end of the small bow and decorated the arrow with colorful stripes just like ones used by Indians. He ignored a rabbit that dashed back in its hole and continued searching for tracks of deer or elk. So eager was he to see his father's look of pride when he returned with such bounty, he gave little consideration to how he could bring back the burden by himself, or the skill required to kill large game with a bow and arrow.

Looking up through the overhanging branches, he squinted at the sun beaming down from the center of the sky. He'd promised his mother he would be back in time to study his reading lesson with Glen before the noon meal. He knew he'd ventured too far from home and started retracing his tracks.

As he approached a large clearing, he stopped abruptly, straining to see through the distant grove of cottonwoods trailing the stream back to his family's homestead. Why did everything look so dark and hazy? His gaze lifted higher. The sight raised the hair on the back of his neck. Ominous billows of black smoke rose above the treetops and swirled across the pale blue sky. An acrid smell wafted through his nostrils.

Swallowing his fear, he continued walking at an even pace, but he couldn't convince himself that only some dry brush had caught fire. Something much larger was burning. Something in the direction of home.

Suddenly, a scream split the air, followed by the sharp crack of a musket. No longer able to hold back his fear, David hurled aside his bow and arrow and raced through the tall grass. He reached the far side of the glen, jumped a ditch, and scrambled up the other side. He clawed through the thick under-brush, thrashing his way closer to the acrid smoke. Sweat mixed with tears of fright stung his eyes.

Piercing yells echoed through the thickets. When he reached the open road next to the corral, the sight yanked the breath from David's lungs. He stood frozen. His home was ablaze, flames leaping out the windows and shooting up through the roof. The fire roared in his ears. From where he stood, he felt its intense heat, yet he shuddered as cold, icy terror took hold of him.

Painted Indians astride shaggy ponies were rounding up the horses and mules from the corral. He recognized their shields and lances. They were the Pawnees he and his father had seen a few days ago on their way to the trading post. Herding the animals into the dense woods, the marauders swiftly made their escape.

David looked around. His insides began to shake with panic. *Where are Ma and Pa? Where's Glen?*

He saw his father lying on the ground next to the corral gate, an arrow pro-truding from his chest. He ran over and knelt beside him. "Pa … Pa?" He lifted his father's head. No words came from his mouth. No sound, no breath. Noth-ing but a thin trickle of blood. He lowered him to the ground and then stood, looking for his mother.

He caught sight of her lying beside the garden. A scream exploded from his throat. "Mother-r-r!"

He ran past the burning house and flung himself down next to her. His mother's beautiful, long auburn hair had been scalped from her head. Blood oozed down the side of her face and her eyes, devoid of any further pain, stared up at the heavens. David looked away, a wave of nausea gripping his stomach.

When he was finally able to look at her again, he saw something in her out-stretched hand. Shaking uncontrollably, he picked up the cameo his mother had always worn and clutched the pendant in his fist.

Turning to look at what was once his home, he cried out his brother's name. "Glen?" His only answer was the howl and hiss of flames devouring the wood cabin.

Shock replaced reality. Time stopped everything but the gentle breeze that tossed David's hair about his face. Dreamlike, he stood and walked back toward the corral where his father lay. The prone, lifeless body of a Pawnee lay sprawled a short distance away, a gaping hole in his back.

Slowly, he scanned the vicinity and there, crumpled against the wall of the stable was Glen, a knife driven in his side, and an arrow sticking into his thigh. Circles of bright red colored the boy's shirt and pants. A musket lay by his body.

David thought how strangely peaceful his brother looked, as if he were sleeping. Squeezing his eyes shut, he bowed his head in despair. Glen wasn't asleep. He was dead. Like Ma and Pa.

The soul-wrenching sight of his family's bloody massacre was too much for him. Shock gave way to fury. He screamed with helpless rage and dropped to the ground. Gripping his mother's cameo, he pounded the earth with his fists.

Tears streamed down his face. His hands throbbed from cuts and bruises, but still he continued to beat the hard earth in a desperate need to release the pent-up rage against this horrible fate—the agony of being left alive but alone, when all he loved and lived for were dead.

David didn't know how long he'd lain in the dirt, his chest convulsing with dry, wracking sobs. The fire was spent, leaving only the smoldering ruins of his home. Numb, he rose to his feet and rubbed his forehead, trying to gain control of his thoughts.

The sound of approaching horses jarred his mind back into focus. More savages came into view. From their garb and weapons, David knew they were a different tribe than the Pawnee raiders.

Fear propelled him toward the protection of the woods. He tripped and stumbled his way along the high bank of the stream. Stealing a glance over his shoulder, he saw the small band stop to look at the destruction. Then several of them pointed in his direction.

Desperately, David searched for somewhere to hide. Hearing the horses picking up speed and getting closer, he leaped over the edge of the steep embankment. Sliding down the rocky slope, he spied a large, empty burrow and crawled inside. He tried to conceal himself by tucking his legs under him. Then he turned his face toward the opening.

Minutes later, horses' hooves thudded to a halt directly above the small den. Dirt and rocks tumbled around David. As the seconds crept by, he wished with every beat of his pounding heart that he were a wolf hiding in his den.

He sucked in a deep breath when a pair of buckskin-clad leggings and moccasinned feet slid in front of his cramped hideout. Suddenly, a bronze face appeared in the opening. Vermilion-painted cheeks lifted into a stiff smile, and animal black eyes stared into David's grey ones.

Hours later, as the small army patrol rode past the charred remains of the ravaged homestead, a pall of grey smoke floated around the soldiers like an eerie fog, and every man sensed death before actually seeing it.

The lieutenant in command dismounted and stood in front of the first body they found. Near him lay a second body, an Indian.

"Damn Pawnees again," he said to the soldier who had dismounted beside him. The lieutenant looked past the corral. "Search the area, Sergeant. I suspect we'll be burying more than these two."

It took only a few minutes after the sergeant had issued the order for the dragoons to find two more bodies—a woman bludgeoned to death and scalped, and another lying next to the stable, an arrow and knife protruding from him.

"Damn shame. This one's only a kid," the officer said, peering down.

Frowning, the sergeant knelt and took hold of the boy's wrist, then opened one of his eyelids. "My God, sir, he's still alive!"

Pennsylvania, 1845

Five-year-old Laura Westbrook swung her legs over the side of the bed, tucking her favorite dolly under her arm. She peered through the dawn's waning darkness at Alex lying in his bed opposite hers. His rust-red hair had fallen across his closed eyelids, and a skinny arm hung over the bedside. She could hear Papa and Mister Dan's voices downstairs.

Laura crossed the room and quietly opened the door. She eased through the narrow opening. Mister Dan's voice grew louder. Quickly, she closed the door behind her, not wanting to awaken her brother.

"John, I've taken about all the city life I can handle."

Laura knelt by the banister at the top of the stairs. She leaned against the wooden post, clinging to it with one hand, the other holding her dolly. She looked through the open doorway of the kitchen where Mister Dan sat at the table opposite her father.

"More to the point, I've taken about all of your mourning for Lucy I can handle. I'm sorry for being so blunt, but it's been six months since the accident. It's time to stop brooding about the past, my friend, and start—"

Wham! Her father slammed his fist on the table. "Enough! You've said enough!" He rose abruptly, sending the chair clattering backward to the floor. Grabbing his cup from the table, he walked to the cook stove.

Laura bit her lower lip. Papa was upset again. She watched him pour himself more coffee. Since Momma had gone to heaven, he'd changed. He didn't seem to know she and Alex were still living there. He no longer read stories to her or helped her brother with his school work. Aunt Sarah kept saying he would soon be like the Papa Laura had always loved—happy and laughing. She remembered how he would sneak up behind Momma and kiss her on the neck, making her happy and laughing, too.

The sound of chair legs scraping across the floor interrupted her thoughts. Mister Dan stood and bowed his head. He was very tall with massive shoulders. Laura had been frightened by his size when she first met him last year, but she liked him now, especially after he'd given her the baby doll for her birthday.

Often he came over to sit in the parlor with Papa in the evenings while Aunt Sarah washed the dishes and put her and Alex to bed. Sometimes he'd eat Sunday dinner with them at Aunt Sarah and Uncle James's house.

Dan released a deep sigh. He walked around the table and set Papa's chair upright. "John … make up your mind." Her father remained tight-lipped, staring out the window, his gaunt figure supported by a thin, outstretched arm braced against the wooden frame.

"I can't stay any longer. Are you leaving with me or not?" Dan demanded.

"Yes, damn it! God, yes, I need to get away from here." John shook his head. "I'm no good to anybody, least of all my kids. Be best if Sarah took them to raise."

Laura's eyes widened. Her father's words resounded up the stairs, their meaning slapping her in the face. *I need to get away from here.* Her fingers tightened around the banister. Papa was leaving!

Hearing the door at the front of the house open, Laura scurried out of sight. When her aunt stepped into the hallway, she quickly returned to her bedroom, closing the door behind her.

Standing in the entry, Sarah Osbourne removed her shawl and bonnet and placed them on a chair. She rubbed her hands together to ward off the chill from her early morning walk to her brother's house. "Landsakes," she whispered, "that wind is brisk."

She noticed a light in the kitchen and called out to her brother. "John, are you—" She faltered when Dan stepped out from the doorway. Clasping her hands, she asked, "Daniel, why are you here this time of day?" Her gaze darted from him to the kitchen, then back to him. "What's the matter? Is John all right? The children …"

Dan laid a hand on her shoulder. "The children are fine. They're still asleep. I came over to talk to John." His eyes met hers. "Sarah, I'm leaving tomorrow."

"Leaving … tomorrow?" she repeated, her voice breaking. She skirted around him and into the kitchen.

John stood at the window. He gave Sarah a cursory glance before returning his gaze outside. Taking her apron from its hook beside the cook stove, she cleared her throat. "If you two men will give me a few minutes, I'll fix some breakfast."

"I'm not hungry," muttered John.

It was the way he said it. No, more than that, it was the way he'd spoken to her for the past six months. Pitching the apron aside, Sarah spat out her words in a voice seething with anger. "John, I can't take your self-pity any longer! It's those children upstairs you should pity. But you don't seem to care about *them* anymore." Her voice trembled with emotion. "Lucy is gone and, God knows, I've understood your grief and heartache. But Laura and Alex are not gone. They need, more than ever before, love and understanding. Harboring this deep depression is not only destroying you, it's affecting your children."

Strong hands gripped her shoulders from behind. "Sarah," Dan said in a firm voice.

She put her hand over her mouth, ashamed of her outburst. She turned and hurried from the kitchen.

Dan heaved a sigh and glanced at John whose head was bowed.

After a tense moment, the silence was broken when John reached for his jacket off a peg and said, "Got some papers to sign at the office. Then I'll be back." He looked over at Dan. "Please, go talk to Sarah. Tell her … well, you know what to tell her."

Dan watched John walk out the back door. "Do I?" he questioned under his breath. "I'm not so sure, old friend."

Across the hall, he found Sarah seated in the open parlor, staring into the fireplace. He sat on a settee facing her. "What you said about John is true." He leaned forward, resting his forearms on his thighs. "That's why he wants to go with me. I'm heading back west out to Oregon Country."

At her groan of protest, he raised a hand. "Now before you get all riled up again, hear me out. I know he'd be leaving his family and law practice. But you said it yourself. In his present state, he's neither a decent father nor a good lawyer. John's not only fighting despair but guilt. He's torn between wanting to leave with me and thinking he should stay for the children's sake."

He stood and walked over to the fireplace. Resting one boot on the raised hearth, he propped his arm on the mantel. "And yet you, Sarah, are the one Laura and Alex need most. If John did stay, you'd still be running from your house to this one to care for them. He's convinced it would be best if you took the children into your own home."

All the while Dan spoke, Sarah had kept very still, her hands clutching the arms of the chair. Now she stood and began pacing. "Daniel, Lucy's tragic death was a terrible blow to us all." She sighed. "And yet, I actually feel blessed in being given the opportunity to care for Laura and Alex. I love them as if they were my own children."

Dan understood. Barren all these years, Sarah was grateful to have her niece and nephew fill that void in her life. Compassion for her welled up inside him. For an instant, he wanted to take her in his arms and remind her that once he had wanted her to bear his children. Instead, he pulled his gaze away from her and picked up an iron poker.

"How would James feel about their living with you?" he asked, idly stoking the fire.

"James is a good and generous man. He would welcome the children into our home. He loves them as much as I do."

"Then it seems they'd be well taken care of, doesn't it? You know John will provide for their financial needs as well."

"Yes, Daniel, but tell me, how long will John be gone?"

Dan shrugged his shoulders. "That I can't answer. We'll be traveling clear across the continent." For the first time that morning, he smiled at her. "Hey, don't go worrying your pretty head. I'll make damn sure nothing happens to your brother."

Nodding, Sarah tried to smile back. "In time, I hope he meets someone else. John needs a woman to love and care for him."

Dan placed the poker back in the stand. "Most men do, but I never found anyone else."

Not giving Sarah a chance to respond, he strode into the hallway where he lifted his hat and jacket off the coat rack. Before letting himself out, he turned and said huskily, "Tell little Laura and Alex good-bye for me." His gaze lingered on her face. "Take care of yourself, Sarah."

CHAPTER 1

Missouri, 1860

The years of youth are a memory.
So quickly those footprints fade.
The future lays a path for me.
Which one, my chosen destiny?

Laura Westbrook read and reread the poem she'd composed on the first page of her journal. Releasing a long sigh, she got up from her chair and walked to the window, her eyes straining to see through the dirt that coated the glass on the outside. With a couple of jerks and a loud "umph," she forced the window open, admitting the various sounds from the main street below.

In the town of St. Joseph, it was the beginning of another busy day. The distant clangor of a blacksmith hammering iron on his anvil was superseded by the noise of two loaded buckboards rumbling their way past the hotel. Several restless horses hitched to a rail snorted and stomped, seeming eager for their riders to return so they, too, could be on their way.

As Laura gazed down at the horses, her wistful smile widened into a grin. "I bet I'm more anxious than you are to get going."

She turned to see Aunt Sarah twist away from the dresser, both hands pushing pins into her hair. "What did you say, dear? I can't hear you with that window open."

With another grunt and two hard pushes, Laura shoved the stubborn window shut and faced her aunt. "I was just thinking out loud."

Seeing Sarah still clothed in only her dressing gown, Laura sighed again, walked back to her chair, sat down, and opened her journal to the second blank page. After she wrote, *May 7, 1860*, she slowly tapped her pen against the paper, searching for the right words. As the minutes passed, her thoughts whirled, but she made no attempt to write them down.

"I can hardly believe it," she said, a tremor of excitement in her voice. "Soon we'll be traveling clear across the continent in a wagon."

Sarah glanced at Laura's reflection in the dresser mirror. "I wish I were as enthusiastic about it as you." She shook her head. "Two thousand miles to California seems an impossible distance."

Laura picked up the *St. Joseph Gazette* from the table beside her and pointed to an article. "The government estimates the number of emigrants who have traveled to California and the Oregon Territory by the end of this year will exceed two hundred thousand."

Sarah's brow lifted. "It's no wonder your father's law practice has grown. He said in his letter he's taken on a partner."

Setting the newspaper aside, Laura tried to picture them arriving at their final destination, Placerville, and seeing her father for the first time in fifteen years. "You know, I can't even remember what Papa looks like. If it weren't for his letters, I'd be meeting a total stranger."

Noting her aunt's frown, she added, "But I promise to judge him for who he is now. Not the father I didn't have." Her words held a stubborn tinge of bitterness.

Sarah rose and walked over to rest a hand on Laura's shoulder. "He did what he thought was right for you and Alex at the time, dear. Sometimes the strength of love is measured not by how one holds on to it, but by how one let's go." She gave Laura's shoulder a gentle squeeze. "One thing's for sure. Your father will have no problem recognizing you. You're the perfect image of your mother—her auburn hair, her emerald eyes. Why, she even had those same tiny freckles sprinkled across her nose."

Returning to her dressing table, Sarah continued, "Laura, I've been slow as molasses this morning. Since you're dressed, how about going down to the hotel desk to see if Daniel left us a message? I'm sure he knows our steamboat didn't dock until late yesterday. He probably doesn't want to disturb us, thinking we might be sleeping late. As one woman would have liked to have done," she quipped, rolling her eyes upward.

Laura ignored her aunt's last remark. She, herself, had been awake and dressed for what seemed like hours. "Good idea," she replied, gathering up her journal, pen, and ink. She placed them inside the carved wooden box, a special gift Uncle James had given her shortly before he died.

"He could be waiting for us in the lobby right now." Laura got up and walked to the door. "Although I guess I wouldn't recognize him, even if he were."

"Oh, yes, you would!" exclaimed Sarah. "Unless Daniel's changed, a man that well-built you couldn't miss."

Letting herself out, Laura laughed. Of course, how could she forget! As a little girl, she'd thought he looked like a giant out of a fairy tale.

When she returned five minutes later, Sarah stood at the bedside in her petticoats and camisole. Looking at two dresses spread across the bed, her aunt frowned. "Honestly, Laura, I don't know what's the matter with me. I've never been so indecisive. Nothing looks right on me." She waved a hand in frustration. "Well, never mind. Did you see Daniel?"

"No, but he did leave us a message." She handed Sarah a note.

Sarah read it aloud, "Hope you ladies have gotten enough beauty rest. I'll have your wagon in front of the hotel at noon to load up and ferry you across the river to our campsite. Dan."

"So, while you finish dressing," Laura said, "I'm going to take a look around town. I'll be back before noon."

"I don't think you should be traipsing around a strange town by yourself."

Laura pursed her lips in annoyance. "I won't traipse ... I'll walk in an appropriate, ladylike fashion." She could tell her aunt didn't appreciate her sarcasm, but refused to give in. "Sarah, for heaven's sake, I'm twenty years old and quite capable of taking care of myself. Haven't we had enough discussion about you allowing me my independence?"

"Yes ... yes," Sarah replied resignedly. She shoved aside the dresses and slumped on the edge of the bed. "It's just that ... well, you're all I have left." Her voice wavered, barely above a whisper. "First your brother was sent to that godforsaken outpost. And then James ..." She shook her head in despair. "I still can't understand how a healthy man, a physician himself, could die from pneumonia so quickly."

Tears welled up in her eyes as she shrugged her shoulders. "Then selling the house—all my possessions. This past year hasn't been an easy one, Laura. I've had to let go of so much that was a part of me."

"I know," Laura said, her own eyes misting. "But we still have each other." She leaned over and embraced her aunt. "We're making this trip together, remember? Before too long, we'll be stopping to see Alex at Fort Hendricks. Then a few months later, we'll be reunited with Papa."

Sarah nodded, putting her fingers to the corner of her eyes to catch the tears. "You're right, of course. Please forgive me for being such a goose this morning."

Laura walked to the door. "Sarah, you're not a goose. A mother hen perhaps," she teased, "but not a goose."

She had dropped the customary use of the word, aunt, before Sarah's name long ago. Aunt and niece had been determined through family ancestry, but years of living together had created a bond like mother and daughter, and thus, an acute awareness of each other's feelings.

This morning Laura sensed her aunt's uneasiness at seeing Dan Driscoll again. After they'd arranged to join his wagon train to California, Sarah's past memories surfaced, prompting her to confide in Laura about her brief, passionate affair with Dan before her marriage to James.

Now as she let herself out into the hall, the thought occurred to her, *maybe fate is bringing Sarah and Dan back together so they can re-ignite those flames.*

She shut the door and hurried down the stairs and through the lobby. As soon as she stepped out the front of the hotel, her eyes and ears were filled with the sights and sounds of the bustling town. People were everywhere. With purpose in their steps, they walked up and down the street along the wooden sidewalks.

Laura moved out from under the shaded overhang of the hotel, and the bright mid-morning sun glared its greeting. A light breeze blew its warmth over her face and ruffled her hair. She watched a covered wagon roll past her and wondered what it was going to be like spending the next six months in one of those things. Lifting the hem of her skirt, she ran across the road before another rumbled by from the opposite direction. She grinned when she reached the other side. She wasn't traipsing, but she doubted her mad dash had been very ladylike, either.

In a remote part of Kansas Territory, the Indian maiden, Stargazer, walked out of the woods and down the bank to the edge of a narrow river. As she knelt to fill her water sac, she spied two bear cubs cavorting along the embankment downstream. Obviously they had not caught wind of her scent, for they continued to frolic and nip at each other. Their antics were so funny she laughed aloud.

But then, as if by magic, they disappeared. In the next instant, she heard muffled wails and realized the cubs had tumbled into the concealed pit her brother, Swift Eagle, had dug to trap pronghorns.

Though her mind cautioned her, she couldn't help feeling sympathetic to their howls and started toward the pit.

Suddenly, a loud roar filled the air, and a huge, dark form burst from the trees. Stargazer came to an abrupt standstill. Charging toward her was an enormous grizzly. It slid to a halt not ten steps from her. Hackles up and ears flattened, the bear opened its mouth to reveal deadly fangs.

Stargazer's mind whirled in fear. When the beast reared up on its hind legs becoming twice her height, she knew that here stood death itself. Letting her trained, spiritual mind take over, she closed her eyes and dropped to her knees in surrender to the Great One Above.

Behind her came a shrill war cry. "*Hi-i-ya!*" A second later, a lance whizzed past her head, its iron point piercing deeply into the middle of the grizzly's chest.

Stargazer scrambled to her feet as Grey Wolf leaped between her and the raging bear. Clad only in a breechcloth and moccasins, he faced the massive animal, a long-bladed knife in his right hand.

Not diverting his eyes from the bear, her brother spoke in the Cheyenne language he'd learned so well. "Run, little sister!"

"But, Grey Wolf, she will kill you!"

"Go! Get Swift Eagle."

The grizzly bellowed her anger. She swung her huge arm across the protruding lance and snapped the end of the pole from its embedded point.

Stargazer's eyes widened in horror. She dashed into the woods, wasting not another word or backward glance.

Grey Wolf knew there would be no time for help to reach him. Sending Stargazer after their brother was only a ploy to ensure her safety.

He watched the mother bear lower herself again on all fours. She snorted and swayed back and forth, as if sizing up this new threat standing between her and her young still whining in the pit. Fierce black eyes glared out from her massive head. White froth foamed from her mouth.

Grey Wolf crouched low and shifted slowly to one side only a few steps from the bear. The grizzly lunged. Grey Wolf jumped back, but not far enough. Her giant claws raked bloody gashes across his stomach, the powerful blow knocking him to the ground. Before he could recover, she pounced and sank her fangs into his left arm.

Struggling under her huge body, he tasted the vileness of fear in the back of his throat. He thrust his knife hard into her abdomen, yet knew it would take a strike to the heart to kill her. He yanked the weapon out of the tough hide and wrenched his other arm from the grizzly's jaws. The flesh tore away from the bone, but there wasn't time to react to the searing pain. He pushed away from the beast and rolled to his feet.

The bear roared her anguish, blood foaming from her muzzle. She rose again to her full eight feet. Swiftly, Grey Wolf lifted his uninjured arm as high as he could and with all his strength, plunged the knife into the mortal side of the bear's chest.

In her final death throes, the crazed animal flung her mighty arms around him and sank vicious fangs into his shoulder. The excruciating pain and pressure he felt from her powerful jaws consumed the last of his strength. The convulsing mass of fur and muscle plummeted to the ground, pinning him beneath it.

Time seemed suspended as Grey Wolf's life flashed before him. He struggled to grab hold of the cameo strung around his neck. Just before darkness closed around him, he wrapped his fingers around the treasured medallion and prayed for God to join his soul with his beloved family of long ago.

Laura lay awake staring up at the arched canvas cover as the first rays of morning seeped into the wagon. Her aunt slept soundly a few feet away on the same type of makeshift bed as hers, a thin pallet stretched atop a long wooden box. Underneath they'd stored their linens, household items, and personal belongings, including Uncle James's medical supplies. Without a doctor this trip, Dan was counting on Laura's nursing skills to help see them through.

Her father had paid Dan for their wagon, mule team, and provisions last winter in California. He'd also instructed Dan to purchase a mount for her. Laura wondered if it would be a mustang, a small, sturdy horse often used on the frontier. She was amused at Dan's apology yesterday for having to buy a western saddle since no side-saddle could be found anywhere in St. Joe. If he only knew how often she'd ridden bareback at home.

The clink of spurred boots approaching drew her gaze to the rear of the wagon. The canvas flap rustled. "Wake up, you two! Time to rise and shine. This is the big day you've been waiting for."

Sarah's eyes slowly opened. She winced as she rolled to her back. "Land sakes, I can see it's going to take a while getting used to sleeping on these boards," she muttered, swinging her feet to the floor.

"Hey in there," Dan bellowed, "you up?"

Uncorking a bottle, Sarah pulled out a match and lit the lantern beside her. "Barely!"

Dan chuckled. "Henry has breakfast ready, and his coffee is just the right color of mud. Meet you at our wagon."

"Dag nabbit! Where in tarnation are they?"

Coming around the back of Dan's wagon, Laura slowed her steps. Beside her, Sarah shot her a wavering glance, signaling to hang back out of view.

Hunched next to a campfire, a small, wiry-looking man fanned smoke with his hat. "Hell, serve 'em right if the whole damn mess burned up!" The man stood and crammed his hat back on his head. Tufts of straggly grey hair stuck out over his ears, the hat's brim flattened against the front of the crown.

Dan sauntered out of the woods, opposite the campsite. "Whoowee … you're cussing mighty early this morning, Henry."

Alongside him, his young scout, Lucky, laughed aloud. "What's he fussing about now?"

Dan shook his head. "Beats me."

Henry's bushy brows twitched up and down. "Humph!" he belched and squatted back down. Grabbing a fork, he flipped over some pan bread that was turning from shades of brown to black inside the skillet. "If those little ladies of yorn don't get their tender hides over here, they can forget this breakfast. I can't keep grub hot all mornin', ya know."

Dan threw Lucky an amused glance. He then picked up a tin cup off a rough-hewed stool and walked over to a smaller fire. Taking the boiler from an iron hook secured to a tripod, Dan poured coffee into his cup. Just as he lifted it to his mouth, he caught sight of Laura and Sarah standing beside the wagon.

Lowering the cup, his appreciative eyes gave Sarah the once-over from head to toe while Henry continued to prattle away.

"No sir, I never hired on to cook for no uppity women!"

Dan frowned in Henry's direction as tinware clattered from an overturned box. He raised his voice. "Good morning … you gals are sure looking bright-eyed and bushy-tailed."

"Good morning, Daniel," Sarah responded, wrapping her shawl tighter around her shoulders as she stepped around a large water barrel.

Abruptly, the noise stopped, and Henry lurched to his feet.

Laura glanced purposely from Henry to Dan. "Hope we're not late."

Dan smiled. "Nope, not at all." He gestured with a nod of his head toward two stools, both newly sanded. "Have a seat." Reaching for the boiler, he poured coffee into two more cups. He gave Sarah a wink and handed her a steaming cup. He gave the other to Laura.

As he rested his hands on his hips, Laura noticed the holstered gun at his side. The scout had one too. Neither of them had worn the guns yesterday when they'd loaded their wagon in St. Joe and ferried them across the Missouri.

Lucky touched the brim of his hat. A dimpled grin emphasized his boyish good looks. "Morning, ladies."

"Henry," Dan said, "this is Sarah Osbourne and her niece, Miss Laura Westbrook."

Henry wiped his hands on a towel and swung it over his shoulder. He was actually blushing. "It's, ah … right good to meet ya." His head bobbed up and down as if it were attached to a spring. "Big D has spoken of ya often … yep, he surely has."

Smiling, Laura echoed her aunt's "hello," and sat on the stool next to her. Taking a sip of coffee, she made a mental note to fix herself tea tomorrow morning. As for the food, she really didn't care what it tasted like, just as long as it filled her empty stomach. Neither she nor Sarah had eaten much yesterday. Like the other travelers, they'd been too busy loading supplies in preparation for their long journey. In all, twenty-seven wagons and seventy emigrants had signed onto Dan's wagon train.

Laura hadn't more than scooped up the last of her scrambled eggs, when Lucky came around the side of the wagon leading a dark bay-colored horse. He held out the reins to her. "He's all yours."

Setting down her plate, Laura rose and walked over to take the reins. "Lucky, he's beautiful." She slid a hand over the animal's glossy neck as his intelligent eyes watched her. He was finely built and stood a good fifteen hands high.

"His name's Sonny."

Dan stepped beside her. "He's a Morgan. Don't see many in these parts. Your father wanted me to buy you the best I could find. 'Not some cayuse bred on the plains,' he told me."

A familiar twinge of bitterness stirred inside her. Just another atonement like the other gifts my father's sent me over the years, she thought. Still, she returned Dan's smile, not wanting to seem ungrateful.

She lifted the hem of her full skirt and set her boot in the stirrup. Thank goodness she'd left those silly crinolines stashed in her trunk. She waved off Lucky's offer to help her up and with one hand on the pummel, easily swung into the saddle.

Dan grinned. "Well, looks like Laura's ready to hit the trail." He turned to Lucky. "What you gawking at, boy? It's time to turn those eyes westward. Let's get the wagons forming a line up the St. Joe road."

CHAPTER 2

❀

Inside the lodge, Stargazer watched her mother, Woman-With-Smart-Hands apply a fresh dressing of moss to Grey Wolf's wounds as he lay unconscious. She'd always marveled at the rich, golden color of his skin and the expanse of curly brown hair covering his chest. *But look at him now,* she thought remorsefully. Because of her, a mass of gaping wounds and dark bruises scarred his body.

Her gaze lifted to his face. With each day, he looked more like a stranger. The sickly pallor of his skin was in stark contrast to the heavy, dark stubble covering his chin. At puberty, Grey Wolf had not plucked his facial hair, as was the custom of her people. Instead, every day he had shaved it off using a finely honed knife.

She knelt beside him opposite her mother and picked up the oval stone strung on a rawhide thong around his neck. With a cloth, she gently wiped blood from the woman's white face carved on it. She dared not remove the necklace, for he'd worn the talisman for as long as she could recall.

"Oh, Holy-One-Above," she prayed, "please do not claim Grey Wolf's spirit so early in his life."

She wiped a tear from her cheek and turned to watch Chief Black Arrow drop sage and sweet grass into the fire. Smoke swirled above her head, wafting its way up the center pole and through the top of the large tipi. It was the Cheyenne's way of cleansing the air in preparation for Nightwalker, the clan's seer and medicine man.

"Father, is there nothing more we can do?"

"You and your mother have done all you can to help my chosen son," said Black Arrow. "He needs one close with spirits as well as strong in medicine."

Seemingly the clan's medicine man, Nightwalker, had been awaiting those very words, for the front flap of the tipi opened, and in he stepped. The Indian's burly frame cast a giant shadow inside the lodge, intensifying his aura of mystery and power. He wore a buffalo-horned headdress and around his neck hung several small bundles tied with rawhide.

"Wife, daughter, leave us," Black Arrow commanded as he lifted his eyes in reverence to this most sacred man.

Obediently rising, Stargazer straightened her tunic of soft, tanned deerskin. She stole a last worried look at Grey Wolf before following Woman-With-Smart-Hands from the lodge.

For several moments, Black Arrow listened as the medicine man stood beside Grey Wolf and called to the Great Spirit, his voice rising and falling in a rhythmic cadence. Up to now, Nightwalker's medicine had not been effective, and his son's fever had increased.

"What is your plan, Great One?" Nightwalker asked, thrusting his head back, with eyes closed and arms held high. "Will Grey Wolf walk again among our people or go forever into the spirit world?"

A lingering span of charged silence hung in the air before Nightwalker opened his eyes. "Grey Wolf wanders in a strange place." He leveled his gaze upon the chief. "Not of our world, not of the spirit world, but with people of his own race."

Black Arrow glared deeply into the dark eyes of Nightwalker's, trying desperately to see the vision he had seen, to understand the words he had spoken.

Nightwalker laid a hand on Black Arrow's shoulder. "My friend, you must remember your son was bred from white seed. Only his God who gave him life can decide whether he should live on this earth or travel to the afterworld of his ancestors." Nightwalker looked down at Grey Wolf's unconscious form. "He must be with his own people for this to be determined. There is nothing more I can do for him. If your son stays here, he will die, his spirit to wander the vacant skies, lost forever."

Though Black Arrow had not experienced the seer's vision, the revelation of his words hit him with a powerful force. He understood full well what he must do.

"But it is not right!" Stargazer pleaded, clinging to Woman-With-Smart-Hands' arm. "Grey Wolf does not even know what is being decided for him. Mother, you cannot allow this. Please talk to Black Arrow."

Woman-With-Smart-Hands shrugged Stargazer's hand from her arm. Squatting, she scooped up sand and sprinkled it over the outside cook fire, careful not to snuff the buried embers that would be rekindled in the morning. "Does my daughter question her father's decision?"

"I … I do not mean to. But I love my brother and do not want to see him leave." A tear rolled down her face. "Where will Black Arrow take him?" The tone in Stargazer's voice revealed her resignation to the inevitable.

"Near the big mud river where many white villages are." Woman-With-Smart-Hands smiled compassionately as she pushed to her feet. "I have packed things he will need. Perhaps you have time to make him a good luck token."

Her suggestion brought a spark of hope back into Stargazer's heart. She'd make him a special gift. A headband decorated with red beads, the life color. She'd work all night on it. Surely such an amulet would help give him the strength to endure.

Stargazer looked anxiously at her mother. "And after their Great Spirit heals Grey Wolf, then he will return to us?" Her eyes searched her mother's for confirmation.

Woman-With-Smart-Hands sighed. "If that is his choice." She cast her gaze past Stargazer to the distant horizon. "But you must understand, my daughter, when Grey Wolf finds himself among the white people again …" she paused, "he might wish to stay."

Stargazer bowed her head, indicating she understood. But inwardly she clung to the belief there was no reason for Grey Wolf to want to stay with the white people. After all, they were strangers to him.

Laura doused her hanky with water from the barrel's spigot at the side of the wagon and wiped her face and neck. The trail so far had been long and dusty. Every day Dan rotated their wagon farther down the line, bringing ones from the rear to the front. That way, everyone took their fair turn at breathing the dust from the wagons rolling ahead of them.

After crossing a wide stream, they'd stopped to freshen their water supply. Now it was time to push on, which meant eating the grit once again. Lifting her eyes to the heavens, Laura silently prayed for rain.

"Don't forget to use some of this lotion," Sarah said, peering down from where she sat high atop the wagon seat. From a bottle, she poured a dab of creamy substance in the palm of her hand, and then tossed it to Laura. "Out here our lotions are a necessity, not a luxury," she reminded her curtly.

"I'm aware of that," Laura replied, a note of irritation slipping into her voice. She smoothed a generous portion on her hands and face, smelling the sweet scent of almond oil blended with the basilicum ointment.

"Wearing a hat is a necessity, too, but I hardly ever see it on your head," Sarah added.

Laura chewed her bottom lip. After handing up the bottle, she reached over her shoulders and grabbed her hat hanging down her back by its neck strap. She plunked it on her head, cinched the strap under her chin, and pasted a smile on her face.

When Sarah opened her mouth to speak again, Laura threw up her hands. "Never mind, I know!" She dug into her jacket pocket and whipped out her leather gloves.

At the sound of a horse approaching, she turned to see Lucky ride up. "Ol' Ace and I thought Sonny might like to look at something beside the back of your wagon." He gave his horse a pat on the neck. "How about it, Laurie … ride with me?"

"No, Lucky, I think I should—"

"Drive again?" Sarah interrupted. "Why? It's my turn, and I don't need you up here beside me."

"That's right, Mrs. Osbourne," Lucky said in hearty agreement. "You can do just fine on your own. I have to say, both of you caught on how to handle that mule team in no time."

"We had good instructors," Sarah replied, smiling. "Where's Daniel, anyway? It's time for him to be yelling for us to get the wagons moving."

"Well, ma'am, the boss went back to remedy a problem. Seems there's a straggler or two slowing us down." Lucky dismounted and walked over to untie Sonny's reins from the tailgate. "Come on, Laurie. We can ride up ahead of the wagons."

Sarah frowned. "Oh, I don't think Laura should—"

"Should what?" Laura countered.

"Ride ahead," Sarah finished lamely. She gave Lucky a conciliatory look. "But then, I guess, you're safe with Lucky."

"You can bet your pretty bonnet on that, Mrs. Osbourne."

Lucky held the reins while Laura mounted. When he stepped away, she gladly set her heels to Sonny's flanks, and the horse took off at a gallop.

"Hey," Lucky shouted, "who said anything about a race?"

Black Arrow held up his arm, signaling his two warriors to halt. Behind them, Grey Wolf's pinto whinnied and pawed the earth seemingly impatient with the delay. The proud stallion was adorned with eagle feathers tied to his black mane and tail. Poles, secured to his sides, held the travois carrying Grey Wolf. Bundles of his possessions, a lance, shield, and bow, and a full quiver of arrows were strapped to the pinto's back.

Grabbing a water sac, the chief slid from his horse. He knelt beside Grey Wolf and cradled his head in his arm. He tipped the sac, allowing water to trickle into his son's mouth.

Grey Wolf opened his eyes. Their silver glaze reflected the fever raging throughout his body. "Where are you taking me?" he rasped.

"Nightwalker said I will find trusted white people to care for you. Only their Great Spirit who gave you life has the power to heal you."

"But where …" Grey Wolf coughed, and then grimaced.

"Do not talk, my son. Save your strength."

Grey Wolf's eyes closed, the fever once more pulling him under. Black Arrow's brow creased with worry. He must travel two more suns to reach the missionary. His son would never make it.

He stood and looked far down the hill where a long line of white men's tipis rolled across the prairie. Watching, he again pondered the meaning of Nightwalker's prophecy.

Laura reveled in the exhilaration of riding Sonny at a full run. The wind whipped past her face and threatened to pull her long hair from its combs. Laughing, she stole a glance behind her. Lucky rode fast at her heels, his blue roan about to overtake the Morgan.

"Laura, stop!" Lucky yelled. He leaned over and grabbed her reins, yanking both horses to a jolting halt.

"What do you think you're doing?" she railed.

Lucky raised an arm and pointed. "Look what's coming down that hill. The way you were riding, you'd have been on top of them."

"Oh, my stars, is that … are they …" Her heart lurched with a giddy flutter. "Indians?"

Lucky squinted his eyes. "Cheyenne, I'd say."

Three Indians made their way down the slope, their horses' legs completely hidden in the tall, swaying grass. A riderless horse trailed behind the leader.

Lucky twisted in the saddle and looked back. "Here comes Dan. He's good at parleying with the Indians. Knows how to use their sign language." He eyed Laura sternly. "You better go on back to the wagons."

Laura caught the way he fingered the handle of his holstered gun while he followed their progress down the hill. "Do you think there might be trouble?"

"Ain't enough of them to take on a whole wagon train, so it's not likely. Then again, you never know what goes through those savages' minds. They're not exactly pleased with us tramping over their hunting grounds."

Laura gripped the reins tighter, restraining Sonny's skittish prance as Dan halted his horse close by. "I'm surprised to see the Cheyenne this far east," he said. From the even tone of his voice, he didn't sound worried.

Reaching the open road, the Indians veered in their direction. "Looks like they're pulling a travois with somebody on it." Dan gestured with a jerk of his head. "Laura, you go on back. Lucky and I'll see what they want. I told the folks to circle up for the night. Couple wagons need repair anyway."

Telling Lucky to stay behind him, Dan urged his horse forward. He halted in front of the lead Indian who wore a tanned-hide shirt, heavily fringed and decorated with an elaborate design of colored beading across the shoulders and down the sleeves. More beads ran the length of his fringed leggings and covered his moccasins. A wide breastplate made of bones hung from his neck. At the end of each long, black braid of hair, two large white and black-tipped eagle feathers were tied. But it wasn't just his colorful clothing and ornaments that marked this Indian a chieftain; more evident was the stoic pride chiseled on the Indian's face.

Mesmerized by what she saw, Laura had no intention of turning tail and running. These weren't some glorified pictures in a book, but real-life Indians. She eased Sonny closer, wanting to hear their conversation.

"I meet as friend," Dan said, his English words pronounced slowly in conjunction with the movement of his hands. He waited for the Indian to indicate his acknowledgment, and then continued signing. "I lead my people north to flat river and west over mountains," he said, lowering his hands to his sides.

Lacking any facial expression, the Indian made several motions with his hands and fingers, then spoke in what must have been his native tongue. He slid from his horse, his look indicating he expected Dan to dismount, too.

They walked past the large pinto and knelt beside the travois. The Indian continued to talk and gesture with his hands.

Lucky turned in his saddle and glared back at Laura. "Confound it, Laurie, get back to the wagon," he said under his breath through clenched teeth.

"Why?" Laura demanded, her eyes boldly meeting his.

"Because Dan said to. It could be dangerous."

"They don't look dangerous," she whispered. She stood up in her stirrups, stretching to see past the two other Indians astride their horses. "There's someone lying on that litter. Do you suppose the person's sick?"

Lucky frowned. "How should I know?"

Laura dismounted and started toward the travois. She'd taken only a few steps when the two Indians vaulted from their horses and leaped in front of her, their long lances braced horizontally across their bodies.

"Laurie!" Lucky jumped from his horse, grabbed her arm, and swung her around. "For God's sake, girl, haven't you got a lick of sense?"

"Let go!" Laura pried his fingers from her arm.

"Just where in blazes do you think you're going?"

She turned to Dan who'd stepped around the pinto. He looked a bit bewildered, while the older Indian seemed to glare right through her. "All I want to do is take a look at him. Maybe there's something I can do."

Dan signed to the chief. "She means no harm. She—"

"Dan," Laura interrupted. She tried sidestepping the two Indians, but they countered her every move. She sighed with impatience and looked between them. "Dan, why don't you tell him I'm a nurse?"

Dan walked around the Indians whose eyes remained riveted on her. "Listen, Laura, you've got to understand how unusual it is for them to see a white woman …" he hesitated, frowning, "especially one with your looks, sashaying around them and speaking out like you're doing!"

He turned to Lucky. "We could have a problem on our hands. That man lying over there is Chief Black Arrow's son. He's badly injured, and the Indians think white man's medicine can heal him."

"Then why don't you tell the chief there might be something I can do for him?"

"It isn't that easy. Once you touch the man, it means I've agreed to be responsible for what happens to him."

"How was he injured?"

"He was mauled by a grizzly."

Laura inhaled sharply. "My Lord, I must go to him," she said, darting past Dan and Lucky before they could stop her.

Just as the warriors lunged for her, Black Arrow's stern shout stopped them. Knowing she'd have to get past the chief, she cautiously stepped up to him. She pointed her thumb to the middle of her chest and said her name. Boldly determined, she pointed behind the big pinto, and then waited, her eyes seeking his for permission.

For the longest time, Black Arrow watched as the wind blew long strands of her hair about her face. Laura supposed its bright auburn color held his fascination. He reached out and fingered a lock of it. After his gaze roamed over her from head to toe, he spoke, the words rolling off his tongue in that rhythmic high-low pitch. Then he moved aside for her to pass.

Laura lowered her eyes, sensing it was the respectful thing to do. Relieved she'd met with the Indian's critical inspection, she stepped around the pinto.

As she knelt beside the travois and looked at the man, she gasped aloud. A dark beard and mustache covered the man's pale, white face. Long, golden-brown hair brushed the top of his shoulders with a few damp strands straying over his forehead. Nothing about him resembled an Indian except for a red-beaded band circling his head.

"Why ... he's a white man!" she exclaimed.

CHAPTER 3

"Yeah, he is," Dan said, an edginess apparent in his voice as he hovered over her. "The chief referred to him as his chosen son. Seems he adopted him."

Laura tugged at the rope holding the blanket in place. "Lucky, help me with this."

Kneeling beside her, he grabbed the rope from her hands. "Laurie, do you always do what you damn well please?"

She didn't answer, concerned only with getting the binding untied. But when Lucky pulled back the blanket, she recoiled from the sight.

"A bear did this?" she gasped. She'd helped her uncle treat bullet and knife wounds, but never injuries that looked like these.

"A grizzly can be a hell of a beast when he's provoked," Dan said.

The ravages of the bear's attack were most evident on the man's shoulder and left forearm. The arm was red and swollen, the torn flesh obviously the result of the grizzly's teeth, as were deep punctures in the thick muscle of his shoulder. Lacerations across his abdomen showed the only signs of healing.

Upon further scrutiny, she noticed an oval cameo nestled in a mat of dark hair in the middle of his chest. It hung on a cord of rawhide circling his neck. Admonishing herself for taking time to observe such a thing, peculiar though it was, Laura returned her attention to the man's injuries.

Steeling herself, she examined the jagged wound on his left arm. Though crusty from dried blood and the application of some kind of moss, it didn't appear to be infected. However, when she touched his shoulder, a viscous, yellow fluid oozed from a deep wound. Laura leaned closer. As she pressed and probed, the man's face contorted. A groan vibrated from his throat.

Black Arrow grunted and moved up next to her. She sensed the chief's anxiety and withdrew.

As she pulled a handkerchief from her pocket and wiped her hands, the man's eyes slowly opened. So overwhelming were they in their silver intensity, Laura could almost feel the fevered heat emanate from them as he stared up at her. He seemed to want to speak, but when he lifted his head, his eyelids fluttered and closed, and his head slumped back again.

Laura took hold of his hand and pressed her fingertips to his wrist. His pulse was weak and his breathing, labored. Compassion tugged at her heart for this man who suffered, yet stubbornly clung to life.

She stood and faced the chief. His coal black eyes drew her to him like a magnetic force. She swallowed hard, trying to find her voice. "He'll die if he doesn't get medical attention right away." Her words were for Dan, though her gaze never wavered from Black Arrow's.

"You really think you can save him?" Dan's question held a strong note of opposition.

Laura frowned, wrenching herself from the chief's stare. "It doesn't matter what I think. What matters is that I try!"

"Laurie, just what is it you plan to do?" Lucky put in. He raised a mocking brow. "Take this man, this Indian … whatever he is … back and nurse him in your wagon?"

Laura couldn't believe what she was hearing. Dan was actually questioning what to do with this man's life. And Lucky sounded as if it would be a damned inconvenience!

"Dan, how can you turn him away?" She searched his face for some show of compassion. What she found was a close-mouthed, guarded look. "For God sake, he's a white man!" Her voice trembled. "If you send him away, he won't last another day dragged behind that horse."

There was a moment of brittle silence before Dan's expression wavered, and he heaved a deep sigh. He looked at Black Arrow who hadn't flinched. Raising his hands, he said firmly, "We agree to take your son with us, if you understand that even with this woman's medicine, he still might die."

The chief leveled his gaze on Dan as he spoke solemnly and signed his words.

Dan's mouth flattened into a grim line.

"What did he say?" Laura asked.

"He said his son came into this world white. If it is his time to die, he asks that we honor him with the white man's burial." Dan crossed his one forefinger over the other as Laura had just seen the chief do. "With crossed sticks above his grave."

She clenched her fists at her sides and said in a quiet, determined voice, "There'll be no grave, not if I can help it."

Dan nodded, offering her a rueful smile. He lowered his gaze to the travois. "Black Arrow gave him the name, Grey Wolf. He's lived with the Cheyenne ever since he was a little boy."

Laura shuddered, assailed with a deep sense of pity. *Lord, what a tormented life he's led. And now, to end up like this.*

A short time later, the two warriors and Black Arrow rode back up the grassy slope. Though hardly a word was said between Black Arrow and Dan before they left, Laura had witnessed an earnest exchange of friendship. The chief gave Dan two buckskin shirts covered with beaded designs and a small pair of soft deerskin moccasins, the latter given with a pointed finger toward her. After Dan accepted the gifts, he shook the Indian's hand. Laura found it both touching and amusing to see the stern-faced chief pump his arm up and down in an awkward attempt to mimic Dan.

Mounted on Sonny, she twisted in her saddle, looking at the travois behind the pinto stallion. *"Grey Wolf,"* she whispered, mulling the name over in her mind. She hoped he was as strong and tenacious as the animal he was named for. His life would depend on it.

As the sun descended toward the horizon, the bright, blustery day changed into one of soft shadows and a gentle breeze. The emigrants bustled about their wagons, by now quite adept at the daily routine of preparing their campsites.

"Unharness them mules, son," a man yelled.

"Tom, Jed, get washed up for supper," a woman's voice rang out.

But when Laura rode past each of their campsites with Dan leading the pinto and travois, their activity stopped abruptly. Everyone stared, mouths agape. As the procession moved on, a buzz of whispers followed.

"Who's that lying behind that horse?" she heard one ask.

"Seen Driscoll talking to some Injuns up the road. Guess he's one of them." answered another.

"Now why, in heaven's name, would Mr. Driscoll be bringing a sick Indian back to our train?" The muttered voice was full of disdain.

Dan halted in front of his wagon. "Lucky, get someone to help you remove the extra crates from our wagon. You can store them in the buckboard under heavy oilcloth."

"Right, boss," responded Lucky, riding past him.

Laura nudged Sonny forward. "We're wasting time. Let's get this man to my wagon."

"Grey Wolf stays here."

"But you told the Indian chief I would be taking care of him."

"You will." Dan dismounted. "In this wagon." He glanced at her over his saddle, a glint in his eye. "Tell me, if we were to put him in your wagon, whose bed would he lie on, yours or Sarah's?"

"Well, I ..." She cast an uncertain look back at Grey Wolf.

"Laura," Dan clenched his mouth in annoyance, "I'm not going to allow a strange man to bed down in your wagon, injured or otherwise."

"I suppose not," she replied sheepishly.

Walking back to the pinto, Dan began untying one of the poles holding the travois. "Henry, where the hell are you?" he bellowed.

The short, craggy man seemed to pop out of nowhere. "I'm right here, Big D, right here ... don't need to holler."

"If you're right here, how come you're not giving me a hand?" Dan snapped. "This wagon's been a hospital before. We need to get it set up again. Can't you see we got a patient?"

Henry's eyebrows did their up and down twitch. He looked from the foot of the travois to the man's whiskered face. "He sure is a peculiar one, ain't he?"

"Just get your hiney over here and help me lower these poles to the ground." He peered over the stallion at Laura again. "And you best be getting your medical supplies."

Minutes later, standing beside the mule team, Sarah set down the animals' feed bags and wiped her hands on her apron. "Well, I'm certainly glad you're back, Laura. That was no place for you up there with Dan and those Indians."

Laura tethered Sonny to the side of the wagon and climbed inside the back.

Sarah came around and stood at the open tailgate. "A moment ago, I heard someone say they saw Dan bring back a sick Indian on a litter."

Laura picked up her uncle's medical case and handed it to Sarah, then opened a chest and retrieved an armload of towels.

"Laura, I'm speaking to you."

She held the towels out to her aunt as well. Sarah plunked the case down on the ground. "Young lady, answer me right now!" she admonished, snatching the towels.

Grabbing a small valise, Laura lowered herself from the tailgate. "You don't have to shout. A man's been injured. But he's not an Indian." She gave Sarah an impatient glance. "However, he was raised by them."

Her aunt looked somewhat perplexed. "I don't have time to explain." Laura picked up the medical case. "Come and see for yourself."

Inside Dan's wagon, Laura sat on a wooden box next to the improvised bed on which Grey Wolf lay, still unconscious. A blanket covered him to his waist. After she removed several surgical instruments from her case, she glanced up at Sarah standing beside her. "I need more light."

"I've got it," came Dan's reply behind her. He lit another lantern and held it above her.

Laura wrung out a cloth from a small wash basin. As she cleansed Grey Wolf's shoulder, blood rolled down his arm. Wiping the flesh surrounding the wound, she spoke quietly. "This afternoon I discovered what I suspect to be the reason this wound isn't healing." She handed the bloody cloth to Sarah and reached for a clean one.

While restricting the flow of blood as best she could, she used a probe to examine the festered area. Bracing Grey Wolf's muscular shoulder, she exchanged the probe for a small pair of forceps. As she eased the instrument into the wound, a low moan rumbled in his throat.

Suddenly, his eyes opened and flashed a wild look like those of a trapped animal. Laura withdrew the forceps, but before she could lift her arm away, he grabbed her wrist.

The strength of his grip was unbelievable considering his weakened condition. He glared at the instrument, then at her. For a brief moment, those luminous eyes penetrated her very soul.

Dan moved beside her. "I think I'd better restrain him."

Unexpectedly, Grey Wolf released her wrist. Remaining still, he watched her. "No, I don't think that's necessary," she answered.

"Well, at least let me give him a couple slugs of pain-killer." Pulling a bottle of whisky out of a box, Dan poured some in a tin cup and stepped around her. He held the cup to Grey Wolf's lips.

Grey Wolf had no sooner taken a swallow when a grimace shot across his face, and the whisky spewed from his mouth. He turned his head and spat again, his expression one of loathing.

"I'll be damned!" Dan exclaimed, setting the cup aside and stuffing the cork back in the bottle. "Never knew an Indian who didn't like the taste of whisky."

"He's not an Indian," Laura corrected, meeting Grey Wolf's narrowed gaze. "Don't put it away, Dan. I can use it later to help fight the infection."

Hoping Grey Wolf would allow her to continue, she leaned over and again applied the forceps. She pressed deep, trying to grasp the hard thing imbedded in the thick muscle of his shoulder, all the while, aware of the pain constricting his face and the sweat beading his forehead. When she finally pulled the forceps out, he sucked in a quick breath.

She pressed a clean cloth firmly over the wound with one hand and held up the forceps with the other. As Dan swung the lantern closer, Sarah let out a gasp. In the tongs' grip was a broken fang, almost two sharp, deadly inches of it.

"Good God," muttered Dan, "how'd you know that was in him?"

"As I said before, I thought I saw something inside the wound when I first examined him this afternoon." Laura caught the amazed glint in Grey Wolf's eyes as he, too, observed the thing which had caused him so much torment. She shuddered and dropped the gruesome fang into the basin.

Sarah shook her head. "No wonder he's been delirious with fever."

Grey Wolf's body slackened as he again slipped into unconsciousness. His face was alarmingly pale under the mask of dark beard.

"Let me help," Sarah said, a sense of urgency in her voice. "I can make a poultice of alum to stanch the flow of blood."

Acknowledging her with a nod, Laura reached inside her case for a needle and catgut. Her work to save him had only begun. She still needed to close the wound after thoroughly cleansing it, get his fever down, as well as tend to his other injuries.

That evening, Lucky stood for the third time and stalked past the campfire. Shoving his hands in his pockets, he watched the shadows waver within the flickering light of the wagon. "What are they doing in there, boss?" He looked over at Dan who'd just dumped out the dregs in his coffee cup. "Jesus, it doesn't take that long to sew him up. He'll either live or die. No need watching him every minute!"

Dan didn't answer. Instead he glanced at Henry who was whittling on a chunk of wood. "Henry, how about a fresh pot of coffee?"

"I could sure use some about now," Sarah said, stepping down from the wagon. She smiled wearily at Dan.

Laura appeared behind her, brushing back strands of hair from her face and tucking them into her side combs. "I was able to get some laudanum down him. He'll rest easier now."

Lucky took her by the arm and lead her to a stool. "Enough attention's been given to that Indian for one day. You need to rest yourself." He turned to Henry. "These women need to eat. Where's that poor man's stew you fixed?"

Henry stopped shoveling ground coffee into the boiler and pointed a gnarled finger. "In that pot, youngin … close to you as it is to me. Serve 'em up some."

The next morning Laura walked into Dan's camp to find Lucky sitting on a stool, tugging on his boots. He looked up and gave her a smile. "Morning, Laurie. You're up early."

She nodded to him, then to Henry who was laying a match to a fresh pile of kindling. "Morning. Where's Dan?"

"Making sure those wagons got repaired," Lucky replied.

Hugging her arms across her chest to ward off the damp chill, Laura shot a worried glance over her shoulder. "How's Grey Wolf?"

"Alive … leastwise, he was when Dan checked on him a while ago." Lucky stood and stretched. "The old man will have breakfast going before long."

"Oh, please don't fix anything for me, Henry," she said. "I need to look in on Grey Wolf myself."

Lucky yanked his hat farther over his forehead and turned to Henry. "Don't fix me anything either," he snarled and stalked out of camp.

"Hey, you whipper snapper!" Henry yelled after him, "what about those flapjacks you were so all-fired hungry for a minute ago?"

Laura grinned as she pivoted toward the wagon. Those two sure liked to ruffle each other's feathers, she mused.

She climbed inside and quietly lit a lantern, then set it on top of a wooden box. Grey Wolf was asleep, his bearded face, peaceful and relaxed, relieved of the pain that consciousness brought.

Pressing a hand to his forehead, she felt his fever transmit its heat to her cool palm. Her hand lingered a moment longer while she watched the lantern flicker its golden glow over his muscular chest. The cameo lay in the center of him, as if it truly belonged there, the woman's white silhouetted face shimmering against his bronze skin.

Unable to stop, Laura's gaze roamed the length of him. A line of hair trailed from his chest, down his flat stomach, past the red claw marks, around his naval, and disappeared under the blanket. So deeply disturbing was the sight of his raw masculinity, it was all Laura could do to discipline her mind back to the task of cooling his fever.

With a quick glance away to impose her self-control, she stripped off her jacket and rolled up the sleeves of her blouse. Tucking towels under him as best she could, she then bathed his face and upper torso with witch hazel. Afterwards, she applied clean dressings to his arm and shoulder.

Just as she finished, his eyes opened. Like bright shards of glass, they glared up at her. Then without warning, he lunged for her. Laura leaped backward, almost upsetting the lantern beside her. He snatched blindly at the towels and growled like a madman, struggling to get up.

Realizing Grey Wolf wasn't cognizant of what he was doing, Laura collected her courage and reached out to stop him. "You mustn't get up." She tried to push him back. "Please, lie down. You're going to open those wounds if you don't—"

Suddenly, he grabbed her arms and slumped to the cot pulling her on top of him. Laura froze. Her face was inches from his, yet she was afraid to move. Her heart thudded against his chest. Heaven help her as to what he might do next.

CHAPTER 4

❀

Prickles of fear crawled up Laura's spine as she lay over Grey Wolf, imprisoned in the circle of his arms. Strange words rumbled from deep in his throat, his breath blowing hot against her cheek. Still, Laura remained like a fallen statue, too frightened to move or speak, while the fevered sweat from Grey Wolf's chest seeped through the front of her cotton blouse.

Slowly the intensity in his silver eyes grew dimmer, deep creases furrowing his brow. Relief settled over her as his eyelids fluttered, and then closed, his hold on her slackening. Yet she waited, not daring to pull away until she was sure he was asleep.

"Are you all right in there?"

Laura twisted around to see Dan looking in, his face marked with concern. She worked to untangle herself, lifting Grey Wolf's heavy arms from around her waist. "Yes … I am now," she stammered, pushing to her feet.

Dan seated himself on the opened tailgate, his gaze flitting from Grey Wolf to her. She smoothed her blouse into the waistband of her skirt and sighed. "I was trying to keep him from getting up. He's still quite delirious."

"I was bedded down near the wagon and heard him tossing around earlier this morning," Dan said, frowning. "Until we know more about him, Laura, I'd feel better if you weren't alone with him."

Nodding, Laura took a deep breath, forcing herself to relax. She sat beside him, her legs dangling over the side of the tailgate. "It must be a real shock for him to wake up in a covered wagon and see strangers hovering over him," she said, thinking about the way he'd reacted yesterday when he awoke. She hadn't been frightened at all when he'd grabbed her then.

But now ... She glanced at him. Now, she wasn't sure. A few minutes ago, when he'd opened those extraordinary eyes, he looked so ... so savage. Even if he didn't know what he was doing, he'd shown a violent side of himself.

What was he really like? A man who'd lived with Indians practically all his life. Seeing Lucky and her aunt approach, she pushed the errant thoughts aside.

"Well, how's the medicine woman doing?" Lucky asked, leaning against the side of the wagon, a lopsided grin dimpling his cheeks.

Sarah stepped beside him. "And how's the patient doing?"

Laura shrugged. "He's not out of the woods yet, but I believe we got to him in time."

Dan crooked an eyebrow. "More like he got to *you* in time!"

The wagon creaked and groaned on its wheels as the mule team clip-clopped along the hard dirt road. Perched atop the driver's seat, Laura held a loose rein while she scanned the landscape. To her right, an ocean-like expanse of grassy meadows rolled like waves all the way to the horizon. To her left, the tree-lined river flowed parallel to the trail they'd followed for the last couple of days.

She looked ahead at Sarah riding astride Sonny and wondered if the big man riding alongside had anything to do with the change she'd seen in her aunt. Even the way Sarah dressed lately indicated a difference in her. A knitted shawl no longer draped her shoulders, the sleeves of her blouse were rolled up, and the raised hem of her calico skirt revealed an exposed leg. Her bonnet hung forgotten down her back, loose strands of hair blowing about her face.

Laura smiled. No doubt Daniel had everything to do with it! Maybe old flames could be rekindled.

As her gaze shifted to the wagon ahead of her, her thoughts returned to the man lying inside. Endless questions continued to nag her. Who was he? Why had he been raised by Indians? What happened to his real family?

Now that his wounds were healing and his fever had diminished, she'd stopped the doses of laudanum. Finally this past noon while seeing to his personal needs, Dan was able to exchange hand signals with him. But to Laura's disappointment, Dan informed her that the few words Grey Wolf spoke were Cheyenne, no English words at all.

He'd given no response to Dan's telling him Black Arrow had left him and returned to his people. When Dan signed who he was and where his wagon train was going, Grey Wolf's face remained hard-set. Dan told her the only time he showed any expression at all was when he'd offered to shave off his beard. To that, he gave his eager consent.

As the caravan veered from the road, Laura snapped the reins with a sharp flick of her wrist and turned her team in behind Dan's wagon. They were heading closer to the river meaning the end of another day's trek. Dan wanted them to make twenty miles today. Judging from the stiffness in her backside, Laura was sure they'd traveled every blessed inch of that and then some.

Later that evening, Laura sat before the campfire stirring a small bowl of porridge she'd made from oats, cornmeal and molasses. Beside her, her aunt sipped tea while opposite the fire, Henry contentedly dunked a piece of cornbread into his cup of coffee. A few yards from them, Lucky worked at adjusting Ace's cinch.

"Where'd Daniel go?" Sarah asked, peering at Lucky over her teacup.

"He's assigning guard duty." Lucky jammed his foot in the stirrup and swung into the saddle.

"And where are you going? You haven't eaten a thing," Laura put in.

"Not hungry." His gaze swept the distant grasslands. "Thought I'd round up a foraging party while there's still some light. Grouse and turkey in these parts. The smell of one of them birds cooking over a fire might improve my appetite." He gave Laura a pointed look. "What are you making?"

"Grey Wolf's supper," she said, pouring some hot water from a kettle into the bowl to thin the gruel's consistency.

Lucky snatched up his reins. "That's what I figured." He spurred Ace in the flanks and rode off.

Henry shook his head and gave a snort. Laura supposed he'd noticed Lucky's quick switch in temperament at the mere mention of Grey Wolf's name.

"Are you going to stay in camp?" Sarah asked Henry. Laura caught the concerned look her aunt gave him, rolling her eyes in the direction of Dan's wagon.

Henry winked. "Yes, ma'am, ain't goin' nowhere."

"No one has to stay on my account," Laura said. She faced her aunt. "Sarah, I hope you're not like some of the others on this train. They're already gossiping about Grey Wolf. Saying since he grew up an Indian, he's just another savage and can't be trusted."

"Why, I wouldn't say anything of the sort! I only thought someone ought to be here in case you need some help with him." She set her cup on the ground. "Isn't there anything I can do?"

"No," Laura answered curtly, picking up the china bowl from her lap and rising.

Shrugging, Sarah stood. "Then I'm going to our wagon. I want to darn Daniel's socks. He's been walking around with holes in them for much too long."

Laura didn't miss the way Henry's wiry eyebrows shot up at her aunt's remark about Dan's socks. He was probably wondering the same thing she was. When, in heaven's name, had Sarah seen Dan with his boots off?

As her aunt left, Laura leaned over, plucked a clean linen towel out of a box, and headed toward the wagon. Behind her, Henry cleared his throat. "Now, little Missy, if he gives you any trouble, you just holler. I'll be right out here."

Grey Wolf didn't have to open his eyes to know the woman had entered the wagon. He could smell the sweet scent of her.

Cautiously, he peered at her beneath veiled lashes. He guessed he'd been unconscious for some time, but gazing upon the beauty of this white woman assured him he was now fully awake and in control of all his senses. Indeed, weak as he was, he felt his body respond to her presence.

As he watched her move a wooden box next to his bed, he tried to recall when he'd last seen a woman of his own race. Ah yes ... last year at the trading post. Two army soldiers brought in their wives. He remembered their curious stares. "A half-breed," the women had called him, not caring if he heard.

The name didn't surprise him. That's what he was to both whites and Indians who didn't know him. They had no conception of the true blood that coursed through his veins. They saw a brown-haired, grey-eyed man who dressed, acted, and spoke like an Indian and so judged him a half-breed.

As the woman sat beside him and placed a lit candle on top of the box, Grey Wolf continued to study her under the concealment of his hooded eyes. The light from the candle's flame flickered over the rich red-gold of her hair, almost the same color as his mother's. And like his mother, she wore hers pinned back with a few loose curls framing her face.

She had a rare and pretty face. Creamy white skin with a rosy flush to her cheeks, tiny freckles sprinkling her nose, and full pink lips curving up softly at the corners. When she leaned closer and lifted her eyes, Grey Wolf couldn't help but be transfixed by the most radiant eyes he had ever seen—the color of fresh, spring grass.

As Laura turned around, she felt the weight of Grey Wolf's penetrating stare. When she looked down at him, it was all she could do not to stare herself, so astounded was she by the remarkable change in his appearance. Without his beard, his face was lean, a strong, angular chin protruding below well defined lips. He was much better looking without the beard. In fact, he was downright handsome.

To break the spell of their bold gazes upon each other, Laura returned her attention to the bowl cradled in her lap. "It's good to see you're fully awake." She dipped a spoon into the gruel. "You must be hungry."

There was no response.

"Up until now, all I've managed to get down you is tea and broth. You have to eat to get your strength back." She held up the spoon.

Grey Wolf's gaze never left hers, though his expression remained flat and unreadable.

Laura girl, he doesn't understand a word you're saying. Just go ahead and put the food in his mouth!

She lowered the spoon to his shapely lips. Grey Wolf slowly opened and closed his mouth around it, all the while looking at her.

A shiver slithered up the back of Laura's neck as she slid the spoon out of his mouth. She dipped it back into the porridge and again guided the spoon to his parted lips.

Lordy, she was trembling like a newborn calf. If he just wouldn't stare so. If he'd say something. Anything. Even those strange Indian words.

Just then, to her utter embarrassment, a small portion of the porridge slipped off the spoon and plopped on his chest next to the cameo. "Oh dear, how clumsy of me," she moaned, grabbing a towel. As she wiped it off, his muscles flexed beneath the cloth.

Setting the towel aside, she scooped up another spoonful. This time when she brought it to his mouth, he reached out and clasped his long brown fingers around her wrist. Her breath caught in her throat as he steadied her hand and sipped from the spoon. Only when he released her hand, did she release her breath.

Setting the spoon back in the bowl, Laura still felt the warmth of his touch. She couldn't continue to feed him this way. It was too awkward ... and too intimate.

As if he read her mind, Grey Wolf braced himself on his good arm and pushed back into a sitting position. Laura grabbed his pillow and propped it against the box behind him.

Pain contorted his face as he leaned back. He clenched his teeth and closed his eyes a moment, then reached out and took the bowl from her lap.

Released from his intense stare, Laura observed Grey Wolf while he ate. No longer a mask of sickly paleness, his face was a warm, deep bronze. She supposed his years of living in the rugged outdoors had carved that look of strength into his features. His long mane of sun-streaked, brown hair hung over his shoulders, with an unruly lock curling over his smooth, square forehead. He no longer wore the red headband.

"I'd be glad to make you more," she said when he'd scraped the last bit of porridge from the bowl. "But first, I want to put salve on that arm and shoulder." She knew he didn't understand her, but talking to him somehow seemed to ease the tension.

She took the bowl from him and set it aside. She then swung around for her medicine case on the floor behind her. As she bent over, a flush of heat crept into her face. On the bed not six inches from her, Grey Wolf's lower torso was exposed, save for a breechcloth barely covering his loins. The quilt lay at his feet, shoved there when he'd slid into a sitting position.

Laura felt the color drain from her face. Never before had she been so affected by one man's presence. She was vividly conscious of every masculine contour of his body—from his broad chest and well-developed arms to the rigid muscles of his flat abdomen, from his bare hips to his sinewy brown legs.

He looked so powerful. She swallowed, her throat dry. *So primitive.*

Anxiously, she peered up at his face. He gazed at her knowingly. And when their eyes met, he raised one dark, brazen eyebrow.

Laura knew her face had regained its color, surely now a beet red. She lurched forward and yanked the quilt from his ankles up to his chest. "You must stay covered. I'm not saving your handsome hide only to have you die from pneumonia!" she said, blurting out the words before she could stop them.

Well, he doesn't understand a thing I say anyway, she mused. Gathering her composure, she bent over again to open the medicine bag. As she searched for the jar of salve, she contemplated the look on Grey Wolf's face a second ago. Was it her imagination or did she see his mouth twitch in amusement? And hadn't there been the slightest glimmer in those iron-grey eyes?

"Need any help, Miss Laura?" Henry asked from the rear of the wagon.

"No, everything's fine, Henry." She offered what she hoped was a reassuring smile. "I'm just going to redress Grey Wolf's wounds."

The old man scratched his whiskered chin and peered over at the Indian. "Well, I'm a heifer step away, if you need me," he said and sauntered off.

Swiveling around on her stool, Laura gave a start as Grey Wolf reached out a hand to touch her. Instinctively, she drew back. He frowned at her, a muscle quivering at his jaw.

His eyes were so crystal clear Laura swore she could almost see through them. How she wished it were possible to see into his mind and know what he was thinking.

When he reached out again to touch her face, she batted his hand away and swooped to her feet. "I think I should leave now." Not taking time to gather up anything but her medicine bag, she scurried outside.

Standing beside the wheel of one of the emigrants' wagons, Dan wiped his hands on a rag. "The axle wasn't your problem, Lester. The hub wasn't seated right. Should roll fine now." Glancing up, he saw Lucky approaching.

"Boss," the scout broke in, "we need to talk."

"Can it wait? I was going to give Lester a hand greasing these wheels."

Lucky eyed Lester and the missus looming over her husband's shoulder. He leaned in close to Dan's ear. "Let the ole coot grease his own wheels. You can't do everything for him."

"Yeah, suppose you're right." He handed Lester the rag. "Got something to tend to. The grease bucket is in my buckboard, help yourself."

Making their way through the campsites, Dan and Lucky passed various members of the train, most of them seated around their cook fires.

"Good evening, Mr. and Mrs. Parkinson," Dan said, touching the brim of his hat as he walked by the elderly couple.

At the next wagon, he smiled. "Howdy, Jed. How are you doing?" The young man mumbled that he was fine. Dan nodded and continued on, aware Lucky hadn't said a sociable word to anybody.

As they reached a stand of trees not far from their wagon, Lucky suggested they stop and have a private talk.

"I can see something's got your dander up," Dan said. He braced an arm against the trunk of a tall pine tree. "Let's have it."

Lucky hooked his thumbs over his belt. "Did you notice how thick the air was when we passed most of the wagons?"

Dan gave him a blank look, not sure what he was getting at.

"You know, sort of a tense feeling among the folks."

"Boy, quit talking in riddles and come out with it!"

"All right. When I was with some of the men hunting this afternoon, they told me a lot of the people don't like having a half-breed on the train. They think he's a threat to their safety."

Dan pushed away from the tree. "First of all, Lucky, he's not a half-breed. He's as white as you and me. And second, he's no threat."

With a jerk of his head, Lucky gestured toward the other campsites. "Yeah, well, you'd better explain that to them."

Dan shook his head in agitation. "I don't owe anybody an explanation. Hell, they can think what they want. Grey Wolf is in my wagon, and he's not bothering a soul." He shot Lucky a pointed glance. "Except for maybe one. Tell me, what do you have against the man? I see your ears laid back every time his name comes up."

Lucky squared his shoulders. "I don't like him, that's all."

Dan rubbed the side of his chin. "Hey, I know you're not keen on Laura looking after him. But don't worry; I'm keeping an eagle eye on him."

The next morning Grey Wolf sat on the side of the cot, waiting for dawn to cast its first hazy light into the wagon. If he'd known where the bright-eyed woman stored the matches, he could light the candle propped in the candleholder next to the cot.

The fragrant bayberry candle brought back a memory of his childhood. His mother would mark a groove in one of her scented candles, and then have him read aloud from his lesson book until the flame burned the wax down past the groove.

As the morning light filtered into the wagon, he picked up the silver spoon he'd used the night before. Its thin, embossed handle felt comfortable between his fingers. Setting it down, he perused the multi-colored patchwork quilt at the foot of the cot. It looked similar to the one his mother had been working on so long ago. Abruptly, he looked away. A quilt she never had the chance to finish.

That all-too-familiar hurt began to burn its way up Grey Wolf's chest. He slipped the cameo over his head and turned it over. He could barely read the worn inscription engraved around the gold-rimmed frame. *To Mary, Love Glen.* The pendant had been a birthday gift to his mother from his father.

Hearing footsteps approaching, he squeezed his eyes shut to force away the memories. He looped the cameo back around his neck, grabbed his buckskins and stood up. Instantly everything whirled out of focus. He reached for the sideboards just as he heard Dan's voice.

"Better take it easy there, boy." Dan climbed inside the wagon. "It's going to take a while for you to get all your strength back, you know." He gestured the signs for *future time* and *strong body*. As he wrapped a supportive arm around him, Grey Wolf heard him mumble under his breath, "Not sure how much you understand, but I suspect more than you let on."

As he allowed Dan to help him out, a revitalizing breeze swept through his hair, its coolness a welcome relief from the stale confinement of the covered wagon. His gaze was drawn to the river beyond the trees. Its cold water would feel welcome too, cleansing his body and renewing his soul as well.

"Guess I know where you're heading," Dan said, nodding in the direction of the river. "Here, I have some clothes for you." He gathered up a checkered shirt and pair of corduroy trousers from the tailgate and held them up.

Grey Wolf shook his head and held up his buckskins. He winced as a sharp pain shot through his arm.

"Your shoulder's still not healed," he said, signing the words simultaneously. "Laura ..." He placed a hand beside his head and curled his fingers. He stroked downwards as though combing long hair, the Indian sign for woman. "Wants you to put on these clothes. Big shirt with buttons. Easier for her to put medicine on you."

Grey Wolf frowned. He set the buckskins on the tailgate and took the trousers from Dan. Looking at them a moment, he remembered seeing them on the young scout. He thrust them back, took the shirt, picked up his buckskins and started for the river.

He hadn't gone far when he heard Dan yell, "Hey, better not get that shoulder wet."

Not bothering to turn and acknowledge that he understood, Grey Wolf smiled to himself and kept on going.

CHAPTER 5

Laura and Sarah walked into Dan's camp. "Why, Henry, you've already started breakfast."

"Yep. Been hankerin' for some pancakes and didn't need you ladies to show me how to make 'em." He squatted down and laid a cast iron skillet on the white-hot stones nestled in the smoldering fire. The embers popped and snapped, sending sparks shooting upward through a curl of smoke. "Take a seat and I'll have a batch ready in no time." He glanced up. "And before ya ask me where the men folk are, I'm gonna tell ya." He directed his gaze to Laura. "Grey Wolf is down at the river." He shifted to Sarah. "And Big D ... er, that is, Daniel's gone down to see if he wants to eat with us."

Picking up a large bowl of batter and a wooden spoon, he continued, "As for Lucky, he's laying in a supply of wood. Won't be finding much once we get to the Platte River, ya know. We'll be using dry weeds and buffalo chips to keep the fires burning then."

Laura smiled down at the wiry little man as he dropped a thick spoonful of batter onto the sizzling, hot skillet. "I can't wait to taste those pancakes. We've heard you flap the best jacks this side of the Missouri." She turned to her aunt who was selecting eating utensils from a box beside her stool. "Sarah, I didn't get a chance yesterday to change Grey Wolf's bed linens. This would be a good time. It will only take me a few minutes. You go ahead and eat. I'll be right back."

After climbing inside the wagon, Laura looked around for the linens she'd set on top of a wooden crate the day before. She noticed they'd been shoved to one side. Laying next to them were several bundles made from tanned hide. One was partially opened, its leather straps loosened. Assuming they must be some of Grey Wolf's personal belongings, she turned from the box, chastising herself for even thinking of looking inside the bundle.

She stripped the soiled sheet off the straw mattress, and then spread the fresh linen over the bed, all the while trying to ignore her nagging curiosity. As she tucked in the sides, she frowned. What sort of things would be in those bundles?

She stepped back over to the crate. One little look couldn't hurt, she reasoned. Laura pulled the straps farther apart and peered inside. Shrugging off her guilty conscience that demanded she not touch a thing, she picked up what appeared to be a porcupine's tail tied to a stick with sinew. She lifted it to the side of her face and brushed it through a loose curl, marveling at her discovery. The stiff bristled tail made a crude hairbrush.

Putting it aside, she fingered several other implements inside the pouch, one of bone, another of wood, a few of scrap metal. None were recognizable, save for what looked like a long, smoking pipe. The stem was painted blue with several colorful bird feathers tied near the mouthpiece. The opposite end was carved into the shape of an eagle's head with its open beak forming the pipe bowl.

There were two smaller pouches. She unfolded one and found a variety of dried leaves, grass, and roots; in the other, wads of meat were mixed with some kind of berries. She wrinkled her nose. The contents looked putrid and smelled worse!

Worried he might return at any moment, she refolded the pouches and partially closed the bundle just as she'd found it. Any feelings of guilt she had for invading his privacy were overpowered by the fascinating thrill of secretly touching some of his personal possessions, strange as they were.

As she turned to leave, she spotted a long bow and a quiver full of arrows laying on the floor next to a barrel. She hadn't seen them before, either. Nor the lance balanced atop the barrel. Laura's eyes widened at its length. The hand-forged iron blade had to be at least twelve inches long. Attached to its wooden shaft, the lance was much longer than she was tall. Cautiously moving around it, she climbed down from the tailgate.

Just as Sarah announced the pancakes were ready, she saw Grey Wolf coming out of the woods. The sight of him made her catch her breath.

His stature was even more impressive now that he was standing. Walking next to Dan, he was as tall and broad in the shoulders, but slimmer in the waist. He had on one of Dan's shirts, the left sleeve hanging empty, his arm tucked inside. Long, wet hair clung to his neck, errant locks dripping over his forehead. He wore a breechcloth over fringed buckskin leggings that molded tightly around his muscular thighs. Moccasins decorated with colored beading covered his feet.

Following Laura's gaze, Sarah shook her head. "Daniel, that wasn't the smartest thing for Grey Wolf to do. He could catch a chill." She scooted a stool closer to the fire.

"Shoot, Sarah," Dan said, "Indians are used to cold water. They bathe in icy rivers in the middle of winter."

Laura frowned. "I best get him a blanket."

Returning from the wagon, she noticed Grey Wolf had ignored the stool Sarah offered and was sitting on the ground with legs folded, eyes closed.

"Grey Wolf?"

As he opened his eyes and lifted his head, she caught a gleam of interest in his face. But when she circled the blanket around his shoulders, he gave her only the slightest nod, his expression clouding over like a smoke screen again.

Laura pursed her lips and turned to Dan. "Even if he can't say 'thank you,' wouldn't you think he could at least manage a smile to show his appreciation for all we're doing for him?" Her voice was tight with frustration. "Tell me, don't Indians ever smile or is that an expression only whites use?"

Dan's mouth quirked in amusement. "Sure they smile. They're human beings just like us. I've seen them laugh, too."

She gave Grey Wolf a disgruntled look. "I hate to say it, but I think that wooden face of his would split in two if he smiled."

"Say, is anybody gonna eat these flapjacks or do I have to eat 'em all myself!" Henry exclaimed.

Needing no further prompting, Laura arranged several pancakes on a plate. After spreading honey over them, she gathered up a knife and fork. She walked over to Grey Wolf and held out the plate and utensils in front of him.

He shrugged off the blanket and took them from her. Tossing the knife and fork on the ground, he scooped up one of the honey-drenched pancakes and took a big bite.

Laura's eyes narrowed. She leaned over and whispered close to his ear, "Fine with me. Eat with your fingers like a cave man."

Henry flung the long whip high over the mule team's heads, the coiled end unfurling with a resounding snap. "All right, you ornery ninnies," he bellowed, "get a move on … ain't long, we'll be calling it a day."

Riding on the front seat beside Henry, Grey Wolf smiled inwardly. The old man's voice and actions reminded him of Jeremiah.

He wondered where his old friend was right now. On his visit last summer, Jeremiah was excited about the discovery of gold down the South Platte River. Said he planned to grubstake a partner in the hopes they'd get lucky.

A sense of foreboding channeled through Grey Wolf. Trained to interpret such feelings as warnings from the Great Spirit, he promised himself that after he rejoined the Cheyenne, he'd check on his one and only white friend.

But for now, there was nothing he could do but concentrate on getting well. He stretched his arm and flexed the thick rope of muscles from wrist to shoulder, trying to work out the stiffness. Though his strength was returning, he didn't feel up to riding his horse, Four Winds.

Henry continued to jabber nervously to the mules. The sooner I leave, the better, Grey Wolf thought. Like this man, there were others on the wagon train who didn't trust him. Walking past their campsites, he felt their stares. Some were only curious, but most glared at him with open hostility.

From the time Grey Wolf had regained consciousness and found himself among these white strangers, he'd remained impassive to their stares, silent to their repeated questions. It was his best defense from the harsh reality that even though he was of the same race, he didn't belong. A time span of fifteen years had changed that. The white world he'd lived in as a child wasn't his now.

Tired of being jostled about, Grey Wolf swung down from the slow-moving wagon. Pain knifed through his shoulder, but he ignored it. After the woman called Laura removed the stitches, it would be time for him to leave.

Laura ...

Just thinking of the bright-eyed woman sent heat racing through his veins. Whenever he was around her, he tried his utmost to conceal his desire. He could tell by the remarks she'd made that she had plenty of spirit. He liked that.

But what truly held his fascination was her beauty. Her creamy white skin, her green eyes, her curly auburn hair—all traits of a white heritage.

Traits of his heritage.

Quickly, he cast the thought aside. His people were the Cheyenne.

Still, he regretted not expressing his gratitude to the woman who'd saved his life and to the white leader who'd offered his friendship. But then, what did it matter? A few more moons, he'd be on his way, never to see either of them again.

As he walked alongside Four Winds tied to the back of Dan's wagon, the thought of rejoining the Black Arrow clan stirred him with excitement. He would return in time for the summer hunts. Grey Wolf patted the side of the stallion's neck affectionately. How good it will be to feel the strength and speed of Four Winds again, the two of them becoming one in pursuit of the shaggy-mane buffalo. The horse was truly an extension of his own body. Without him, he would be like an eagle without wings.

The last few days he'd slept at night in a camp away from the others, Four Winds's reins tied to his wrist. He took no chance on his most valuable possession being stolen by some enemy—be it white man or Indian!

Early the next afternoon, Laura came into Dan's camp to find Henry kneeling over a board, cleaning a mess of fish. "My heavens, who caught all the fish?"

"He did," Henry said with a jerk of his head.

Laura glanced over to where Grey Wolf was tying several mules to a picket line between the trees. "You mean Grey Wolf?"

"Yep," Henry replied, sliding a long knife under one of the fish's gills. With a practiced hand, he made filleting the trout look like easy work.

Laura sat on a stool and placed her medicine case on the ground beside her. She sensed rather than heard Grey Wolf approaching. He had the remarkable ability to move without making a sound.

When she turned and looked up at him, his sultry eyes bored down into hers. Like countless times before, Laura's heart fluttered in response.

Without a word, he knelt in front of her and removed the sleeveless, deer-hide vest. Laura sighed resignedly. Why should he act any differently toward her today than he had any other day? She'd long since given up trying to ease the tension between them with words or gestures.

Henry stopped what he was doing and eyed Grey Wolf critically. "Something, Miss Laura, how he's come to expect it, ain't it? Just squats there waiting for ya to tend to him, never no sign of thanks or nothing."

Though Laura agreed with Henry, she didn't say so aloud. Directing her attention to his shoulder, she removed the bandage and examined the wound. The stitches had held together well, the redness and swelling almost gone. Soon she could remove them.

Reaching into her case, she lifted out a jar of salve. She rubbed the healing cream first over his shoulder, then down his arm. As her fingers traced the line of veins along the inner side of his powerful forearm, Grey Wolf turned his hand over and opened it. An undercurrent of excitement rippled through her. She hesitated, her gaze slowly climbing to his face. His eyes took on a softness as he slipped his hand into hers and linked their fingers. With the slightest squeeze, he released her then and rose to his feet.

A warm ache settled in Laura's chest. Was this his way of communicating his thanks to her? She picked up his vest off the ground and handed it to him. He averted her gaze, shrugging into the vest, not bothering to tie the front laces. Her glance skipped to the cameo pendant centered in the middle of his chest. The white Grecian face stared back at her, a smile carved into her delicate features.

"M-m-m! We could smell those fish frying all the way down by the river, couldn't we, darlin'?"

As Laura stepped back from Grey Wolf, Dan and Sarah walked into camp. Dan smiled at Grey Wolf. "I saw you hook those trout this afternoon. You made it look like child's play."

Laura watched Grey Wolf's demeanor change as Dan signed his words. He squared his shoulders, his face expressing obvious admiration for the older man.

"Why, the way you're getting around, son, you'll be good as new in no time," Dan continued amiably.

Instead of responding with his typical stiff nod, this time Grey Wolf faced Laura and spoke in a low, resonant voice flowing with a rhythm of strange, syllabic words. At the same time, he motioned with his hands. It was the first time she'd heard him say more than a word or two of Indian, and even then, they'd always been spoken to Dan.

When he finished, Dan grinned broadly. "Grey Wolf says to tell you, Laura … ah, I think he called you, Bright Eyes … that he doesn't have with him the many horses and buffalo hides it would take to pay you for saving his life. He asks that you accept his humble thanks and his prayer that the Great-One-Above will reward you with a life of happiness."

Grey Wolf's sudden openness took Laura by surprise. She was touched by his words; especially by the name he'd called her.

"Tell Grey Wolf I am pleased to accept his words of thanks and his beautiful prayer. But he's alive and well because of his own willpower and strength as much as anything I did."

After Dan signed her words to Grey Wolf, an awkward silence ensued. Some indefinable emotion settled upon Grey Wolf's face as his gaze remained fixed on her.

Feeling uneasy under his scrutiny, she turned askance to Dan. He wrapped an arm around Sarah and motioned toward the campfire where Henry stacked fried fish on a platter. "Well now, what's say we eat?"

Later that night while Sarah went with Dan to visit another family, Laura relaxed on her bed, content to be alone with her journal. With the lantern propped beside her, she read the dozen or more pages she'd written. The last several pages sounded more like a personal diary than an itinerary of her trip.

There were fewer details on the day-to-day happenings and far more on her private thoughts and feelings about Grey Wolf. Never had she seen a more handsome man in all her life. He exuded virility beyond belief. Even his strange, incommunicative behavior added to his masculinity.

She wrote how that evening Grey Wolf, for the first time had let down his guard and expressed gratitude for what she'd done. Laura smiled, remembering the warm feel of his hand around hers, the deep resonance of his voice and the poetic words he'd used to thank her. Finally she'd witnessed a gentler, more civilized side of him.

She touched her pen to her lips, her smile fading. But how disappointing when moments later, he'd again grown quiet, saying not another word to any of them. He had taken some of the fish Henry had prepared and returned to his separate camp among the trees to eat alone.

Laura sighed. In a matter of days Dan said Grey Wolf would probably leave. She'd know no more about him then than she did now. The white man with an Indian name would forever remain a mystery to her.

Her gazed down at the open journal in her lap. So what purpose did it serve to write down these meandering thoughts about him? She closed the pages, her mind made up not to write another word.

Besides, she didn't like the way he'd been affecting her lately.

Oh, yes you do, an inner voice protested. *Face it, you're attracted to him.*

No! He's been brought up by Indians, her more sensible side countered. *You must forget him.*

Returning her journal and pen inside the small chest, Laura forced her more practical mind to the forefront, banishing all romantic thoughts.

Or so she hoped.

CHAPTER 6

The caravan of wagons continued along the Little Blue River, gradually closing the distance to their first important waypoint, Fort Kearny, popularly called "the gateway to the plains." From one campsite to the next, the emigrants' routine was the same; tend to the animals, gather fuel and water, cook and care for their families, and then fall exhausted into bed.

After a particularly arduous, albeit monotonous day's journey, a prospector named Slade Brandt sat with his back against a tree and watched a thick cloud drift past the moon, shrouding him in darkness. Restless and on edge, he was by no means ready to hit the hay.

Uncorking a bottle and tipping it to his mouth, Slade welcomed the burning sensation as the whiskey rolled down his gullet. After a few swigs, he felt better; the gnawing in his belly subsided, and his hands were steadier. As he wiped his mouth with his sleeve, a vision of a young woman's shapely body floated through his mind. He rubbed the front of his crotch, his body responding to his carnal thoughts.

From the time this trip started, he'd wanted to saddle up to that fiery-haired woman. Trouble was, whenever he'd sought her out, she was either with her aunt or at the Driscoll wagon nursing that damn savage.

Slade snorted in disgust and took another pull from the bottle. Driscoll was a damn fool. Plenty others on the train thought so, too. He'd heard the gossip. The man was white, yet the son of a Cheyenne chief. Shit, the son of a bitch was a stinkin' traitor, that's what he was!

How'd that wagon master know for sure the Injun wasn't used as a spy? Yeah, he'd heard the man was hurt bad. Still, Injuns were cunning. After he got better, and the people on the train were used to seeing him around, he could catch 'em off guard ... some night, signal his Injun friends and run off with their livestock. Hell, might even wake up one morning with arrows rainin' down on 'em!

Slade took one last gulp and corked the bottle. He jammed it back in one side of his saddle bag, and then reached in the other side and pulled out a cracked mirror. The clouds had thinned out with enough moonlight to see his reflection. He scratched his black whiskers, wondering if he should shave. His mouth twisted into a sneer. Maybe the woman liked the feel of rough whiskers against her lily-white skin.

Again, a vision of her appeared. This time he imagined her shoulders bare and her breasts outlined beneath a thin, lacy undergarment. His organ began to swell and pulsate, signaling its need.

He groaned and clambered to his feet. Impatient, he looked out beyond the small campfire. The last time he'd checked, she was visiting that Swedish family camped close to the trees. As the low cloud drifted by, he peered up at the full moon and cursed its returning brightness.

After helping Katrina Sorenson with the dishes, Laura thanked the woman and her husband for their hospitality. They'd insisted she join them for supper after she'd relieved their child of a painful stomachache that afternoon using a remedy of carbonate of soda. As she bid them good-night and moved away from their campfire, she became aware of the beauty of the moonlit night. Tired of the amenities of social conversation, but not yet ready to return to her wagon, she sought solitude among the trees lining the river bank.

Admiring the night-blooming primrose growing in abundance, Laura bent down to pick a few of the flowers. The sudden crackle of leaves behind her made her jump. As she swirled around, a man stepped between the thickets.

"Well now ... didn't 'spect ta see a woman out here thish time a night," he slurred. The moon shining through the trees dappled his heavy-jowl face and cast harsh shadows below his eyes. "Not lost are ya?"

Laura took a step backwards. "Why no, of course not. Dan went down to the river for water. I'm waiting for him here."

"Oh, really? I just came from the river. Didn't see nobody." His thin lips stretched into a repulsive, gap-toothed grin. "Laura's the name, ain't it?"

She hitched her chin, refusing to cower. "Miss Westbrook to you." She issued a curt "excuse me," and started past him, only to be halted by the man's iron grip around her arms.

"You'd better let go of me, mister." She swallowed the panic rising in her voice. "Dan will be back any minute."

His hands slid up her arms. "Hey ... why don'tcha cut the actin', huh?" He made an effort to square his stooped shoulders and winked at her. "I know Driscoll ain't nowhere around here." He licked the spittle from his mouth. "Now, how about you and me gettin' better acquainted? The name's Slade."

Laura had enough of his foul-smelling breath. She jerked her hands up and shoved him, throwing Slade off balance. She swept up the hem of her skirt and turned to run.

"Hold on, damn it!" he said, grabbing a handful of her hair and yanking her backward. He pulled her against him and wrapped an arm around the front of her. Hiking up her breasts, he leered over her shoulder.

Laura's heart pounded at a frantic rate. She knew full well what he wanted. A scream crawled up the back of her throat, but before she could release it, he let go of her hair and slapped his hand over her mouth. Instinctively, she clamped her teeth into his flesh and bit down hard, tasting both blood and satisfaction.

Cursing, Slade wrenched his palm from Laura's mouth and spun her in his arms until she faced him. Hair combs flying, her hair tumbled around her face and down her shoulders.

"A damn wildcat, ain't ya? Well, ya know what ... that works me up even more, woman!"

He slammed himself hard against her. "Ya feel that!" he growled, arching his body so she could feel his full erection rubbing against her abdomen. "Well, ol' Slade wants more than just a feel." He thrust his mouth over hers, forcing his slobbering tongue between her lips.

Laura wrenched her face away. With her arms pinned to her sides, she tried to kick him. But her legs and skirt became entangled with his legs, and they both toppled to the ground.

Her head struck the earth so hard, tiny lights flashed behind her eyes. Before she could recover enough to focus clearly, Slade heaved his body on top of her. He clawed at her breasts, ripping her blouse. Trapped beneath him, Laura gasped for air and screamed as he then reached down and yanked up her skirt.

In the next instant, a powerful force lifted his body off her and hurled him, head over heels. As Laura shook her head to clear it, Slade started to get to his feet.

Behind her a hard, masculine voice filled the night air. "When you stand, you die!"

Slade froze on his hands and knees. Stunned, Laura turned and stared up at the towering figure of Grey Wolf. *It was he who had spoken!*

He drew a knife from the sheath at his waist and held it out so Slade could see the sharp, menacing blade illuminated in the moonlight. Then with a flick of his wrist, the knife flew through the air.

Slade didn't have time to flinch before the iron blade stuck in the ground midway between him and Grey Wolf.

"Does the snake strike a woman, but squirm away from a man?"

Again Grey Wolf's deep-timbre voice echoed in Laura's ears. The shock of hearing him speak assailed her senses. English ... he spoke English! Astonishment and confusion compounded the turmoil already rioting within her.

Seconds later, Dan darted out of the woods. "What the hell ..." His glance cut from Laura to Grey Wolf, and then to Slade. "Watch out!" he yelled as Slade lunged for the knife the second Grey Wolf shifted his gaze to Dan.

Before Laura could blink, Grey Wolf swung his leg around and slapped his foot into Slade's wrist, knocking the knife out of his hand. He then followed his body's momentum and came around with the other leg. Ramming his heel hard into the man's gut, he kicked him backward into the bushes. Bloodlust in his eyes, Grey Wolf grabbed his knife and leaped toward Slade.

"Stop, Grey Wolf!" Dan demanded. He yanked his Colt from his holster, cocked the hammer and pointed it at Grey Wolf. "Don't move." The weapon conveyed his message better than any sign language.

Groaning, Slade struggled to his feet. "Agh ... I think the damn heathen broke my ribs." Clutching his belly, he staggered toward Grey Wolf.

Dan shifted his aim. "Don't you take another step either, Brandt! I don't know what's happened here, but from the looks of Laura, I'm sure as hell about to find out, and one or both of you are going to pay!"

"It was him," Slade rasped. He coughed and spat on the ground, then leered at Grey Wolf. "He was trying to hump her. Hell, if it wasn't for me, that animal—"

"That's a lie!" Laura railed, scrambling to her feet. She brushed the hair from her face and straightened her clothing. Standing beside Dan, she faced her attacker. "You're the animal!"

Grey Wolf stepped closer to Slade, his body coiled, ready to spring. Dan motioned with his gun. "Drop your knife and back away, Grey Wolf."

Grey Wolf glared at Slade long and hard before tossing his knife on the ground and retreating.

"Did he hurt you, Laura?" Dan asked, his voice lined with contempt as he kept his gun on Slade. He stole a glance her way, his eyes giving her the once over. "I mean, did he—"

"No," Laura said firmly.

Dan cast a doubtful look.

"Honestly, Dan. Grey Wolf stopped him before he had a chance to …" her gaze sought out Grey Wolf, "to do anything to me." She wished he'd say something. But he remained silent, his attention focused on Slade who was doubled over, still cursing and groaning.

Dan jammed the Colt back in his holster. He stomped over to the man and grabbed his arm. "You've been nothing but trouble ever since you joined my train."

"Agh … quit jerkin' me," Slade rasped.

The sudden sound of heavy footsteps diverted Laura's attention to Lucky bounding through the trees. His glance shot from Grey Wolf to Dan holding an iron grip on Brandt. "Damn, what's going on here?" When he saw Laura, his expression turned to utter astonishment.

"Laurie, what happened?" Stepping over to her, he grasped her arms, his gaze lowering as did his voice. "Are you all right?"

Self-consciously, Laura folded the torn collar of her blouse inside her neckline. "Yes, I'm all right, really," she replied, resting her hands on his chest. Thankfully, the throbbing in her head had subsided.

Dan shoved Brandt ahead of him. "Lucky, take this sorry excuse for a man back to our camp. Tie him up somewhere close enough for me to keep an eye on him, but far enough so I don't have to smell him."

Lucky gave Laura a reassuring squeeze and then released her. Stalking over to Brandt, he pulled out his revolver. "Move it!" he growled, thrusting the gun in the man's side.

Laura shuddered, allowing herself for the first time to think of what the man would have done to her if Grey Wolf hadn't stopped him. She turned to where Grey Wolf was standing. But he was gone, his knife no longer on the ground. "Where'd he go?" she asked, straining to see into the woods.

Dan shook his head and shrugged. "Just like an Indian. He can vanish faster than a shadow in the dark."

"He speaks perfect English, you know. I heard him."

"Yeah, well, I'm not surprised. I had a hunch he could." Dan rubbed his chin, his brows drawing together. "I need to get you back, Laura. Hate to think how upset Sarah's going to be when she sees you and hears what happened."

Scouring the riverbank, she caught sight of Grey Wolf's tall profile silhouetted against the moonlit water. Maybe he'd talk with her now. Maybe she could learn more about him.

"Do me a favor, Dan. Tell Sarah what happened. You can tell her in such a way she won't blow everything out of proportion. Otherwise," she gave him a bleak smile, "I can see myself chained to my wagon for the rest of this trip."

She picked up her combs from the ground. Gathering hair from the side of her face, she tucked them in above her ears. "I'll be along shortly. I'd like the chance to thank Grey Wolf for what he did."

Dan nodded. "If you're asking me to smooth the way for you, I guess I can try." He smiled at her understandingly before disappearing through the shadow of trees.

Laura walked toward the river. Nearing a large willow, she frowned. That's strange; a moment ago he was standing here by this tree. She stepped to the other side of the willow and called out, "Grey Wolf?"

"Have you not learned?"

She whirled around. He stood only a few feet from her, his arms folded across his bare chest. He was a sight to behold. She caught her lower lip between her teeth as a delightful shiver raced through her. The moonlight shimmered over the contoured muscles of his body, gilding his golden skin with a magnificent sheen. Even the exposed scars across his shoulder and arm added to his virility.

"By now you should know it is dangerous for you to be out alone at night," he said.

Boldly, she lifted her gaze to his face. "But I'm not alone."

CHAPTER 7

❁

The willow's swaying limbs brushed against Laura's arm; while the sound of the river's steady current swirled past her. As Grey Wolf's keen eyes met hers, a moment of doubt flashed in her mind. Good Lord, what *was* she doing? Not a half hour before, she'd been brutally man-handled by that horrible Slade Brandt. Now, here she was, standing in the woods with a man she knew little about.

Yes, but there's a difference, her subconscious argued. *Your heart isn't pounding with fear this time. Instead, it's fluttering with excitement.*

"What do you want, Bright Eyes?"

The name caused a sweet ache to settle in her chest. "I ... I wanted to tell you that I'm very thankful for what you did."

"It is a small deed compared to all you have done for me."

The deep tone in his voice marked the sincerity of his words. But even more important was the fact he could say them—that he spoke perfect English. "Why did you lead me to believe you couldn't understand me? That the only language you knew was Cheyenne?" The more she thought about his deception, the more it annoyed her. Her voice rose. "When I talked to you, when any of us talked to you, you understood every word." She tossed her head and thrust a hand on her hip. "Why, in heaven's name, didn't you speak up?"

Lifting a brow, Grey Wolf reached out his hand and cupped her chin. "You are a woman of many faces. First your beautiful eyes show approval, and your sweet voice speaks gratitude. Now your tongue sharpens, and your body hardens with displeasure. Do all white women display their emotions so openly in front of a man? Such behavior I would not see from an Indian maiden."

"You ... you didn't answer my question," she insisted.

He traced his fingers along the side of her face, over the surface of her forehead and down the other cheek. "To touch the shape of a woman's face is the Indian's way of telling her she is pretty."

An unwelcome blush flared through her cheeks. Laura drew away from his hand, determined not to be affected by his words or his touch. "Until tonight, except for sign language and a few Indian words, you chose to remain silent. I want to know why?"

"My father taught me that when a man's tongue is still, he hears and sees more."

She frowned, frustrated by his evasive reply. "When you say your father, do you mean the Indian chief, Black Arrow?"

He nodded.

"But what about your real father? Your family? Where are they?"

Grey Wolf stiffened. "You ask me why I have kept silent." He leveled a piercing glare on her. "So I could avoid questions like the ones you ask me now."

Laura knew she'd overstepped her bounds. "I'm sorry. I didn't mean to offend you." Dropping her gaze, she reached out and plucked one of the willow's slender leaves. "It's just that tonight, when I found out you spoke English … well, I thought we could get to know each other better." She skimmed the leaf lightly over her bottom lip, its tickling effect somehow easing her tenseness. "Maybe become friends." Glancing back at him, she shrugged dismissively. "But I suppose it doesn't matter, you'll be leaving soon."

He cast her a long, lingering look and then turned in the direction of the encampment. "You should return to your wagon. You will be safe. I will not be far behind."

Laura sensed an invisible wall had been raised between them now. A wall Grey Wolf would not allow her to penetrate again. She opened her hand and watched the leaf flutter away in the breeze. Then lifting the hem of her skirt, she stepped past him into the woods.

Back at the campsite, Sarah stared out into the darkness. "Oh Daniel, I'm so relieved no real harm came to her." She cast him a baleful glance. "But still, you shouldn't have left her at the river alone with Grey Wolf."

Hunched on his stool near the campfire, Dan rested his forearms on his thighs. "She just wants to talk to him. There's no need for you to worry, she's safe. My God, the man rescued her from that no-account Brandt."

"Yes and I'm thankful for that. But you don't understand. Laura has become infatuated with him. I can tell by the way she's been acting lately. There's a certain look in her eyes when she talks about him."

Straightening, Dan crooked an eyebrow. "Infatuated?"

"Daniel, Laura's very inquisitive. She has been ever since she was a child. That's fine in some respects, but combined with that impetuous nature of hers, it can get her into trouble." Sarah sighed, returning her gaze to the distant cottonwoods dusted with soft moonlight. "When do you think Grey Wolf will be leaving?"

Dan rose from his stool and stretched. "Well, he's definitely getting his strength back. He does anything I ask him. You know, Indians don't like to stay beholding to anyone, so he's been working around the camp to pay us back for taking care of him." He walked around the fire and stood in front of Sarah. "Honey, it wouldn't be right for me to order him off the train." He clasped her shoulders. "I know he's anxious to rejoin the Cheyenne. Soon, he'll be mounting that pinto of his and riding off, never to be seen again." He smiled down at her. "I'm telling you, all this worrying of yours will be for nothing."

Did Sarah read something more than reassurance in the glint in Dan's eyes? "Besides," he continued, sliding his hands down her arms and giving them a gentle squeeze, "I don't like to see that frown mess up such a beautiful face." When he lifted one hand to her face and brushed a knuckle alongside her cheek, she knew intuitively he wanted to kiss her.

"Boss, that drunk ain't going anywhere!" Lucky exclaimed, stomping into camp. "I tied him to a tree every which way but upside down. And Henry's guarding him."

As Lucky walked over to the water bucket and pulled the dipper out, Dan frowned, his gaze returning to Sarah. He seemed reluctant to release her.

Lucky tipped the dipper to his mouth and took a quick gulp. "When I told Henry what Brandt had done to Laurie," he swiped the back of his sleeve across his mouth, "it was all I could do to keep the old cuss from bashing his head in with an iron skillet."

Lowering his hands, Dan stepped back from Sarah. He gave a tight laugh. "Yeah, I believe that."

"So, what are you going to do with Brandt?" Lucky asked, pitching the dipper back in the bucket with a loud splash. "Wait until we get to Fort Kearny and let the army deal with him?"

Facing the young scout, he rubbed the back of his neck. "I gave that some thought, Lucky, but I know from past experience they'd only let him go in a day or two. They don't have the room to jail every drunk in the territory." He returned to his stool, lifted a booted foot on top, and propped an arm over his knee. "He didn't break any law. If he'd hurt Laura, then it'd be a different story. He'd be punished."

Lucky threw him a perplexed look. "Then what are you going to do with him?"

"Come dawn tomorrow, I'll see that he packs up his gear and leaves."

"You're turning him loose? Boss, you can't do that!"

"Yes, I can, too," Dan snapped. "It's a few days before we reach Fort Kearny, and I'm not carrying him another mile. Tomorrow we're laying over. Brand will be well on his way by the time we start out the next day." Straightening, he took his foot off the stool. "All he's talked about since he joined this train was going to Pikes Peak and dig for gold. With trouble being that man's next-of-kin, the only thing he'll be digging is his own grave."

Sarah scowled. "Well, I say, good riddance! I don't want my Laura to have to see the man again."

"Yeah, you're right, Mrs. Osbourne," Lucky conceded. "I'll follow him and make sure he's out of our hair. I bet those other prospectors will ride out with him. They've been complaining we're going too slow. Can you imagine that? Shoot, we're ahead of every wagon coming out of St. Joe."

"That's why we're staying in camp tomorrow," Dan said. "I expect the women would like to catch up on their washing, mending and the like."

"Did I hear you say we won't be traveling tomorrow, Dan?" Laura asked, stepping into the firelight. Before Dan could answer, her aunt rushed to her side.

"Laura, dear …" Sarah gave her a critical once-over from head to toe, her gaze flitting back to her torn collar. Tears glistened in her eyes. "Daniel told me everything, and I just thank the Lord that awful man didn't … well, that nothing worse happened." She fell silent for a moment while she wrapped her arms around Laura and embraced her. "It's late and I know you want to get cleaned up." She gave her a final hug and then released her. "You go on to our wagon, and I'll fetch you a basin of fresh water."

"You heard right, Laura," Dan said. "We're laying over tomorrow. Think everyone could use some time to catch up on their chores." He looked past her into the darkness. "Did you have a talk with Grey Wolf?"

"Yes." Laura's gaze followed Dan's. "I got a chance to thank him, but I was hoping to learn more about him." She pursed her lips in disappointment. "It's obvious he doesn't want anyone to see behind that fierce Indian exterior of his. It's a shame. I think he keeps a lot of his feelings locked inside."

"What do you care, Laurie?" Lucky broke in. "The man is about as strange as they come, and you shouldn't have a thing more to do with him. I don't care what he did back there. Heck, any man seeing a lady in distress would've done the same thing." He frowned in disgust. "If it'd been me, I'd have shot Brandt where it counted most and been done with him!"

"Lucky, that's enough," Dan said, placing a hand on the scout's shoulder. "Let's not keep Laura any longer. I'm sure she wants to put this night behind her." He nudged him. "Come on; let's go see if Henry's flattened Brandt with that frying pan yet."

Giving Laura a half-hearted nod, Lucky then aimed a scowl at Dan who prodded him forward.

The next morning, holding an armload of clothes, Laura hummed merrily as she weaved in and around the bushes lining the bank of the river. Scanning the area, she could see why the other women, including her aunt, had chosen to do their wash down river where it was more open. The water along the bank here was covered with a dense growth of tall reeds.

Still, she purposely sought a more secluded spot away from the others. She was sure their main topic of conversation would be her unfortunate run-in with Slade Brandt. Sarah would never bring it up, but a few gossip-hungry biddies would like nothing better than to pump her full of questions. And though Laura certainly had nothing to be ashamed of, she preferred putting the whole sordid experience behind her.

Earlier that morning, she'd stopped by and drank a cup of coffee with Henry. She was relieved to hear Brandt had been banished from the train and had, along with his cronies, left before sun-up with Lucky tailing them.

By now, Brandt's expulsion and the reason for it would have spread like wildfire. The only positive thing that might come out of the incident, Laura hoped, would be a little more respect shown toward Grey Wolf for what he did. All she'd seen so far from most of the people were sneers of disapproval and continued avoidance of him. She suspected many feared him.

Laura glanced up river where she'd stood with Grey Wolf the night before. *You just can't stop thinking about him, can you?*

She sank to the soft grass near the water's edge and set the bundle of clothes beside her. Idly combing fingers through her hair, she stared at the moccasins on her feet and thought about the Indian chief who'd given them to her. She recalled Black Arrow's deep concern while she'd examined Grey Wolf. It was still difficult for her to believe a white man could be an Indian's adopted son.

She pulled off the moccasins, shed her jacket, and then stood. Grasping the back hem of her skirt between her legs, she brought it up and tucked it firmly inside the front of her waistband. She rolled her drawers above her knees. Observing where the river flowed clear of the reeds, she gathered up her laundry and stepped into the water.

Her breath caught in her throat. "Ye gads, it's freezing!" How could Grey Wolf stand to swim in this? She plodded forward a few feet, the water rising above her ankles.

Suddenly, a bullfrog leaped past her. He rolled his bulging eyes, his croak sounding indignant at having been disturbed. Laura giggled. "Sorry, Mr. Frog."

She took another step, and a rock in front of her came to life, sprouting legs and a green head. "And hello to you, Mr. Turtle." It scrambled away, ducking into deeper water. Laura smiled and continued to inch deeper through the thick reeds.

She did not find the next specimen of nature's abundant wildlife so humorous. "Oooh!" she wailed, watching the snake slither past a growth of waist-high grass in front of her.

Frantically, she looked to her side, then behind her, trying to decide which way to go. When she checked back to see which way the snake was going, the thing had disappeared. "Horrors! Get me out of this jungle!" She clutched her belongings to her chest and started to retreat when a burst of hearty laughter filled the air.

Surprised, Laura swirled around. The next instant, her feet slipped on the mud-slick bottom. As her arms flailed about in a desperate attempt to catch her fall, her clothes sailed through the air.

Though Laura managed to keep from completely submersing herself, the front of her blouse and skirt were drenched.

Another hearty belt of laughter rang out.

Sputtering, she regained her balance and looked up. On the bank, Grey Wolf stood chuckling with amusement. Well, how about that, the man knows how to laugh. Still, at the moment, she was more concerned with the whereabouts of one long, slithering reptile.

"Do you see it?" she asked, glancing around anxiously, not caring that her laundry lay tangled in a clump of nearby reeds.

"Unlike the snake you met last night," Grey Wolf said, "this one will not strike. It is harmless."

"But where is it?" she demanded, a remnant of fear clinging to her voice.

"Do not be frightened, Bright Eyes. It is already on the other side of the river."

Giddy with relief, Laura realized how silly she must have looked a moment ago. When Grey Wolf stepped to the edge and extended his arm, she grinned. "I guess I looked pretty funny, huh?"

He cocked his head as if he was unsure of her meaning. Taking her hand, he pulled her onto the bank. "You look pretty, yes."

For the life of her, Laura didn't know why she wasn't more embarrassed. Her wet camisole and blouse clung to her breasts, her nipples puckering from the cool air ... or was it the way Grey Wolf looked at her?

As she met his probing gaze, Laura felt something strange and wonderful pass between them. He pulled her close and lifted her hand to his mouth. He pressed his warm lips to the center of her palm and then kissed each one of her fingers. "Every time your soft, healing hands touched me," he whispered, "I ached with pleasure, not pain." He slid his mouth over the inside of her palm again. His heated breath sent goose bumps up her arm. Words eluded her.

Releasing her hand, he threaded his fingers into her hair. "Now it is your turn to feel the pleasure of my touch." He drew her face nearer, his mouth lowering to hers.

Oh, Lord, this was what she'd been waiting for.

His first kiss was soft, like a whisper. The next, like the stroke of a feather across her mouth. He sipped at her upper lip, licked her lower lip, tasting, teasing, taking a little more of her with each kiss. A wild, delicious sensation skipped along Laura's spine, making her shudder.

Grey Wolf lifted his mouth from hers. "You are trembling, Bright Eyes. You are not afraid of me, are you?"

"No," she murmured. Her glance drifted to the ever-present cameo laying against his broad chest. She rested her hands on either side of the necklace and leaned into a towering wall of muscle.

Wrapping her in his arms, he lifted her off the ground. As she curved her hands around his neck, his mouth slanted over hers, his tongue parting her lips. Laura had never, ever been kissed like this. One chaste kiss or two by a beau on her aunt's front porch was all she'd experienced. Entranced, she opened her mouth a little more. Immediately, Grey Wolf's tongue slid deeper, bringing her another wild shiver of pleasure.

Fire surged through Grey Wolf's veins. Fighting for control, he uttered a deep groan and pulled his mouth from hers. He set her down and laid a kiss at her temple. As her soft auburn hair brushed his face, he breathed in its seductive scent. It was no use. Like a man lost in an inferno, there was no chance he could battle the flames. Nor did he want to. He nipped at her ear lobe, and then seared a path of kisses down her slender neck.

"Grey Wolf, you … m-m-m," she moaned as he eased a hand around the front of her and cupped her breast, his thumb teasing her taut nipple beneath the wet fabric.

"Please, I—"

Grey Wolf sought her lips again, smothering her words. His hands curved around her slim waist and down her hips, molding her against him.

"No …" she dragged her mouth from his and pushed against his chest, "you must stop."

Her words were like cold water thrown over hot flames. Grey Wolf withdrew his hands. He searched her eyes, looking for the desire he'd seen moments ago. "You want this as much as I do," he said huskily.

"No …" Laura frowned. "I mean, we shouldn't …"

In the distance, Grey Wolf heard voices. Above the embankment, he sighted two men walking through a thick stand of trees. They soon passed, their voices receding.

Smiling down at her, he reached out to finger the silky hair on her shoulder. Now he understood. She didn't want anyone to see them. "When the sun climbs down the sky, we will meet again."

"You mean, tonight?"

He nodded, continuing to play with her hair. He sensed her indecision. But he also saw the ardor still sparkling in her green eyes. He gave her one last look that bespoke more than words, then climbed the embankment and slipped into the woods.

The moment Grey Wolf left, Laura felt the loss. She realized she could no longer deny the strong feelings she had for him—feelings from the very first time she'd laid eyes on him. Now more than ever, she wished to know and understand this man who seemed more Indian than white. She strained to see beyond the trees hoping to catch another glimpse of him. But with his usual animal-like stealth, he'd vanished.

You shouldn't meet him again, she told herself. She rubbed a fingertip over her lips and smiled when they tingled.

You shouldn't … but you will!

CHAPTER 8

Late in the day, Grey Wolf packed for his departure the next morning. Kneeling beside a smoldering campfire, he shoved the last of his belongings into a leather pouch. Grasping his brush, he absently ran a hand over its stiff bristles. Why did he feel so distracted? He stared at the hair brush. A smile tugged at his mouth. *Bright Eyes.*

Days ago he'd found a tell-tale strand of her long auburn hair entwined in the brush. He had smelled her scent on some of his other things as well. Knowing she'd been through his personal belongings didn't bother him, though with anyone else, he would have been furious. In some strange way her touching them brought her closer to him.

He dropped the brush inside the pouch and tossed it aside. *Yes, because of her,* he chided to himself, *your mind is in the clouds and your insides rage like a brewing storm!*

He was sure one reason he found her so attractive was because she was white. Not even the half-French woman, Morning Dove, would have measured up to her beauty. She had been the first, many summers ago, to show him the pleasure between a woman's legs.

He settled back against a tree and closed his eyes. He could only imagine the pleasure Bright Eyes could give him … but tonight he would know.

Dan lifted the boiler off the iron tripod. As he poured the steaming coffee into a cup, he wrinkled his nose at the strong odor. It seemed he'd spent a damn lifetime drinking Henry's over-cooked coffee.

He took a swig from the cup. He was satisfied with the day's accomplishments. Repairs were made to a few wagons, wheels greased, and most of the animals reshod. People had stocked up on their supply of wood and filled all their water barrels. Once they reached the Platte Valley, the trees thinned out considerably, and the North Platte River was hardly fit to drink.

He set the coffee aside and glanced toward Grey Wolf's camp sheltered among a stand of oaks a short distance away. The man sat on the ground, his back reclined against a tree.

Dan sauntered over. "Guess there's no need to sign my words anymore," he said, leaning a shoulder against a tree opposite Grey Wolf.

Grey Wolf stopped sharpening his knife on a stone and looked up, his attentive expression indicating he waited for Dan to continue.

"I reckon you got your reasons for staying so tight-lipped." Dan hitched his chin toward the people milling about their camps. "For one thing, I figure you're a might uncomfortable around those folks." He hiked the front brim of his hat higher on his forehead. "You know, they aren't too sure what to make of you either."

Grey Wolf slid his knife back in its sheath at the side of his waist. "Most of them look at me the same as a half-breed," he said matter-of-factly. "They are right. I lived ten summers as a white boy and fifteen as an Indian." He wrapped the whetstone in a small cloth and tucked it into the pouch beside him. "My boyhood does not count for much. The man in me is Indian. I do not belong in the white man's world."

"I can see how you might feel that way. Fifteen years is a long time." Dan folded his arms across his chest and eyed Grey Wolf sharply. "Tell me then, how is it you speak such good English? Seems like you would've forgotten most of it after that many years."

In one fluid motion, Grey Wolf rose to his feet. He seemed to weigh his words carefully before he spoke. "A man named Jeremiah who owned a trading post took an interest in me. More than a friend, he became my tutor. He encouraged me to keep up with my reading, writing, and ciphering. He supplied me with books, newspapers, anything with the printed word." He hesitated, then added, "For the past fifteen years he is the only white man I been around; until I found myself in your wagon."

Dan didn't miss the poignancy of Grey Wolf's words. He reached into his trouser pocket. "I have something for you. Wanted to give it to you before you left." He held out his hand. "I got hold of it before Laura had a chance to throw it away." In his palm lay the bear fang. "Thought you might like to have this."

A slow, steady smile spread across Grey Wolf's face. Taking it from Dan, he held it between his thumb and forefinger. "The tooth of a grizzly is highly valued by the Cheyenne. They believe its power and strength is passed on to the man who possesses it." His fist curled around it, his appreciative gaze returning to Dan. "Only a true friend would think of giving such a token."

"Tell me, did you kill that bear or did he get away?"

A spark of pride gleamed in Grey Wolf's eyes. "One of the last things I remember was my brother, Swift Eagle, telling me its magnificent hide was on the drying rack."

"Glad to hear that," Dan said, sending a glimpse to Grey Wolf's forearm and shoulder. "Hate to think you got those battle scars for nothing."

A moment of silence fell between them. Grey Wolf looked off toward the horizon. Dan detected a note of sadness in the young man's voice when he said, "I will leave before the next sun."

"Do you know where Black Arrow is?"

"Yes. Plans were made with the Arapahoe to meet along waters that run northwest of the red river you call the Republican. Buffalo herds graze there during Moons of the Green Grass and Red Berries."

Dan nodded. "I know the area. I used to hunt and trap along there. Not much more than half a day's ride to the South Platte River where my train will be crossing in a couple weeks."

"Will you stop at the soldiers' fort?" Grey Wolf asked, squatting down. He tucked the bear tooth inside the smaller of several pouches laying on the ground.

"You mean Fort Hendricks? Lordy, yes. Sarah and Laura will have my head if I don't. Laura's brother, Alex is stationed there, and she's real anxious to see him. They're mighty close brother and sister."

Dan lifted his hat from his head, combed his fingers through his hair a couple of times, and then readjusted his hat. "You see, they lost their mother when they were kids. Their father placed them in his sister, Sarah's care, and he left with me. Now he lives in California. He's a lawyer in a town called Placerville."

After stuffing the smaller pouches into a larger one, Grey Wolf stood. "That is where they are going? To Placerville?"

"Yep, that's right."

Grey Wolf raised a brow. "The woman, Sarah … she is your woman?"

Dan shot him a pointed look and shook his head. "No, but I'd sure like to think someday she will be. Her husband died about eight months ago." A meaningful smile curved his lips. "I've known her most of my life."

"And Bright Eyes? Is she promised to anyone?"

"Laura?" Dan chuckled and shook his head again. "No man has laid a claim on her that I know of. Though from what Sarah has told me, a few back east have tried."

"Your scout has feelings for her," Grey Wolf stated flatly.

"Yeah, Lucky does," Dan said, hooking his thumbs over his gun belt, "but I don't think Laura feels the same about him." He shrugged. "It's a long way to California, though. Who knows what might develop between them by then." He looked past Grey Wolf. "Speaking of the boy, here he comes."

"Darn it, boss, I've been looking all over for you!" Lucky walked around Grey Wolf, hardly acknowledging him save for a sideward glance. "I need you to look at Ace. I'm worried about him. I've never seen him act so strange. His eyes are watering something awful, and he won't eat."

"Why sure, let's go have a look." He turned to Grey Wolf. "It was good talking with you. See you later on."

The sunset transformed the blue sky into layered colors of pastel pinks and muted reds. Before Grey Wolf reached the line of picketed horses, he stopped to watch the yellow ball of fire the Indians called the Father of Life sink below the earth. As it disappeared, he gave thanks to the Great Spirit for the day that had passed. Then he set out again, cautiously approaching the scout's horse.

He stood a few steps away from Ace and waited for the animal to become accustomed to him. He spoke calmly in the soothing voice his pinto, Four Winds, liked to hear. "*Na-vesene* … easy, my friend." Moving closer, he gently stroked the white blaze on its broad nose. The horse's dull, listless eyes closed.

He opened a small parfleche tied to his waist and dipped his fingers into its contents. Cupping the grey powder in his palm, he grasped the horse's halter and blew several wisps up the animal's nostrils.

The horse didn't flinch or try to back away. "Good, my friend. You are smart to accept this powerful medicine. You will—"

"Get your hands off him!" The words were punctuated by the sound of a gun being cocked.

Grey Wolf released the halter and slowly turned around. Not bothering to look at the scout's face, he fixed his gaze on the revolver in his hand. He knew the deadly power of the weapon, having used one of Jeremiah's to kill game.

"Just what in hell do you think you're doing?"

"I heard you tell Dan your horse was sick." Grey Wolf spread his palm, keeping his eye on Lucky's hand. "I have medicine to cure him." Relief skidded down his spine as the scout's thumb eased off the hammer, and he holstered the gun.

"Ace doesn't need your primitive, useless medicine," he said, walking over to the horse. He took hold of the halter and wiped the powder from the animal's muzzle.

Grey Wolf heard the disgust in Lucky's voice. He knew the real reason why this man hated him. *Bright Eyes.* Every time she came near Grey Wolf, the scout bristled with jealousy.

He tossed the remainder of the powder on the ground and slapped his hands clean. "By morning you will find out how useless my medicine was," he said, shouldering his way past the scout.

Laura sat in Sarah's Boston rocker behind their wagon, pen in hand, journal in her lap. Beside her, the flickering lantern propped on a barrel served as a poor substitute for daylight.

"Getting too dark to write, isn't it?" Sarah asked, stepping down from the tailgate.

"Yes, I suppose so."

Sarah glanced at the journal. "It amazes me that you find so much to write about. Why, by the time we get to California, you'll have penned an entire book." She smoothed the front of her gingham skirt. "You should join us at the Horton wagon. Mr. Horton promised to entertain us with his melodeon, and Henry's gone to get his fiddle. Dan said some music would be a great way to bolster everyone's spirits before we start out again tomorrow. He's passing the word along for anyone who'd like to join us."

"Sounds fun. I'll be by in a little while." Laura leaned over and picked up the small wooden chest from the ground. She placed the journal, pen, and ink bottle inside and closed the lid. "First, I need to tidy up some of my things. I don't know how you manage to keep your side of the wagon so orderly."

Arching one eyebrow, Sarah smiled. "Seems I don't have as many things to occupy my mind as you do." She gave Laura's shoulder a pat. "Don't be long. We'll be looking for you."

After her aunt left, Laura rested her head against the back of the rocker and folded her hands on top of the chest. She hadn't missed the true meaning behind her aunt's remark. Guess she hadn't been too successful in hiding what had really been occupying her mind. She wished she could confide in her aunt about her true feelings for Grey Wolf. But she knew Sarah wouldn't approve;

the fact he lived as an Indian was too hard for her to accept. Who was she kidding? She, herself, found it hard to understand.

Laura shrugged dismissively. The sky was darkening rapidly. Already a dozen stars twinkled high overhead. She sighed, wondering if she'd see Grey Wolf tonight. Earlier that evening, Dan told her he would be leaving before sunrise. He would be going back to the Cheyenne Indians. She bit her lip, feeling the ache of disappointment crawl up her chest and into her throat. Dear God, why? Why did he want to return to a tribe of Indians when he could live a much more civilized life with his own kind?

"Hello, Bright Eyes."

Laura jerked her head up. Grey Wolf stood a few feet away.

"You watch stars, like my sister, Stargazer. She has names for many of them." His glance swept the sky. "They are like hundreds of eyes watching what we do at night."

Grey Wolf's strong, deep voice was hypnotic to her ears. Her gaze slowly traveled over him. A perfect match to his powerful looks.

His clothes molded his body so exactly they must have been sewn especially for him. He wore a long deerskin shirt over leggings made of the same tanned deerskin. The shirt's neckline opened into a wide, deep-V to the middle of his chest, the cameo claiming its place a few inches below the hollow of his throat. A sash circled his waist, both it and the shirt heavily encrusted with geometrically designed beadwork of many colors. The beading stretched across the breadth of his shoulders and down his long arms. His moccasins were trimmed with the same decoration.

As her gaze lifted to his face, Grey Wolf's eyes glowed with arrogant pride. He knew so well the effect his appearance had on her. It was no wonder. Never did he look more handsome.

Long, golden brown hair framed his face, the red headband circling his forehead. Entwined in his hair behind one ear, two white and black-tipped feathers fluttered in the evening breeze. Laura curled her hands in a tight grip around the ends of the rocker's wooden arms. *And never did he look more Indian.*

"Did you say your sister's name is Stargazer?" Laura asked, hoping she sounded calmer than she felt.

Grey Wolf nodded.

"It's a pretty name."

"She has hair black as night, soft brown eyes, and copper skin. Very different from your beauty."

A warm flush crept into Laura's cheeks as she pushed up from the rocking chair. She carried the chest to the wagon, leaned over the lowered tailgate and set it on the floor. From the corner of her eye, she caught Grey Wolf's gaze linger on the rocker tilting to and fro. She wondered what he was thinking. She waited until he looked at her again and then asked, "How did you get the name, Grey Wolf?"

Folding his arms across his chest, Grey Wolf regarded her thoughtfully. He came tonight knowing she would ask him more questions. He stepped closer to her. "I was hiding in a small den when Black Arrow found me. Thinking my light eyes resembled those of a wolf, he named me Grey Wolf."

"How long ago was that? How old were you?"

"Fifteen summers ago. I was ten." His eyes sought hers. Next would come the questions he knew had to be foremost in her mind. What had happened to bring about his capture? And what happened to his parents?

Grey Wolf had never told anyone of that traumatic day. Not even his friend, Jeremiah had asked him about it, sensing his reluctance to speak of it. He'd tried to keep the pain and sorrow of that dark day buried in the deepest corner of his heart.

Laura fidgeted with a button on her blouse. "What was your name before then? The one your parents gave you?"

The unexpected question caught him off guard. It had been a lifetime since he'd spoken his white name aloud to anyone. He lowered his arms, his fists bunched at his sides. "David," he said, the word barely audible. The name sounded foreign and saying it almost made him physically sick. He swallowed, tasting the bile in his throat.

"David?" She reached up and softly pressed a hand to his cheek. "David," she repeated and smiled, "it fits you."

Turning his face from her, he stared into the night. "No one has said that name … since …" His voice faltered.

For the first time in his life, here was someone he could pour his heart out to. Tell it all to. All his deep-seated emotions, all his divided feelings. He could explain how the boy, David, became the man, Grey Wolf. How he learned to share his white soul with the trained body and mind of an Indian.

But he had hidden all those feelings behind an emotional wall for fifteen years. His gaze drifted back to Laura. And he knew not even Bright Eyes could help him tear it down.

He drew in a cleansing breath to clear his troubled thoughts, aware she was speaking to him again.

"… I know it's hard to talk about. Perhaps I could ask you something else. Since you lived with the Indians most of your life, how come you speak English so well?"

It was natural for her to be curious about him, just as Dan had been. And she deserved an answer, as he did. "During my third summer with the Cheyenne, I met a white man named Jeremiah who owned a trading post. He never tried to persuade me to leave the Indians, but he told me it was important not to forget my book learning. I went to his place whenever I could, so he could teach me."

A mental image of the crusty old man surfaced. Grey Wolf smiled; glad to be recalling fonder memories. "Jeremiah T. Hornbuckle is his full name. He still gives me books when I go to see him. They belonged to his wife who was a school teacher back east before she died. My favorite is James Finemore Cooper's *The Last of the Mohicans*." He shook his head. "I read it so many times, I can recite it."

He looked down at Laura, surprised at how relaxed he felt now. "Enough talk." He took her slender hand in his. "Walk with me while the moon and stars watch over us."

CHAPTER 9

Hand in hand, Laura and Grey Wolf walked through the tall grass. Hearing a fiddle strike a tune, she slowed her steps and looked up the line of wagons to where a crowd gathered around a blazing bonfire.

"Are they having a special ceremony?" he asked.

Laura shook her head. "It's not really a ceremony."

"When I approached your camp, I overheard your aunt. She wants you there."

She glanced at his large hand encircling hers. A sensual current rippled up her arm as he rubbed his thumb back and forth over her fingers. Her gaze lifted to his face. "I'd rather be with you." Their eyes held, and for a moment, their silence said more than any spoken words could. Then Grey Wolf clasped her hand tighter and led her away from the wagons.

When they reached a spot bearing a lone cottonwood, he knelt down and indicated for her to sit on a mat of short, tufted grass beside him. An owl hooted from a branch high overhead. "Except for him, we are alone," he said, smiling.

Laura sat on the ground and curled her legs under her full skirt. Her heart pounded so hard she was certain Grey Wolf heard.

"You smell like summer flowers," he said. He hooked a finger under her chin, his gaze on her lips. "And I am drawn to the nectar." His mouth lowered and he kissed her lightly. Then coaxing her to lie back, he stretched out beside her and slid his forearm under her head. He kissed her again, this time his open mouth covering hers fully. Several times he drew away, only to return, each kiss more demanding than the one before.

Cocooned in the warmth of his embrace, Laura slid her hands up his chest to his shoulders, feeling his heat through the buckskin shirt. Beneath her palms, his corded muscles flexed and tightened. Her fingers delved into the thickness of his long hair, and she breathed in his maleness. Her whole being reeled with the look, the strength, the scent of him.

He circled a hand at the base of her throat, his thumb skimming over her throbbing pulse. He lifted his mouth from hers and while holding her gaze captive, he lowered his hand over her blouse and cupped the swell of her breasts.

Dear Lord, she shouldn't allow him to touch her this way. It could only lead to intimacies she knew little about. But as Laura stared with longing at him, an unbearable, instinctive need welled up inside her. Tomorrow this man whom she cared for deeply would be gone. Before he left, she wanted more than empty dreams to remember him by. She searched his face as he looked at her in silent expectation. *David.* Yes, the name suited him. And tonight she would give herself to him.

Clinging to his shoulders, she thrust herself upward so he could hold the fullness of each breast. A deep groan emitted from his throat as he responded to her invitation.

Passion fueled the fire burning inside her. She wanted his heavy touch without the constraints of her blouse hindering the feel of his strong hands. Somehow reading her thoughts, he began to undo the buttons. But numerous and small, they were difficult to work free. Nudging his fingers aside, Laura unbuttoned the rest, then sitting up, stripped off the blouse.

Grey Wolf placed a gentle hand at her side. When he turned her body to face him, he drew in his breath as he scanned her bare shoulders and cleavage above her camisole. Laura knew the three-quarter moon lent more than enough light to see her.

He took hold of one of the thin straps and slipped it off her shoulder. She shuddered when his fingers glided down her arm. Lowering the other strap, he watched the garment fall to her waist. His heated gaze swept across her breasts, lingering a moment before he reached up and pulled out the two combs holding her hair in place. Thick tresses tumbled over her shoulders, the ends fluttering in the warm evening breeze and tickling her flesh.

"*Ne-peva-tamaahe,*" he said.

Laura tilted her head questioningly.

Grey Wolf laid the combs on the ground, and then pulled her down beside him. Braced on one elbow, he leaned close to her ear and whispered, "You are a beautiful woman." He laid a callused hand over one breast and cradled its roundness in his palm while his soft lips skimmed the side of her neck.

Laura closed her eyes, delicious tremors swirling inside her. She set her hand over the top of his, reveling in the feel of him holding her so intimately. Her nipple tingled beneath his coarse fingers, becoming hard and erect. She rolled closer, her other breast aching to be touched and held the same. As Grey Wolf's responsive hand stroked her flesh, a satisfied moan escaped her lips.

Lost in the magic of his loving, Laura draped her arms around his neck allowing his hand to move down her waist. At the same time, his mouth and tongue mated with hers, delving and devouring, their pleasures building with breathtaking intensity.

But as he gathered her skirt off her thigh and slipped a hand underneath, the sudden memory of Slade forcing his hands up her dress flashed through Laura's mind. Instantly, she stiffened. Breaking their kiss, she pulled back and looked into Grey Wolf's face. The understanding she saw put her mind at ease even before he spoke.

"Do not be afraid, Bright Eyes. I want only to bring you the pleasure your body craves as much as mine." He lowered his head and swirled his tongue around the tip of one nipple, then crossed to the other and suckled gently to the rhythm of her heartbeat.

Laura relaxed, the stars blurring overhead as a warm darkness engulfed her. "David … oh, David," she murmured.

Grey Wolf lifted his head and stared down at her. "Why do you call me that?"

Laura blinked up at him, confused by the sudden harshness in his voice. "David? It's your name."

"*Was* my name." He flashed her a chilling look of disdain. "*Was!*" he repeated. He abruptly rolled away from her.

Suddenly cold in places where she'd felt warm only seconds ago, Laura sat up and shrugged back into her camisole. "What do you mean?" She laid a tentative hand on his shoulder. "It still is."

"No! David is *not* my name. It was a child's." His stone-grey eyes bored into hers. "A child who died with his family fifteen years ago. He is a memory," his gaze drifted past her, "part of a nightmare I have tried hard to forget."

Laura watched the torment cloud his face as he stared, unblinking and unseeing, into the darkness. Now she knew. His family had died. But how? Were they killed by the Indians? Maybe the very Indians who captured him?

Oh Lord, how she wished she could ask him. Then she would understand the kind of suffering he'd been put through.

In one swift motion, Grey Wolf rose to his feet. "We should go back," he said in a monotone voice, schooling his expression to hide the turbulence Laura knew festered beneath the surface.

She hurriedly buttoned her blouse. It wasn't supposed to be like this, she lamented. She had wanted him to love her, and to love him back. It was to be a night to remember. *Their night.*

She wished she hadn't called him David, though she didn't understand why that should affect him so. She scooped her combs off the ground and jammed them back in her hair. But then, she supposed she hadn't gone through what he had. Yes, she lost her mother at a young age, and her father left, but she'd been raised by loving relatives, not Indians.

When she stood, he reached out and swung her around to face him. "Remember, the man who held you in his arms tonight was Grey Wolf, a Cheyenne warrior."

She lifted her chin, leveling a piercing glare on him. "And Laura, not Bright Eyes, was the woman Grey Wolf held."

His powerful hands tightened around her shoulders. He looked as if he was about to say something else, but instead he turned and started back the way they'd come. A few steps behind him, Laura stared at his broad back, one question continuing to nag her. Why in the world would he want to go back to those Indians who, for all she knew, killed his family?

As they drew closer to camp, she realized Grey Wolf was leading her to the Horton wagon where a throng of people danced and clapped to the music. Nearby the bonfire shot tiny sparks into the night sky like Fourth of July fireworks. Laura hung back, in no mood for the merrymaking.

"Laurie, I've been looking for you," Lucky said, emerging from the crowd. The firelight glittered in his clear blue eyes as he smiled and took hold of her hand. "Your aunt said you'd be along, but I was beginning to wonder."

"I had a few things to do before tomorrow," she offered, trying to look far more composed than she felt. She hoped he didn't notice they hadn't come from her wagon.

Lucky threw Grey Wolf a withering glance. "You might as well go on back to your camp, Grey Wolf. I know how awkward you must feel around civilized folks."

Laura cringed at Lucky's remark. She looked back, again hoping Grey Wolf would say something to her—anything that might heal the rift between them. But he said nothing, a dark, enigmatic look on his face.

Lucky tugged her arm. "Come on, Laurie."

As she allowed him to lead her away, she stole a last glance over her shoulder. Grey Wolf stood, staring after her. Regret tore at her heart. Was this the way they were meant to part? With nothing more said between them?

Laura kept her miserable feelings to herself. On the surface, she gave the appearance of enjoying the music and laughter. But in the back of her mind, the image of Grey Wolf lurked, dressed in all his Indian finery.

Why, she wondered sadly, does he want to cling to that image of himself, denying all ties to his white heritage? She plunked down on a spindled back chair, while Lucky went to fetch her some apple cider. Oh, what's the use in getting upset, she chided herself. The man came into my life a stranger and a stranger, he'll leave.

But deep inside, she knew better. One doesn't have strong feelings for a stranger. She knew something else. Because of those feelings, she would never be the same again.

"Laurie?"

"… hmmm?" Laura raised her head, reluctant to allow Lucky's voice to infiltrate her thoughts.

"Here's your cider," he said, standing in front of her, a cup in his hand.

She sighed, letting go of memories she knew she would later retrieve time and again. "Thanks, Lucky," she said and offered him a smile as she took the cup from him.

He pulled a stool beside her and sat down. Taking off his hat, he propped it on one knee. He looked around at the group of adults and children singing and clapping to a chorus of *Oh Susanna*. "Looks like everyone's having a good time. Dan likes to get people on the train together like this every so often. The journey's a long, hard one and the better folks get to know each other, the better they tend to pull together when the going gets rough."

Laura nodded as Ed Horton struck up *My Old Kentucky Home* on his melodeon, his hands pumping the sweet-sounding notes from the instrument's bellows. Beside him, Henry played the fiddle. Several couples circled the bonfire in a slow, swaying waltz.

In the shadow of the trees, Grey Wolf listened to the music. He had never heard such strange instruments. He watched the men swing the women around in their arms. How different from the movements of the Cheyenne who danced to the rhythmic beat of drums—up and down on their toes, stomping, leaping, howling their tribal songs.

Jealousy tightened every muscle in his body when the scout wrapped Laura in his arms and danced in the same manner as the others. Bowing his head, Grey Wolf clenched his jaw. *The man has more right to her than you do. He belongs in her world. You don't.* Forcing himself not to look back, he stalked away toward his camp.

As the music receded, the sharp trill of a bird slowed his steps.

He listened intently. There it was again. A cold knot twisted in Grey Wolf's stomach as he broke into a run.

Meanwhile back at the party, as Lucky swirled Laura around the other dancers, she tried to get into the spirit of the evening. "You surprise me, Lucky. I didn't know you liked to dance."

"There's a lot you don't know about me, Laurie. Maybe now that Indian is leaving, we'll have more time to get acquainted."

"He's not an Indian. He was born white, the same as you and I," she replied.

"Yeah, well that doesn't change who he is now. Do you think he dresses that way for the fun of it?" Lucky bumped into another couple, threw them a quick "Sorry, folks," and swung Laura on by them. "I'll tell you one thing. If Indians were to attack this train, I bet I know whose side he'd be on!"

"Lucky, how can you say that!" She stopped dancing. "You're wrong. You don't understand him."

"And I suppose you do?"

"Well, I—"

"Looks like you two are having a good time," Sarah broke in, smiling radiantly over Dan's shoulder as they waltzed by. "I didn't think these two trailblazers knew how to dance, did you, Laura?"

Before Laura could respond, a man pushed through the crowd, shouting, "Driscoll! Hey, Driscoll, you gotta come quick. Indians stole some horses!" Abruptly, the music ceased. "They got away, except for ..." he shot Laura a furtive glance, "that savage Miss Westbrook patched up."

Dan's face was a mix of alarm and disbelief. "Slow down, Seth. Do you mean Grey Wolf?"

At Seth's nod, Dan bristled, his right hand settling over the handle of his holstered gun. "Where is he?"

Seth lifted an arm and pointed. "Yonder, at the last picket line. The men got him tied up and fixing to hang him. But I thought you should be in charge of any hanging that's gonna take place."

"Damn!" Dan turned to Lucky. "Come with me." He glared at the crowd of onlookers. "I'll handle this. Everyone stays here," he commanded with a strong tone of authority. Then he turned on his heels and hurried off with Lucky and Seth.

Laura stared wide-eyed at her aunt. "It can't be. It just can't be," she beseeched above the loud whispers buzzing around them. "I have to go to him."

"You can't go back there!" Sarah protested.

"But they've made a mistake." Laura picked up the hem of her skirt and escaping her aunt's grab for her arm, rushed past her.

"Laura, come back here! Laura!"

Seven men, hell-bent on quick justice, hovered around Grey Wolf.

"Well, what are you waiting for?" one of them snarled to the man beside him. "Shit, give me the damn rope!" He snatched the noose out of the man's hand and circled it over Grey Wolf's head.

With hands tied behind his back, Grey Wolf stiffened as the leader of the mob cinched the rope around his neck. Anger burned like fire in his chest. "I did not help those Indians steal your horses," he said, glowering at the man. "They are—"

"Shut up, heathen! You think any of us are going to believe you—a white man who prefers living with Injuns?" He leaned over and spit in Grey Wolf's face.

As the spittle rolled down the side of his cheek, Grey Wolf's hands doubled into fists behind his back, but he held his tongue.

"Frank, keep your rifle on him in case he tries anything," he said to one, then barked at another whose young, frightened eyes avoided Grey Wolf's cold stare. "You, boy, bring that horse over here under this tree."

"Jake, don't you think we ought to wait for Driscoll before we hang him?" the boy questioned nervously.

"There'll be no hanging, so every one of you back away from Grey Wolf," Dan shouted, halting a few feet from them, the scout behind him. "Jake, I said move away from Grey Wolf *now*! And you, Frank, drop your rifle!"

The one man tossed his weapon, while the others stepped back. But Jake held his ground. "Driscoll, this man's a horse thief. We have every right to string him up."

"The hell you do! Not on my wagon train."

"Even when we have proof?" Jake looked at Frank. "Tell him what happened."

Frank cleared his throat, averting Dan's narrowed eyes. "Well, I walked to my wagon to fetch some water. I was just getting back when I saw two Injuns scattering with five of our horses. Hell, by the time I grabbed my rifle, darkness had swallowed them up." He glanced at Grey Wolf. "That's when I saw him. He was standing next to the other horses and mules tied to the picket line." He shook his head. "He knew he didn't have a chance of getting away when he saw my rifle pointed at him. I told him to throw down his weapons and—"

"Me and my friends," Jake interrupted, "weren't at your little party, Driscoll, so when we heard Frank yelling for help, we come a'running. It was too late to chase after the Injuns, they were long gone. But Frank caught this one ..." he snorted, glaring up into Grey Wolf's face "red-handed." He turned his angry gaze on his men. "He's a traitor to his own kind. I say we lynch him here and now!"

"Yeah," Frank growled, "let's get it over with!"

Jake made a grab for the rope around Grey Wolf's neck as the men closed in, one leading the horse. In the same second that Dan drew his gun and fired a shot into the air, Laura burst from the trees.

"No!" she shrieked, pushing her way between the men and Grey Wolf, a wildcat look in her eyes. She slapped her hands to Jake's chest and shoved. "Get away from him!"

With a show of disgust, Jake retreated, as did the others.

Laura grasped the rope and tugged on the knot, her hands shaking with anger. "Are ... are you all right?" she asked, her voice cracking.

Grey Wolf answered with a stiff nod, keeping his features deceptively composed to hide his anger and humiliation. He inclined his head for her to remove the noose. He felt degraded that she should find him like this, tied up and unable to defend himself. He wished she didn't have to see the hatred these people had for him. They didn't want to hang him because they believed he was a horse thief. They wanted to hang him because he was an Indian.

CHAPTER 10

"Laura, move away from him."

She looked at Dan, bewildered. "But you know Grey Wolf didn't have anything to do with stealing those horses." She bit her lip trying to steady her voice. The rope slipped from her hand, the ugly hangman's noose coiling at her feet like a serpent's head. She kicked at it and stepped back. How could any of them believe he would do such a thing, especially Dan?

Laura was mortified to see the same contempt on Lucky's face that she saw on the other men's faces. "Boss, there's something you ought to know," he said. "Late this afternoon, I caught Grey Wolf at the other picket line. Gave me some lame excuse he was giving Ace medicine to heal him. Now I wonder if he wasn't planning on stealing him."

Dan's gaze cut to Grey Wolf. "I want to hear your side of this."

"Hey, Driscoll, over here! Look at this!" All heads turned as one of the men swung a lantern behind some scrub brush.

Dan walked over, Laura and the others close on his heels. Sprawled between the bushes, an Indian lay with an arrow protruding from his back. "Things just became a little clearer. That's Grey Wolf's arrow."

Jake stepped closer. "How you know that?"

"From the white ring painted below the feathers. Same as the other arrows in Grey Wolf's quiver."

"Why would he kill an Injun?" Jake asked, disbelief punctuating his words.

"He is Pawnee!" came the cold, brittle response. "He is my enemy."

Grey Wolf approached, his hands still tied behind his back. He walked around the bush and kicked the body over on its side. Blood gushed from the hole where the arrowhead and shaft jutted out of the Indian's chest.

Laura cringed and looked away, rancid bile stinging the back of her throat. It was clear his hatred toward this Indian went far deeper than mere resentment for stealing their horses.

Dan moved behind Grey Wolf and began untying his hands. "Looks like we owe you our thanks for stopping the Pawnees before they had a chance to steal anymore of our livestock."

"You think they'll come back tonight?" Lucky asked.

Dan shook his head. "They got what they wanted. Pawnees usually don't attack large wagon trains outright. They just like to sneak in and out with a few horses." He yanked the knot loose from Grey Wolf's wrists. "You're free to go, son." His eyes narrowed in Jake's direction. "You're lucky I don't kick you off my train for inciting this lynch mob."

He thrust the rope into the man's hand, and then looked around at the others. "I'm the law on this train and don't any of you forget it! As for the horses, there isn't any way we can get them back now. I'll find out who they belonged to and replace them from my own stock until we reach a way station where we can get replacements. Now, all of you go on back to your wagons. We're heading out early in the morning."

Grey Wolf picked up his weapons off the ground. Laura saw the way Jake and the other men gave him a wide berth as they passed by. His size alone was threatening. Combined with his savage looks, those cunning grey eyes, and that animal-like stride, it was no wonder they feared him. After all, hadn't she been frightened of him at first, before she became accustomed to him?

Yes, and then he had an entirely different effect on her, didn't he? Fear turned into attraction. She watched him sheathe his knife and sling the bow and quiver of arrows over his shoulder. *And now into what . . . ? Love? Was she falling in love with him?*

As he headed away from the wagons, she stared after him. His moonlit form disappeared into a shadow of dense thickets.

And all she could do was stand here and watch him walk out of her life.

"Wait!" Laura called, starting after him. She'd taken only a few steps when Lucky seized hold of her arm.

"Laurie, let him go."

"I'll thank you to let me go!" She pulled from his grip. "What's the matter with you, Lucky? How dare you accuse Grey Wolf of stealing those horses! You're no better than those suspicious weasels back there. Trying to pin something on him just because he looks and acts differently from you."

"Laurie, that's not it at all. I don't have anything against the man except ..." Lucky hesitated, his shoulders sagging as he let out a heavy sigh. "Look, maybe I was wrong. But I still don't think you should be around him."

"Well, I do!" Brushing past him, she hurried to catch up with Grey Wolf.

In the background, she heard Dan issue orders to double the night guards. She was thankful when his next order was for Lucky. "Hey, kid, give me a hand digging a shallow grave for the Indian or the next thing we'll have is a pack of wolves breathing down us."

Far from the wagons, Grey Wolf stalked toward his camp, anger and bitterness in every step. Great Spirit Above, he might have been swinging from a tree by now if Dan hadn't stopped those men.

The image of the dead Pawnee sprawled on the ground brought a grim smile to his lips. He had once more avenged the deaths of his white family. If he'd been any place but here, he would have taken the Indian's scalp for his war belt.

His steps slowed as his thoughts turned to Laura. He remembered how she flung herself between him and those men. The significance of what she did made him realize that her feelings for him must be more than a physical attraction. And what about his own feelings? Did not his admiration for her reach deeper than the color of her eyes and the beauty of her skin?

"Grey Wolf, please ... wait!"

He halted and turned; surprised she had gotten so close behind him without his hearing her footsteps. *Thoughts of the woman deafen your ears,* he chided himself.

"Why do you follow me?"

Laura stepped closer. "Because I wanted to tell you how much I hate those men for what they did to you. I never for one minute believed you helped those Indians steal our horses." She cast her eyes downward. "Dan told me you're leaving tomorrow morning. I didn't want to let you go without saying good-bye. I thought after all we'd been through together, what we've done for each other ..." She lifted her head, sweeping a lock of hair behind her ear. "What we've shared ..." Her voice wavered under his steady gaze.

The night grew still, quiet.

Uncertainty crept into her face. "Didn't our being together earlier tonight mean anything to you?"

He couldn't restrain himself any longer. It was impossible for him to hold back his feelings when this woman—this beautiful, spirited woman spoke to him this way. With one swift jerk, he pulled her to him. "Yes, Laura, it meant something to me. Much more than I wanted it to." He kissed her then, hard, almost angrily.

Grey Wolf's steel grip on her arms hurt, but Laura didn't care. She returned his savage kiss, glad to be in his arms again, to hear him speak her name and say those words.

His mouth ravished hers, spreading her lips apart, thrusting his tongue deep. She heard a groan of frustration low in his throat. Then as abruptly as he'd swept her into his arms, he set her away from him. His eyes, dark, troubled looked into hers. "This ... what we are feeling ... it is wrong. I am not the man for you." He slid his hands down her arms and squeezed her, tenderly this time. "I do not want to hurt you."

"But surely you know by now how much I care for you?" She clung to him, a tightness clutching at her throat. "I don't want you to leave."

"Laura, listen to me and accept what I have to say. Fate brought us together, tempted us. But that does not make it right. We are worlds apart. You need a man who can promise you a future, not someone who hunts buffalo for survival and fights tribal enemies; whose only possessions are his tipi, weapons and horse."

He released her with a finality that brooked no argument. "Tomorrow you will go on to California with your people. And I will go back to mine."

But Laura wouldn't give in, not when it hurt so much. "Why do you call those Indians your people? They *aren't*. The color of your skin is the same as mine." She didn't mean to sound so harsh, but she was exasperated by all he'd said. "David is your name, more so than Grey Wolf. Why do you deny it? Why deny your heritage?"

Grey Wolf flashed a look of disdain and fired back, "Heritage? What heritage? My heritage was wiped out in one morning—gone forever!"

Laura saw the raw hurt in his eyes before he swung away from her. Oh, God, what had she done? Had she pushed too far? Instinctively, she reached out to him only to draw her hand back.

"It must have been horrible."

He stood silent, unmoving.

"Grey Wolf, please, don't shut me out. I want to understand. The Indians killed your folks, didn't they?" She pursed her lips together, surprised to find them swollen from his kiss. She reached out and laid a hand on his shoulder. "How can you remain loyal to the people who killed them?"

He turned back to her, his face solemn. "Black Arrow's people did not kill my family. Pawnees did."

She frowned. "But they're still Indians."

"The man who tried to hurt you … the men who wanted to hang me … they are white. Yet, you do not turn away from other whites because of them."

Laura's features remained clouded with what Grey Wolf knew to be concern for him. He clenched his jaw as he fought the mental anguish clawing at his insides. She wasn't going to let up, was she? Did she think saving his life gave her the right to question it? Maybe it did. And didn't he care enough about her to want her to understand why he must go back to the Cheyenne?

Taking hold of her hand, he led her to his camp. He had never talked to anyone about his loss, his feelings, his years with the Cheyenne. Maybe it was time he did.

Once there, Laura settled on a blanket he'd spread on the ground. A shiver skipped up her arms as a cool breeze sent a cluster of leaves whirling around her. Grey Wolf wrapped the ends of the blanket about her shoulders, and then knelt in front of the charred remains of his campfire.

He cupped his hands around the center of the coals and blew gently. Fascinated, Laura watched him exhale slowly, even breaths and utter soft, Indian words. Like magic, bright embers appeared. He held some dry grass over the embers and continued to blow. In no time, flames licked at his fingers. After adding some twigs and branches on top, he sat cross-legged opposite her.

Staring into the fire, his crystal-grey eyes turned golden. "I do not remember much about my childhood," he began. "What I do remember seems like a dream. My mother and father. My brother. The place where I lived. They are all a dream that fades more and more with time." Bowing his head, he cleared his throat. "But one memory never fades. The day Pawnees massacred my family and burned my home."

He leaned over and tossed another piece of wood into the fire. The flames leaped higher, sparks crackling and popping upward. "I was hunting in the woods, when I saw the smoke. I ran as fast as I could, but by the time I got there, it was too late." His eyes closed, and Laura knew he was reliving it all over again. "They were dead."

He curled his fingers around the cameo pendant. "For a long time, I blamed God for not letting me die with them." He seemed unaware he was clutching the cameo until he opened his eyes and noticed her looking at his hand. He lifted the stone out in front of him. "My father gave this to my mother for her birthday. I found it in her hand."

"It's beautiful," Laura said, her voice barely a whisper.

"Cheyenne wear tokens and charms to give them luck or special powers. This gave me the strength and courage to go on when fear and hatred threatened to destroy me."

She hung on his every word. She could tell by the tightness in his voice, this was hard for him to talk about. Yet she hoped by bringing his feelings out into the open, he'd gain some sort of relief. "When were you captured?"

"Not long after the Pawnees left. Black Arrow and his warriors were tracking them. They are the Cheyenne's tribal enemy. When Black Arrow rode in, he saw the destruction. He told me later he would never have taken me if my family had survived."

"Did you try to escape?"

"I wanted to, but it was impossible since I was tied behind the warrior I rode with. We traveled many suns. I tried to keep my bearings, but the land was unfamiliar. When we reached their campgrounds, they imprisoned me inside a tipi for several weeks."

He picked up a stick and stirred the embers. "They treated me good. They fed and clothed me. But I hated them. It did not matter they were Cheyenne and not Pawnee. They could have been Shoshone or Kiowa for all I cared. To me, they were ..." his glance met hers, "savages."

Laura caught the mockery in his tone. She knew his bitterness wasn't directed at her, but to others who had called him by that word.

"I was watched closely by one woman. She was Chief Black Arrow's wife. I helped her and other women do menial tasks around the encampment, while the men and older boys went off to hunt. I envied them, but did not have the skills or strength even the boys my own age had. As months passed, although I still looked for a way to escape, I found myself wondering what it would be like to ride their fast ponies and hunt the buffalo."

He tossed the stick into the flames. "I do not know when I stopped wanting to escape. I guess when I finally accepted the fact I had no family to go back to."

Engrossed in what he was telling her, Laura hardly moved, not wanting to distract him.

He smiled. "Black Arrow's wife, Woman-With-Smart-Hands, was a wise woman, very patient and understanding. Before I knew it, she was swaying me to their ways, teaching me their language, their customs." He grew quiet a moment, drawing his lips together thoughtfully. "Eventually, I saw them not as a tribe of Indians, but as individuals. The warriors were husbands, fathers, and brothers. Alongside them, their women worked hard, their children taught with discipline and love."

Grey Wolf shook his head. "Even so, it was hard for me to accept Black Arrow as a father. When he tried to teach me the necessary skills to become a man, I rebelled. I guess I was afraid I would not live up to his expectations. But as I watched his son, Swift Eagle, train to become a warrior, I realized not only did I want to learn; I wanted to be better than Swift Eagle. I wanted to prove I could be as good a warrior as any Cheyenne. And so I became more like them every day."

"Did Black Arrow really adopt you?"

"It was two seasons before I moved into his lodge to live with his family. During a simple ceremony, he honored me with the name, Grey Wolf." He held out his right hand. "And he did this." A thin white scar ran the full width of his palm. Unsheathing the long knife from his waist, he traced the pointed edge of the blade along the scar. Laura sucked in her breath, imagining the searing pain such an incision would cause. "Black Arrow cut my hand, then his own and Swift Eagle's. Afterward, he pressed my hand to theirs, mixing our blood."

He drew Laura's eyes to his. "It sealed a bond between us forever."

Laura nodded. She understood what he was telling her. His home was not just with the Cheyenne, but with a father and mother, a brother and sister. They'd taken the place of his lost family. Looking at him across the fire, she again observed the intricate beadwork sewn on his hand-made shirt; the feathers woven into his long hair; the red band circling his forehead. The evidence was there—not written on some formal adoption papers—but in his clothes, in his face, in his eyes. He was a proud Cheyenne warrior.

She understood now why he didn't want to change. Nor did she want him to. She loved him for who he was. And for that reason, she must let him go.

Grey Wolf rose to his feet. Stepping around the fire, he offered her his hand. The blanket slipped from her shoulders as he pulled her up. He tilted her chin with his thumb and forefinger. "I will not forget you," he said, his gaze sweeping over her face.

"I'll never forget you," she replied in a tremulous voice.

His hand tightened around hers, while his other hand cradled the side of her cheek. His glance lowered to her lips, and her pulse quickened, waiting for him to kiss her.

Instead, he let go of her and stepped back. "You better leave." The longing and regret in his eyes matched what she felt in her heart. "Good bye, Laura."

"Good-bye, Grey Wolf. Godspeed." Blinking back tears, she turned from him and walked toward the wagons.

CHAPTER 11

Urging Four Winds up the crest of the hill, Grey Wolf halted the pinto between a stand of scrub oaks. The horse danced and snorted, his black and white coat slick with sweat from another hard day's journey across the sun-scorched plains.

The panoramic view below sent a surge of exhilaration through Grey Wolf. Tipis numbering well over two hundred dotted the grasslands. The Arapahoe and Cheyenne had met as planned, their villages separated by tribe, bands and families. Smoke wafting through the tops of the lodges created a blanket of haze that drifted across the azure sky.

Spying movement in the underbrush a short distance down the hill, he reined Four Winds behind the trees and dismounted. Holding the horse's muzzle with one hand to quiet him, he gripped the handle of his knife with the other.

When a familiar figure stepped into the open, his apprehension gave way to a smile. The young girl wore a knee-length tanned, doeskin tunic. Her braided black hair swung over her shoulders as she leaned down to pluck a few berries from a bush and drop them into a basket cradled in her arm.

Grey Wolf looped the reins over a branch, then picked a handful of berries off a nearby bush and tossed them above the girl's head. As the fruit rained down, she frowned, her wary eyes searching through the tall shrubs.

When he circled the trees to reveal himself, Stargazer gasped in surprise. "*Ma-hta-sooma!* Mystery of mysteries! Is it a spirit who stands before me?" she asked, blinking her eyes.

Grey Wolf laughed. "No, my little sister," he said, easily slipping into their native tongue. "I stand before you, flesh and blood."

Scurrying up the hill, she paid little attention to the berries spilling from the basket. The sunlight glittered in her brown eyes as she looked up at him. "I prayed every night. I prayed you would come back to us."

"It is the strength of those prayers that helped bring me back. And this …" He touched his forehead.

"You knew I made the headband?"

"Red beads with a yellow-winged bird in the center … who else would make me such a gift?"

Stargazer openly appraised her brother from head to foot. He was bare-chested, wearing only a breechcloth and moccasins. As her gaze traveled over the scars on his forearm and in the thick muscle of his shoulder, she was reminded of the cruel wounds he'd endured in his deadly fight with the grizzly. She observed the talisman hanging from his neck and his long-bladed hunting knife sheathed at his waist. By all outward appearances, he looked the same. But only time would tell if being among the people of his own race might have changed him in other ways.

She closed her eyes, quickly thanking the Great One Above for allowing Grey Wolf to return alive and well. Then she cast an excited glance toward the villages. "I cannot wait to see the look on everyone's face when they see who walks beside me."

Grey Wolf untied Four Winds, and the two headed out of the thicket and down the grassy slope. As they passed the first encampment, a group of children darted around them giggling and pointing, while a dog nipped playfully at their heels. Women tending the cook fires outside their tipis turned in their direction. Some showed surprised recognition, others, curiosity.

Stargazer told Grey Wolf most of the men were away, either hunting or competing in games of skill, but that Black Arrow had remained in camp to plan summer ceremonies with the other leaders.

Walking the perimeter of tipis encompassing their own village, Grey Wolf heard someone call out his name. Stepping around the pinto, he recognized their clan's arrow maker, Runs-Like-Deer seated in front of his tipi. Branches, lengths of sinew, and a small pile of arrowheads were arranged beside him.

Nodding to his long-time friend, he handed Stargazer the pinto's reins and knelt down to examine one of the long, narrow branches. "Wood from the ash tree makes good weapons."

Runs-Like-Deer laid aside the arrow he was working on and arched a brow. "So, it is true, Black Arrow left you with white-eyes."

Grey Wolf tested the strength of the wood by bending the branch in the middle. It gave a little, but didn't snap. "Yes, Nightwalker instructed my father to take me to people of my own blood so that I might live," he replied, setting the branch down and rising to his feet.

The Indian cast Grey Wolf a sly look. "I am glad you are back. I will make you many fine arrows. In exchange, maybe you give me something from land of whites?"

Grey Wolf remembered the hand tools Dan insisted on giving him. Runs-Like-Deer could put a chisel to good use in shaping hard flint into arrowheads. He nodded. "Come by Black Arrow's lodge tonight."

As he took the reins from Stargazer and moved on, she quickened her steps to keep up with his long strides. "What about me? Have you brought me back something?"

Grey Wolf grinned at his sister's forwardness. Customarily reserved around male members of her family, Stargazer had never been so around him. "Yes, little one, I have something special for you." He no longer needed the lotion Laura gave him for his wounds. Stargazer would like the soft feel of it on her skin, as well as its fragrance. Reaching into a parfleche hanging from Four Winds's back, he pulled out a bright green bottle. When he held it out for her to see, her eyes widened in delight. The colored bottle would have been a gift even if it were empty. He uncorked it and poured some lotion on his fingers, then rubbed it on top of her hand. "Smell it," he urged.

Stargazer lifted her hand to her nose. A quizzical smile touched her lips. "Hum, it smells like a field of prairie flowers after summer rain." She took the bottle from him after he recorked it. "I thank you, my brother."

Ahead of them, an elder member of the clan approached. He squinted his eyes, adding more creases to an already well-lined face. In sudden recognition, he rushed forward and laid a gnarled hand on Grey Wolf's shoulder. "Welcome back. Glad to see you looking so well."

"Thank you, Grandfather. It is good to be home." The words expressed the genuine warmth and contentment he felt at that moment. Yes, here in this village with these people, he was indeed, home.

The old man glanced in the direction of a large tipi in the center of the village. "Does my son know you have returned?"

Grey Wolf followed his gaze. Outside the lodge, Black Arrow's familiar shield, lance, and bow were mounted on a wooden tripod. "No, I am on my way to see him now."

The Indian turned to Stargazer, a sparkle in his craggy eyes. "Granddaughter, are those berries for me?"

"I can think of no one I would rather give them to," she replied, handing him the basket.

Taking it, the elder said to Grey Wolf, "Do not let me stop you. News will travel fast and I do not want it to reach Black Arrow's ears before his eyes see you first." He smiled and shuffled away.

"Mother is visiting her sister," Stargazer said. "I will go and tell her of your return. That is, unless someone else has already told her. Then I will see her coming, her legs running faster than Runs-Like-Deer!"

Laughing, Grey Wolf tugged one of her braids. "Go, then. I will see you later."

As he neared the family dwelling, Grey Wolf lifted his chin and pulled his shoulders erect. With the respect due an Indian chief and the pride due an Indian father firmly set upon his face, he swept back the entrance flap and stepped inside.

Black Arrow sat cross-legged on a buffalo hide at the rear of the tipi, ladling stew from a kettle into a wooden bowl. When he glanced up to see who had entered, his gaze penetrated Grey Wolf's. Silence floated in the air like steam from the kettle while his father continued to stare at him. In all the years he'd known Black Arrow, he never could tell what the man was thinking or feeling from his expressionless face. He always had to wait for him to speak.

"Come, sit. To share food again with chosen son brings me great pleasure."

As custom dictated, Grey Wolf walked around the center fire and behind his father to sit at his left side. Black Arrow handed him the bowl. "Especially since I thought I might have lost him."

"Did my father think I would die?"

Black Arrow ladled stew into another dish. "You are strong. I was sure with white man's medicine you would live. But in my heart, I did not know if you would return to our people."

Grey Wolf bowed his head, hurt by his father's words. Did he mean he didn't know how strong Grey Wolf's loyalty to the Cheyenne was? But had he not considered staying? And for only one reason … a woman.

Refusing memories of Laura to take shape in his mind, he watched Black Arrow take the first bite, then picked up a buffalo horn spoon and delved into his own. No further words were spoken while they ate. Woman-With-Smart-Hands was a better cook than Henry. He was so hungry he could have filled his bowl twice more with the delicious venison stew, but instead set it aside when his father finished.

"Father, I brought you white man's tobacco." He pulled out a leather pouch tucked into the back of his waistband. "And this." After loosening the draw strings, he took out a small clay pipe and handed it to Black Arrow.

The older man's onyx eyes gleamed as he fingered the pipe's polished stem and bowl. He filled it with tobacco from the pouch and lit it with a flaming stick from the center fire. After several deep draws, he grunted. "White man's pipe good." He gave a final puff and laid it aside. "Not easy to take son away from his family and leave him in hands of white strangers. But seeing him here beside me means decision was right one."

"I am very grateful to you, Father. And to Nightwalker for his infinite wisdom and power to understand and guide you with his vision."

"Was it woman who healed you? One with hair like a young deer's in the sunlight and eyes like budding leaves in springtime?"

Frowning, Grey Wolf looked at Black Arrow. "How do you know her? Was she in Nightwalker's vision?"

"No, my son. I saw her when I met white leader. I knew woman possessed strong powers, and it was she Great Mystery had led me to."

No longer able to repress his thoughts, a vision of Laura formed in Grey Wolf's mind. As the memory became more vivid, he turned his face from Black Arrow. Closing his eyes, he saw her long auburn hair falling over creamy white shoulders; saw the camisole slipping over young, firm breasts. A flare of heat surged through his loins, bringing him abruptly to his feet. Yes, she possessed strong powers. All the time and distance he'd put between them and what did it matter? She could still control him—heart, mind, and body.

Aware of his father's watchful eye and intuitive mind, Grey Wolf banished his thoughts of Laura and regained his composure. Grabbing a water sac that hung from one of the poles, he took a long drink, and then turned back to Black Arrow. "I will go now to the sweat lodge."

Black Arrow nodded his assent. "Tonight we will talk more about white people and their leader who crosses our land."

Later that afternoon inside the sweat lodge, Grey Wolf poured water over the hot stones. They hissed and sizzled, spewing a cloak of steam around him. He settled back and closed his eyes, forcing the saturated air into his nostrils. Sweat streamed down his neck, over his shoulders and down his naked torso. It was good to be inside this place where a man renewed himself, where the body was cleansed and the mind revitalized, where evil spirits and poisons were driven out. And where unbidden memories could be flushed away as well. At least, for a time.

He steered his thoughts to the days ahead. He was eager to join Swift Eagle on a buffalo hunt and wondered when his brother would return. A familiar voice outside the sweat lodge gave him his answer.

"If my brother stays in there too long, he will look like the shriveled meat our mother cooks over coals!"

Grey Wolf leaped up and flung back the thatched door. Standing before him, Swift Eagle wore a wide grin that mirrored his own. As their eyes met, it struck Grey Wolf how much this man meant to him. He'd been a brother-friend all through their years of growing up—as boys playing, learning and competing together, then as warriors fighting enemies side by side.

He slapped Swift Eagle's shoulder affectionately. "I did not expect you back so soon." He grabbed a cloth hanging next to the entrance and wiped the sweat from his face, then wrapped it around his waist. "Was your hunt successful?"

"We have not found herd, only strays." A glint of satisfaction entered his dark eyes. "Your return is good omen. You will change our luck."

Grey Wolf gathered up his buckskins folded on the ground. "Come to the stream while I rinse off. I want to hear about our friends, the Arapahoe who have joined us this summer."

"Yes, and I want to hear about the flame-haired medicine woman Black Arrow spoke of."

The monotony of the landscape and the increasing summer heat made traveling the Platte River Road an arduous journey. Knowing this, Dan had made camp early to give everyone a long deserved rest.

Next to their wagon, Sarah relaxed in a rocker with her stitchery while Laura settled on a blanket a few feet away. She had just started to thumb through a copy of *Harper's Monthly Magazine* when out of nowhere, a coil of rope dropped from overhead and lashed her arms against her sides. She let out a gasp, instant fear racing up her backbone. As she snatched at the rope, she caught the oddly curved smirk on her aunt's face.

The realization dawned on her, bringing her frantic heart rate back to normalcy. Before she'd even followed the length of rope to its end, she knew who held it. "Lucky, you scared me half to death! What in heaven's name do you think you're doing?"

Dan was standing next to him, chuckling. "Looks like you lassoed a mighty nice filly."

Lucky gave the rope a slight jerk, causing Laura to pitch to one side, the magazine slipping from her lap. "Yep, sure does."

Righting herself as best she could with her arms pinned to her sides, Laura didn't find his boyish antics that humorous. "Get this rope off me!"

Looping the rope into his hands, he sauntered closer. "Seems the little filly could use some taming though."

"This is crazy. Let me loose right now."

Standing over her, he tugged upward on the lariat. "Why should I?" he asked. She had no choice but to struggle to her feet. "Now that I finally got your attention, I ain't too quick to give it up." His blue eyes glittered under the low brim of his hat, his gaze settling where the rope fit snugly under her breasts.

Laura tossed back her head. "And just how long do you plan on keeping me tied like this?"

He took his time lifting his gaze to meet hers. "Tell you what. I'll let you go if you promise to spend the afternoon with me."

Laura quirked her brow. "If you don't untie me right this minute, Lucky Phillips, you can forget you ever knew me, much less we spend time together."

He grinned. "All right, no need to get uppity." Loosening the rope, he lifted it over her head.

She pushed back a strand of hair from her face. With that devilish, lop-sided grin planted on Lucky's face, it was hard to stay miffed at him. "Just what do you have in mind? There isn't a whole lot we can do in this god-forsaken country, you know."

"Oh, I wouldn't say that. Take off those moccasins and get your riding boots on. I'll go saddle Sonny for you."

As Lucky left to get the horses, and Laura climbed into the wagon to change, Dan turned to Sarah. "Well, how about it? Will you spend the afternoon with me?" He removed his hat and ruffled his dark hair. The silver strands at his temples gleamed in the sun. "Or do I have to hog-tie you, too?"

Laying her embroidery in her lap, she looked at him coyly. "And what did you have in mind?"

CHAPTER 12

Dan fitted his hat back on his head and held out his hand. "Let's walk over by the river."

Rising, Sarah set the embroidery on the rocker and allowed him to lead her to the shade of some cottonwoods near the river bank. The secluded trees not only offered them welcome relief from the sun, but a privacy that sent a strange ripple of excitement surging through Sarah's body.

She glimpsed back between the branches at Laura mounting her horse. "Are you sure they'll be all right, Daniel? There's not a landmark to be seen beyond this river. If they go too far, they could get lost."

Facing her, Dan hooked his hands over a branch above her head and settled his gaze on her. "All the scouting he's done for me, the kid's never gotten lost."

Sarah frowned. That was just it. They were both mere kids, hardly into their twenties. She could sense Dan reading her thoughts.

"Darlin'," he said, "did anyone ever tell you that you worry too much?"

She gave him a meek smile. "Yes, as I recall you told me that years ago. Remember how worried I was when my brother agreed to come west with you?"

Letting go of the branch, Dan lowered his arms. "And how about a few years before that? When I asked *you* to come west with me." His eyes met hers. "Remember then?"

Sarah looked away, uneasy with where this conversation was leading.

"You were so concerned about upsetting your parents and hurting James ..." He hesitated, tucking his thumbs over his gun belt. "You never considered my feelings."

Sarah stepped to the edge of the river. This was the first time he'd ever brought up their past. "That's not true. It was just that I had an obligation to my folks … and to James's family." Her gaze drifted across the river where long-stemmed yellow wildflowers swayed in the stiff breeze. "I explained to you then that our parents had always planned for James and me to get married." She swept from her eyes an errant lock that had pulled free from her chignon. "I did consider your feelings. I knew I couldn't become the kind of frontier wife you needed."

"You were a stronger woman than you ever gave yourself credit for, Sarah." Dan paused. "But you were right to marry James," he conceded, his tone huskier. "He gave you what I couldn't. A home, security … a future. I just couldn't see it at the time, I guess."

Absently kicking a few pebbles with the toe of her shoe, Sarah thought back to that crucial time in her life, when she was torn between Daniel's young, impetuous love and James's safe, comfortable companionship. Yes, she'd made the right choice, but still she wondered … what would it have been like if she'd married Daniel? She glanced up to find him watching her. At forty-two, he was still quite good-looking, the age lines around his mouth and near the eyes adding a touch of gentleness to his dark, rugged features.

She hugged her arms across her chest, not liking where her thoughts were taking her. After all, she was still in mourning, her poor James not dead a year yet. As a warm smile curved Dan's lips, again she wondered if he was reading her mind.

"Why don't we sit here on the bank and watch the sunset?" he suggested, gently taking her arm and motioning toward a grassy area.

As Sarah settled on the ground with her legs folded beneath her, Dan took his hat off and lowered his large frame next to her. Stretching out his legs, he crossed one boot over the other and leaned back on his elbows.

To their left, the sun was descending rapidly, gilding the edges of the low-lying clouds with its last golden rays. Crossing the shallow river downstream, two familiar figures on horses were silhouetted against a distant, rose-tinted horizon.

"Laura's a fine woman," Dan said. "Make some man a good wife one day." He chuckled. "A mite different from the young ladies I've been around, though. Got a lot of spunk."

"Yes, she's certainly more adventuresome than I was at that age." She watched the two ride over a short rise and down the other side. "As a child, Laura was a real tomboy. Put as many holes in her pinafores as her brother did in his knee pants." She shook her head. "Lordy, talk about me worrying. I remember when she was ten, she nearly broke her neck trying to prove she could ride as well as Alex by jumping his thoroughbred over a neighbor's fence." She shrugged. "But nothing she did ever seemed to bother James. He called her a free spirit. 'We mustn't restrain her enthusiasm for life,' he'd say.

"I used to quarrel with him over his letting her accompany him on calls at all hours of the day and night. The year before his illness, he relied on her assistance more than me. I had compassion for the sick, but he knew when it came to the sight of blood, Laura had the stronger constitution."

Sarah was quiet a moment, plucking at a few blades of grass beside her. "It's funny," she said, the realization sinking in for the first time, "but I think I've learned more from Laura than she has from me in the last couple years. Her attitudes have influenced mine." She looked at Dan, her eyes seeking his. "It was Laura's idea to leave Pennsylvania, you know. She was the one who wrote John and asked if he knew when you'd be leading another train to California." She sighed, raising her knees and smoothing her skirt over them. "Truth is, I think she's more anxious to see Alex at Fort Hendricks than her father in California."

Dan nodded. "I think I understand why. From what I've gathered, she's very close to her brother." He pushed himself from the ground and stood. "On the other hand, she hardly knows her father, except for what she's read in his letters."

"Yes, I suppose you're right," she replied.

He offered his hand and pulled her up. She wondered if his heart quickened the same way hers did every time they touched.

"What about you, Sarah? Are you anxious to get to California?" Keeping her hand in his, he urged her a step closer. "Is that the *only* reason you joined my train?" His gaze probed hers, demanding an answer. Old familiar feelings stirred deep inside her.

She cleared her throat, pretending not to be affected by his nearness. "Well, I ..."

He didn't wait for her answer. His hand reached out and circled the nape of her neck, his mouth lowering to hers. Willingly, Sarah parted her lips, wanting to taste his kiss; wanting to remember what it was like to be in his arms again.

Arching against him, she felt his rigid thighs press against her. His powerful arms encircled her, his hands spreading across her back. Dear God, yes, the feel of him was so familiar. Strong. Demanding. How could she have ever forgotten?

As their kisses became hungrier, deeper, all the years melted away, and that special magnetism they'd felt for each other resurfaced. Within seconds of their embrace, Sarah knew Dan's love for her had never died, and her love for him could be reborn.

But for Sarah the realization that their bodies could respond with renewed passion so quickly unnerved her. After all, they'd only been on his wagon train a few weeks. Things were happening too fast. She twisted within his arms, pushing away. "Daniel, please, we mustn't."

He refused to let her go. "Sarah, honey …" As she turned her face, he cupped a hand under her chin. "Don't fight it. It's right for us this time." He forced her to look at him. Unmistakable longing flared in his eyes. "You still feel something for me, don't you?"

"Oh yes, yes, I do, but—"

"But what then?" When she tried to turn away again, he cradled her face in both his hands. "Honey, don't you see? We have a second chance." His lips brushed her forehead as he spoke. "I love you. All these years, I've never stopped."

"Oh, Daniel …" Her throat constricted as she stepped back. It was so hard to admit her feelings—feelings that seemed to betray the love she'd had for James. A long moment passed before she said, "Daniel, it's true for me, too. All these years you've held a special place in my heart." She sighed, blinking back tears. "But still, don't you see? It doesn't mean things can work out now, just because I'm no longer married. We're older and so many things have changed."

"Darlin', that's just it. Things *have* changed. I've changed. I'm tired of wandering back and forth across the country. It's time I settled down and built that ranch I've been saving for … before I get too damn old to do it."

Dan hesitated, seeming to weigh his words carefully. "I lost you once, and I couldn't bear to lose you again." He smiled down at her. "Please, give us a chance, Sarah. You'll see."

Beside the shallow river, Laura watched the horses lower their heads for a drink while Lucky searched in his saddlebag for his canteen.

"Lucky, I can cup my hands in the river to get a drink."

"Naw, that water ain't any good. All you'll taste is sand. I got it here somewhere."

Laura gazed out over the luxuriant grasslands studded with summer flowers. She'd enjoyed the afternoon with Lucky. To her surprise, he'd shown her wildlife she hadn't yet seen: a colony of squirrel-like animals called prairie dogs, popping their heads out of tiny burrows, then scurrying back inside; a pack of antelope that galloped past them swifter than race horses; and the greatest thrill, a huge herd of buffalo numbering in the thousands grazing downwind from where they watched atop a hill.

But now as her eyes surveyed the far-reaching plains, she wasn't looking for animals. No, instead she found herself wishing a certain man would ride into view astride his pinto, like she'd imagined so often in her dreams.

"Beautiful sunset, ain't it?"

Laura swung around to see Lucky holding the canteen. "M-m-m, yes, it is." She took the canteen and sipped from it, then glanced toward the bright orange sun about to touch the western horizon.

"Something the matter, Laurie? You're awful quiet."

"I'm just admiring the sunset, like you." She took another swallow of water and handed the canteen back to Lucky.

He lifted it for a quick swig. Then he wiped his mouth with the back of his hand. "Laurie, I been wanting to ask you …" He looked at her hesitantly.

"Yes?" Laura urged.

"Well, I was wondering if you had a beau back in Philadelphia."

The question shouldn't have surprised Laura. She'd guessed Lucky might want more than a casual friendship. "No, no one special."

Lucky took another gulp from the canteen and fitted the cap on. After returning it to his saddlebag, he stepped over to Laura. "Maybe it's time you did." He smiled, his blue-eyed gaze resting on her lips. "You sure wouldn't have to look far." Before Laura could stop him, he swept her into his arms and laid his mouth over hers.

His lips were soft, his kiss unhurried, and for a few seconds Laura accepted the pleasant feeling it gave her. But when he pressed her more firmly against him, she realized what she wanted, what she needed, couldn't be found in Lucky's arms. That special kind of feeling existed only in Grey Wolf's embrace.

Before he could deepen the kiss, she stiffened, pulling her lips from his. He drew back, giving her a long, questioning stare, then released her and turned away.

There was a tense moment of silence before Laura reached out and touched his arm. "Lucky, I'm sorry, I—"

"Don't apologize," he blurted, his voice strained. "I'm the one who should apologize."

Laura stepped around to face him. "Lucky, the first day we met, we became friends. And over the weeks, I've gotten to know you better, especially these past few days. I've grown very fond of you." She smiled. "You remind me of my brother, Alex."

Lucky's mouth flattened into a grim line. "Your brother, huh?" He gathered the horses' reins and led them from the riverbank. As he handed her Sonny's reins, he cast a rueful glance. "That ain't exactly what I wanted to hear." He hitched his chin toward the horizon. "Sun's down. Better head back."

Riding at a slow gait toward the campfires visible in the distance, Laura was concerned Lucky might still be feeling the sting of her rejection. She was relieved when he finally spoke up.

"You know I, uh, didn't get the chance to meet Alex last year when our train stopped at Fort Hendricks." He smiled over at her. "Now you got me curious what he's like."

"Oh, I'll make sure you meet him," she said, glad the friendly ring in his voice had returned. "How long is it before we get there?"

"Not long. A few more days."

"What's the fort like? Is it as big as Fort Kearny?"

"Yeah, it's an important way station for the wagon trains. A good place to stock up on supplies."

Laura tried to envision their arrival. She was so anxious to see Alex that even a few more days sounded too long.

CHAPTER 13

The morning sun emitted a broad fan of light rays over the hazy Nebraska plains. Across the uneven terrain, a platoon of twenty-five soldiers of the 1st US Cavalry rode their horses southward in sets of two, led by commanding officer, Captain Glen Herrington.

The captain's pride and arrogance was reflected in the blue uniform he wore with hardly a crease showing, the epaulets laying flat and squarely above his shoulders. Even the yellow striped facings on the sides of his pant legs ran a neat line along his muscled thighs, curving at the knees and into polished black leather boots.

Riding in from the western flank, a lone soldier swiftly closed the distance between himself and the captain. As soon as he reined his horse alongside Herrington's matching bay, Lieutenant Alex Westbrook raised a dusty blue-sleeved arm and pointed back from where he'd come. "Captain, sir," he reported in a voice loud enough to be heard over a hundred trotting hooves, "there's a man driving a buckboard mighty fast in our direction. He's just the other side of that rise."

Captain Herrington turned in his saddle and ordered Sergeant Avery behind him to halt the men.

"Troop halt!" bellowed the sergeant, lifting his arm high. His shout was heard halfway down the line of soldiers, a chain reaction stopping the rest.

Herrington squinted toward the horizon. "Just one man driving a wagon, Lieutenant Westbrook?"

"Yes, sir. But he's riding like there was a swarm of bees on his tail. He should be in sight any minute now."

His words were no more than spoken when the wagon appeared in a billowing cloud of dust over the crest of the hill. Herrington held a vigilant eye on the fast approaching wagon as well as the road behind it.

The driver yanked his team to a stop a few feet away. "Am I glad to see you!" His round face was flushed, his beady eyes wild with excitement. "About a half hour ago three Injuns rode into my camp demanding whisky and tobacco. One of the damn redskins was wearing a derby!" He drew a quick breath and then continued, "I blasted two of 'em, by God, but the one with the hat got away before I could get an aim on him. I don't rightly know what tribe they—"

"Your name, mister?" Herrington demanded.

The man gave him an impudent glare as he snatched a soiled bandanna from his back pocket. He took his time wiping his face and neck.

"I asked your name."

The man wadded up the bandanna and stuck it back in his pocket. "Clayton … Robert Clayton."

"Where did this happen, Mr. Clayton?"

"About two miles back. I was finishing my breakfast when—"

"You say you shot two of them?" Herrington interrupted, his voice sharp with impatience. He'd had a feeling when he left the fort yesterday that this was going to be anything but a routine patrol.

"You're damn right! Sent 'em both to hell where they belong!"

Herrington turned a raised eyebrow to the man on his left. His army scout, Tucker, remained expressionless, slouched over his saddle, his arms folded atop the pommel. A former trapper and fur-dealer, the man never wore anything but loose-fitting fringed buckskins. At fifty, he knew this country better than Herrington ever hoped to.

"What do you think, Tucker? Cheyenne, maybe?"

"More than likely. Large encampment south of here."

Herrington motioned to his sergeant. Immediately, Avery urged his bay forward.

"Take Mr. Clayton and a squad of ten back to the fort by way of the main road. See that Clayton gives a full report to Major Williams. I'll proceed with the rest of the patrol to the campsite."

"Yes, sir." Sergeant Avery saluted, then turned his horse and rode down the line of cavalrymen calling out names.

Herrington's sharp, assessing gaze shifted back to Clayton. He'd noticed the equipment and supplies loaded in the man's wagon—another prospector likely heading for the mining camps at Cherry Creek.

"Mr. Clayton, my men will escort you to Fort Hendricks. There you will tell the post commander what happened."

With a grumbled response, Clayton flicked his reins sharply, sending the horses and wagon bolting forward.

Easily following the wagon tracks, Captain Herrington and his patrol found the two Indians, their bodies lying some fifty feet apart. Two spotted ponies grazed on tufts of grass a short distance away.

With no order to dismount, the soldiers remained in their saddles while Captain Herrington, Tucker and Lieutenant Westbrook walked over to the first Indian. Clad in a breechcloth, he lay spread eagle in a pool of blood, buffalo flies swarming overhead.

"Yep, Cheyenne," Tucker said.

Herrington removed his buckskin gauntlets and tucked them over his belt. As they walked toward the other Indian, he noticed marks in the dirt indicating the Indian had crawled to where he was now lying face down. He watched for movement. When it came, he was ready.

The instant the Indian rolled, Herrington had the Colt out of his holster. Lightning-quick, he hit the hammer and fired. The Indian's head snapped back, a hole appearing in the center of his forehead. Several of the soldiers' horses, already uneasy with the smell of blood in their nostrils, panicked and reared at the sound of the pistol's loud repercussion. Their riders fought to restrain them and bring them back into formation.

"Damn!" Alex exclaimed, staring in astonishment. In the Indian's hand was a sawed-off rifle. "How'd you know he was hiding that rifle under him, Captain?"

"I didn't," Herrington answered flatly, fitting the Colt back in his holster.

Alex shook his head. "He was aiming right for me. If you hadn't reacted so fast, I'd be a goner."

As Herrington's gaze traveled over the Indian's lifeless body, fragmented pictures flashed before him, all of them horrible, gut-wrenching memories. He squeezed his eyes shut, forcing his mind to clear. "Don't ever trust an Indian, not even one you think is dead," he said in a ruthless voice. He stepped around the body, trying to ignore the nagging ache in his leg that served as a constant reminder of his haunted past. "See that both corpses are strapped to their ponies. We're taking them back to the fort."

"What the hell for?" Tucker drawled. "That Indian will probably be back for 'em, Cap'n. Cheyenne usually take their dead to their burial grounds."

"Incidents like this have got to stop, Tucker. I want you to go to their village and tell the chief to come to the fort for the bodies. You can tell him Major Williams wants to offer his personal condolences." Herrington leaned over and picked up the rifle. When he looked at Tucker again, his voice hardened with contempt. "Of course, what the major should tell him is to keep his damn braves away from our people or there'll be more bloodshed."

Alex frowned. "Think instead of coming in peaceful, they might retaliate and attack the fort, sir?"

"Naw," Tucker interceded, "the Cheyenne ain't gonna wage war with a whole U. S. Army regiment over the loss of a couple bucks." He scratched his unshaven chin. "The chiefs have a hard time controlling these renegades. They're like stray bullets—can't keep 'um from veering off in the wrong direction."

A fly buzzed around Herrington's face, then swooped down and lit on the corpse. "Get on with it, Lieutenant," he said before turning back to the patrol.

High atop the pole located at the nucleus of Fort Hendricks, the stars and stripes fluttered in the afternoon breeze. As Herrington crossed the parade ground on his way to the post commander's office, a trumpeter standing near the flagpole sounded his horn. The captain paid little notice to the soldiers who responded to the routine call, hustling to the stables to groom and water their horses.

Entering the administrative office, he removed his felt slouch hat and hung it on a peg inside the doorway. "Afternoon, Yates," he said to the adjutant sitting behind his desk. "Is the major in his office?"

Yates rose to attention and saluted. "Yes, sir. At the moment, so is his wife, sir."

"I see. Then I'll come—"

Just then the major's door swung open and Martha Williams stepped out. "Adam, at times you're as stubborn as a ..." She wavered a moment at the sight of Captain Herrington standing on the other side of the staff officer's desk, then turned to her husband and said, "See you in time for supper, dear."

Facing Herrington, she smiled. "Captain, glad to see you safely back."

Herrington gave her a stiff nod. "Mrs. Williams."

Mrs. Williams picked up her skirts and stepped past him, allowing Yates to escort her outside.

Through the office doorway, Herrington saw Major Williams straighten in his seat behind his flat-top desk and motion for him to enter. He stepped inside and saluted.

"At ease, Captain. Take a seat."

"Thank you, sir." Herrington laid his two-page report on the major's desk, and then pulled up a chair and sat down. He winced as the aggravating pain shot through his leg.

The major picked up his pipe and laid a match to it. After sitting back in his chair and exhaling several puffs of smoke, he said, "So, tell me what happened out there today. All I have is the prospector's story."

"About fifteen miles south of Banner's Bluff we came upon two Cheyenne braves. One was dead, the other, wounded."

The major's eyebrows lifted. "One was alive, you say?"

"Not for long. He had a sawed-off rifle hidden under him. When he made a move in Westbrook's direction, I had to finish him."

Williams's eyes darkened. "Better him than one of ours, Glen."

Herrington shifted uncomfortably in his chair. The major often called him by his first name—something he had a hard time getting used to.

Since orphaned at age fifteen, he'd lived within the confines of a rigid army life—a life in which he was most often addressed by his surname. In his teens, he'd lived at Fort Leavenworth working for the post commander. Then he spent four years at West Point, four years at Fort Belknap, Texas and this last year and a half at Fort Hendricks. Fifteen years of strict army protocol—with no one to call him by his namesake.

That is, with the exception of his last year at West Point, when he met and fell in love with the senator's daughter. *Jennifer.* He could still remember her calling him by his name, her soft lips curving into an intimate smile whenever she said it. If only he hadn't been transferred.

"Glen?"

Herrington jerked his head around to find the major standing next to him.

"Lost you for a moment there, didn't I?"

"Sorry, sir." Herrington cleared his throat. "You were saying?"

"I was asking if you thought Clayton might have misjudged the intentions of those Indians and reacted too quickly when they first rode into his camp?"

Herrington exhaled loudly. "With one carrying that rifle, I'd have to lean toward Clayton's side."

Williams laid his pipe in a tray on his desk and walked to the window facing the parade ground. Herrington could see the mail wagon just arriving. Within minutes, soldiers would flock around it eagerly awaiting their names to be called.

"Yes," the major said, "I suppose if Clayton had waited too long to decide if they were friendly or hostile, he may have been the one lying in the dirt. As for you, of course, killing the Indian was a matter of self-defense." He turned around abruptly. "That's the damn trouble. It's difficult to separate the peaceful Indians from the hostile ones. And you put the shoe—or moccasin—on the other foot, they find it just as hard to trust us."

Frustration creased the major's face as he stepped over to a large map of the United States hanging on the wall. Glaring at it, he spouted, "Millions of square miles of frontier out here, and only seventeen thousand soldiers expected to cover and protect it!"

Herrington didn't comment, preparing to listen respectfully to the major's well-worn complaints which he'd heard a dozen times before from other army commanders.

"The government sends us out here with no official strategy, no guidelines, and tells us to protect our people, but keep peace with the Indians." Williams shrugged resignedly and sat back down at his desk. He looked across at Herrington. "Tell me, do you think it's possible to live in peaceful coexistence out here with these Indians?"

Herrington rose stiffly and walked over to the window. Outside the men were ripping open their mail the minute it was handed to them. Smiles formed on some faces, not on others. He glanced over his shoulder. "You want my gut-honest opinion, Major?"

"That's what I expect from you."

"The Indians have roamed this land free for too long to want to share it with anyone. And they sure as hell aren't going to tolerate much longer our telling them where they can live, where they can hunt, and where they can die."

Williams shook his head. "Makes you wonder how it's all going to end."

Herrington turned to face the major, unable to keep animosity from his voice. "Right simple to me. Sooner or later the Indian will be forced to give in to the domination of the white man."

Major Williams sighed. "It all comes down to American patriotism pitted against Indian pride. And you're right. This whole country's destiny will end up in American hands. I have no doubts about that."

He relit his pipe and inhaled a deep draw of smoke. "Glen, how about you coming over for dinner tonight? Martha promised to have the cook prepare a hen, and she's going to bake a pie herself." He leaned forward, resting his arms on his desk. "She loves having you over, you know that."

Herrington moved away from the window and smiled, glad the subject had been changed. "I've never turned down an invitation to taste one of Mrs. Williams's pies, you know that, sir." He came around to the front of the desk. "What time?"

"Seven o'clock, and for God's sake, dress informal this time." The major stood and gestured at the papers on his desk. "I'll read your report and if I have any further questions, we can discuss them tomorrow. Call it a day, Captain."

"Yes, sir." Herrington saluted, then pivoted and walked out of the office. The uneven sound of his footsteps on the floorboards emphasized his right leg's shorter stride. He acknowledged the adjutant who snapped a salute and lifted his hat from its peg.

As he stepped outside, he looked over at a separate wood frame building at the end of the walkway. He'd been inside Major Williams's living quarters several times. At the entry, handmade rugs covered the planked floor. In the front room, embroidered table scarves graced the tabletops. A leather parlor chair, old and worn, set opposite an upholstered settee. Silver candlesticks and tea service sat on a mahogany sideboard, daguerreotypes of their two married daughters and three grandchildren displayed on a shelf above it.

Herrington's eyes narrowed in annoyance. Why did such insignificant things bother him so much? Adjusting his hat on his head, he stepped off the boardwalk and started across the parade ground. That's just it. They aren't insignificant. They're possessions that represent home and family. *Things he'd lost a long time ago and never have had since.*

"Captain Herrington?"

He halted as Westbrook hurried to his side. "Yes, Lieutenant?"

"I have a stack of official mail and a personal letter for Major Williams, sir. I thought you might want to take them to him."

"No, I just came from his office. Give them to Sergeant Yates. If any of the business pertains to me, the major will send for me."

"Yes, sir."

Westbrook continued standing there.

"Something else?"

The young man's face relaxed into a smile. "Remember I told you I had a sister and aunt back in Pennsylvania?" He held up a separate envelope. "They're coming here. I mean, they're going to California, but they'll be stopping here on their way. Traveling on Mr. Driscoll's wagon train. You remember him, sir? He came through last year."

"Ah, yes, Driscoll. Hell of a good man. Would've made a good officer."

"Indeed, sir." Westbrook grinned. "I sure want you to meet my sister and aunt."

Herrington gave a brief nod. "I'll look forward to it. Carry on, Lieutenant." Westbrook saluted and made an about face toward the major's office.

Glen headed across the quadrangle. As a small work detail marched past him, he picked up his stride, not allowing his leg to falter.

Once inside his quarters, he removed his gun belt and laid it on top of a rickety wooden table. After stripping off his navy blue jacket and hanging it over a peg on the wall, he sat on a spindle-back chair and massaged the taut, aching muscle in his thigh. It seemed the older he got, the more the damn leg bothered him.

After several minutes and no relief, he gave up. He knew the only thing to ease the pain was in the cupboard. Moving from the small front room to the meager kitchen, Glen removed a bottle and glass and poured a liberal amount of the amber liquid.

CHAPTER 14

Inside his tipi, Grey Wolf prepared for his first council meeting since his return. He adjusted his breechcloth front and back, and then sheathed his knife at his side. Quickly and methodically, he braided two eagle feathers tipped down into a section of his hair before securing the red band around his forehead.

He made sure the cameo necklace hung low on his chest. Then he strung the polished bear fang on a shorter cord around the base of his throat. All who saw it today would know the bravery and strength it stood for, and the powerful medicine it bestowed him.

The previous day, the Cheyenne warrior, Yellow Dog had returned reporting two braves had been shot and killed. Later in the day, an army scout rode into the village and spoke with Black Arrow. Immediately following the scout's departure, his father had sent a message to selected leaders and warriors residing in the summer villages to meet in his council lodge this morning.

Walking through camp, Grey Wolf saw several warriors heading his way, the one known as Yellow Dog leading. He wore a black hat with a rounded crown and narrow brim. He would have looked comical if it weren't for the menacing scowl etched on his face.

As Grey Wolf turned toward the council lodge, Yellow Dog stepped in front of him. His black eyes bored into Grey Wolf's. "You should have stayed with your own kind, paleface. Except for the old man in there and some of his weak-minded followers, none of us wanted to see you back among our people again."

Hands clenched at his sides, Grey Wolf glared back at the Indian. Yellow Dog had been his enemy ever since he'd become Black Arrow's son. His jealousy and hatred had festered over the years as Grey Wolf became the superior warrior, his battle trophies outnumbering Yellow Dog's by far. Brandishing him with a searing look, Grey Wolf shoved past him and entered the lodge.

Inside, a large group of men sat around a central fire. A few were Arapahoe, the rest Cheyenne. Grey Wolf sat next to Swift Eagle.

Discounting Yellow Dog and his cohorts who entered with him, the Indians present regarded Black Arrow as their supreme leader and the council's head spokesman. They all turned respectfully toward him and waited for him to speak.

"We have come together today as one people," Black Arrow began. He held up a long stem pipe. "Before we talk, we will smoke pipe to bring our thoughts together." Passing the pipe was his father's way of easing some of the tension that had built up among the bands since Yellow Dog had returned with the news.

When it had made the circle, Black Arrow said, "It is with great sorrow that we are here. Thunderhawk and Little Elk are dead. All night, we have grieved with their families and felt their loss." He looked across the council fire. "Now Yellow Dog has come to tell what he saw."

Grey Wolf knew Yellow Dog was eager to speak. No doubt this would be his chance to incite more hatred toward the white men and their soldiers. "Me, Thunderhawk and Little Elk hunt the buffalo. We come across twenty killed by white men's rifles. They lie forgotten on ground, only two stripped of their hides, the rest, a rotting waste for vultures and wolves to feed upon.

"We pass many white men heading toward mountains to dig for the yellow rocks. We stop at camp of one to ask for food and tobacco. He does not honor us with reply. Instead, he fires gun at us. Thunderhawk and Little Elk fall from their horses, but I escape."

Beneath the council's rapt attention, an undercurrent of animosity began to stir. Grey Wolf frowned with contempt. This was exactly what Yellow Dog had hoped for. Though the warrior was honor bound to tell the truth, he would twist it to his own advantage.

"When I go back," he continued, "I see the bluecoats. I hide and watch. Thunderhawk, lying wounded, asks for help." Yellow Dog pointed to the middle of his forehead. "Instead, bluecoat fires his weapon into Thunderhawk's head. Then they put him and Little Elk on their ponies and take them to fort."

Indignation rumbled through the council like summer thunder.

Yellow Dog's face contorted in anger. "We must avenge the killing of our warriors! Rise up against the white men and soldiers who cut them down like animals."

Several Cheyenne braves nodded in agreement, one speaking out. "The whites go through our sacred lands like prairie fires, destroying everything in their path. They muddy our rivers and flatten our grasslands. They dig the earth from under our feet."

A young Arapahoe scowled. "More and more come to dig for the yellow rocks. And they do not leave after they find them. They stay and build wooden villages everywhere."

Grey Wolf grew concerned with this kind of talk. Though most of what these men said was true, it did nothing but bring more anger and unrest, fueling the fires of war again. He bowed his head. The Cheyenne have had enough war. One of the worst occurred three years before when three hundred warriors were defeated by an enormous cavalry of soldiers at the Solomon Fork River. Such a severe setback prompted their chiefs to seek a more peaceful existence. But still, retaliations by small war parties continued, usually made up of young, undisciplined braves like Yellow Dog, eager to fight for any cause.

Across from Grey Wolf, an Arapahoe leader spoke out, his voice tempered with resignation. "It is true many whites cross our lands. More than we have numbers for. So many, we can no longer rid ourselves of their presence. We must learn to keep peace with them."

Grey Wolf knew his father had purposely allowed the others to have their say first. Now it was time for him to speak in a frank manner.

Black Arrow held up his hand. "Hear me, my friends. To avenge the deaths of two would endanger the lives of many. We cannot allow that. A peace treaty was signed by our people and theirs. We will honor it."

"I did not sign that treaty!" Yellow Dog retorted. "No one in this council did, not even you. We do not have to live by its rules!"

Grey Wolf clenched his mouth to keep from lashing out at Yellow Dog. The warrior was young and foolish, a trouble maker. He'd told his story the way he wanted others to hear it. It was a much different account than the one told to his father by the white mountain man, Tucker, whose word many leaders trusted over the years.

"You, Yellow Dog, know the Arapahoe and Cheyenne leaders who signed the treaty," Black Arrow said. "You must abide by their decisions as I and other members of this council do." He gazed around the circle. "The soldiers have kept their part of the treaty. They have given us clothing and food in return for using our land."

Ignoring Yellow Dog's grunt of disgust, he continued. "This day, I go to soldiers' fort and meet with their leader. I will bring back Thunderhawk and Little

Elk so their bodies can be wrapped in robes, and their spirits can walk the path of their ancestors."

"They were my cousins," Yellow Dog said stiffly. "I must go, too."

Grey Wolf frowned at Black Arrow's consenting nod. He wasn't sure how the Indians would be received by the soldiers. And he feared Yellow Dog might cause trouble for Black Arrow. "It is my brother's and my wish to accompany you as well, my father. I can interpret the soldiers' words."

Black Arrow nodded again.

There was another reason for Grey Wolf wanting to go to Fort Hendricks. He'd estimated the number of days it would take Driscoll's wagon train to travel the North Platte River and then down the South Platte. They should be near the fort by now.

Inside the sutler's store at Fort Hendricks, Sarah skimmed her hand over the colored muslin stacked on a table. "Laura, they have sewing needles and thread. And here are some bolts of cloth."

Beside her, Laura uttered a quick, "Yes, I saw them," before turning her attention back to what was going on outside the store window. She watched a line of soldiers marching across the parade ground. None of them were Alex.

They had reached Fort Hendricks before noon, the wagon train setting up camp about two miles outside its perimeter where there was plenty of grass for the animals. After getting settled, Dan drove Laura and Sarah to the fort in the buckboard and left them at the sutler's while he went on to the commander's office. Now waiting impatiently inside the store for Dan's return, Laura hardly cared about sewing needles or bolts of cloth.

"Daniel shouldn't be long," Sarah said, glancing over at her niece understandingly. She peered out a second window. "Oh, look, here he comes now."

Elated, Laura hurried past her aunt and out the door. "Where is he?" she asked before Dan had reached the wooden walkway. Her heart dropped when she saw his somber expression. "Don't tell me the commander wouldn't let Alex greet his aunt and sister. Surely—"

Dan held up a hand to silence her. "Major Williams would've been glad to send Alex over, except he's not here."

"What do you mean, he's not here?"

Sarah stepped beside Laura. "Where is he, Daniel?"

"He left on patrol early this morning."

"Did the major say how long he'd be gone?" she asked.

"No. We were interrupted by a sergeant who seemed anxious to talk to the major privately, so I didn't get a chance to ask him."

"Ooh," Laura moaned, biting her lower lip. "What if we don't see him before we leave?"

"I plan to keep the train here a few days," Dan said, "so chances are, you will."

Laura brightened a little. "We're staying a few days?"

Dan nodded. "We have to wait for a shipment of supplies to arrive so we can stock up on what we need to get over the mountains, most of the horses and mules need to be reshod, and besides that, the folks will be glad for the time to post a few letters back to the states."

Sarah circled an arm around Laura's shoulders. "I'm sure Alex will be back soon, dear."

"The major mentioned he and his wife would like to meet the both of you," Dan said. "He asked us to come over to his private quarters later and—" He halted in midsentence, his gaze sweeping past Laura. "Now I see the reason that sergeant was in such an all-fired hurry to talk to the major."

Laura turned her gaze in the direction of Dan's. Four Indians on horseback were riding unimpeded through the fort's arched entrance, passing two sentries posted at the guardhouse. One was fully clothed in buckskins and wore a feathered headdress. The other three riding abreast wore only breechcloths with bows and quivers slung over their bare backs. The Indian on the far side wore an outlandish derby hat atop black braided hair, while the one on this side had long brown hair flowing to his shoulders.

She drew in a quick breath, her hand pressed against her chest. "Oh, my God, it's him!"

"Is that Grey Wolf?" Sarah asked, staring in astonishment.

"Yes," Laura answered in a tremulous whisper. As the Indians crossed the quadrangle, her gaze followed the man with the broad golden back and muscled legs bracing the pinto stallion. Yes, it was him all right—she'd recognize him from a mile away.

"Why do you suppose he and those other Indians are here?" Sarah asked Dan.

"Beats me." Dan pulled his hat further over his forehead, shading his eyes. "That's Black Arrow beside him. Grey Wolf told me his village wasn't far from the South Platte."

A surge of excitement rippled up Laura's spine. Never in her life had she expected to see him again. She stood, not moving an inch, yet wishing like crazy she could race across the parade ground after him.

But of course, she couldn't. Certainly not in front of all these soldiers. Besides, what would she say? Nothing had changed between them. They'd already said everything there was to say.

Still, her gaze remained riveted on him. Seated on his horse beside the other Indians, he looked so primitive and menacing. It was hard to believe he was the same man who'd held her in his arms with such tenderness only a few weeks ago.

She watched them approach the soldiers standing outside the commander's office. "Is the older man, Major Williams?" she asked Dan, trying to compose herself.

"Yeah ..." Dan rubbed his chin, "sure wish we could hear what's said. From the look on those Indians' faces, I don't reckon they're paying a social call."

CHAPTER 15

Soldiers stationed around the fort stopped what they were doing to watch the Indians ride across the parade ground, turning their horses toward the post's main headquarters.

"What do you think, sir?" Sergeant Avery asked, standing on the boardwalk next to the major. "Are they going to cause trouble?"

"Hope not, Sergeant." Williams scrutinized the Indian with the feathered headdress. "The chief's name is Black Arrow. I met him at Fort Laramie when their annuities were handed out last summer. Seemed peaceful enough then." His brows drew together. "Of course, there's no telling how peaceful he feels right now."

As the Indians halted their horses in front of him, Williams exchanged glances with Black Arrow, but neither spoke. A hush settled over the garrison, not a sound heard other than the Indians' horses shifting restlessly. He took note of the warrior with grey eyes and light brown hair. Seemed he'd heard tell of a half-breed sighted in these parts. The Indian with the derby was evidently the one Clayton said got away.

A sudden shift in the wind banged a loose clapboard against the side of a building ending the silence as well as Williams's observations. He gave a nod to Black Arrow. "I'm Major Williams, commander here at Fort Hendricks. We met at Fort Laramie." He signed the words as best he could.

Black Arrow motioned with his hands and replied in his native tongue. Williams frowned, not catching all of what he said. He wished Tucker hadn't left with Herrington. The scout spoke Cheyenne fluently.

"My father says he remembers you."

The major nodded, relieved the half-breed spoke English. "You say the chief is your father?"

The breed lifted his chin and answered in a firm, articulate voice. "Yes. My name is Grey Wolf." He gestured to the Indians beside him. "With us is Yellow Dog and my brother, Swift Eagle. We come for Thunderhawk and Little Elk."

Williams nodded to Sergeant Avery who, in turn, whispered to a corporal who hustled away. He looked up at Grey Wolf. "Tell your father that I regret what happened yesterday. The man who shot the two braves said he was afraid for his life. When the three men, including the one you call Yellow Dog, rode into his camp demanding tobacco and whisky, he thought they were going to shoot him."

The major peered over at the Indian wearing the hat. The evil scowl on the man's face left little doubt in Williams's mind that what Clayton thought about him and his friends was probably true.

He waited for Grey Wolf to translate. "Tell Black Arrow that when the soldiers got there, one brave was still alive. When he tried to shoot one of my men, another soldier was forced to kill him."

The corporal returned, stepping to Williams's side, a sawed-off rifle in his hand. The major took the weapon and held it out. "This belonged to the Indian."

Grey Wolf slid from the pinto. He examined the rifle, then handed it up to Black Arrow speaking rapidly to him.

The chief's expression darkened. He turned to Yellow Dog, his words to the warrior spoken in clipped, harsh tones. The Indian stiffened, but said nothing.

Black Arrow threw down the rifle and spoke again to Grey Wolf. When he finished, Grey Wolf turned back to the major. "My father also regrets what happened. He hopes you do not think all his people are like the few who act foolishly and cause trouble. The Cheyenne respect the treaty their leaders have signed and want to keep peace with your people. He says there is plenty sky, earth and water for everyone."

Williams met Grey Wolf's gaze. He wondered if the half-breed believed what his father said. Hell, the peace treaty he spoke of probably wouldn't be in effect much longer. Already there was talk in Washington of getting the Cheyenne and Arapahoe to sign a new treaty which would restrict the territory they could live on. He suppressed a sigh. Well, those things were up to the politicians, not him. He was just one soldier trying to appease the Indians the best way he knew how.

"Tell Black Arrow we also continue to honor the treaty. This summer, blankets, food and tobacco will be given to your people."

After Grey Wolf repeated his message, Yellow Dog blurted something out, his voice full of contempt.

"What did he say?" Williams demanded.

"He asks if we will receive rifles and ammunition that were promised to hunt game."

"No," the major answered sharply with an emphatic shake of his head. "There will be no rifles or ammunition. Not until we are assured that there will be no more incidents like the one yesterday. I will let time be the judge of that."

Standing outside the store with Dan and Sarah, Laura viewed the entire proceedings with awe. Though she wasn't able to catch any of the conversation between Major Williams and Grey Wolf, she understood the gravity of the meeting, particularly after a soldier brought two horses around from the rear stables. Slung over each animal's back was the unmistakable form of a corpse wrapped beneath a blanket.

She watched Grey Wolf approach the major and speak to him again. Her heart skipped a beat when the major pointed in her direction. It skipped another beat when Grey Wolf turned and looked at her. And when he swung up on his horse and rode toward her, she thought sure her heart would stop completely.

As he closed the distance between them, she became oblivious to everyone and everything around her. He reined in Four Winds a few feet away. He said not a word, yet his crystal-grey eyes said everything. Subtly, they roamed over her figure conveying his wish to touch her, to hold her.

It seemed forever before he finally broke the spell between them and looked at Black Arrow who'd ridden up beside him. The other two Indians rode on past with the laden horses in tow.

She wondered if one of them might be Swift Eagle, the brother Grey Wolf had spoken about. She hoped he wasn't the sinister-looking one with the hat, who, when she gave him a brief glance, leered back at her. Glad to see him ride out of the fort, she directed her attention back to Grey Wolf and the chief.

Acknowledging Dan by holding up two fingers, Black Arrow shifted his eyes to Laura. His expression seemed almost reverent as he spoke in a smooth, even tone. He ended his words by closing an outstretched hand into a fist.

A strange look of discomfort wavered across Grey Wolf's face. "My father wishes to thank you for saving my life. He says one who saves another's life has touched that person's soul." He hesitated, a muscle quivering in his jaw. "He says, Laura, you have become my guardian spirit …" his voice lowered, "and control my destiny."

A warm flush crept up her cheeks. Even though the words were Black Arrow's, it was Grey Wolf's expressing them that unsettled her. "Tell your father it was with the help of our God that I saved your life. Through Him, I was able to touch your soul and become your guardian spirit." She met Grey Wolf's eyes straight on. "But never can I control your destiny. Only you can do that."

A smile overtook Grey Wolf's features. Black Arrow's face reflected the same approval when his son translated her words. In fact, the chief's expression was much like what she'd seen the first time she'd stood before him on the trail.

Grey Wolf looked at Dan. "When do you leave?"

"Not for a few days."

As Four Winds tossed his head and pawed a hoof at the hardened ground, Grey Wolf tightened his grip on the reins. He gave Laura a sharp, parting glance. Then he nodded to his father and they reeled their horses into a gallop and rode out of the fort.

Watching them leave, Laura felt no sadness. She remembered Grey Wolf's eyes and the promise they held—a promise that she would see him again.

Martha Williams returned to the living room carrying a silver tray stacked with cups and saucers. Placing it on the breakfront, she smiled at Sarah and Laura. "It's so nice to have someone to share tea with. Adam prefers coffee like Mr. Driscoll." She poured the tea into two cups, handing one to Sarah, the other to Laura. Both women sat on a green upholstered settee opposite Dan, his hulking frame dwarfing the parlor chair he sat on.

"Thank you, Mrs. Williams," Sarah said, returning her hostess' smile.

"Please, call me Martha."

"Well, Martha, I can tell you it's a treat for us to drink out of china cups instead of tin, isn't it, Laura?"

Laura nodded appreciatively. After taking a sip, she lowered the cup and saucer to her lap. Major Williams stood by the fireplace, one arm propped on the mantel, the other hand holding a pipe. He'd been explaining the troubling events that brought Black Arrow and his warriors to the fort.

"Sounds like my brother would have been shot by that Indian if it hadn't been for Captain … what did you say his name was?"

"Herrington. Captain Glen Herrington."

"Well, be sure to give Captain Herrington my heartfelt gratitude, Major."

"You can tell him yourself when he and your brother return, Miss West-brook."

"And when will that be?" Laura asked, trying not to sound too anxious.

The major waited while Martha served Dan, and then placed his own cup on the mantel. "Should be back in a day or two. They took a detail out on another patrol." He laid his pipe aside and picked up the cup. "As a preventative measure. The more those young bucks see of the army, the better off we'll be."

He took a quick sip, frowning as he set the cup down. "I believe Chief Black Arrow wants peace, but I'm not so sure about some of his warriors. I must tell you, I didn't like the looks of the one with the derby propped on his head called Yellow Dog. The chief better keep a tight rein on him." Williams sent Dan a wary glance. "Can't say I put much trust in that half-breed, either. I was surprised when he recognized your train camped outside the fort. Might I ask how he knows you?"

Dan lifted a brow at Laura indicating he knew she didn't like Williams's comment about Grey Wolf. "It's rather a long story, Major, but I'll keep it brief. First, I should tell you, he's white, not a half-breed. He was taken in by the Cheyenne when he was a boy, after his family was killed by Pawnees."

Martha, seated next to Sarah, let out a gasp. "Oh my, how tragic!"

"Yes, ma'am, it was. But the man's not looking for pity." He turned back to Williams. "Nor should anyone distrust him."

Williams shrugged. "I'll take your word for it, Driscoll, though I still wonder where such a man's loyalties lie—with the whites or the Indians." He picked up his pipe and a match. "Interesting enough, Captain Herrington lost his folks at the hands of Indians, too. But he was a whole lot luckier. The army took him in." He struck the lucifer against the mantel and relit his pipe. "You still haven't said how you know him?"

"We met him on the trail. He'd been severely injured by a grizzly, and Black Arrow was taking him to a missionary. Their medicine man had convinced Black Arrow his survival depended on white man's medicine. Laura took one look at him and knew he didn't have a chance if something wasn't done for him right away. Since she'd been trained by her uncle who was a doctor, I figured she knew what to do. And the chief was agreeable to leaving him in her care." Dan smiled at Laura. "Got to hand it to her. Nursed him back to health, good as new."

Williams listened attentively continuing to blow puffs of smoke from his pipe.

"Grey Wolf left us then," Dan continued, "but while he was on the train, several things happened that proved his worth to me."

"Well, if I ever see him again, I'll remember what you said, Driscoll." Williams gestured toward Laura and Sarah, his smile communicating his desire to lighten the tone of the conversation. "Now tell me, how about Miss Westbrook and Mrs. Osbourne staying at the fort while you're camped here. Martha would sure enjoy their company. Besides, it would be only proper, seeing they're family to one of my finest officers. Our guest quarters aren't much, but I know they beat the inside of a wagon."

Dan grinned. "They'll have to speak for themselves, though I can pretty much guess their answer."

"My goodness, what do you think, Laura?" Sarah asked. "Should we accept the major's kind offer?"

Laura set her teacup on a doily-covered table in front of her and grinned. She couldn't have been happier if the invitation had been to stay at a fancy hotel. "I'm just worried that once I sleep in a real bed again, I won't want to go back to that wagon. I may stay here and enlist."

Williams chuckled. "Miss Westbrook, I wish you could. We have one physician assigned to two forts, this one and Fort Laramie. Martha helps out best she can."

Laura grew serious. "If there's anything Sarah and I can do while we're here, please let us know."

"Well, thank you. We've been rather fortunate, though. Haven't had any illnesses or injuries that couldn't wait until the doctor got here."

Martha placed a hand on Sarah's arm. "I'm so happy you both will be staying."

"Tell me, do you get any periodicals from the states?" Sarah asked. "I have some editions of *Harpers' Weekly*, if you'd like to read them."

"Oh, bless you. I haven't read one since I left to come out here over a year ago. The army delivers eastern newspapers from time to time, but that's all."

"Well then," Dan said, pushing up from his chair, "how about we ride out and get your things?"

Major Williams retrieved his hat from a nearby table. "First, let me show you ladies the guest quarters. They're in the building next to us. Both rooms are cleaned and inspected regularly since quite often we have dignitaries come through, congressmen and the like, eager to see this part of the frontier."

Laura and Sarah rose from their seats and after repeated thank-yous to Martha, followed Dan and the major out the door.

A short while later, Dan drove the buckboard out of the fort with Sarah and Laura beside him. They hadn't gone far when Dan raised his hand and pointed. They looked to the top of a ridge where a horse and rider moved parallel with them along the rim. This time Sarah didn't have to ask who it was.

As Dan pulled to a stop in front of their campsite, Grey Wolf descended the bottom of the hill. Dan helped Sarah from the seat, Laura lowering herself from the other side. "I'll unload the buckboard," he said, eyeing Sarah with his familiar stop-your-worrying look. "You get your things together."

Sarah nodded, but when she turned expectantly to Laura, she was walking out to meet Grey Wolf. Sarah's heart fluttered anxiously as she watched Grey Wolf lean aside his horse and with one arm, lift Laura up behind him. The breadth of his chest and shoulders were so wide, Laura's slender form was hidden behind him.

Grey Wolf reined his horse in front of Sarah. "I would like to talk with your niece privately. I will bring her back when the sun sets."

Sarah wasn't sure whether he was asking her or telling her. "Well, we were planning to return to the fort."

"Not until later," Laura put in before Sarah had a chance to say more. "Please, would you pack a few things for me? I'll ride out tomorrow if I need anything else."

Dan gave Sarah a reassuring wink. "I don't see a problem with that, do you?"

The look stamped on Laura's face convinced Sarah there was no use to protest. She was going to do what she wanted whether Sarah approved or not. She smiled lamely. "No, I suppose not."

Dan sharpened his gaze toward Grey Wolf. "Be back by dusk."

Grey Wolf answered him with a single nod, then swung the stallion around and rode away.

CHAPTER 16

As Grey Wolf guided Four Winds up the steep hill, rocks and dirt tumbled around the horse's hooves. Laura started to slide backward. "Hold tight," he said over his shoulder.

Circling both arms further around his bare chest, Laura felt the thick muscles of his upper torso flex as he held the steed on course. Her heart thudded, but not from her perilous ride, rather from the pressure of her body pressed against his.

Finally clearing the top, Grey Wolf swung the pinto around and rewarded Laura with a bird's-eye view of the plains. Directly below them, the wagons formed a wide circle of white dots. To the left, Fort Hendricks stood proud, its buildings patterned in a square, and in the distance, the azure-blue river curled its way to the horizon.

Grey Wolf glanced at her out of the corner of his eye. "We can have privacy here." He prodded Four Winds toward an outcrop of large boulders.

After he halted the horse on the shaded side of the granite formation, he swung his leg over the animal's head and dropped to the ground. Facing her, he held out his arms. She placed her hands atop his shoulders as he grasped her waist and eased her down.

Their gazes locked as he slowly and deliberately slid Laura down the front of him, her skin igniting when he dragged her over his hard chest. She shuddered as he pressed her against his rigid thighs, and when her feet touched the ground, her mouth mated with his in a desperate attempt to quench the fire burning deep inside her.

Passion and need, relief and happiness flooded through them both. Up on tip-toes, Laura clung to Grey Wolf, while their lips sucked, their tongues swirled, and their moist breaths heated each other's face. Swallowing deep moans and soft whimpers, they kissed again and again while the memories came flooding back as to how good they felt in each other's arms. Grey Wolf's large hands caressed her sides while hers moved over his chest, the mass of coarse hair tickling her fingers before she rested them beside the cameo.

"Ah, you feel so good …" his mouth slid to the side of her cheek, his voice ragged, "better than my dreams." He kissed her earlobe, and then buried his face in her hair. "And you smell so sweet."

Delightful shivers followed the path of his hands along her spine. "Lilac sachet …" was all she could manage to say, her legs weak and rubbery.

Grey Wolf steadied her, guiding her a few steps to the wall of the large boulder. "We will take it slow and make this time we have together last," he said, bracing her against it. He kissed her forehead, and when she closed her eyes, he softly brushed his lips over her lids. "I have missed you, Bright Eyes."

Laura's heart skittered in her chest at the sound of the familiar endearment. "I never thought I'd see you again. I couldn't believe my eyes when you rode into the fort." She allowed a flirtatious smile to touch her lips. "I knew the way you looked at me, you'd find a way for us to be together."

As his gaze swept over her face, flecks of silver danced in his eyes. "I had to see you one more time." He squeezed her arms. "Wait here." He walked over to Four Winds and pulled the top blanket off the animal's back, then gave the pinto a slap on his hind quarter. The horse trotted off a few yards to nibble on a clump of grass.

Grasping Laura's hand, he led her around the side of the boulder where the ground was level. He swept stones away with a moccasinned foot and laid the blanket down. As she settled herself upon it, he unsheathed the knife at his waist and set it on a rock nearby. He sat cross-legged opposite her.

Laura scrutinized the scar on his shoulder. It was thinner and smoother now. Leaning over, she touched it lightly. His skin quivered beneath her fingertips.

A glint of something drew her attention to an unusual object on a second strip of rawhide clinging tightly to the base of his neck. She hadn't noticed it before, and it took a second before she recognized it. "Why, that's the bear fang I removed from your shoulder. But how did—?"

"Dan gave it to me before I left. He knew Cheyenne revere the teeth of animals, especially the bear."

"I … see," Laura said hesitantly. She didn't fail to catch the all too familiar note of Indian pride in his voice.

"Remember the last time you sat on this blanket, Laura? I told you almost everything about me." He reached out and skimmed a knuckle along her cheek. "Now it is your turn to tell me about you."

Laura clasped his hand and pressed it against the side of her face, reveling in the feel of its size and strength. "There's not much to tell. My life hasn't been half as exciting as yours."

"I want to know about it," he said emphatically, sliding his fingers through her hair and fanning it out beside her face. "I want to know what made you the woman you are." His eyes softened. "You are so trusting, so open. So sure of yourself."

"Sure of myself?" She eyed him critically, uncertain why he would think that. "If there's anyone more sure of himself, it's you."

Frowning, Grey Wolf withdrew his hand abruptly. He shifted to his side and propped himself on an elbow. "Tell me where you came from."

Laura leaned back against the boulder and gave him a short description of the town in Pennsylvania where she was born. She told him about her mother's death, and her father leaving them when she was only five. She talked some about her brother, Alex, and about their fairly easy childhood under the guidance and love of her aunt and uncle. She explained to him that it was her uncle who'd taught her about healing and medicine.

"And now I'm going to California." She sighed, her expression becoming somber. "You talk about my being so sure of myself …" She gave him a wane smile. "The closer we get, the more uncertain I am about why I'm going there."

Grey Wolf's brow creased. "What do you mean? You are going to see your father. You will live with him, won't you?"

She shrugged. "I guess. In his last letter, he wrote he had a lady friend, a widow who'd lost her husband some years back. Sounded as if they may get married."

"Your Aunt Sarah, she will live with you?"

"Yes, but I have a feeling not for long. I'm pretty sure she and Dan will be getting married, too." She brightened. "I hope so, anyway."

He smiled. "They would make good mates." An earnest look overtook his features. "You will be with family who loves you, Laura, your own flesh and blood."

She realized what he was saying. She should be grateful for what she had. He, on the other hand, would never see his own flesh and blood again.

Grey Wolf patted the blanket next to him. "Come over here," he beckoned.

Scooting closer, Laura's gaze flitted over the length of him. His body, exquisitely male and all but naked reclining beside her, sent fervent messages to every part of her. None were more urgent than her hands that ached to reach out and touch him.

Grinning, Grey Wolf arched one brow and cocked his head. "Does the woman like what she sees?"

She laughed and admitted shamelessly, "From the first time I examined you in Dan's wagon."

"For a while in that wagon, a fog circled my head, things were not clear. I do not remember much until that first time you fed me." His grin widened. "You were not too sure of yourself then, dripping hot porridge on me."

"Well, goodness, you looked so …" she hesitated, "savage."

"Savage, huh?" He leaned over and growled into the side of her neck, nipping at her skin playfully with his teeth.

Laura giggled, goose bumps popping up along the nape of her neck. She lifted a hand and pushed against his chest.

Grey Wolf stopped and drew back. His expression sobered. "Is that what I look like to you now, Laura? A savage?"

Her eyes lowered, as did her voice. "What was the Indian word you said to me the last night we were together?"

"You mean the word, beautiful?"

"Yes, how did you say it?"

"*Ne-peva-tamaahe,*" he said, his eyes meeting hers.

Laura reached out and traced a finger lightly over the bicep of his arm. "*Ne … peva … tamaahe,*" she repeated. As she splayed her hand across his wide chest, his muscles bunch tightly beneath her palm. Even in the shade of the rocks, his skin shone like smooth, polished gold. Fascinated, she moved her hand further down to touch the rigid flatness of his stomach.

Suddenly with an intensity that startled Laura, Grey Wolf clamped an iron hand around her wrist and held her hand still. "Do you know what you are doing to me?" He shifted slightly so that she could see the real evidence of his maleness in the bulge under his breechcloth.

A warm, erotic sensation fluttered through the inner recesses of Laura's body. Yes, she saw what she was doing to him. But she knew she was helpless to stop. Call it curiosity, call it yearning. Call it want, need, desire. From Grey Wolf's first kiss, it was all these things … and more. It was much, much more.

She wanted to learn the passionate secrets her dreams had only alluded to. She lifted her face and stared into those crystalline eyes. And to have this man—this very special man—be the one to teach her.

His grip on her wrist tightened.

"Grey Wolf, I … I want …" She faltered, taken back by the fragile sound of her own voice.

He pulled her against his chest. "Sweet Laura, I know what you want. I want you too." Releasing her hand, he clasped the nape of her neck and drew her face to his. His gaze lowered to her lips. Gently he guided her mouth to his, circling his lips over hers, expertly taking possession of what she so willingly offered.

As he slipped his tongue into her mouth, he rolled her onto her back. Cradling her in his arm, he plied her with ardent kisses along her temple, over her ear, in her hair, each one arousing Laura's instinctive passion.

She wrapped her arms around his neck, a warm flood of desire cascading over her. The anticipation caused her breasts to ache and swell even before he touched them. Wonderfully possessive, his hand caressed one, then the other. She couldn't help the low moan emitting from her throat as she rolled herself against the pressure and felt her nipples harden beneath her bodice.

Reaching for the top button of her dress, he drew away and murmured, "I remember you were better at these than I."

The memory of his hands on her bare flesh and the ecstasy it brought sent Laura's fingers fleeting down the row of buttons. Grey Wolf raked the dress off her shoulders, and they both tugged the camisole and dress to her waist, all in a matter of seconds. Then settling back on the blanket, they began to relive that memory.

Grey Wolf cupped one breast in his hand, then the other. He lifted each one high, caressing it almost reverently and lathing his tongue over its peak.

Laura became lost in the exquisite feel of his mouth and tongue sensitizing her flesh everywhere he touched her, from the tip of her breasts to the valley between them, from the pulse point at her throat to the fine hairs along the side of her neck, then returning to her hungry lips.

With a hand on her hip, Grey Wolf clenched the folds of her skirt in his fist and spoke into her open mouth. "Like a flame, you are setting my body on fire."

Laura tasted the beads of sweat above his upper lip, smelled a pleasant, muskiness emanating from his body. Sliding her palm over the slick, silkiness of his shoulder, she understood his meaning. The same intense heat was consuming her, and it wasn't the summer sun that made their bodies perspire.

As she buried her fingers into his long mane of hair, Grey Wolf stretched his hand further down her leg. But when he pulled the hem of her skirt to her thigh, he stopped abruptly. Leaning back, he looked at her questioningly.

"My drawers," she whispered, her smile tentative. "I don't suppose Indian girls wear them?"

Raising up on one arm, Grey Wolf slid his hand over the thin cloth to the apex between her thighs. "No," he said as he cupped his hand over her.

Laura closed her eyes, releasing a soft moan as he rubbed her gently. Now she was discovering where her desire was centered, where all her passion flowed … here, where Grey Wolf held her.

Throbbing and craving for what, Laura wasn't sure, she lay waiting for him to show her. But to her frustration, he suddenly removed his hand.

Her eyes opened to find him staring at her intently. When he spoke, his voice was so low she strained to hear him.

"I need to know, Laura."

"Know what?"

"Has any man—"

"No, never," she blurted, heat flushing her cheeks. "You are the only …" The right words eluded her. She knew her virginal innocence had to be stamped all over her face.

"An Indian maiden who has never been touched by a man wears a protective rope." His gaze clung to her. "It is the Cheyenne way. Only her husband can remove it."

The meaning of his words tore at Laura's heart. He was still fighting the differences between his world and hers. Like before, his Indian ways were coming between them.

Vowing not to allow it to happen again, she took his large hand in hers and pressed it to her breasts. "I'm not an Indian. And I wear no such rope." Without shame, she moved his palm back and forth over her skin. She shuddered, her breathing becoming uneven. "What we're feeling is so good, so right." She pressed his hand over the special place where it had been a moment ago and in a trembling voice filled with unrestrained passion, pleaded, "Grey Wolf, make love to me."

CHAPTER 17

Laura's provocative encouragement and persuasive words were more than Grey Wolf could bear. With far less gentleness than before, his mouth came down over hers, hot and urgent. "Ah, Laura," he rasped, forcing her name against her lips as he reached between her thighs. He felt her moist desire already dampening her drawers and knew his last vestiges of restraint were gone. Lifting his mouth from hers, he gave her a penetrating look and whispered, "What have I done to deserve you?"

"It's not what you've done, it's who you are," she replied in a throaty voice full of feeling. "You're a very special man, Grey Wolf." She flattened her hands against his chest. "And I know I'll never, ever meet anyone like you again."

Her words struck a sensitive chord, but in the heat of passion, Grey Wolf ignored the possibility that she knew him better than he knew himself. Drawing apart from her, he pulled her to a sitting position and took hold of the dress and camisole bunched at her waist. "Raise your arms." Her gaze clung to him as she complied, allowing him to lift the clothes over her head.

He watched her full breasts raise and lower with the movement of her arms. Her hair tumbled around her shoulders. He swallowed hard, trying to force down his lust that threatened to take control. He wanted to make this first time good for her. And the only way was for him to take it slow and easy.

After setting her clothes aside, he held out his hands. "Give me your foot," he instructed.

"My foot?" she asked hesitantly.

"Yes, both feet, so I can remove your boots." He smiled, touched by her innocence. Laura twisted from his side and stuck one foot in front of him.

Stretching the elastic gussets, Grey Wolf pulled one boot off, then the other and set them beside the blanket. He sensed a shyness about her as he rolled her stockings over her slender ankles and stripped them from her feet. Her alluring innocence made her even more desirable and stirred a wealth of emotions in him that he never knew existed—feelings that tugged at his heart as well as his body.

Tenderly, he caressed her delicate feet, his fingers messaging the sensitive skin along their arch. "I want to touch you all over," he said, kissing the inside of one ankle before setting her feet beside him.

He kicked off his moccasins and rolled closer to her. He ran a palm up the side of her leg to the curve of her hip where he gripped her tightly. Drawing her to him, he reclaimed her lips, needing to feel their reassuring warmth against his.

Circling her arms around his neck, Laura opened her mouth and brazenly matched the stroking of his tongue with her own. He felt her passion build as she crushed her breasts against his chest and uttered urgent, muffled sounds inside his mouth.

Laying her back on the blanket, Grey Wolf clasped the waistband of her drawers and tugged gently. The tie loosened enough for him to push the undergarment over her hips and part way down her legs. He lifted his mouth from hers and watched his dark hand skim over her ivory belly. His fingers burrowed into the triangle of auburn hair between her legs.

Laura opened her eyes, a small gasp escaping her lips. He smiled. "You are as soft as rabbit's fur."

Laura clung to him desperately as deep quivers rippled through her crevice under his hand. Unable to stop her body's responses, she parted her thighs. Grey Wolf delved a long finger between her, and it was as though she'd been ignited with a torch. She gave a jolt and heard herself cry out. With wonder in her eyes, she looked up at him, and he returned her gaze with one of understanding.

He caressed her warm moistness. "Relax, Laura ... let your body relax."

As glorious sensations overpowered her, she closed her eyes and gave into the erotic mastery of his touch. Her pelvis rode his sensual up and down strokes while the rest of her body grew loose and languid.

"Do not close your eyes," he beckoned. Lifting her lashes, she met his hot, sultry gaze. "In them, I can see how much I please you."

Laura combed her fingers into his long hair while an all-consuming pleasure flowed through her, spreading, growing in intensity. "I never thought ... I never dreamed it could feel like this." But as she arched her body in a passionate need for more, the source of her pleasure slipped away.

"Grey Wolf, don't, oh, please, don't stop ..."

"Easy, Laura. We have only begun." He leaned over and stripped the drawers from her feet, then with a jerk of his hand, removed the cord around his own waist and slung the breechcloth aside.

Laura's gaze never left his face as he moved over her, bracing an arm either side of her. Barely touching her, he rested his weight on his forearms, allowing her to grow accustomed to the size and length of his body hovering above her. Then he gradually lowered his chest to her breasts, the cameo dropping between them. As his legs straddled her hips, his pulsing manhood pressed against her abdomen. Wordless seconds passed as they looked into each other's eyes.

"Feel me," he whispered, moving over her in a slow, stimulating motion, "feel how much I want you."

Tentative at first, Laura lifted her hips in response to his. His long, turgid shaft rubbed against her, its steady throb matching her own body's rhythm. Her hands that had been around his neck, now wandered down the firm muscles of his thighs.

Dear God, his body is so big, so powerful.

Grey Wolf buried his face into the side of her neck, his breath hot against her skin. "Do not be afraid. Take hold of me. Feel what your body wants." But this time she was unable to do his bidding, her hands remaining still, clinging to his hips.

His mouth covered hers at the same time he took hold of her hand and pressed it to his heated flesh. And when her fingers closed around the length of him, his mouth ground into hers even harder, his tongue thrusting and reaching deeper.

With newfound understanding of lovemaking, Laura accepted his demanding kisses as her hand became bolder, caressing his slick, silky manhood. She discovered the stroke of her hand mimicked the stimulation of his hand, and even though their bodies were very different in form, they were very much alike in their response to each other.

Grey Wolf wrenched his mouth from hers. "Bright Eyes ... ahh," he groaned, the sound of his voice a strange mixture of agony and pleasure, "you learn quickly." To her bewilderment, as the thrill of stroking him aroused her own desire to fever pitch, he jerked away, twisting out of her grasp.

Struck with the horrible notion that maybe she'd done something wrong, Laura cast him a worried look. "What's the matter? Did I do it wrong?"

A chuckle rumbled in his throat. "No, you are not doing anything wrong." He shifted his weight to one side and laid a hand lovingly under one breast. "It was beginning to feel too good."

Her breath caught in her throat as he lowered his mouth and licked the crest of her erect nipple. "But how …" she tensed, her flesh prickling as he popped her nipple between his lips and sucked, "can you feel *too* good?"

Lifting his head to look at her, his eyes darkened seductively. "I will show you."

His words hung in the air like an echo, as his hand began its journey down her body to the place that beckoned him most. Parting her legs, Grey Wolf's fingers probed her wetness, circling and stroking the core of her womanhood. Laura's eyes drifted shut, her head lolling from side to side in sheer, wanton rapture. "My God, what are you doing to me?"

She was sinking within herself, drowning in delicious sensations deep beneath his fingertips. Her nails dug into his arms, and she clung to him as if he were her only lifeline.

"Let yourself go, Bright Eyes. Do not hold back."

She said his name, maybe screamed it, she wasn't sure, as wave upon wave of spasms engulfed her. She tried to get her breath, but there seemed no time, as ecstasy filled her from head to toe. She opened her eyes, watching Grey Wolf's body cover hers and his hot, satiny length probe her throbbing entrance. Instinctively, Laura spread her thighs wide and arched her hips, her body ready for the ultimate fulfillment.

Hovering above her, Grey Wolf barely held himself inside her and in a shuddering voice warned, "It may hurt at first, Laura."

Clutching the blanket on either side of her, she cared not about any such hurt, so fierce was the need for him to take her now. "It's all right, please, oh please," she beseeched, communicating her trust in him through her eyes.

The corded muscles in his chest and shoulders rippled as he moved in and out, deeper and deeper. Laura gasped, not from the pain already subsiding, but from the torturous storm of pleasure that threatened to drive her out of her mind as he spilled himself into her, one thrusting surge after another. She knew he held nothing back, giving her all he had until the aftershocks of his climax finally coursed through his body. Then burying his face in the side of her hair, he lowered himself next to her and whispered intimate words, both Indian and English into her ear.

Unable to distinguish every word, Laura smiled, knowing they all held special meaning; for while their bodies lay entwined and their hearts beat as one, they were not in his world, nor her world, but their world. And in this sweet aftermath, as he gazed into her eyes and her body still tingled and quivered inside, she wished they didn't ever have to leave it.

"There is no one I would rather have for my guardian spirit than you, Laura," Grey Wolf said, kissing her with a new kind of tenderness.

"And could you be mine as well?" she asked, feeling such an abiding bond with this man to whom she had given herself so completely.

A smile curved the corner of his lips. "I have already decided I am." Raising up, he took hold of his cameo necklace and pulled it over his head. Laura's heart all but stopped as he circled the thong over her head and laid the cameo between her breasts.

"Grey Wolf, I can't. It was your mother's and you've worn it—"

He pressed a finger to her lips. "I have worn and cherished it for a long time. Now it will mean more to me if you wear it."

Oh God, how could she refuse him? Her eyes reached deep into his, marveling at all this man was. So prideful, so fierce; yet so gentle, so sensitive. Yes, she would keep it, for in doing so she would be keeping a part of him.

She smiled, a tear fluttering down her cheek. "Thank you. I shall wear it always."

He leaned over and kissed the tear away. "Good. That is what I wanted to hear." His gaze sharpened. "Now you must give me something in return."

His request warmed Laura's heart. She would like to give him something in return, but what? What did she have that could equal the sentiment of his cameo?

"But I have nothing of value with me."

"Ah, but you do." He lifted a hand and gently combed his fingers through her hair. "My mother's hair was like yours, beautiful and wavy, like the color of fire." His voice was low and tender. "Can I have a lock of your hair?"

A simple gift, Laura thought, yet for him it would be the perfect one. Bringing her hand to the side of his jaw, she drew his mouth to hers, her answer touching his lips. "Yes, of course you can."

The instant she kissed him, Grey Wolf pulled her to him and deepened the kiss. Uttering a low, guttural moan, he then dragged his mouth to the side of hers. "Sweet Mother Earth, I cannot get enough of you." He set her apart and let out a long, resigned sigh. "You are a very passionate woman, Laura. No matter how many times I made love to you, it would never be enough." His light-hearted smile seemed forced as he skimmed an index finger down the bridge of her nose. "We should get dressed. I need to take you back." Retrieving his breechcloth, he rose to his feet.

Laura sat up, amazed to find herself feeling not at all inhibited by her nudity even though she was no longer in Grey Wolf's arms. She looked around her, and it was as though the world had come alive for the first time. Nearby a large black crow flapped its wings and strutted across the ledge of a boulder rendering its familiar "caw-caw" to several of its flock pecking on the ground at the base of the rock. Lifting her face to the bright western sun, she savored its warmth while she watched white wisps of clouds make their sojourn across a Dresden blue sky.

Grey Wolf moved into her line of vision, returning her attention to him once again. He wrapped the breechcloth around himself and tied the rawhide cord at his waist, then slipped his feet into his moccasins. After he picked up his knife off the rock and slid it into the sheath at his side, he set his hands on his hips and stared down at her.

"If you do not put those ..." nodding toward the blanket, he arched a brow, "drawers on, I will not be responsible for what happens next."

With a grin, Laura shimmied into them.

"And what is this little piece of nothing called?" he asked, squatting down and picking up her camisole. He held it at arms length, a twinkle in his eyes.

Laura tried to grab it out of his hand, but he jerked it away. She giggled. "It's a camisole."

He turned it this way and that. "Are they always decorated with a pink ribbon?"

This time when she reached for it, he let her have it. "No, some are plain with no ribbons at all." She fitted the garment over her head and arms, allowing it to fall over her breasts. Through her lashes, she could see Grey Wolf following her every move. She was enjoying the playful banter between them. "Some camisoles are decorated with lace," she said, her glance meeting his coyly.

"What is lace?"

His question threw her. He didn't know what lace was? But then why would he? His mother may never have worn anything with lace. And for sure, Indians didn't use it.

"Lace is a delicately woven fabric sewn on clothing. It's very pretty."

Grey Wolf reached out a finger and traced the edge of her neckline. His smile faded. "I wish I could see you in lace." Then as if the cloth had burned him, he snapped his hand away, stood and backed off the blanket. "While you finish dressing," he said in a clipped voice, "I will get us water."

Though Grey Wolf could have brought the stallion to his side with a whistle, he walked to the horse instead, taking the time to collect his thoughts. He didn't like what was running through his head. Stepping beside Four Winds, he untied a water sac from the strap above the animal's shoulder. Even though he had been the first man to love Laura, he would not be the last. Who would be next to ignite the flames within her? Would it be the young scout on the wagon train? Or someone she has yet to meet in California?

Loosening the sac's long drawstring, he tipped it above his mouth and let the water roll down his throat, wishing the liquid would wash away his jealousy as easily as it did his thirst. After wiping his mouth with the back of his hand, he yanked the drawstring closed. His jealousy, he thought resignedly, wasn't only toward the man who'd possess her body, but the one who would possess her heart.

Returning, he found Laura standing next to the blanket fastening the last of her buttons. The cameo hung over the rounded collar of her dress. Looping the water sac over his shoulder, he moved to her side.

Her fingers stilled as she looked up at him. He took hold of the necklace and dropped the thin cord under the neckline of her dress. "I want you to wear it here," he pressed his palm to her chest, "close to your heart."

Her smile gave him the assurance that she understood the poignancy of his words. The cameo was more than a gift; it was a declaration of how strong his feelings were for her.

"And my hair?" she asked, fingering a lock curling over her shoulder. "Where will you keep it?"

Grey Wolf pulled the knife from his sheath. "I will put it in a medicine bundle and strap it to my thigh." The edge of the knife was razor sharp and it took but a second to cut the lock of hair she held up for him. "I will take it off only when I bathe," he said. Sheathing the knife, he then looped the long strands into a loose knot, refraining from telling her that such a bundle worn around an Indian's thigh was regarded as potent love medicine.

He handed Laura his water sac, then turned and let out a shrill whistle. Immediately, Four Winds swung his head up from where he was grazing and trotted over. While he tucked the lock of hair into a pouch secured to the pinto's back, Laura looked at the sac somewhat dubiously.

"Here," he said, coming over and taking it from her. He pulled open the drawstring. He held the narrow rim of the vessel between her lips and lifted it.

"M-m-m," she murmured. She wiped some droplets from her chin. "Whatever that is, it certainly keeps the water nice and cool."

"It is the lining of a buffalo stomach."

"Buffalo stomach!" Taking a step backward, she spat and stuck out her tongue, a sudden foulness invading her mouth.

He eyed her, smirking. "It is better than those rusty canteens whites drink out of."

Laura wiped her mouth with the back of her sleeve. It may be white man's blood running through Grey Wolf's veins, but in his heart and mind, she reminded herself, he will always remain the unrelenting and ever proud Cheyenne warrior.

Watching him retie the sac on the pinto, she recalled the major's words earlier that day. *I wonder where such a man's loyalties lie—with the whites or the Indians.*

"Why do you look at me that way?" he asked, the reproachful tone in his voice cutting into her thoughts.

"What way?" she asked warily.

"Like you are looking for something. What is it, Laura? Or should I say *who* is it? David?" He gave a final yank in the knot. "Are you still hoping to find David somewhere inside me?"

"No," she shook her head, "no, of course not." She bit her lip and looked away. *Oh, but wasn't she?* It seemed he read her thoughts far better than she read her own.

CHAPTER 18

Grey Wolf clenched his mouth, suppressing the urge to say anything more. He had to face the fact Laura would never understand the life he led. He stepped around her and picked up the blanket. After spreading it over the buffalo hide atop Four Winds, he rested his forearms across the stallion's back and looked pensively far beyond the ridge to where the Platte River flowed.

My life is like that river. The South Platte veered away from the North Platte steering its own endless course across the plains. So too, his life years ago had made an abrupt change and now wanders across the plains just as aimlessly.

Laura's gentle hand on his shoulder coaxed him out of his reverie. "I didn't mean to make you feel uncomfortable," she said. "It's just that ... there's a part of you I can't seem to reach."

He understood what she meant. But it was a part of him he didn't want her to invade. A place of heartache and nightmares—a place better left alone.

Schooling his expression to mask his inner feelings, he inclined his head and teased her with a smile. "Believe me, a few minutes ago you reached every part of me." Lifting his brows suggestively, he took her hand and squeezed it. "And if we do not leave, I will have you reaching for me again."

Laura grinned at his play on words, but she wasn't swayed by them. She tugged her hand from his, her grin fading. "I don't want to leave yet. Please, let's talk some more." She walked to a grassy mound a few feet away and sat down.

Following her, Grey Wolf settled on the ground beside her. His gaze swung to the sun hovering lower in the sky. Like Laura, he didn't want their time together to end. He wished he could stop the sun from setting, stop time altogether. Then they could stay there forever. He wasn't aware his mind had drifted to such hopeless musings until she spoke his name.

"Grey Wolf, will I see you again?"

"I think you know the answer to that."

A frown creased her forehead. "But I'll be staying several days at the fort. You could come there."

Resentment knifed through him. He was barely able to contain his anger for Laura's sake. "Did you see the way the soldiers glared at me when I rode in today? Even in Major Williams's face, I saw the distrust. No, Laura, I will not go back there."

She nodded, both disappointment and understanding reflected in her eyes. "The major thought you were a half-breed, until Dan explained. He told him how we met you." She offered him a reassuring smile. "Dan spoke very highly of you."

"Dan is a fair and honest man. Too bad there are not more like him."

Laura cast a somber look toward the distant horizon. "Where is your home? How far from here?"

"South. It will not take a full sun to ride there. Before I go back, I plan to see Jeremiah. He is on in years and I worry about him."

She plucked a long blade of grass and toyed with it between her fingers. "He means a lot to you, doesn't he?"

"If not for him, I would not be sitting here talking to you. I will always be grateful he convinced me not to forget the English language."

"Where does he live?" she asked.

Grey Wolf regarded her for a moment, reaching out to brush a lock of hair from her face. "Bright Eyes, always full of questions," he said with a slight grin. "Jeremiah's trading post is not far from my village." He stood, held out his hand and pulled her to her feet. "What else do you want to know?"

An uneasy flush crept into Laura's face. "It's about what happened at the fort today. The major told us about those two Indians who were killed. Since they were Cheyenne, I guess you knew them?"

He had expected Laura to ask him about what she'd seen. He could avoid answering her, but deep down he wanted to explain why such a thing happened, especially now that he knew the major had told his version.

"Yes, Thunderhawk and Little Elk were relatives of Black Arrow."

"Did you know that one of them almost shot Alex? My brother could have died." Her eyes filled with contempt.

He stared at her, astonished. "Laura, I am sorry. I did not know." A tense moment of silence stretched between them. His gaze clung to an unfocused spot far below the ridge as he hunted for the right words to say. "Please do not resent all Indians because of the actions of some. Many clans, including Black Arrow's, try to keep peace with the whites. But there are those, especially young warriors like Thunderhawk and Little Elk, who are angry and bitter. They do not want to be told by the whites where they can and cannot go."

"And what about you?" There was no mistaking the challenge in her voice. "How do you feel?"

His first thought was to tell her he wanted to see a lasting peace between the Indians and whites. But that was not what she asked. She wanted to know which side he was on.

"My people have always thought of this land as something free for everyone, like the sky and sun," he said with quiet emphasis. "Not to own for only themselves and keep others away, like the whites are trying to do." Facing her, he met her intense gaze. "If it were the whites' whose land and livelihood were being taken from them, as well as their freedom and pride, I am sure they would be angry and bitter too."

Laura drew in a breath. She hugged her arms across her chest. So, she had her answer. Grey Wolf hadn't come right out and said it, but he might as well have. His loyalties were with the Indians. And the strange thing was, she agreed with everything he said. Rubbing a hand up one arm, she responded hopefully, "I heard the major tell Dan that our government wants to sign a new treaty with the Indians. Maybe that will improve things."

"Only if it is fair and both sides honor it," Grey Wolf replied, his voice sounding none too hopeful. "According to the last treaty, the government is supposed to give the Indians monies and goods, but they give far less than they promise. Today Major Williams told Yellow Dog we would not receive any rifles or ammunition, even though that firepower helps kill buffalo faster and easier than with spears or arrows."

She remembered the major telling her Yellow Dog had been with the other two Indians. "Yes, but in the wrong hands, those guns could cause more trouble, like what happened yesterday."

Grey Wolf reached out and taking her by the shoulders, pulled her closer to him. "I do not like to think what might have happened to Alex." Torment flashed across his face. "I would not want you to feel the pain of losing a brother as I have."

"That's why it's important for me to spend time with Alex before we go on to California. I don't know when I'll see him again." Her glance made a broad sweep of the plains. "I'm hoping he'll be back in the next day or two."

With a nod toward the setting sun, Grey Wolf squeezed her arms. "You see where that sun is? I better take you back before Dan comes searching for us."

Laura looked deep into Grey Wolf's eyes. The longing she saw in them made her wish she hadn't. She tried to hide the misery from her own eyes, but she couldn't. Neither of them spoke. They both knew words would change nothing and only make leaving that much harder.

They remained silent as Grey Wolf led her to Four Winds. He lifted her onto the stallion's back, and then swung up behind her. Circling an arm around her waist, he settled her close against him.

As he urged the pinto down the hill, Laura leaned back into his strong embrace, wishing she could ride that way forever. But all too quickly they neared the wagon train. The haunting sadness she'd experienced when Grey Wolf had left the train before seeped into her heart once again. She was relieved when he halted Four Winds a discreet distance away and thankful too, that Sarah and Dan were nowhere in sight.

He dropped the reins, his one arm gripping her waist. Sweeping her hair off her shoulder, he buried his face in the side of her neck and pressed his lips behind her ear. Her skin prickled as his mouth grazed her earlobe, his breath warm and moist when he spoke. "Your spirit will be with me always, Laura …" his hand moved over her breasts possessively, "as mine will be with you."

Her heart thumped beneath his heavy caress while desire and despair intermingled, creating havoc with her senses. Before she knew what was happening, he lowered her from the horse. Then without so much as a glance her way, he swung Four Winds around and galloped away.

Laura lifted her hand in a silent farewell, fighting back the tears. The borrowed time they'd shared had been wonderful and meaningful. That was what she would remember, not the sadness of his leaving.

Back at the fort, Laura stood at the open window of the guest quarters and looked up at the stars twinkling above the coppery moon. The night was eerily quiet, save for one sentry calling out the hour, and another farther along the perimeter of the garrison echoing his answer with a dulcet, "… all's well."

Ever since earlier that afternoon when Grey Wolf rode away, she felt strangely detached from everybody and everything. Though she hadn't shed a tear, inside her heart was broken.

Earlier that evening, she'd gone through the motions of arriving at the fort and settling into her room. When Mrs. Williams brought over a tray of dried fruits, biscuits and hot tea, the three of them sat in Sarah's room making light conversation while they ate. She'd acted politely interested in what was said, but neither cared then, nor remembered now what they'd talked about. Finally, when a corporal brought them large basins of heated water and fresh towels, Martha departed and Laura withdrew to her room next door to bathe.

Like Sarah's, her quarters were small and sparsely furnished with a bed, washstand, square table and lamp. Located at the end of the building, the room had a single window with faded blue muslin curtains draping the sides.

Laura glanced at the bed. Its thick mattress and clean linens beckoned her to lie down, but she knew if she did, she would only toss and turn ... and dream. She closed her eyes, the familiar ache seeping into her chest. That was all she could do now, wasn't it? Dream of him. His dark hands touching her, his warm lips kissing her, his smooth, intimate voice whispering Indian words ...

"Laura?" Tap, tap. *"Are you awake?"*

Her aunt's voice came to her as if from a distance. She pressed the heels of her hands to her eyes waiting for the look, the feel of Grey Wolf to recede before tightening the sash of her cotton robe and going to the door.

When she opened it, Sarah looked at her, smiling apologetically. "Dear, I hope you weren't asleep. You did say to give you about an hour, and then come over. Something else you wanted to talk to me about, remember?" At Laura's hesitation, she inclined her head. "You were asleep, weren't you? We can talk another time."

"No, I wasn't. I ... uh, I was just looking out the window admiring all the stars. It's such a beautiful, clear night." She moved aside so Sarah could enter and for the first time, realized how dark the room was. Stepping over to the bedside table and picking up a match, she struck a flame, then lifting the glass lamp, lit the wick. As she blew out the match and set the lamp down, she glanced at her aunt.

Sarah's smile lingered. "You miss Grey Wolf already, don't you?"

Laura dropped her hands to her side and released a heavy sigh. "Yes," she replied, allowing her desolation to take hold completely.

"Is that what you wanted to talk to me about?"

Laura nodded and crossed to the window. She curled her fingers around the folds of the curtain and peered out. "I thought I hurt after Alex left for the army, but it never felt like this."

Sarah stepped up behind her and touched her shoulders. "Oh sweetheart, I do know what you're going through. All those years ago and I can still remember how much it hurt when Daniel left. It took a long time for James to fill the emptiness in my heart." Shrugging her shoulders, she shook her head. "And now isn't it strange ... Daniel's come back into my life, filling the void left by James."

She moved to the other side of the window opposite Laura. She glanced out the window for a moment before turning to Laura. "Do you love him?"

Laura's hand tightened around the curtain. She swallowed, the ache in her chest rising to her throat. Go ahead, admit it, say it out loud. *No sense to deny it any longer.* She bit her lip to keep it from trembling. "Yes, I love him."

She looked for Sarah's reaction, but her aunt showed neither surprise nor disapproval. Instead she nodded, her eyes expressing not judgment but understanding. Relieved and needing her comfort, Laura stepped into the circle of her sympathetic embrace.

"I think I knew you loved him before you did," Sarah said, hugging her. She smiled, tilting her head to look into Laura's face. "I recognize the symptoms." She patted Laura's shoulder, guiding her to the bedside where they both sat down. "At first, I wanted to believe it was only infatuation but finally admitted to myself that you were old enough to have much stronger feelings."

Laura leaned her head back and glimpsed upward, trying to blink back the tears stinging her eyes. "I love him so much, but I know he doesn't feel the same about me." She shrugged. "I think he could, but he won't let himself. He told me it could never work out for us, that our lives are too different."

She straightened, releasing a sigh. "He sees himself as an Indian, and he shuts me out whenever I try to remind him of his birth heritage. It's like he has this wall around him, and he only lets me in certain doors." Resignation slipped into her voice along with the sorrow. "Anyway, it doesn't matter, he's gone now."

Sarah sat quietly for several seconds before speaking. "Dear, I know there's not much I can say to help how you're feeling right now, but there is one thing I've found to be true. Please believe that things have a way of working out for the best." She took Laura's hand in hers. "And I surely do admire the man for caring enough to consider what is best for you." A sudden light twinkled in her eyes as she patted Laura's hand. "Say now, there's something I've been meaning to ask you. Where did you put James's watch? We don't want to forget to give it to Alex."

"Oh, my gosh! It's still in my reticule in the wagon. I'll ride out tomorrow and get it."

Standing, Sarah clasped her hands together. "You know, I had this wonderful premonition that we'll see Alex tomorrow."

"Glory, I hope so. I could use his freckle-faced smile about now."

Sarah laughed. "It's getting late, time we turned in." She walked to the door. "Good night, Laura."

"Good night. And thank you for listening. It helped."

"Anytime, dear," she said, letting herself out.

Laura walked back to stand in front of the window. She pulled the cameo from beneath her robe and curled her fingers around it. Sarah's attempt to steer her mind from Grey Wolf had only worked temporarily. She gazed out into the darkness. "Good night, my love," she whispered.

CHAPTER 19

The next morning, a stiff breeze sent a cluster of leaves swirling over Grey Wolf's head, arousing him from a deep, dream-laden sleep full of ethereal visions of Laura holding out her hand and calling for him. Stretched out on his side on the ground, Grey Wolf watched the blue haze of dawn filter through the swaying boughs of the trees, while darkness still clung stubbornly to the shadows. Overhead a jaybird's sharp cry sliced through the last remnants of his dream. He tensed. Behind him, the sound of footsteps crept very slowly, barely audible.

With every muscle coiled, he held his breath and waited for the person to come closer. Then wielding his knife, he leaped and flung the intruder to the ground. Inches apart, eyeball to eyeball, they stared at each other as Grey Wolf held the point of the blade against the man's throat.

"Blast it!" the man croaked, trying to catch his breath pinned beneath Grey Wolf. "Ease up, boy. It's only me."

The early morning sun lent just enough light for Grey Wolf to discern the lean, bearded face. "Jeremiah, you crazy fool! I might have killed you!" He rolled and stood, hoisting his friend up.

The older man dusted leaves and dirt off his pant legs. "Naw, I know you. You wouldn't have used your knife until you saw who it was."

"Wrong, my friend. If it had been any darker, your head would have been rolling into those bushes," he jammed the knife back into its sheath, "*then* I would look to see who it was!"

Jeremiah grinned. What started as a chuckle turned into a deep cough that took him a minute to suppress. "You're always sneaking up on me," he said, clearing his throat. "This time, I got you first."

Grey Wolf frowned, concerned for his friend who was at least twenty years older than he. "Are you all right?"

"Shucks, take more than a young pup like you to lick me!" He hitched up the waist of his trousers that were too big for his thin frame. "By thunder, it's good to see you. Been too long since you paid a visit. I was beginning to think something happened to you."

Grey Wolf smiled, putting aside his concern. "How did you know I was camped nearby? Your place was dark when I rode in late last night."

"After answering nature's call a while ago, I caught a glimpse of a horse between the trees. When I crept closer, I recognized Four Winds."

Grey Wolf picked up his belongings off the ground, and then followed Jeremiah out of the woods to a large log cabin, fronted with a wide-roofed porch. Hanging from the eaves above the entrance was a battered wooden sign with the words painted in white: TRADING POST—Jeremiah T. Hornbuckle, proprietor. They walked around to a back stoop which was the entrance to Jeremiah's living quarters.

As Grey Wolf set his things on the single wood step, Jeremiah aimed a pointed look at his shoulder. "Didn't have that scar last time I saw you. One on your arm, too." He glance shifted to the bear fang hanging at his throat.

Grey Wolf ignored the curious lift of Jeremiah's brow. "Is that coffee I smell brewing?" he asked, a hollow ache tightening his chest as he remembered when and where he'd last drank white man's coffee.

"It sure is. Come on in. I have a hunch we got some stories to trade."

Two cups of coffee and a few stale biscuits later, Grey Wolf leaned his chair back on two legs watching Jeremiah pour them yet another cup.

"That woman, Laura, she did a dandy job of sewing up your shoulder," Jeremiah said as he placed the coffee pot back on the stove. He sat down opposite him. "Guess you thought that's good enough reason to give her your mother's cameo, huh?"

Grey Wolf cut him a quick look before settling his gaze on the steaming cup in front of him. The man had a remarkable keenness; although it probably had not taken much insight to pick up on Grey Wolf's feelings for Laura after he'd described her to him. "I did not say I gave it away. Maybe I lost it."

"Did you?"

"No," he answered flatly. He bristled, his jaw tightening. He appreciated Jeremiah's interest in him, but there were boundaries to how much a man like him revealed when it came to personal feelings. At an early age, he had learned to keep his inner self separated from his outer one, and he didn't like anyone seeing the vulnerable side of him, the one that harbored self-doubts and misgivings.

Pushing back his chair, Grey Wolf stood. He walked to the other side of the room where several stacks of books lined one wall. He knelt and picked one up. Opening the leather-bound cover, he read the title centered on the first page: *Moby Dick* by Herman Melville. "What will you do with all these books?" he asked.

"Take them with me, of course. I hauled them this far west." Rising to his feet, Jeremiah braced the table as another coughing fit shook his whole body. He pulled a handkerchief from his pants pocket, spat into it, and then wadded it back into the pocket. Looking over, he dismissed Grey Wolf's worried frown with a wave of his hand. "It's this damp, morning air. Gets me every time." He moved beside him and pointed to the books. "You want some of them?"

Grey Wolf shook his head. "Hard enough to travel from camp to camp with the ones you already gave me. I can help you pack them though." He looked around the sparsely furnished room. "I can help you pack up everything. In the trading post, too."

Jeremiah gave an appreciative nod. "I was hoping you'd say that. I want to get back to the mine as soon as I can. Me and my partner, Charley, have the claim registered all legal and proper, but I don't like to leave him there alone too long. Never know when someone's going to try and jump you and argue the boundaries later. The gulch is filling up fast now that news has spread about finding gold there."

He grinned and motioned toward the table. "Sit back down. I'm going to show you something that will dazzle your eyes right out of their sockets!"

He scurried into the adjacent room and returned a moment later with a small leather poke in his hand. After they both were seated again, Jeremiah opened the drawstring and dumped the contents on the table.

Grey Wolf peered down at the small pile of yellow rocks and granules in front of him. He picked up one the size of his thumb nail and held it in his palm, surprised at the pebble's weight despite its smallness. The gold was shiny in appearance, but certainly didn't dazzle his eyes like Jeremiah said it would.

"Well? What do you think?" Jeremiah flicked a glance from Grey Wolf's face to his hand. "Aren't they the prettiest rocks you've ever seen?"

Grey Wolf let the pebble roll out of his hand onto the table. "No."

"No?" Jeremiah repeated, his crinkled eyes showing his befuddlement.

Grey Wolf settled back in his chair, amused and feeling the urge to tease. "I can get you rocks prettier than those. All different colors—pink, green, black—and shinier, too."

"Yeah, but these aren't just shiny, colored rocks. These are gold, my boy." He picked up the one Grey Wolf had dropped. "This little chunk alone is worth fifty dollars. And there's more where that came from. Why, won't be long and I'll be able to stock a real nice mercantile store in Denver City."

Grey Wolf leaned forward and rested his arms on the table. "One like you had back east?"

Jeremiah's face brightened with a youthful excitement that belied his years. "Maybe bigger." Just as quickly the glimmer faded, his expression sobering. "After Hattie died, I left St. Louis to get away from the memories. Never missed the city life either, not until I started going into Denver. Seeing it grow and prosper, businesses cropping up everywhere, got me wanting to be a part of it."

His smile returned. "Yes, siree, as soon as I hit a little more pay-dirt, I'm going to have me one fine store."

Although Grey Wolf nodded his approval, he had mixed feelings. On the one hand, he was glad that the gold would provide a reliable source of income for his friend, but on the other hand, the cursed gold was cause for much of the animosity and dissension between the Indians and whites.

Captain Glen Herrington lowered the brim of his hat to shield his eyes from the late afternoon sun. As he led his patrol up the road, he narrowed his gaze on a circle of wagons camped to the southwest. Twisting around in his saddle, he shouted above the drum of the cantering horses behind him. "Westbrook!"

The young lieutenant broke formation and urged his horse alongside Herrington's. He followed the direction of Herrington's gloved hand. "Yes, sir, I spied them myself. Could be Dan Driscoll's train."

"You won't know unless you ride over there, Lieutenant."

"Yes sir!" Alex responded, setting heels to the horse's flanks and bolting off at a full gallop.

As Herrington watched Alex ride away, a familiar feeling of envy gnawed at him—envy toward another soldier being reunited with his family. Irritated at himself for harboring such a loathsome feeling, he flicked his reins, quickening the pace of his horse and the sixteen others behind him.

A short time later, he and his troopers filed into Fort Hendricks. As the column crossed the quadrangle, the horses kicked up a trail of dust, blowing and snorting in eagerness to reach their stables. After Herrington gave the order to his sergeant to dismiss the detail, he swung in front of post headquarters where he dismounted and handed the reins to an awaiting soldier.

"Give him a good rub down, Private." The young trooper saluted and led the horse away.

Approaching Major Williams's office, Herrington caught sight of a woman standing in front of the guest quarters. Even at a distance of thirty yards, he could tell by her youthful figure she was in her early twenties. She flung her bright auburn hair away from her face and hurried toward him. He quickly conjured a guess as to who the woman might be.

Reaching the boardwalk, she lifted her gingham skirt and stepped up beside him. "Pardon me, sir, may I have a moment of your time?"

He pulled off his gauntlets and tucked them over his belt. "The name is Captain Glen Herrington. What can I do for you, ma'am?"

"I was looking for Lieutenant Alex Westbrook. I didn't see him ride in with your patrol."

"Would it be too presumptuous of me to ask if you're his sister from Pennsylvania?"

Meeting the captain's eyes, Laura was struck by their color; stone-grey tinged with black. She offered an apologetic smile. "I'm sorry, Captain. Allow me to introduce myself." She extended her hand. "Yes, I'm Laura Westbrook, Alex's sister."

"A pleasure to meet you, ma'am." Herrington clasped her hand gently, and then released it. "Lieutenant Westbrook told me he was expecting you and his aunt to arrive soon. It's my fault he's not here at the moment. Under my directive, he went to see if the wagon train camped outside the fort was yours. Once he learns that you're here, it won't take him long to ride in."

She noted his slight wince when he shifted from one leg to the other and wondered if he'd been injured. Just then, Sarah stepped onto the boardwalk, an anxious look on her face.

"Laura, dear, where's Alex? Have you seen him?"

"No, but the captain said he should be here shortly." She placed a hand on her aunt's arm. "Sarah, this is Captain Glen Herrington. Captain, my aunt, Sarah Osbourne."

"Ma'am," Herrington said, tipping the brim of his hat.

"I've been looking forward to meeting you, Captain," Sarah replied.

Behind her, Major Williams appeared from his doorway and approached them. "Couldn't help overhearing your conversation from my office window." He returned Herrington's perfunctory salute. Then he smiled at Laura and

Sarah. "Won't Lieutenant Westbrook be surprised to find out you're staying here?"

Sarah nodded and faced Captain Herrington. "I'd like to take this opportunity to thank you, Captain, for what you did. Major Williams told Laura and I that if it hadn't been for you, that awful Indian might have killed Alex."

"Westbrook would have done the same for me, ma'am," Herrington replied, matter-of-factly.

The major folded his hands behind his back. "Mrs. Osbourne and Miss Westbrook had just arrived at the fort yesterday, Glen, when Chief Black Arrow and three of his warriors came to claim those bodies you hauled in. One was the Indian Clayton had seen get away; the other two were the chief's sons. Interesting enough, the one son I mistook for a half-breed was, in fact, a white man Black Arrow adopted when he was a boy. Found that out from Driscoll, the wagon master. He met them on the trail a few weeks ago. Miss Westbrook here, treated the white man who had an unfortunate run-in with a grizzly."

Herrington frowned. "I've heard tales of whites living with Indians, but I've never come across any." He looked at Laura, making no attempt to hide the obvious disdain from his voice. "He must've been a difficult one to deal with."

Laura stiffened her shoulders. "Not difficult at all, Captain. He spoke good English, and we ..." she met her aunt's furtive glance, "um, we got along very well."

"Actually, Captain," Sarah put in, "he was quite a remarkable man, not at all the kind of person one might think, given his upbringing."

Clearing his throat, Major Williams acted somewhat uncomfortable, giving the captain what seemed a warning look before addressing Laura and Sarah. "I'm sure Westbrook will be here shortly. Would you like Captain Herrington to escort you back to your quarters?"

"That won't be necessary," Laura replied.

"Well then, if you'll excuse us, ladies, we'll be getting back to work." After giving a slight bow, Williams retraced his steps through the doorway.

Herrington nodded politely to Sarah, then fixed his gaze on Laura. His cinereous eyes were sharp and direct. "Miss Westbrook," he said, inclining his head again. He made an about turn and walked into the major's office.

Starting back to their rooms, Sarah asked, "Did you notice Captain Herrington walked with a limp?" She slowed, frowning at Laura. "Why, what is it, dear? You have the oddest look on your face."

"Oh, it's nothing," she said, erasing the frown from her face as well as a vague feeling of familiarity that had crept over her when the captain looked at her. "Yes, I did notice he favors one leg. I also got the impression he doesn't have much sympathy for the Indians—or those who befriend them."

As they neared their rooms, three men rode into the fort. A cry of joy burst from Laura's lips, recognition making her heart beat double time. "Alex!" she shouted, waving and leaping off the walkway. She dashed around a detail of soldiers passing by and ran into the middle of the parade ground.

Her brother jumped from his saddle before his horse had skidded to a full stop and swooped her into his arms. "Sis ... ah, Sis ... God Almighty, it's good to see you!"

Tears swam in her eyes as she laughed and cried at the same time. The last time she saw him, he was resplendent in his new blue cavalry uniform board-ing a train with transfer orders in his hand, waving good-bye to her, Sarah and James. That same pride for her brother still radiated inside her, although with a quick once over she saw his uniform was a lot worse for the wear. "You scoun-drel, if you aren't a sight for sore eyes." She leaned back within his strong embrace and grinned. "But you haven't changed. Always the last to arrive. And one who likes to keep the women waiting."

"Me? As I recall, it was you, little sister, who usually kept the gentlemen waiting." He swung her into the crook of one arm, and then turned to Sarah who was rushing up, all misty-eyed too.

"Aunt Sarah!" He pulled her into his other arm and hugged her. "I can't believe you're both finally here. It seems an eternity since I've seen you."

"It has been," Sarah said, dabbing her eyes with a floral hanky.

With his arms around them, Alex lifted his face to Dan and Lucky who'd been watching from astride their horses. "Men, these here are the two prettiest women ever to grace a fort."

Dan exchanged a glance with Lucky and chuckled. "Shoot, you're not telling us anything we don't already know."

Flushed from excitement more than their flattery, Laura smiled up at Lucky. "I'm glad you finally got to meet my brother."

"Knew who he was the moment he rode into camp," he said. "You two look like you were cut from the same mold."

Alex dropped his hand to Laura's waist and squeezed her to him. "Yeah, except she has softer and rounder curves," he said and laughed.

She slapped at her brother playfully. "Oh, Alex, that's enough!"

Dan gathered his reins and motioned to Lucky. "We need to get on over to the blacksmith and see when he can start reshodding the horses and mules."

"Right, boss." Hauling his horse around, he cast a quick glance back at Laura. "I'll have Sonny stabled here at the fort in case you want to ride out to the camp."

"Thanks," she answered. As they rode away, she heard Martha Williams's voice behind her.

"My, my, now there's a happy threesome!"

Alex withdrew his arms from Laura and his aunt and turned an about-face, his stance straight and erect. "Good afternoon, ma'am," he said, making a slight bow as he touched the brim of his hat.

"Good afternoon to you, Lieutenant." She smiled at Laura and Sarah. "Well, what do you think? Has he changed in a year's time?"

Laura lifted a hand to conceal her impish grin. "His manners sure have."

Alex shot her a look that said, I'll get you for that.

"I think he's grown," Sarah commented, eyeing him up and down.

"It's the boots," Alex said. "Makes me look taller."

Laura watched him pull off his buckskin gloves and like Herrington, fit them over his belt. "Are you through for the day?"

"I don't know until I report to Captain Herrington."

"We met the captain a little while ago. He was going into the major's office when I stopped him to ask where you were."

Under the brim of his hat, Alex's brows dipped in apparent disappointment. "I'd hoped to have the pleasure of introducing you to him myself."

"Well, we didn't get to talk very long," Laura added.

Martha leaned in Laura's direction. "I'm afraid the captain isn't much for small talk anyway."

Alex nodded in agreement. "The sooner I report, the sooner I can get cleaned up and—"

A sudden uproar behind Laura cut her brother off in midsentence. She whirled around just as a heavily laden wagon rumbled through the fort entrance, two soldiers from the guardhouse bounding after it, shouting.

Horror bolted up her spine when she saw the wagon's driver slumped back in his seat, the long feathered shaft of an arrow jutting out the front of his body.

CHAPTER 20

Seeing the driver no longer in control of the reins, Alex raced toward the team of horses. He grabbed one of the bridles and dug in his heels. With the aid of the other soldiers, he pulled the horses to a halt.

He hoisted himself up onto the wagon seat and cradled the driver's head, relieved when he saw his eyes open. The man was Ed Fuller, a civilian wagoner hired by the army to deliver supplies.

"Easy, Ed. You're all right now."

"Lieutenant …" he rasped, struggling to speak, "couldn't stop the wagon. Not much s … strength with this damn thing poking in me."

Alex looked at the arrow lodged below his right shoulder. Blood oozed from the wound, the front of his blue checkered shirt a solid red. No telling how far the injured man had traveled.

"Give me a hand, Corporal," Alex yelled to one of the guards. "Let's get him down from here."

As soon as they lowered the driver to the ground, Laura hurried over and knelt beside him. Grasping his wrist, she felt for his pulse while she assessed the arrow's point of entry.

The man peered up, his glazed eyes widening. "Well, looka here." His mouth pulled into a weak grin. "An angel came down from heaven."

Laura smiled back. His talking gave her hope. Thank goodness, the arrow appeared high enough to have missed his lung.

Captain Herrington crouched beside her on one knee. He laid a hand on the man's arm. "Ed, can you tell me if anyone else was with you? Any other wagons?"

"N-no … just me." Fuller drew in his lips and grimaced. "They ambushed me along the Old Summit Trail."

Herrington glanced over at Alex. "Same trail Clayton was on." He looked again at Ed. "How many were there?"

"Four, five, maybe. Come out of nowhere."

"Were they Cheyenne?"

"Can't say for sure."

His pain-filled gaze sought Major Williams leaning over the captain's shoulder. "Wasn't gonna let 'em get your r-rifles, Major. I got away, but one of 'em got off a lucky … a lucky …" His eyelids fluttered, and then closed.

Laura felt his wrist again. "If we don't get this arrow out, he's going to bleed to death."

Williams lurched around. "Sergeant Avery!" he barked.

"Sir!"

"Get Fuller to the infirmary." He flashed a look at his wife. "Martha, you hurry ahead and make sure there's a bed ready."

He turned to Alex. "Westbrook, send our best horse and rider to Fort Laramie to get Doc Simms. Have the trooper report to my office first, and I'll have a message ready to deliver to the post commander." Alex responded with a hasty salute and hustled away.

The major turned to Laura. "Miss Westbrook, it'll be over two days hard riding before my message will reach Fort Laramie and the doctor can get back here. What do you think? Has Fuller got a chance?"

Dan, Lucky, and a small crowd of soldiers stood beside him. All eyes were on her, including Captain Herrington's. "Yes," she answered, stricken by the sudden flashback of another life she'd worked so hard to save. She rose to her feet, dispelling the bittersweet memories. "Let's get him to the infirmary."

She watched the soldiers carefully lift Fuller's prone body onto a litter and start across the parade ground. "One thing in his favor, the arrow is too high to have pierced any vital organs."

She didn't know what medical supplies the fort had on hand. Not wanting to waste time, she sought out Dan and asked him to ride out to her wagon and get her medical cases. "Sarah, you best go with him to make sure he finds everything," she said, then turned to follow the soldiers.

Captain Herrington fell in beside her. She was aware of the shorter stride in his right leg, his left boot making a more pronounced sound as he walked.

"Your brother told me you assisted your uncle with his practice back east," he said, his eyes fixed directly ahead. "However, Miss Westbrook, I doubt you have ever removed an arrow before. Let me forewarn you, it's not a pretty sight."

Laura detected a hint of reproof in his tone. Did he think her incapable of dealing with this kind of emergency? "I've never removed an arrow, but I've removed a bullet from a patient before. And I've performed surgery on countless other injuries." *Including removing a bear fang,* she thought, but didn't say.

Staying close behind the soldiers, they passed between the officers' quarters and the sutler's store to a small building in the rear. Laura slowed her steps. Lifting her chin, she looked up at him. "I assure you, Captain, I will do my very best for Mr. Fuller."

As they stepped under the raftered porch shading the front of the small infirmary, Herrington's keen eyes met her glance and held it. "I'm sure you will, but you'll need my help."

Laura regarded him speculatively. "Have you had medical training?"

"No, none at all." After the soldiers had maneuvered Fuller through the narrow doorway, Herrington removed his hat and held the door open for her. "But I've had first hand experience at pulling out arrows," he said. He motioned for her to follow the men inside.

Laura entered, trying not to show her dismay at the captain's words. *Pulling out arrows,* he'd said. Just how many had he pulled out? And out of whom? The thought made her skin crawl. She glanced back, hoping he hadn't seen the involuntary shudder that rippled up her spine. Lord, she better get hold of herself. If the mere thought caused such a weak-kneed reaction, how did she expect to handle the emergency before her?

Summoning both her courage and her confidence, Laura walked over to the bed Fuller had been placed on. Martha Williams leaned over the semi-conscious man and uttered a word of encouragement. Much to Laura's consternation, the woman's face was almost as ashen as Fuller's.

Seeing Martha's trepidation inspired the opposite in Laura. A sense of strength came over her and her apprehension lessened. She pulled up a chair beside Fuller.

The man's eyelids fluttered open. "Are you a … a lady doctor?"

"No, but I've been trained by one of the best and worked side by side with him for over two years. Until the doctor gets here, Mr. Fuller, I'm going to take care of you."

"C-call me, Ed."

As she unbuttoned his shirt, she smiled. "My name is Laura. Now I want you to lie still, Ed, and save your strength."

She gave a quick glance to Martha. "I need scissors."

Within seconds, Martha was back at Laura's side, handing her a pair of scissors, color returning to her face. "I'll also need several basins of fresh water, soap and plenty of clean cloths," Laura added as she started cutting through the shirt.

Herrington signaled to one of the soldiers. "Miller, fetch the water."

"Yes, sir," the soldier responded and sped out the door.

"We have bandages and cotton gauze, too," Martha said, crossing the room and opening a large cabinet.

"Good," Laura said. "Set everything on this table."

Herrington stepped closer to the bed. "Sergeant Avery, go to my quarters and get a bottle of whiskey out of my kitchen cupboard and bring it here on the double. You two privates can return to your duties."

Herrington set his hat aside and walked around the bed opposite Laura. He waited while she carefully peeled the blood-soaked shirt away from the shaft of the arrow, and then knelt beside Ed. "I guess you know taking this arrow out isn't going to be any picnic."

Fuller gave a grimacing nod. "You and the little lady do what you have to. Sure could use something for the pain, though. It h-hurts like blazes."

"Avery's getting it right now."

The minutes seemed like hours as Laura and Herrington waited for Miller and Avery. When Miller returned with a pail of water, Laura assisted Martha with filling the basins. Another minute, the sergeant was back with the whiskey.

Dismissing the soldiers, Herrington popped the cork off the bottle. He knelt again and slid a hand under Fuller's head. "Here, Ed, swallow some of this." He tipped the bottle to the man's lips. Whiskey trickled out the side of Ed's mouth as he took a swallow.

Setting two basins on the bedside table, Laura liberally lathered her hands with a cake of soap and rinsed them in one of the basins. As she dried them with a towel, she watched Herrington hold the bottle to Fuller's lips, allowing him to take several more gulps.

She bent over and murmured, "Must you inebriate him, Captain?"

He shot her a rueful glance. "Like to put him out of his misery, if I can."

Conceding the point, Laura allowed him to ply her patient with more whiskey while she dipped a cloth into another basin of water and wiped the wound around the arrow. She couldn't wait for Dan and Sarah to return with her supplies. Right now the important thing was to get the arrow out of Ed, and she didn't need surgical instruments or medicines for that, just a steady hand and a strong constitution.

With a forthrightness she hardly felt but was determined to show in front of her self-appointed assistant, Laura sent Herrington a stern look. "I know this is going to be quite painful for Mr. Fuller." She leaned over Ed who'd lapsed into unconsciousness. "If you'd please hold him down while I extract the arrow," she instructed, grasping the wooden shaft.

Herrington clamped a restraining hand around her arm. "Not that way," he said, his sudden action and acid tone causing her to flinch.

She frowned, annoyed by his interference. "The arrow has to come out, and soon, Captain Herrington, or it'll cause infection."

"I know," he retorted. His grip tightened on her arm, forcing her to withdraw her hand. "But it's been inside Fuller too long. The sinew holding the point has softened." He released her arm. "If you pull on the shaft, the arrowhead will come off and remain embedded inside him. It should be pushed the rest of the way through him."

For a split second, his expression darkened, some kind of inner torment flickering in the back of his eyes. "Believe me, I know. If they'd pushed the arrow through my own leg instead of having to dig out the point later, today I might not be walking with a limp." Unbuttoning his cuffs and rolling up his sleeves, he looked down at the arrow. "It's directly beneath his collarbone. You said yourself it hasn't pierced any vital organs. Shouldn't take much to force it through."

Martha cleared her throat. "I, ah, think I'll see if I can find some more towels." The woman was out the door before Laura could tell her they had plenty.

"You don't have to stay and watch either, Miss Westbrook," Herrington said, his voice sounding more compassionate. "I'll take over."

"I don't want to stay and watch." Above her patient, Laura met Herrington, eye to eye. "I want to stay and help. What you say makes sense. Tell me what I can do." She offered a quick smile. "And please, call me Laura."

Herrington's eyebrows lifted a fraction. "All right, Laura." He stood over Ed and started to slide his hands underneath the man's back. "Let's roll him on his good side."

"Captain, your hands ..." she hesitated, hoping not to offend him, "you should wash them first."

He paused, and then nodded in agreement. He rose and walked around to the basin. His intense expression relaxed momentarily. "The name's Glen."

She noticed as he lathered his hands and forearms that the skin above his wrists was stark white. An image of Grey Wolf's strong golden arms flashed through her mind, but an instant later Herrington's voice snapped her back to the present.

"Let's get this over with," he said. He tossed a towel aside and returned to the opposite side of the bed. He rolled Fuller's inert body over, his front facing him. "You brace his back. He's unconscious, but be ready in case he comes to. He might fight us." Laying a hand firmly on Fuller's shoulder, he grasped the shaft of the arrow with the other.

Laura hadn't more than positioned herself when he thrust the vile weapon clear through the man's body. He stiffened and arched violently, his agonized wail filling the room. Then he passed out again.

Laura stared at the triangular arrowhead jutting out above his shoulder blade a few inches from her hands. Blood spewed from his torn flesh, running between her fingers and onto the bed. She wanted to turn away, but couldn't. Fighting for control, she bit her lip hard. The taste of drawn blood coated her tongue.

With a sharp snap, Herrington tossed the feathered end of the shaft aside. Leaning over, he grasped the bloody point and pulled the rest of the broken arrow out of Fuller.

Laura exhaled a breath she hadn't realized she'd been holding. In less than a minute, the deed was done.

An hour later, sitting on the porch outside the infirmary with Sarah and Martha, Laura was more hopeful about Ed's recovery. When Dan and Sarah had returned with the medical supplies, she'd immediately administered a small dose of ergot extract to control the hemorrhaging. She then sutured the two wounds and sealed them with a styptic poultice of alum. After dressing the injury with bandages, she gave him a limited amount of opium to relieve the pain. Now he was resting much easier.

Alex, whose last duty for the day had been to summon Herrington to Major Williams's office, stepped onto the porch and braced a shoulder against the thick wooden post supporting the overhang. "Sis, the captain told me he was impressed with what you did for Ed."

Laura shook her head. "He's the one who did it all. If he hadn't been there, I'd probably still be trying to surgically remove the arrowhead from his shoulder."

"Yes, my dear," Martha said, leaning over and patting her arm, "but the tending you gave him afterward was just as important."

Martha had made her timely return after the gruesome arrow had been pulled out, bringing with her enough towels and linens to accommodate another ten patients. Even so, she'd been a big help to Laura and Sarah while Herrington and Dan looked on.

Laura frowned, her thoughts returning to the captain. She couldn't think of him by any other name but Captain Herrington, even though he'd told her to call him, Glen. It didn't seem proper to address a cavalry officer by his first name, especially one with such a commanding air.

"Alex, did you know the captain's limp was caused from an arrow?"

"Yeah, Sergeant Avery told me. He served with Herrington at another post. Known him a long time. Pawnees raided Herrington's homestead when he was just a kid. Avery said his parents were killed, and his younger brother was lost in a fire that completely destroyed their house. The captain was found unconscious and taken to Fort Leavenworth."

"I recall the major mentioning something yesterday about the captain losing his family at the hands of the Indians," Sarah put in.

"Tragic, isn't it? He's the second person we know who's been through such a horrifying experience."

"Second?" Alex asked.

Laura glanced at her aunt before answering. "Yes, a white man named Grey Wolf. His family was massacred by Pawnees when he was a child. Right after that, he was taken in by the Cheyenne. We met him on the trail a few weeks ago. He was injured and I took care of him. Yesterday he came to the fort with Chief Black Arrow and two other Indians to claim the bodies you and Herrington brought in."

Alex rubbed the stubble on his chin. "You're saying this man is white but lives with the Cheyenne of his own free will?" Laura nodded. "And he came with them to claim the dead Indians?"

Nodding again, Laura clasped her hands tightly in her lap. She thought she heard scorn in her brother's voice

"You see, Alex," Sarah interceded, "Chief Black Arrow is the man's adoptive father."

Alex pushed away from the post and frowned. He gestured toward the major's office. "The captain took those pieces of arrow to show the major. He thinks those renegades were Cheyenne."

Laura hadn't forgotten what Grey Wolf had said yesterday. He'd expressed their wanting rifles to hunt the buffalo. Had Indians from Black Arrow's village attacked Ed, hoping to steal the rifles?

She met Alex's probing gaze. "Well, Grey Wolf certainly didn't shoot Ed. I've seen his arrows and all of them have a white ring painted below the feathers. The one the captain has is marked with a yellow line down the shaft."

Alex shrugged. "I sure hope he didn't, him being white and all. Then again, living with those Indians for so long, maybe—"

"He wouldn't do such a thing! He's not a renegade!" Laura realized she'd raised her voice and looked away.

Alex arched a brow. "Hey, Sis, I'm sorry." He lifted his hands in a defensive gesture. "I didn't mean to imply anything. But I wouldn't be surprised if those Indians weren't from Black Arrow's clan. They lost two warriors and some of them may be out for revenge."

Laura rose abruptly. "I need to check on Ed."

"I'll go with you, dear," Martha volunteered, following her inside.

Alex gave Sarah a pointed look. "How come I get the feeling this Grey Wolf means more to Laura than just someone she nursed back to health?"

Sarah pursed her lips. "It's really not my place to explain their relationship."

"Then there *is* something between them?"

"Was," she corrected, picking a speck of lint off her dress, "but it's over now."

Alex leaned against the post again. The way his sister reacted, it didn't seem over to him.

CHAPTER 21

The cannon fired its volley outside the infirmary just as Laura was about to lay a damp compress across Ed Fuller's forehead. She straightened with a jolt, not yet accustomed to the army's sunrise ritual. Hearing the bugler play reveille, she peered down at her patient. Heavily sedated, he didn't budge.

"I thought I'd find you here."

Laura swung around to see her brother standing in the doorway. "How's he doing?" he asked.

"Sleeping more comfortably since I gave him laudanum. So far, there's no sign of infection." Drawing the sheet to Ed's chin, she recounted the last time someone had depended on her care. "If he has half the recuperative powers Grey Wolf has, he'll be fine." She retrieved her towel on the bed next to Ed and neatly folded it, then laid it beside the wash basin. "He'll sleep most of the day. I'll look in on him later."

Alex held the door open for her, and they walked outside. "After I assign the work detail, I'm off duty." He smiled. "Captain Herrington's orders."

"Alex, that's wonderful. We'll finally be able to spend some time together."

"Yeah, so I was thinking. How about I take you and Aunt Sarah on a little picnic?"

"A picnic?" Laura hesitated, but shook her head. "No, I shouldn't. Ed can't be left unattended."

"He won't be. Mrs. Williams will be here. She sees to the men who report to the infirmary after sick call. And Doc Simms will be here soon." He clasped her shoulders. "We won't be gone that long. You can check on him before we leave. I'll scare up some food from the commissary and see you around mid-morning. How's that sound?"

"It sounds wonderful, but I'll have to ask Sarah." She looked across the parade ground. "We're having breakfast with Martha and Major Williams. Come by there and I'll let you know."

With hat and gloves in hand, Alex was ushered into the dining room by Williams's Spanish maid. The women and the major were seated around a large mahogany table.

"Good Morning, Lieutenant," Williams said. "Miss Westbrook said you'd be stopping by." He gestured toward a vacant chair. "Take a seat and join us?"

"Thank you, sir, but Captain Herrington expects me in his office in a few minutes." He directed a nod at Laura and Sarah. "I've come to ask if my aunt and sister would like to go on a picnic."

Sarah's eyes glistened with exuberance. "I think it's a grand idea, Alex. I was telling Martha and Major Williams how often we used to pack a picnic lunch back home." She smiled. "Such fond memories."

Laura glanced across the table. "Martha, are you sure—"

"My dear, don't you worry about Ed. I'm the one to be looking after him now. You've already done far more than was expected of you. Doc Simms will hardly have a thing to do when he gets here. Isn't that right, Adam?"

Pushing back his chair, the major gave an affirming nod. "He looked a darn sight better last night than when he rode in yesterday afternoon, that's for sure." He rose, saying, "Ladies, have a nice day," then turned toward Alex. "Lieutenant, I'll walk out with you."

Alex gave Laura a quick wink before following Williams out of the dining room. When they neared the front door, the major faced him, a stern look creasing his forehead.

"Westbrook, I'm sure I don't have to remind you, there are a few renegades out there bent on causing trouble. Granted, the hostilities have occurred miles from the army's reservation, but be on the alert just the same. You can't be too cautious."

"Yes, sir, I plan on staying close to the river. We'll be back by two o'clock."

Williams seemed satisfied. Retrieving his hat off a brass hook, he preceded Alex out the front door.

They'd followed the river for only a short time when Alex pulled the wagon to a halt. Seated beside Sarah, he pointed. "How about we spread a blanket over there near the edge of the bank?"

Riding beside the wagon, Laura drew in Sonny's reins and settled back in her saddle. She shaded her eyes from the glaring sun and looked to the spot Alex indicated. "Isn't there a place where the bank's not so steep and rocky?"

Sarah fanned a hanky in front of her face. "And maybe a shade tree or two."

Alex wiped the beads of sweat from above his upper lip with the cuff of his sleeve. "Well, there are some trees where a stream joins the river. Even have some wildflowers and gooseberries growing along the bank."

"How much farther?" Laura asked.

"About a mile." He frowned. He hadn't planned on going that far, even though they'd still be on army land.

"It won't take us long. Come on, I haven't been berry picking since you and I used to sneak into old man Huckster's blueberry patch!" Straightening in her saddle, Laura kicked Sonny into a trot.

Sarah threw Alex an amused look. "She hasn't changed. Never takes no for an answer."

"Yeah, I can see that," he said, shaking his head. Flicking the reins, he whistled at the mare and the wagon rolled forward.

When the tree-lined area came into view, both women gave exclaims of delight. Cottonwoods hugged both sides of a broad stream with clusters of bluebells and wild roses dotting its banks. Stopping the wagon between the grove of trees, Alex scanned the region, looking upstream, across to the other side, then downstream to the river.

Laura breathed in deeply as a cool breeze wafted through the branches, ruffling the leaves. It's so nice, like finding an oasis, Alex."

Yellow Dog hid with his followers behind a crop of boulders at the top of the knoll. As they watched the wagon stop under the trees, he recognized the woman riding horseback. The color of her hair was unmistakable. Long auburn tresses whipped about her head like flames of fire.

Yesterday had not gone well. They did not get the rifles. But today promised to be better.

Yellow Dog uncovered the derby from its protective cloth. Whatever he wanted, he took—even if he had to kill for it. He grinned broadly. In fact, killing made his possessions all the more valuable.

He fitted the hat securely atop his head. Its uniqueness made him stand out from the rest of the tribe. He always wore it on hunts and during celebrations.

He glared down at the woman, her pale face held high. Indeed, he thought, this was a time to celebrate. Soon he would touch what Grey Wolf had touched. She would not be his guardian spirit as Black Arrow had told others. Instead, she would be *his*!

Seated across the blanket from his sister and aunt, Alex felt more at ease than he did an hour ago. They'd shared stories while eating their fill of smoked ham sandwiches, canned peaches and Mrs. William's fresh baked molasses cookies. He'd related some funny and not-so-funny times he'd had since stationed at Fort Hendricks, and Laura and his aunt had talked about their experiences on the wagon train.

Not much was mentioned about the white Indian, Grey Wolf. Alex had asked Laura about him, but his questions were answered rather curtly. No doubt, it was a touchy subject, one he decided not to press her about.

Reaching into a box that served as a picnic basket, Alex lifted out the jar of lemonade, another rare treat donated by Mrs. Williams. "I felt bad that I couldn't get back for Uncle James's funeral." He uncapped the jar and poured some into each of their cups. "I still have a hard time believing he's gone." He looked at Sarah. "I know how much you miss him."

"Yes, I do." She glanced at Laura. Her smile held a touch of sadness. "But your sister finally made me realize life has to go on." Sighing, she picked up her cup.

"Dan's been a great support to her," Laura offered.

Sarah's gaze flitted self-consciously down to the cup in her hand. "Yes, he's been a wonderful friend." She sipped at the lemonade. "Laura," she said, the lilt in her voice sounding more cheerful, "why don't we give Alex his gift? You brought it, didn't you?"

"Indeed, I did," she answered, unfolding her legs and rising to her feet. "It's in my reticule in the wagon. I'll get it."

A minute later she returned and handed Sarah a small cloth pouch. "You give it to him."

Sarah held it out to Alex. "May this be as much a part of you …" tears sprang from her eyes, "… as it was a part of your Uncle James."

Alex gathered from her expression, this was something very special. Unfolding the flap, he pulled out a watch attached to a long fob chain. He fingered the intricate scrollwork engraved on the gold lid.

"Uncle James's pocket watch," he said, his throat tightening. He opened the lid and read the familiar inscription inside: *Time is golden.* The watch face was white with black numerals and a gold hour and minute hand. He put it to his ear and listened to its rhythmic ticking. "Thank you," he said. "I'll treasure it always." He closed his hand over it, snapping it shut. He gave the pouch to his aunt. "Won't need that," he said, tucking the watch deep inside his trouser pocket.

He saw Laura swipe a tear from her eye before rising and walking over to the bank beside the water. A brief silence ensued, broken only by the peaceful flow of the stream and the chirping of birds in the cottonwoods.

"Where are the gooseberry bushes, Alex?" Laura asked, raising her voice above the current.

"There's a big crop down a ways, on the other side of the stream."

"Do you know how deep the water is?"

"Yeah, I've crossed it a time or two. In the middle, it's about belly deep on a horse."

Laura retraced her steps and stooping over the blanket, picked up the tin that had contained the peaches.

"What are you going to do?" Sarah asked.

"Cross the stream and pick some berries." Laura walked over to the tree where Sonny was tied. After putting the can inside her saddle bag, she pulled the reins free and swung into the saddle. "I remember Martha saying she loves to bake pies." She grinned, nudging the Morgan between the trees with her heels. "A gooseberry pie would taste mighty good."

Alex watched her horse pick his way cautiously down the embankment. "Sis, I really wish you wouldn't cross the stream." She waved at him as Sonny splashed knee deep into the water. "Maybe there are some berries on this side," he yelled.

"Why should she listen to you?" Sarah said, gathering up the plates and utensils and putting them back in the box. "She never listens to me."

Alex kept one eye on Laura while giving Sarah a hand. Laura freed her boots from the stirrups, held her legs above the water and guided Sonny around a large boulder in the center of the stream. Reaching the opposite bank, she turned downstream. He knew she'd found the bushes when she dismounted.

Laura moved cautiously between the shrubs' spiny branches, filling the tin can with the ripe berries. She tasted a few, not surprised to find them tart, but sweetened in a pie, they'd be delicious.

Behind her, a loud splash disrupted the soothing ripple of the water's current. Turning, she saw five Indians on horseback forging the stream. For several startled heartbeats, all Laura could do was stare at them. Then the sounds of shouting farther upstream drew her attention to her brother running along the bank, waving frantically at her.

Her gaze darted back to the Indians. The sudden recognition snapped her out of her stupor. One of the Indians wore a derby hat. A wave of apprehension swept through her. *Yellow Dog!*

She searched for Grey Wolf, but his bronze face and sun-streaked hair wasn't among them. Fear like she'd never known before slithered up her back.

Laura dropped the can of berries and scurried around the bush for Sonny. Snatching his reins, she jammed her boot in the stirrup. The horse shied at her nervous action and side-stepped away from her.

"Steady, Sonny!" Clutching the saddle horn, she tried to get a foothold in the stirrup again, at the same time, craning to see behind her.

Yellow Dog was already urging his pony up the bank. She could see his menacing face, those black eyes leering at her exactly the way they had at the fort.

Finally gaining a seat in the saddle, Laura wheeled Sonny upstream. As her horse's hooves sliced through the water's edge in a hard run, she chanced another look backward. Yellow Dog was charging after her, the other Indians close behind him.

A shot rang out. Across the stream, she saw Alex standing with his arm extended, a gun in his hand. Dear God, he'd fired at them. For Alex to do that meant he feared for her life.

Alex cursed his poor aim. Again he pointed the barrel of his revolver at the Indian rapidly gaining on Laura. Forcing a steady hand, he squeezed the trigger a second time. This time it jammed.

"Damn to hell!" he shouted. He hit the cylinder with his other hand and raised the gun again. "Ah, God, please, no!" Across the stream, the Indian's pony raced neck and neck with Sonny. The other Indians had fanned out on either side of them. There was no way he could risk a shot with Laura in the middle.

Wild-eyed, he tore headlong into the stream, screaming his sister's name. Behind him, he could hear Sarah's screams echoing his.

The Indian leaned over and wrenching the reins out of Laura's hands, he then veered the horse away from the bank. Alex plunged deeper into the stream, willing her to leap from Sonny. But they were going too fast, and he knew if she did, she would risk being trampled.

Taking careful aim, Alex fired again. A white pony stumbled and went down, hurling the rider from its back. But an instant later, the Indian gained his footing and jumped behind another horseman streaking past him.

In a wide sweep around the trees and into open country, the pack quickly vanished from sight down a deep ravine. Alex stopped waist deep in the middle of the stream. There wasn't a chance his sister could get away now. For one excruciating minute, the world closed in around him. Shock, terror, anger, all clutched at his heart, his chest so heavy it hurt to breathe.

Lifting his eyes and pistol heavenward, Alex prayed he wasn't too far out of earshot from the fort and fired the remaining round of cartridges. Then he raced out of the water and up the bank.

When he reached Sarah, she was hardly able to speak for her crying. "Oh, Alex … Alex, you've got to save her!" Her hands clutched his arm in a death grip. "You've got to get her back!"

Alex grasped her hands in his. "I will, Aunt Sarah, believe me, I will. But I can't catch up with them in the wagon. I hope the fort heard my shots and sends a patrol." Putting an arm around her, he led her to the wagon. "We've got to get back."

Sarah pulled away and looked frantically behind her. "But we …" she swallowed, choking back her tears, "we can't leave her."

"And I can't leave you here while I chase after them," he said, reloading his gun from a cartridge pouch on his belt. "God knows, there might be more Indians around. I've got to get you to the fort." He jammed the gun into his holster. "Let's not waste time."

At the first sound of the distant gunfire, Captain Herrington mounted a patrol. They hadn't ridden far before intercepting Lieutenant Westbrook and Mrs. Osbourne.

Laura wasn't with them and by the look of horror on Westbrook's face, he knew he wasn't going to like the reason why. He reined his horse beside the wagon. "Where's your sister, Lieutenant?"

"They … they captured her, sir." Panic, stark and vivid, glowed in his eyes.

"Who captured her?"

"Indians, five of them. That damn redskin with the hat—the one the major said came to the fort with the chief," his words were coming out in an angry rush, "he chased her down and pulled the reins right out of her hands. She didn't have a chance to—"

"Which way did they go?" Herrington broke in.

"The other side of the backwater, heading south along the river."

Beside Alex, Sarah pressed her hands to her face and sobbed aloud. Alex dropped the reins and gathered her in his arms.

Herrington twisted in his saddle. "Corporal Hill!"

The trooper broke from the column and rode to his side.

"Take the wagon and return Mrs. Osbourne to the fort. Make sure Mrs. Williams is with her. Tell Tucker I need him. We'll be following the river south."

He turned to Alex who gently pulled his aunt from the circle of his arms. "Westbrook, take the corporal's horse."

Grasping Sarah's shoulders, Alex looked into her tear-stained face. "We'll get her back," he said, his voice shaking with determination. His aunt nodded, clamping her lips together to keep from sobbing anew.

Not waiting for Alex to mount up, Captain Herrington raised his arm and yelled, "Column, ho!" Immediately, the squadron of twos sprang forward, clouds of dirt whirling in their horses' wake.

CHAPTER 22

Laura's nightmare began.

With Yellow Dog controlling the reins, her horse had no choice but to stretch his neck into a full gallop while she clung to the saddle for dear life, riding farther and farther away from Alex, the fort, and safety.

Traversing a series of rocky ravines, they rode toward the river. As they slowed near its bank where only a few scrub trees grew, Laura swung a hopeful glance behind her. There was no wagon, no Alex in sight. She squeezed her eyes shut and tried to swallow the fear knotted in her throat.

She hadn't expected to see him. He'd be concerned for Sarah's safety now. She remembered hearing successive gunshots soon after she'd been captured. Dear God, maybe more Indians were attacking her brother and aunt. Laura worried for their sake as much as her own.

Lurching to a sudden halt, Yellow Dog grunted something to one of his companions. In response, the Indian slid from his pony and knelt, pressing his hands and side of his face to the ground. He was still for a minute before giving an answering nod.

Yellow Dog swung a leg over his blaze-faced pony and dropped beside Sonny. The Morgan flattened his ears and reared back. Holding on tightly, Laura was heartened by the fact that even her horse sensed this man was an enemy.

Scowling, Yellow Dog pulled hard on the horse's bit, bringing him under control. He handed the reins to his cohort and turned his attention to Laura, his gaze traveling over her with unnerving slowness.

Her flesh crawled along the back of her neck, her hair rising at the nape. She wanted to look away, but couldn't. He stood there, boldly intimidating, his muscled chest gleaming in the bright sun. A diagonal strap held a quiver of arrows against his back. From under the rim of the derby, black hair flowed to his shoulders. His features were rawboned, with gaunt cheeks and a sharp jaw line. The smirk curling his upper lip made his face all the more evil looking.

When he held up a length of rope, Laura sat rigid in her saddle, determined not to show fear. A brave front presented the best deterrent against an attack from a wild animal, and that, she told herself, was exactly what this man was.

Even if she did jump and make a run for it, he was certain to catch her. Her hands curled around the saddle horn so tightly her knuckles turned bone-white. *Dear God ... was he going to rape her? Kill her?*

Yellow Dog snatched hold of her leg beneath her skirt. Gasping, she instinctively pulled away only to have his hand tighten around her, his fingers digging into her skin. He snarled something in Cheyenne, the words sounding like a warning, or maybe a threat, Laura wasn't sure.

Whipping the rope around her calf above her boot, he tied it in a knot, then slipped it under Sonny's belly and tied her other leg. Jerking the horse's reins from the other Indian's hand, he remounted his pony and sent them galloping head long into the river.

From the angle of the sun, Laura guessed it'd been four or five hours since they'd split from the pack. Now it was only her and Yellow Dog.

They'd disbanded after forging the river, the other Indians spreading out in opposite directions while Yellow Dog led her back across the river farther upstream. He made sure their horses stayed in the water, leading them along the shallows for some distance before heading sharply up the embankment toward the hills.

Laura understood his maneuvers. If the army was searching for her, and she prayed they were by now, Yellow Dog was making it as difficult as he could for the soldiers to track them.

Where was he taking her? And when would they stop?

Soaked with perspiration, tired and sore, Laura worried about Sonny as well. Never had she ridden the Morgan this hard and for so long a distance without rest. His coat was streaked with lather. Twice he'd stumbled, struggling to keep up with the more sure-footed animal in front of him that was accustomed to the rugged terrain and Yellow Dog's unrelenting pace.

Laura searched the horizon, wondering where Grey Wolf was now. Still with his friend, Jeremiah or at his village? Her bottom lip quivered. How she wanted to cry out for him.

Instead, she squeezed her eyes shut and turned her cry inward. *Grey Wolf...* her tears were close to the surface, but she fought to hold them back. *Oh, Grey Wolf, if only you knew!*

From somewhere deep inside, she heard his strong, resonant voice. *"Indians wear tokens and charms to give them luck or special powers."*

Laura felt for the cameo beneath her blouse. Tears stung her eyes as she remembered his words before he'd left the wagon train. *"The cameo gave me strength and courage to go on when fear and hatred threatened to destroy me."*

Clutching the cameo tightly in her hand, she prayed for that same strength and courage.

Yellow Dog suddenly reined in his horse. Hastily, Laura concealed the pendant under her blouse. His leg pressed against hers as he pulled her mount alongside his. With one hand still gripping Sonny's reins, he unhooked a sac from the side of his pony and raised it to his lips.

Water spilled out the sides of the bag as he drank. Not bothering to wipe his mouth, he turned his face toward her. Seeing the droplets of water clinging to his chin, she ran her parched tongue across her lips in a vain attempt to moisten them.

Yellow Dog grunted and thrust the sac in front of her. His expression was flat, yet his dark eyes gleamed with savage insolence. Taking hold of the flimsy vessel, Laura tipped it to her mouth. This time she displayed no repugnance for the animal intestine she held, grateful to quench her thirst.

She'd taken only a few swallows when the Indian leaned over and threaded his fingers into her hair. Laura jerked away, a reaction she instantly regretted. Quick of hand, Yellow Dog closed his fist around a thick skein of her hair and pulled.

Her head was bent awkwardly, but every time Laura tugged, he yanked harder. Her fear turned to anger. She grabbed his arm with her other hand. "Let go of me, you beast!"

When he did just that, she almost lost her balance in the saddle. He shot her a scathing look and snatched the water bag out of her hand.

"No, wait," she begged, reaching for it. "I'm still thirsty."

But her plea was to no avail. He looped the sac aside his pony and sent the animal into a dirt-flying gallop, forcing Sonny to bolt and almost unseat Laura again.

The pain knifed through every muscle of her stiff and aching body. "Damn you!" she screamed, clutching the saddle horn. Tears of rage and frustration filled her eyes. "Why ... why are you doing this? What do you want with me?"

Until now, Laura had struggled to keep her emotions in check. She'd tried to remain calm and not provoke him, hoping surely her nightmare would soon be over, that the army was somewhere behind them, certain to rescue her before this day ended. But as she glared at Yellow Dog's back, his long, black hair trailing in the wind beneath that ridiculous hat, her hopes grew dim along with the light of day.

Far over the horizon, dark clouds billowed above the earth. The sunset that once enchanted her with its beauty now looked ugly and foreboding, its shades of purple an ominous warning of approaching nightfall.

Desperately, she scanned the countryside for signs of somebody, anybody who might save her from the clutches of this madman. But there was no one. In fact, no sign of life could be seen anywhere. Not any animals. She looked up. Not even a bird flying overhead. She felt desolate and so alone.

Her eyes returned to the Indian riding in front of her. But she was not alone. And that's what frightened her most.

When the scout, Tucker stopped and dismounted, Herrington stretched his arm high overhead. Immediately Sergeant Avery shouted, "Detail, halt!" As the sound of pounding hooves ceased, the low, intermittent voices of the troopers and snorts from trail-weary horses became more audible. Herrington rode to where Tucker stood.

The scout kicked some horse droppings with the toe of his moccasin. "Trail's gettin' cold, Cap'n."

Herrington prodded his bay with his heels, slowly searching the vicinity. He could barely make out the hoof marks of the two horses, one with shoes and one without. He drew next to the scout again and nudged his hat higher up his forehead. "How cold?"

"Two, maybe three hours."

"Damn it, Tucker, we're losing ground."

"Yeah, well, didn't help none for 'em to scatter like they did back at the river." He lifted his forearm and wiped his brow with a fringed sleeve. "Trackin' is a slow process, Cap'n. That Indian knows where he's goin' and we don't."

From behind him, Westbrook prodded his horse closer to Herrington. "Hadn't we better keep moving, sir?" Tension seeped into his voice. "There are only a few hours of daylight left. I hate to think of my sister with that Indian after dark."

Captain Herrington looked to where the sun hung low in the sky. He wouldn't repeat what he was thinking. Didn't matter whether it was daylight or dark, she was alone with the heathen. No telling what he'd done to her already.

"We're going to keep moving, Lieutenant. Even so, we won't catch up to them before dark." He watched Tucker take a swig from the canteen slung across his chest. "That means another day. Considering how quickly I had to assemble the patrol, our provisions are in short supply. Tell the sergeant I want six men to return to the fort immediately. Collect their haversacks. That'll increase the supply of rations for the rest of us."

"Yes, sir." After lifting his hand in a half-hearted salute, Alex rode back to the column.

Tucker's gaze followed the lieutenant. "Feel sorry for the kid. He blames himself for what happened."

"Shouldn't," Herrington responded with a heavy sigh. "No one can predict the minds of Indians, least of all renegades. Still, it galls me to think they did this practically under our noses."

Tucker nodded toward the east. "Hope those clouds don't shift this way. If it rains, we'll pay hell keepin' a tail on him."

Herrington tugged the brim of his hat lower on his forehead. "If we're lucky, the winds will sweep the storm northward." He gathered up his reins and hauled his mount into a sharp turn. "Press on, Tucker."

A short time later, their luck ran out. Common to the plains, the winds had changed direction with amazing suddenness. Now the storm rolled toward them, its haunting purple clouds covering the earth like a dark shroud save for a narrow band of clear sky clinging stubbornly above the southern horizon.

Rain fell, slowly at first, big single drops pelting the soldiers' dusty hats and shoulders. Then with increasing steadiness, it drenched their backs and sent rivulets of water rolling off their horses' rumps and down the animals' legs.

As Herrington pulled up beside Tucker, a bolt of lightning zigzagged above their heads, followed by a volley of thunder that exploded in their ears. Like a command from Mother Nature, the rain intensified, and the wind blew harder.

Herrington grasped the collar of his shirt and drew it closer around his neck. "Storms that form this fast," he shouted to the scout, "usually blow over pretty quick. Don't like to make camp in the rain if we don't have to. As long as we can see in front of us, let's keep pushing in this direction. Most likely the Indian's still hugging the edge of these hills."

Tucker cocked his head back in order to see beneath the dripping brim of his hat. "That's my guess, too."

Grim-faced, Herrington nudged his horse with his knees, quickening the animal's gait. That's what it'll probably be from here on out, he thought. Guess work. He shut his eyes as another flash of lightning lit the sky. It didn't look good for Laura. Thunder rumbled in the distance. Damn, it didn't look good at all.

Listening to the fading sounds of thunder, Yellow Dog slowed his pace. He'd outrun the storm. He grinned to himself. Several miles of his tracks had been washed away by the rain. The bluecoats would have a hard time picking up his trail now.

The line of his lips thinned as a much different thought entered his mind. Though none of the warriors with him when he captured the woman were members of Black Arrow's clan, word would reach the old man eventually, of that he was certain. And certain, too, that Grey Wolf would find out.

Just how much did the woman mean to Grey Wolf, he wondered. Enough to send him in search of her? Again he recalled the hunger in Grey Wolf's eyes when he'd seen her at the fort.

Yellow Dog's mouth twisted upward defiantly. Let him come. Let him try to take what was now Yellow Dog's. He would welcome the chance, once and for all, to prove who is a true-blooded warrior and who is a white-livered coward, unworthy to live among the Cheyenne.

He halted his pony and dropping the reins, reached for his bottle of whiskey in a side pouch behind him. He lifted it to his mouth for a swallow, then he glanced back at the woman slumped deep in her saddle. She looked asleep with her eyes open, so blank was the expression on her face. After taking another swig, he jerked the reins of her horse.

Immediately, the woman straightened, the curves of her body becoming more prominent. Yellow Dog fixed his gaze on the front of her shirt where deep, shadowed cleavage contrasted with creamy white flesh. He watched her quickly pull a round bead through a small slit, fastening the material together.

As he laid the bottle to his mouth again, his stare met hers. Dull and lifeless a moment ago, now her eyes shone like the color of bright summer moss. And her hair … he marveled at the wavering mass of flames surrounding her face and shoulders. For the Great Mystery to paint this woman's eyes and hair with such colors meant she was blessed with spiritual powers like no other.

He wiped his mouth with the back of his hand. Each time he looked at her the desire to mount her grew stronger. Yet until he knew he was safe from those who would try to take her from him, he must conserve his energy. A woman with such mystical beauty would surely suck him dry, draining him of all his strength.

Yellow Dog looked to where the sky met the earth, the last vista of twilight clinging to its rim. Quickly making a decision, he took one last gulp of whiskey and stashed the bottle back in the pouch. By the next sun, he would reach the timbers. There he would find a place to hide.

His heated gaze returned to find her watching him. He grinned broadly. *A good place to mate with his pretty white squaw.*

CHAPTER 23

The glowing campfire served as a source of light and heat for the troopers gathered near it, but did nothing to lighten their sense of gloom. After they'd set up bivouac and fed the horses, they'd satisfied their own hunger with beans, salt pork, and hardtack. Now slumped on damp blankets and sipping coffee, most were thinking about their comrade's sister, somewhere out in this god-forsaken country with a savage who'd probably sooner kill her than keep her.

Settled around a separate campfire a short distance away, Captain Herrington sat on a sheet of tarpaulin next to Lieutenant Westbrook, while opposite the fire, Tucker lay on the ground, his head propped on his saddle.

"Can't believe the moon and stars found their way out tonight," Tucker commented. "Hell, I thought we were in for an all-nighter with that storm."

Picking up his mess cup, Alex heaved a sigh and rose to his feet. "I'm going to get more coffee. Want any more, sir?"

Seated with one forearm angled across an upraised knee, Herrington stared into the fire. "No thanks."

"Mister Tucker?"

"Naw, son, I've had enough of that belly-wash for one night."

After Alex disappeared into the wavering shadows beyond their campfire, Tucker rolled to his side. Propping himself up on an elbow, he groaned. "Damn it, this is one time I wish I was wearin' a uniform. When these buck-skins start to dry out, they're so gol dang stiff, I feel like one of them King Arthur knights wearin' a suit of armor."

Herrington answered with a distracted nod.

"Cap'n, those wheels been a'spinnin' inside that head of yours ever since we pitched camp. Mind lettin' me in on what you're speculatin'?"

Herrington frowned. "Speculating is about all one can do at this point, Tucker." With a flick of his wrist, he sent the dregs in his coffee cup splattering into the mud beside the tarpaulin. "Before I let you in on what I'm thinking, let me ask you a few questions."

"Shoot, Cap'n."

"The Cheyenne are camped south of here, right?"

"Yeah, but southwest, not southeast like the Indian's been headin'. Course, no tellin' if he's changed directions on us since the storm, but I got a hunch he hasn't."

"Then you don't think he's going to their camp?"

"The way I see it, we know the Indian who grabbed Miss Westbrook is from Black Arrow's clan. And he probably thinks we'll go to the chief's village lookin' for him, so ..." leaning over, he pulled out a chip of dried buffalo dung from a canvas satchel and tossed it into the fire, "... I don't figure he'll go there. Besides, I'm sure he knows Black Arrow ain't gonna cotton to him holdin' her prisoner, much less him puttin' the village at risk by bringin' her there."

Herrington seethed with a mounting anger that had dogged him all day long. "Well, as far as I'm concerned, the whole damn Cheyenne nation is at risk of war if we don't get Miss Westbrook back and damn soon!"

Tucker arched a brow, no doubt taken back by his outburst. The scout paused a moment, rubbing his chin. "Well, I got a strong suspicion he's aiming for the creeks that split the Republican. Easier for him to lose us among the trees and gullies there, than out on the plains. Could even be plannin' to cross over into Smoky Hill country. Plenty of Cheyenne there."

"Then you better hope we snag him at the river. We don't have provisions to go any farther. And if we return without Miss Westbrook, our next orders will be coming straight from the commander at Fort Laramie."

Tucker plucked a couple stones off the ground and rolled them around in his hand. "Cap'n, they don't call me the best tracker this side of the divide for nothin', you know. Tomorrow when I put my nose to the ground, I'm gonna smell that vermin." He pitched the stones into the flames, sending sparks popping up through the smoke. "You can damn well bet on it!"

"I'm not a betting man, Tucker, but I'll hold you to your word."

Tucker eased back against his saddle and looked up at the night sky. "Something else I been thinkin'. Just because one Indian grabbed Miss Westbrook at the river doesn't mean the same one's got her now. Could be one of the other renegades."

"You and I think alike." Herrington glanced at Westbrook who'd returned, his lean form hunkered next to the fire. "Lieutenant, did you get a good look at the other Indians ... besides the one named Yellow Dog?"

"Best I could from across the stream." He shrugged. "They all looked pretty much alike."

"How about your aunt? Did she say whether she recognized any of them?" At Westbrook's perplexed expression, Herrington added, "Any she might have seen the other day at the fort?"

Alex shook his head forlornly. "I never asked her." He idly swirled the coffee in his cup. "Sarah was so frantic and upset, she could hardly speak. It was all I could do to calm her down enough to get her out of there. Besides, she wasn't near the stream. She probably didn't get a very good look at them." He frowned. "Anyway, like I said, those Indians all look alike. The only reason I recognized Yellow Dog was because of him wearing that fool hat."

"There's one that would look different. A white Indian." Herrington waited for Westbrook's astonished gaze to meet his. "You're real sure you didn't see one with lighter skin than the others or different color hair?"

"Yes, sir ... I'm sure."

Herrington noted the tone in the lieutenant's voice wasn't as convincing as it should have been. "Did Laura ever describe to you what that adopted son of the chief looked like?"

A shadow of irritation crossed the young man's face. "I couldn't get my sister to tell me much of anything about him."

Removing his hat, Herrington raked his fingers through his hair. "Well, I know one thing. Whoever the bastard is, when we find him, he's going to damn well wish we hadn't." Dropping his hat beside him, his gaze swept to the other campfire. "Tell Avery we ride out at first light."

Alex poured the rest of his coffee out and set the cup on the ground. Deep in thought, he automatically responded, "yes, sir," then rising, headed toward the sergeant.

Herrington's comments raised some disturbing questions in Alex's mind. In the excitement of the attack, could he have failed to distinguish Grey Wolf from the other Indians? He remembered what Sarah had said to him in front of the infirmary yesterday—that whatever Grey Wolf and Laura's relationship had been, it was over. But what if Grey Wolf didn't want it over? Maybe he had been with those Indians ... maybe she was *his* prisoner, not Yellow Dog's.

Strangely enough, he actually found himself wishing the white Indian did have her. He didn't know much about him, but was sure the man would treat his sister better than Yellow Dog would.

Seated on the top step of the trading post's narrow porch, Grey Wolf settled back against the log wall and gazed up at the midnight sky. The eyes of heaven winked back.

He frowned, hating the desolate feeling that washed over him. But Jeremiah's leaving wasn't the reason for it. Glad for his friend's good fortune, he'd promised to go see his gold mine in a place called Hattie's Gulch, affectionately named after Jeremiah's wife.

No, he smiled ruefully, it was Laura hovering in his mind like a lost shadow after dark. His glance drifted to the moon glistening through the trees. The first time he'd talked to her was under a copper moon like this one. He bowed his head and rubbed the taut muscles at the back of his neck while another vision of her taunted him.

She lay beautifully naked on his blanket beneath a bright afternoon sun. *God Above, she'd been so easy to touch, so soft, so womanly.*

The pounding hooves of a fast-approaching horse snapped him from his reverie. He lurched to his feet. Who would ride so boldly, knowing he'd be heard? He searched the moonlit trees, his body crouched, ready to react.

He tensed when he recognized Swift Eagle. Coming here this time of night meant he must have something urgent to tell him.

The Indian pony skidded to a halt, and Swift Eagle jumped to the ground. "I was sure I would find you here." He laid a hand on Grey Wolf's shoulder. "I bring bad news, my brother. Yellow Dog has captured the woman you call Bright Eyes."

Grey Wolf stiffened, his fists knotting at his sides. He was so stunned, he could hardly think straight. It was all he could do to repeat the dreadful words, "Yellow Dog captured Bright Eyes?"

At Swift Eagle's nod, fiery rage bolted through him. For a moment, his vision blurred, a hundred questions shooting through his mind at once.

But only one mattered. "*Where?* Do you know where Yellow Dog has taken her?"

"I know only what the Arapahoe warrior said when he spilled his shame to our father. He was with Yellow Dog when he took the woman. Before they went separate ways, he heard Yellow Dog say he would seek a safe place along the fat-meat waters where he often hunts. He knew he would never be welcome in Black Arrow's village again. He would go to his brother-in-law's village when winter—"

Not waiting for Swift Eagle to finish, Grey Wolf ran inside the trading post for his bow and quiver. Slinging them across his back, he leaped from the porch and vaulted onto Four Winds. The pinto responded, charging past Swift Eagle and swerving between the trees.

Moments later, as Swift Eagle's horse thundered beside Grey Wolf, he urged Four Winds faster, veering him onto the open prairie, the bright moon lighting their way.

Across the barren plains, up the grassy hills, down the rocky ravines, they rode. And with each and every mile, Grey Wolf's fury escalated, and his heart turned colder. So fierce was his hatred for Yellow Dog; so strong was his fear for Laura.

Awakening, Laura winced as daggers of brilliant sunlight pierced through the overhead trees, blinding her. Lying on the ground face up, she lifted her hands to shield her eyes and discovered that her wrists were bound together. A frenzied panic raced up her backbone until she remembered where she was, and then fear took its place. She glanced down at her feet. Her boots had been removed and her ankles were tied together.

Yellow Dog had dragged her off Sonny early this morning. She remembered staggering behind some brush to relieve herself, thankful he didn't follow her. After he'd tied her, she faintly recalled him making a fire before she had passed out from exhaustion. They'd traveled, God knows, how far without stopping to rest. She'd had little water and nothing to eat since noon yesterday.

She lifted her head, still feeling a bit woozy and searched the woods either side of her. Where was he now, she wondered.

She closed her eyes again, pretending to still be asleep, not wanting to face him. The only sounds she heard were the rustle of wind through the treetops and the sharp trill of a bird overhead. Maybe he'd left. Oh, please, yes, maybe he'd gone on without her.

What was that smell? Smoke? It grew stronger. Cooked meat ... it smelled like cooked meat.

Suddenly something hot pressed against her mouth, burning her lips. Jerking her face to the side, she opened her eyes.

The Indian loomed over her, a chunk of meat in his hand. He grasped her chin and pressed the meat to her lips, but Laura clamped her mouth shut. Hungry though she was, the thought of eating whatever he had to offer turned her stomach. As she twisted and squirmed, he tried to force the food between her teeth while snarling a slew of unintelligible words. She was about to give in, unable to stand the painful pressure of his hand clamped around her jaw when much to her surprise, he bolted upright and tossed the meat on the ground.

At first, she thought he'd given up in disgust. But the sneer on his face changed to a sudden look of wariness. He stood like a stone statue, only his eyes moving, searching the woods directly in front of him.

Laura struggled to a sit up, her gaze following his. He must have heard or seen something. She narrowed her eyes on some brush between a stand of small trees. She gave a quick gasp as the foliage parted slightly. Could there be someone out there? A flame of hope flickered through her mind. Had someone come to save her?

She watched Yellow Dog creep backward. He knelt beside a campfire where the carcass of a small animal was skewered above it. He picked up a bow and pulled an arrow from his quiver. Her heart leaped into her chest, realizing what he was about to do. Looking back toward the bushes, she opened her mouth to scream a warning only to have it die in her throat.

In clear view, a lone wolf shifted from one foreleg to the other, its nose held high, sniffing the air. Laura swallowed hard, her panic turning from a flash of disappointment to a mounting sense of fright.

With its thick grey fur bristling across its back, the wolf bared long, canine teeth and emitted a low, vibrating growl. Dark pupils glittered in the center of crystalline eyes, glaring first at Yellow Dog, then at her.

Slowly, the Indian nocked his arrow and pulled the bowstring taut. Laura held her breath. Before her eyes could track the arrow's flight, she heard a sharp, piercing yelp. The force of the arrow thrust deep into the wolf's chest sent the animal staggering backward on its haunches. It teetered forward in an effort to stand, wobbled on all fours, and then collapsed on its side.

Yellow Dog let out a bellow and looked at her, a triumphant grin on his face. Releasing her breath, Laura shuddered, for at that moment profound relief overpowered any lost hopes of being rescued.

The Indian walked over to the slain animal and squatted beside it. As he took a firm grasp of the arrow and wrenched it free, Laura focused on the long yellow line painted on the shaft. The markings were the same as on the arrow taken out of Ed Fuller.

A minute ago, Laura had felt a strange sense of gratitude, knowing quite possibly Yellow Dog had saved her from being ripped apart by the wolf. But the arrow's tell-tale marks reaffirmed her utter hatred for Yellow Dog. He was the one who'd shot Ed.

The Indian tossed the arrow aside and unsheathed his knife. He jabbed the blade into the wolf's mouth and twisted it repeatedly, then held out his open hand for her to see. In his palm, two curved, bloody fangs glistened in the sunlight.

Revolted by the grisly sight, Laura looked away, remembering too late that to turn from the Indian was to provoke him. Instantly, he leaped beside her and shoved her backward. Her head hit the hard ground with a thudding jolt that for an instant, turned daylight to dark.

Grabbing the end of the rope that bound her wrists, he yanked her arms over her head. He tied the restraints to a sapling behind her, then swung his leg over her skirt and straddled her. He picked up the fangs off the ground next to him and pressed their sharp points to each side of her cheeks.

She froze, not moving an inch for fear he'd dig the teeth into her flesh. Lust smoldered in his black eyes as he slowly drew the fangs along her jaw and down her throat to the vee of her blouse. Laura held her breath, her heart pounding in her ears.

The Indian thrust his hand downward, ripping the top buttons from her blouse. A pent-up cry escaped her lips, anger mounting along with her fear. She bucked and squirmed beneath him, her frightened cry becoming an all out scream of rage.

The stiff, horse-hair rope burned her wrists, and Yellow Dog's weight was too much for her to keep up the struggle for long. In a final show of resistance, she glared up at him with hate-narrowed eyes and spit in his face. "You won't get away with this ..." she yelled, gasping for breath, "the army will find you."

The words meant nothing to him, but saying them bolstered her courage. Even the wicked laugh he gave didn't lessen her hope that somehow, some way she would live through this.

As Yellow Dog's gaze slid down her torn garment, his guttural laugh faded. Tossing the fangs on the ground, his brows drew together. He grasped the thong circling her neck and tugged. The glint in his jet black eyes sharpened as the cameo slid from under her blouse and into his hand.

Instant recognition registered on his face, then a self-satisfied look more triumphant than when he'd killed the wolf. He pulled out his knife and stretched the thong taut over the blade.

Laura shook her head in dismay. "No, don't," she pleaded.

A satanic smile snaked across his face. With a snap of his wrist, he cut through the rawhide.

"No ... you can't. It's mine!"

Her pleas were useless. Yellow Dog snatched up the pendant and tied it around his own neck. Then puffing out his chest, he looked down at her and laughed again.

An ache crawled up Laura's chest to her throat. No longer could she hold back the tears. He'd not only stripped her of her most cherished possession, but her hope as well. Imprisoned beneath him, she was forced to face the truth. There was no chance of her being rescued. With the rain storm and Yellow Dog's crisscross travel, it would be impossible for anyone to find them.

She rocked her head from side to side, clamping her lips to fight back her sobs. She wished he'd stop that demented laughter.

As she blinked back tears, something whirred past Yellow Dog and struck the sapling behind her with a resounding thwack. Craning her neck, she stared wide-eyed at an arrow stuck deep in the trunk a few feet above her head. A blaze of joy shot through her. Painted around the end of its shaft below the feathers was a white ring.

She looked at Yellow Dog.

His laughter died. The triumphant gleam on his face turned to a dark mask of hatred.

CHAPTER 24

Grey Wolf and Swift Eagle stepped out of the woods into the clearing. "You are dead meat, Yellow Dog, like that wolf!" Grey Wolf yelled.

Yellow dog leaped off Laura and whirled to his feet. His gaze shot to Grey Wolf, the shock of being found etched across his face. "If that is so, why did you not kill me when you had the chance?" he countered, a flicker of apprehension wavering in his voice.

Grey Wolf stripped the quiver of arrows off his shoulder and threw it and his bow to the ground. "An arrow in the back is too good for you," he said, the Cheyenne words ground between clenched teeth. His gaze narrowed on the cameo hanging from Yellow Dog's neck. His hand went to the leather sheath at his waist. "I prefer to rip your heart out with my knife."

Withdrawing the weapon, he stole an anxious glance at Laura. With arms stretched over her head, she had twisted on her side to look at him. Even though her eyes brightened at the sight of him, unspoken torment shadowed her face.

"Grey Wolf ... thank God, you're here!" she cried out, a mixture of anguish, fear and relief choking her words.

Grey Wolf looked back to Yellow Dog, his anger intensifying. "Your kind of filth shames our people!"

The warrior held out his knife in front of him. "The Cheyenne are not *your* people!" he railed, stepping away from Laura.

As Grey Wolf stalked Yellow Dog in a wide arc, Swift Eagle moved out of his way. Grey Wolf waved his knife from side to side, testing, taunting, trying to catch the renegade off guard in order to make the first lunge.

Yellow Dog glowered at Grey Wolf who drew closer and closer. "I have taken what Grey Wolf is not man enough to take. She is my woman now."

Fury coursed hot through Grey Wolf's veins. He lashed out with his knife, bellowing, "She will never be your woman! Not as long as I am alive!"

Yellow Dog sprung backwards, avoiding Grey Wolf's strike to his stomach, but catching a gash across the inside of his forearm. Blood spurted from the wound and ran into the hand holding his knife.

He threw Grey Wolf a defiant look and flipped the weapon to the other hand. "Her white loins already drip with my sap," he jeered, "my seed planted deep in her belly."

His shocking words thundered in Grey Wolf's ears. *No! Not Laura ... she was his! Only his!*

He veered with a sudden feint to the left, and then dived to the right, his weight slamming Yellow Dog to the ground. The two rolled over and over, dirt and sweat smearing their bodies. Each grappled for the other's knife while trying to deliver a deadly strike from his own.

Grey Wolf gained the upper position only to have Yellow Dog pitch him on his side at the edge of the campfire. With the flames licking at his flesh, he had no sooner reeled away from the hot coals, when the Indian pounced on him, knocking the knife out of his hand. He caught hold of Yellow Dog's wrist just as the warrior's blade was about to plunge into his chest.

He heard Laura's terrified scream and shouts to Swift Eagle to help him. She didn't know that his brother must honor the fight and would not intervene.

Grey Wolf gripped Yellow Dog's arm tighter, straining inch by inch to force the knife away from his chest. Spurred on by Laura's desperate cries, he overpowered the Indian and wrenched the knife from his hand. He hurled him over his head, then as Swift Eagle emitted a whooping war cry, he pinned the renegade to the ground.

Bloodlust burned in his heart as he held the knife at Yellow Dog's throat. He nicked his flesh with the razor edge of the blade and watched the blood ooze down the Indian's neck.

Everything he felt, all his rage and hatred fueled the iron grip of his hand. One quick, lethal thrust and it would be over. The man he'd despised all these years—dead! He looked at Laura. *The man who'd threatened the very life he valued more than his own.*

"It is a good day to die," Yellow Dog muttered, glaring up at Grey Wolf, arrogance in his voice, no hint of fear.

The Indian's body lurched as Grey Wolf gave a final, deliberate jerk of the blade. The knot split easily, the rawhide thong slipping from around the Indian's neck.

Clutching the cameo, Grey Wolf sneered sardonically at a stunned Yellow Dog. "No, it is not a good day to die." He flung Yellow Dog's knife through the air, the point embedding into the trunk of a distant pine tree. "Slitting your throat is too quick and easy, Yellow Dog. I prefer that you die slowly … rotting in the white soldiers' prison."

Satisfaction welled up inside him as Yellow Dog's face turned pale. The warrior would rather have died now than be caged like an animal in a white man's prison cell.

Swift Eagle handed Grey Wolf his knife. Then he threw a loop of rope around Yellow Dog's neck and jerked him to his feet. "What torture would be fitting before we turn him over to the bluecoats?" Swift Eagle cinched the rope tighter around his neck and yanked it, forcing Yellow Dog to throw back his head and gasp for breath. "I say we castrate him?"

Though Grey Wolf agreed, when he looked past his brother to Laura, fear still clung in Laura's eyes. "No, Swift Eagle, there has been enough torture. It is better that we let the army decide his punishment. Lash him to that tree until we leave for the fort."

He looped the cameo necklace under the waistband of his breechcloth and moved to Laura's side. Kneeling beside her, he cut the rope from her wrists.

Sitting bolt upright, Laura threw her arms around him. "Oh, Grey Wolf …" she gasped, too choked up to say more. She shook as she sobbed into his chest, a flood of relief overtaking her.

He held her until at last, the strength and warmth of his body calmed her. She pulled away and swiped at her tears. "I'd almost given up hope of anyone finding me."

Brushing hair from her face, she cast a worried glance at Grey Wolf. The side of his ribcage under his arm was splotched with black ash. "You're burned—"

"It is nothing," Grey Wolf said, his voice sounding stifled and unnatural. He leaned over to cut free her ankles, and then sheathed his knife.

Laura reached out to touch him. "Let me see how badly—"

Grey Wolf grabbed her arms. "I said it was nothing!" Pulling her up, he held her away from him.

"It is *you* I am concerned about," he said. His gaze traveled uneasily down the length of her.

Laura was bewildered by the irritation lining his face. He seemed ashamed to look at her.

"Yellow Dog said …" Grey Wolf's words fell away as he turned his head, his gaze becoming transfixed on Swift Eagle tying the Indian to a tree on the far side of the clearing. In the forced silence, Laura watched a muscle twitching at his jaw line. When he looked back at her, a fierce light flashed in his eyes. "He said he mounted you."

Laura frowned, not sure what he meant.

He grasped her arms. "He mounted you!" he repeated, his voice lashing out at her like the end of a whip.

A knot formed in her throat as his words sunk in. "No," she cried, shaking her head, "no, he didn't." Still his eyes questioned her. Did he think she was lying?

"Here, just before you came, was the first time he tried to do anything to me," she insisted. "Thank God, you stopped him."

His cold silence tore at Laura's heart. "What did Yellow Dog say to you?" A look of raw anguish crossed his face. She wrenched free of his hold. "Whatever he said, it was a lie. Are you going to believe him or me?" she demanded, trapping his eyes and forcing him to answer.

"I want to believe." He dragged a hand through his hair, deep creases of regret darkening his brow. "Laura, I do not know what came over me. Yes, I believe you." His glance wavered back at Yellow Dog. "But even his touching you makes me …" His jaw tensed, a deep intake of breath hissed between his teeth. "I should have killed him."

She lifted a hand to the side of his face, her fingers touching his hardened features, wanting to smooth away the anger. "No. You did the right thing by not killing him." She stopped short of saying, the *civilized* thing, knowing his sensitivity to such a word.

Grey Wolf slid her hand to his lips and kissed her palm, before gathering her in his arms. "Laura, are you sure you are all right?"

"Yes, really I am. He didn't hurt me." She rested her head against his chest. "What will you do with Yellow Dog?"

"Take him to the fort and turn him over to Major Williams."

Laura slid her hands around his neck. "Grey Wolf," she said, the intimacy of her voice drawing his eyes to hers. "I've only been one man's woman." She paused. "Only one."

The hard angles of his face softened, the last traces of tension melting away. He plucked a leaf from her hair and untangled one of her combs dangling from a loose curl at her shoulder. He held it out to her.

Laura lifted the hair from the side of her face and secured the comb behind her ear. After checking the other side for its mate, she brushed several wayward strands from her forehead.

"I must look a sight," she said, glancing down at her skirt smudged with dirt. The top of her cotton blouse was pulled open where the buttons had been torn off. She drew the collar together in an effort to cover her exposed neckline.

Grey Wolf smiled meaningfully. "Yes, you look a sight. A pretty sight."

His response stirred a memory of the time Laura had fallen in the river and he'd answered her in much the same way. Like then, the same glow of admiration was in those crystal-grey eyes of his.

"It's still hard to believe you're here. How did you find me?"

Grey Wolf touched the tip of her nose with his finger. "I am your guardian spirit, remember?"

"But—"

His finger slid to her lips, silencing her. "I found you, that is all that matters." His thumb brushed away some dirt from her chin. "Come, we will go to the creek and wash off." He took her hand in his.

"Wait …" She lifted the hem of her skirt to reveal her stocking feet. "My boots," she said. As she bent over to retrieve them, he swooped her off the ground and into the cradle of his arms.

"Leave them." Before she could protest, he crossed the campground toward the woods. Thankfully Yellow Dog had been tied to the back of a tree so she didn't have to see him as they passed by.

However, she caught Swift Eagle's curious glance. Squatting down, he said something to Grey Wolf as he pulled a piece of meat from the carcass still simmering on the spit. He grinned broadly when Grey Wolf gave a quick reply. Laura didn't understand their words, but felt her face flush at the knowing look Swift Eagle flashed her just before the woods swallowed them up.

Neither Laura nor Grey Wolf spoke as they moved through the quiet solitude of the forest, each thanking the fates-that-be for allowing them another chance to be together.

With one arm circled around his neck and her body firmly held against the hard wall of his chest, Laura felt Grey Wolf's vigorous strength in every stride he took. She wondered how he found the fortitude after traveling so far and then fighting Yellow Dog. She seemed to weigh no more than a mere child to him.

She heard the sound of a creek's bubbling current as they stepped between the thick border of spruce trees. Grey Wolf set her feet on a mound of smooth stones at the edge of the narrow bank.

The cold water splashed over her toes. "My stockings are getting wet." Leaning precariously against Grey Wolf, she tugged one stocking off, then the other and flung them over one of the low-hanging boughs of a spruce.

Grey Wolf mimicked her actions by flicking his moccasins off his feet onto the moss-covered ground behind him. He pulled out the cameo necklace from the waist of his breechcloth and dropped it inside one of the moccasins. Then to her astonishment, he slipped off his breechcloth and dropped it to the ground. A small pouch that had been tied around his upper thigh was tossed on top.

Balanced on the rocks, Laura gripped his shoulders and felt the heat emanating from his body. It took considerable effort before she could meet him eye to eye.

"That pouch that was around your leg ... what's in it?"

"Your lock of hair."

"Oh yes, I remember when ..." Her voice trailed off. She took a calming breath. "What about Swift Eagle? He might follow us."

"No," Grey Wolf answered matter-of-factly. A smile curled one corner of his mouth. "It is difficult to wash with clothes on."

Why her sudden shyness, she wondered. Because, her inner voice reasoned, making love with him and washing oneself in his presence was two different things. She bit her lip. Well, for certain, she couldn't stand here forever while Grey Wolf waited in all his naked glory.

And glorious he was. Her gaze didn't have to leave his face to know that. She remembered too well the perfect symmetry of that body, a body so near to her now its magnetic warmth radiated from every golden contour.

As a ribbon of excitement rippled through her, Laura's desire for this man, like before, overpowered any lingering inhibitions she had. Again, she wanted to touch ... and be touched.

Practically of their own volition, her hands gathered blouse and skirt, petticoat and camisole, over her head one by one and draped them atop a branch. In Grey Wolf's steadying grasp, she stepped out of her drawers and hung them with the other garments.

Lastly she pulled out her combs, allowing her hair to fall around her shoulders. She stood before him, as brazen and naked as he, the beat of her heart pounding in her chest.

For far too long, Grey Wolf regarded her with a strange kind of solemnness. Then abruptly, he scooped her up in his arms and waded into the middle of the creek.

In waist deep water, he weaved around boulders worn smooth by timeless currents of water flowing over them. When they reached the middle, he sat her atop a large flat boulder, its polished granite barely breaking the surface of the water.

Laura gripped the rounded edges of the rock and sighed with pleasure as she lowered her legs into the water up to her knees. The stream wasn't as cold as she'd expected, and with the rays of the sun beating down on her shoulders, she her whole body relaxed.

"M-m-m," she murmured, leaning over and swirling a hand through the water, "it feels wonderful."

Not saying a word, Grey Wolf took one of her ankles and lifted her foot to the surface, then washed her from her toes to her thigh. As he administered the same stimulating treatment to her other leg, Laura tilted her head back and closed her eyes. It felt like heaven for him to massage her tired muscles.

She breathed in the fresh, cleansing air, rejoicing in the certainty that she was safe now. Freed from Yellow Dog. Rescued by the one man who made her feel more secure than any other—the man who made her happy to be alive.

The drizzle of cool water trickling down the front of her brought her head up and she opened her eyes. Grey Wolf smiled and circled the boulder, cupping water in his palms and anointing her shoulders and back. With each soothing splash from his hands, her body swayed and arched spontaneously.

Returning to her side, Grey Wolf's expression stilled as he drew her eyes up to his. Her nipples tightened into tiny nubs as the warmth of one large hand was laid upon her breast. Gently he palmed one breast, then the other, kneading back and forth over them … washing between them … under them. The friction of his touch brought a soft moan to her lips.

"Lie back, Laura," he said, circling an arm around her shoulders, "let me wash your hair."

Not wanting her sensual bath to end, Laura let him ease her backward. Her hair sank below the water as he braced her head and shoulders. Leaning over her, he combed his fingers through her hair, carefully smoothing out the tangles and giving her scalp a slow, vigorous massage.

"Close your eyes," he instructed. "And your mouth," he added just before he dipped her head under the water.

She came up sputtering and grabbing his arm. "You could have given me a little more warning," she said plaintively, but she was smiling up at him.

He rubbed at what must have still been a smudge on her cheek, his thumb then trailing down the side of her jaw. When his gaze lowered to her lips, she grinned. "Is my mouth dirty, too?" she asked teasingly.

Grey Wolf chuckled. "Yes ..." He leaned over and laved her lips with the tip of his tongue. "Very dirty," he murmured. He then laid his mouth over hers in a swirling, wet kiss.

Laura wrapped her arms around his neck to pull herself closer, but he drew away, raising her to her former position. "Now my turn to be washed," he said, a devilish glint in his eyes.

At Laura's hesitation, his mouth slanted downward in feigned disappointment. "All right, I guess I will do it myself."

He dove beneath the surface and a moment later, emerged on the other side of the creek. He squatted down in the shallow water, scooped up a handful of sand from the bottom, and proceeded to scrub his neck, arms and chest as if it was the most natural thing to do. Laura watched him in awe while he rubbed himself with the sand like she would with soap. Then once again, he disappeared underwater.

Only this time, minutes passed and he didn't come up. Laura scanned the width of the creek. Though the water wasn't deep, the sun's bright reflection prevented her from seeing below the surface. Surely no one could hold their breath that long.

An eerie feeling came over her, the flesh at the base of her spine beginning to crawl. A second later, hands snaked around her waist from behind. Shrieking, she spun around, slipped, and fell into Grey Wolf's waiting arms.

"You! I should have known you'd do something like that," she chided.

His gaze was on her, bold and sensual. A slow grin ruffled his mouth. He tightened his arms around her, fitting her body against his. He was warm and slick, the water making it easy for him to mold her to his muscled body. As her knees rode up his thighs, she slid her fingers around his neck and tangled them into his wet mane of hair. Her breasts flattened against his chest. She could feel her heart thudding counterpoint to his.

Grey Wolf's smile faded. "I need you, Bright Eyes." His hands cupped her buttocks. He spread his legs and pressed her against the rock-hard evidence of his desire. "Be my woman again."

CHAPTER 25

Capturing her lips with his, Grey Wolf delved his tongue into her mouth, determined and insistent. While he firmly clasped her hips, he rubbed his sleek body erotically against hers, side to side, his heated flesh burning a trail across her belly.

Desire swirled through Laura like the currents of water flowing around them. "Yes, I'm your woman," she whispered against his lips. She pressed her mouth to his with an urgency that bespoke her mounting passion.

Their naked bodies moved and mingled, soft skin to hard muscle. They kissed over and over, trying to feed each other's fevered hunger, yet starving for what their mouths alone couldn't satisfy.

As Grey Wolf drew back, their eyes locked. Soft, wanton green gazed into powerful, savage grey.

And they both knew ...

Lovemaking, slow and easy, neither wanted. Not this time.

Grey Wolf gripped her thighs and spread them apart. He then lifted her, wrapping her legs around his hips. Laura clutched his shoulders as he raised them both out of the water. She braced her hands atop his wide chest and straddled him as he leaned backward over the boulder.

He grasped her hips and slid her over the satin length of his erection. "God Above, I need you ... want you," he said, his voice coming from low in his throat.

He stroked the sensitive crevice between her thighs along his heat to ensure she was indeed wet with need. Then he entered her. She gasped, shuddered, not at all ready for the exquisite sensations that flared through her groin.

A rough moan escaped Grey Wolf's lips. He lifted her and withdrew, holding the head of him just inside her opening. "Take me …" he rasped, "take all of me."

Incredible tremors undulated through Laura as her inner core throbbed and reached for him. She spread her legs wider and he surged inside her again. She closed her eyes. She was drowning in a whirlpool of rapture.

She laid her head against the side of his neck, clinging to him as he stretched further back on the boulder. His arms circled her back and he pressed her to him. "I am yours, Bright Eyes … all yours," he murmured in her ear.

As they rocked against each other, Laura felt her orgasm build. "Yes … mine," she moaned, reveling in the rhythm of their bodies. Vibrations deep inside her ebbed and flowed like the water lapping around them.

God, she didn't want it to end, didn't want the flood gates to open, yet knew they must. Yes, right now, they must. She was unable to hold back the tidal wave pulling her under, engulfing her in a wild, mindless climax. She called out his name, needing to tell him she couldn't wait, couldn't stop.

Grey Wolf felt the spasms deep inside her before she cried out. Bracing her above him, he matched her shuddering movements, thrust for thrust, until he was sure she'd reached the very top of the crest. Then he let his body erupt inside her, filling her and he too, calling out her name.

Wave after endless wave they rode, the length of their shared orgasms amazing them both. Grey Wolf sought her mouth and covered her lips with his, muffling her screams of wild ecstasy as well as his own shouts of exultation. After he gave one last tumultuous surge and Laura released a final and glorious shudder, he pulled his mouth away. Both breathed in desperate gasps of air.

Grey Wolf looked into Laura's face as she pushed herself up and balanced her forearms on his chest. He roved his hands down the sides of her soft breasts, around her slender back and over the silky roundness of her bottom.

"Your body fits well," he said. "Every part of you was made for me."

"And every part of you," she responded, gyrating her hips, "was made for me."

Grey Wolf groaned, her provocative movements sending a resurgence of heat through his loins. With a sharp intake of breath, he pulled out.

"What's the matter? Am I too much for you?" Laura teased. Her full breasts brushed against his chest as she hovered over him.

He smoothed back the wet hair from the sides of her face and chuckled. "Never," he growled, the word as much a challenge as was his own suggestive movements beneath her.

Laura's eyebrows shot up, making him laugh. Hoisting her off the boulder, he swung her into his arms and submerged their bodies up to their necks. With a great amount of splashing, he spun her around and around, dipping her in and out of the water. Laura threw back her head, laughing at his antics as they washed their love-drenched bodies and at the same time, cooled their lingering passion.

She continued to giggle as he nibbled at her neck playfully while carrying her out of the creek. It had been so long since she'd laughed and it felt good to be happy again. He stood her on the mossy bank near the spruce trees. A welcoming cool breeze whirled around them.

As Laura's skin began to dry, she shifted her glance to their discarded clothes. "We should get dressed and start back to the fort," she said. She grasped lengths of her hair and squeezed droplets of water from the ends. "I'm sure the army must be looking for me." Anxiety clouded her face. "And I don't know what happened to Sarah and Alex. They were with me when—"

"Do not worry about Sarah or your brother," Grey Wolf interrupted. "One of them who was with Yellow Dog when he captured you told my father that no one else was harmed. You were the only one they were after."

Laura pressed trembling fingers to her lips. "Oh, thank God. I thought maybe they'd been … I didn't know …" Tears sprang to her eyes. "I heard so many gunshots."

He cupped a hand under her chin. "They are safe."

"But they have to be worried, not knowing what's happened to me."

He nodded, his thumb blotting a tear on her cheek. For the first time he noticed the ashen pallor of fatigue beneath her eyes. The terror Yellow Dog had put her through, plus lack of food and sleep was beginning to tell on her.

A pang of guilt constricted his throat. And still she'd given him the love he asked for—had practically demanded of her. How could he be so selfish, so blinded by his own need that he never stopped to think what she had been through?

Yet she gave herself willingly. The assurance that she wanted him as much as he wanted her assuaged his guilt somewhat.

"After we dress, I want you to rest a while," he stressed, soothingly. "It will be a long ride to the fort." He pressed a kiss to her cheek. "I will get your clothes."

After he donned his breechcloth, he gathered up her clothes. He held out the first garment. "Your drawers," he said. Laura smiled compliantly as she stepped into them. He knew she was remembering the last time they were together and how much he enjoyed watching her dress.

"And your camisole …"

She slipped it on, the soft material molding to her breasts.

"Your shirt …"

"Blouse," she corrected. She fastened the buttons, folding the torn collar under.

After he'd handed her the petticoat, skirt and stockings, his hands fell loosely to his sides. *So little time …* he found himself thinking. *So little time left to look at her. To be with her. He must make each moment count, for they would have to last him a lifetime.*

He wasn't aware his mind had drifted until he heard her voice. She was sitting on the ground, her head tilted up, damp ringlets of hair draping her shoulders. "I asked if you found my combs."

"They are next to my moccasins." He lowered himself beside her. "You do not need them. Your hair is still wet."

He waited until she slipped on her stockings. "I want you to lie down," he insisted.

She sighed resignedly. "It would feel good to rest for a little while," she conceded. She stretched her legs in front of her and lay back on the grass.

Grey Wolf propped himself on an elbow next to her. Smiling down at her, he fanned the damp, auburn tresses away from her neck and shoulders. How often he'd thought her hair looked like his mother's. He watched her eyes slowly close, a peacefulness settling over her features.

Even her face resembled his mother. No, not really, he decided. He supposed he thought it because her complexion was ivory, not copper and her features, smooth not angular like the Indian women he had known most of his life.

As Grey Wolf rested beside her and listened to her even breathing, Laura lapsed into an exhausted sleep.

Laura awoke to the feel of Grey Wolf's lips pressing softly against hers. Her heart fluttered from the sheer pleasure of it. How different from the last time she'd been awakened, she thought. Quickly, she chased the awful memory from her mind.

Reclined beside her, he kissed her lightly again, then caressed her cheek with the back of his knuckles. "Have a nice sleep?" he said in that wonderful, deep-timbered voice of his.

Laura circled her fingers around his wrist. Only his strong hand could master such a gentle touch, she thought wistfully. "M-m-m … yes," she answered. "I feel like I've slept for hours." She frowned. "How long have I slept?"

"I cannot tell you." He grinned. "Indians do not carry pocket watches."

She rounded her lips and feigned a look of surprise. "Oh, is that so?" She sat up and ruffled her fingers through her hair.

Grey Wolf sat up and gave a quick glance skyward. "You slept about two hours." He twisted away. "Here, eat this," he said, turning back. He held out a hollowed piece of tree bark containing small chunks of seared meat. "Swift Eagle saved some of the rabbit for us."

So he hadn't remained by her side while she slept. She notice her boots placed near her feet, her combs and the cameo necklace at her side.

Laura picked up a small piece of the meat and put it in her mouth. The meat was warm from the spit and tasted good. Feeling rested, she found her appetite had returned. She ate until only a few pieces were left. When she looked over at Grey Wolf, he shook his head.

"Finish it, I ate while you were sleeping," he said as he picked up the rawhide thong and idly fingered the cameo.

Laura narrowed her gaze on the cameo in his hand. She wiped her fingers on her skirt, and then cupped her hand beside his. "I never noticed …" She leaned over for a closer look at the cameo's gold backing. "Is that an inscription on the back?"

"Yes, but worn and hard to read," he said dismissively. He brushed her hair off one shoulder, circled the thong around her neck and tied the ends. The cord was shorter now, the cameo hanging below the base of her throat.

"Oh, Grey Wolf," she said, fingering it, "an inscription makes it even more special. What does it say?"

He hesitated before replying, as if he found it hard to tell her. "To Mary, love Glen."

His words seemed to float through the air and hang there. Pensively, Laura lifted her gaze to meet his. "To Mary, love …" She paused. *"Glen?"*

Grey Wolf nodded. "Glen was my father. I told you my father gave the cameo to my mother."

A curious thought needled its way into Laura's mind. "You also told me you had a brother who had been killed by the Pawnee Indians, didn't you?"

"Yes," he answered, his voice tight.

Laura could tell her questions were once again dredging up painful memories. Still, she couldn't stop herself from asking as a strange feeling prickled the back of her neck. "What was his name?"

Grey Wolf stood up. Turning his back to her, he stared across the creek. "Glen ... he was named after my father."

Laura drew in a breath, her heart picking up a beat. *Dear God, it was too much to think, to believe that possibly ...*

She rose and stepped closer to him. "You never told me your surname." She swallowed. Her throat felt dry. "What was it?"

Grey Wolf swung around to look at her. His eyes narrowed. "Why are you asking these questions? What does it matter what my last name was?"

Laura didn't answer, her set expression telling him she awaited his answer.

"Herrington." He watched her intently as he repeated the name he hadn't said in fifteen years. "Our family name was Herrington."

Speechless, Laura stared at him. A wave of recognition flooded through her as she imagined his crystal-grey eyes changing to dark steel, and his face transforming into someone with hauntingly similar features.

"Laura? What is it?"

It was a moment before she could recover her power of speech. "Captain Herrington ... Glen ... he's ..." She began to shake, tears stinging her eyes. There was little doubt in her mind now as Alex's words came back to her. *Pawnees attacked the captain's homestead ... his parents killed ... his younger brother lost in the fire.*

A tear rolled down her cheek. "But you weren't in your house when the Pawnees set fire to it, were you?"

"No," he answered, impatience in his voice. He looked at her warily, his hands grasping her arms. "Who is Captain Herrington?"

Laura took a slow, calming breath. How was she going to tell him the brother he thought was dead all these years was quite possibly alive?

"Captain Glen Herrington is a soldier at Fort Hendricks. I ..." Steeling herself, she forced her voice to remain even. "I believe, he's your brother."

Grey Wolf let go of her abruptly. He glared at her, his face reddening with quick anger. "My brother is dead, I told you, killed by the Pawnees!" His eyes were hard, scaring her with their intensity. "Do you want to know how I found him? With a knife in his gut and an arrow in his leg. Blood all over him." He grabbed hold of her again. "Dead, do you hear me, Laura? He was dead!"

Laura shuddered, the torment in Grey Wolf's voice ripping through her heart. She hated to put him through this. But after what he just said about the arrow in his brother's leg, she was more convinced than ever it was true.

"Oh, Grey Wolf, I know it's hard to believe, but don't you see … it all makes sense." She looked at Grey Wolf's straight forehead, the firm slant of his jaw, his eyes—especially his eyes. "He looks a lot like you … he's a few years older," her words ran together, "Alex said his folks had been massacred by Pawnees when he was a boy … that he'd lost a younger brother."

A strange, faraway look clouded Grey Wolf's face. Laura went on, trying desperately to reach him, to convince him. "An army patrol found him unconscious and took him to Fort Leavenworth. Glen told me he'd been shot in the leg with an arrow and they dug it out of him. He walks with a limp."

Grey Wolf rubbed the back of his neck, lines of concentration creasing his brow. Laura could sense the impact of her words working their way into his soul. All those wasted years … neither of them knowing the other was alive. And the twist of fate life had dealt them—Grey Wolf, a Cheyenne warrior, his brother, an army captain.

As he gave a deep sigh, his hands slid down her arms. "Fort Leavenworth was not far from our home," he professed, the words barely audible.

Laura nodded, his statement giving more credence to her belief. She was relieved his voice no longer held any anger. But his eyes were red; his face, pale.

He released her and bending over, picked up her hair combs. When he handed them to her, Laura saw the effort it took to conceal his turbulent feelings by the tight way he schooled his expression.

"We must leave," he said. "The sooner we return to the fort, the sooner I will know for sure."

She fitted the combs into her hair, her heart swelling with excitement. In her own mind, she already knew.

In her heart, and in her soul, she knew.

Captain Glen Herrington and Grey Wolf were brothers.

CHAPTER 26

As Laura followed Grey Wolf through the dense woods back to the campsite, he said very little other than to point out which path to take. It was like him to shut her out of his thoughts and feelings, closely guarding them like walls around a prison. Still, she wouldn't let his detached mood dampen her own elation at witnessing such a heartrending revelation. How wonderful it will be when the two brothers finally meet!

As they stepped into the clearing, Laura's thoughts were diverted by the sight of her horse, Sonny tied to a tree opposite the campsite. Near him were three pintos—Grey Wolf's stallion, Yellow Dog's, and the third, a dappled brown and white she surmised was Swift Eagle's since he was securing a bundle atop the animal's back.

Laura hurried to Sonny's side and reached out an affectionate hand to stroke his head. She hadn't seen him since Yellow Dog had led him away with his own horse to the other side of the thickets that morning.

"Hey, boy," she crooned, her fingers combing through his thick forelock of hair. "Bet you could use something to eat." Laura smiled as the Morgan nudged his muzzle against her shoulder. She was relieved to see him alert after the endless miles he'd traveled. "Lord, how long has it been since you've had water?"

"Swift Eagle fed and watered the horses," Grey Wolf informed her as he knelt next to the campfire. He scooped up several handfuls of dirt and threw them over the flames. Puffs of smoke billowed upward and were caught by a breeze sending them spiraling above the treetops.

The mention of Swift Eagle sent Laura's gaze in his direction. When she saw him untie Yellow Dog from the tree, she clenched Sonny's bridle so tightly her nails dug into her palm.

Grey Wolf must have sensed her apprehension as Swift Eagle led the renegade to his horse. He stepped in front of her and took hold of her arms. Lowering his head to look at her, he drew her eyes to his. "He will never hurt you again, Laura."

An involuntary shudder rippled up her spine. "I know, but I'll feel much better when he's—"

The thunderous sound of rapidly approaching horses drowned out her words. Instinctively, Grey Wolf pulled her to him as a number of mounted soldiers rode out of the woods, their guns drawn.

Laura's glance shot from Alex to Captain Herrington as they abruptly halted their horses in front of them. Before she could express her joy at seeing them, Herrington pointed his revolver at Grey Wolf.

"If you understand English, heathen, let her go now!"

Laura was shocked by the captain's words. Instead of releasing her, Grey Wolf gripped her tighter. Shaking her head, she yelled, "No! Glen, you don't understand. Grey Wolf didn't—"

Suddenly out of the corner of her eye, Yellow Dog raced past them. He jumped over the smoldering campfire and sped for the woods, Swift Eagle close on his heels.

A sense of unreality whirled through Laura's brain as she saw the captain fire his gun and Yellow Dog spin like a puppet, and then plummet to the ground, blood spurting from his back. In the next instant, Herrington was shifting his aim at Swift Eagle.

She felt Grey Wolf's body stiffen. He let go of her and in one enormous leap, hurled himself at the captain, catapulting him from his horse. Both men hit the dirt rolling, Herrington's revolver flying out of his hand.

Reacting simultaneously, Alex and Tucker swung from their horses and drew their guns; her brother's aim was on Grey Wolf, the scout's on Swift Eagle.

Horror-stricken, Laura flung her arms out and screamed at the top of her lungs, "Nooo! Don't shoot!"

In a frenzy to stop Alex and the scout, she lunged forward. Alarm flashed across both men's faces when she threw herself between them and Grey Wolf. Oh God, could this nightmare really be happening? Grey Wolf fighting one brother to defend another, and her own brother about to shoot him!

Just as Grey Wolf backed off and pushed to his feet, Glen bolted upright and rammed his fist into Grey Wolf's jaw. The force of the blow sent Grey Wolf sprawling into the underbrush.

Glen's shoulders heaved as he sucked in a deep breath. "Laura, get out of the way!"

He threw a sharp, expectant look at Westbrook. "Lieutenant!" His voice was pure venom. "Kill the savage!"

"Alex, no!" Laura wailed, her eyes pleading with him. She knew she was asking him to defy his commanding officer's order. Her heart slammed against her chest as she fought for words to convince him. "Grey Wolf's the one who rescued me, Alex. He fought Yellow Dog." Relief trembled through her when her brother eased off the hammer of his gun, Tucker doing the same.

She whirled to face Herrington whose hard, metallic eyes still burned with lethal anger. "You can't shoot him, Glen." She glanced down at Grey Wolf who made no effort to stand. He wiped blood from his mouth with the back of one hand and glared up at his brother. The wretchedness outlining his face split her heart in two. He became a blur as her eyelids filled with tears.

"Oh, Glen, can't you see ... can't you tell?" She gave in to the tears, letting them trail down her cheeks. "Grey Wolf ... he's your brother."

Slack-jawed, Glen stared at her as if she'd taken leave of her senses. Slowly he cast a disbelieving look at Grey Wolf.

Laura swiped at her wet cheeks. She didn't expect him to accept what she'd said. Though simple were her words, far more profound were their meaning.

Stepping closer, she lifted the cameo from her throat for him to see. "He found this laying in his mother's hand after she was killed by the Pawnees."

Stubborn denial clung to Glen's features. Slowly, she reversed the cameo. Then recognition blazed in his stone-grey eyes. Laura knew he didn't have to read the worn inscription to verify the cameo was, indeed, his mother's.

As Glen lifted his gaze above her head, she turned to find Grey Wolf standing directly behind her. She moved aside and waited in the emotion-filled silence as the two men stared at one another ...

Indian to soldier.

Brother to brother.

"David?" The tone in Glen's voice was incredulous.

Grey Wolf felt sweat trickle down the side of his jaw and sting the cut at the corner of his mouth. It took every muscle, every nerve, every fiber of his being to hold his tortured emotions in check. Glen's words, heathen and savage, reverberated in his mind, hurting far worse than his cuts and bruises and prompting his worst fear—his brother's rejection now that he knew who he was. And what he was.

Fists clenched at his sides, he answered simply, "Yes, it is me … David."

"Jesus Christ," Glen uttered, his shoulders sagging heavily as his eyes traveled the length of his brother's sun-bronzed frame.

Laura could tell those around them, the mounted troopers, Alex, even Swift Eagle, were trying to comprehend what they heard and saw. But it was she who understood best the gravity of the scene playing out before them.

These were no longer young boys who could throw their arms around each other in a fit of joy over their discovery. They were grown men who'd led far different lives, and it would take more than blood ties to bridge the lost years between them. It would take understanding and time on both their parts, and Laura suspected far more conciliation on Glen's behalf.

"I never would have recognized you," Glen said, shaking his head.

Grey Wolf leaned over and picked up Glen's cavalry hat. He dusted the brim and handed it to his brother. "I would have known you," he countered. "You are older, taller. Otherwise, just like I remember."

Glen smoothed back his hair and fitted the hat on his head. He forced a smile and said, "Well, you look a damned sight different from when I saw you last."

Spotting the revolver half buried in some leaves, Grey Wolf stepped over to retrieve it. He studied it for a second, feeling the weight of it in his hand. He curled his fingers around the barrel and handed it to Glen.

Glen fitted the gun in his holster and fastened the flap. "Christ, it's hard to believe you're alive."

"I feel the same about you."

"I thought you were trapped in the house after the Indians set fire to it. When I regained consciousness a week later, the soldiers told me there was nothing left but ashes." Glen's voice lowered, sounding gruff. "I never went back."

"What about Mother and Pa? Were they—"

"They're buried in a cemetery outside Fort Leavenworth," Glen broke in. As one of the horses behind him danced and snorted restlessly, his countenance changed, his military veneer abruptly wiping all traces of emotion from his face. He squared his shoulders and turned to Laura. "Are you all right?"

"Yes, Glen, thanks to …" Her gaze flitted to Grey Wolf. What was she to call him now? She caught the quick lift of his chin. "Thanks to Grey Wolf," she answered, realizing nothing had changed. He was David in his brother's eyes, but in his own, he was still an Indian warrior.

"By now Doc Simms ought to be at the fort treating Ed Fuller. He better take a look at you, too."

Laura shook her head. "I appreciate your concern, but I'm quite all right. Yellow Dog may have frightened the daylights out of me, but he didn't hurt me." She smiled nervously. "Although, Lord knows what he might have done if Grey Wolf and Swift Eagle hadn't come when they did." She glimpsed Yellow Dog's body sprawled on the ground. "I saw the markings on his arrows. They match the one we took out of Ed."

Glen eyed his brother. He gave a curt nod toward Swift Eagle who hadn't moved from the side of Yellow Dog's body. "I take it, this Indian's a friend of yours?"

"Swift Eagle is more than a friend," Grey Wolf replied evenly. "He is my brother."

Laura saw the captain flinch. He cast a critical glance at Swift Eagle, then back to Grey Wolf. "So that's why you jumped me," he remarked. "How about Yellow Dog? Any relation?" His tone held a note of sarcasm.

"He was a distant cousin of Black Arrow, but to me, he was an enemy. His disobedience caused trouble many times for the Cheyenne. You gave him what he deserved. My only regret is that he did not suffer more for what he did to Laura."

Alex pulled her into the circle of his arms. "God Almighty, Sis, you had me damned worried!" Then he drew back and keeping her hands in his, he nodded to Grey Wolf. "I'm sure grateful to you for saving my sister. She's mighty special to me."

She is special to me, too, Grey Wolf reflected. He wondered what Alex would think if he knew about them. And what would Glen think?

Probably the same thing he knew in his own heart. He was an Indian who had little to offer Laura. Horses, tipis, and buffalo hides might be enough for a Cheyenne maiden but certainly not for her. She deserved more. Much more. And someday she would find it.

"Sergeant Avery!" Glen's commanding voice cut into Grey Wolf's thoughts.

"Sir," answered a soldier who reined his horse apart from the others.

"There's a creek not far from here. See that the horses are watered. Then we'll start back while there are still a few hours of light left."

"Yes, sir."

Grey Wolf sensed the high esteem the sergeant held for Glen. The soldier quickly repeated the order and led the other mounted troopers through the woods.

"Captain, what do you want to do with that dead Indian?" Tucker asked, moving up beside him. "We gonna take him to the fort or leave him here for the wolves?"

"He will be buried with his ancestors," Grey Wolf said. His voice held a defiant edge.

"I thought you said he was your enemy?" Glen retorted.

Grey Wolf noted a hint of censure in Glen's tight-lipped expression, but ignored it. "He was. But after he makes the journey to the spirit world, he is no one's enemy. All are equal in the eyes of the Great One." He motioned to Swift Eagle, speaking to him in their language. Without a word in reply, the Indian bent down and grabbing the renegade by his arms, dragged him toward their pintos. "We will take him back to our village where he will be prepared for burial."

Glen frowned, a look of dismay on his face. "My God, David, do you think now that I've found you, I'm going to let you out of my sight so easily? I want you to come to the fort. You and I, little brother, have a lot to talk about, a lot of years to cover."

Glen's response was more than Grey Wolf had hoped for. Could it be his brother would accept him for who he was? Knowing that even though their parents had been killed by Indians, he had made a home among them. A part of him wanted to believe it, but a part of him felt that even if they talked, Glen still wouldn't understand.

He looked into Glen's face and saw his father … their father. He never felt more torn, more divided between two worlds than he did right then.

With his thumb, Grey Wolf wiped the persistent trickle of blood from the edge of his mouth. Rubbing its red stickiness between his fingers, he thought a moment longer before answering. "You and I are of the same blood, yet fifteen years apart have made us strangers." His somber eyes lifted to meet Glen's. "If talking can make us brothers again, then I will go with you to the fort."

CHAPTER 27

The next evening inside the guest quarters, Sarah sat on the edge of Laura's bed and clasped her hands in her lap. "It must have been a living nightmare for you, dear."

"Yes," Laura replied and sighed. She circled her pink batiste nightgown over her head. "One I thought would never end." Picking up her wash basin from the stand, she walked to the open window. But it did end when Grey Wolf came to save her.

She parted the muslin curtains and tossed out the water. A smile chased her frown away as she remembered the time they'd spent together at the creek. *That was like a dream she wished had never ended.*

She peered out the window, across the parade ground. Glen had insisted Grey Wolf stay in a vacant room next to the officers' quarters. She wondered how they were getting along.

After returning the basin to the stand, she picked up her brush from the bedside table and sat beside her aunt. She removed her combs and swept the brush through her hair while Sarah went on talking as she'd done practically nonstop since her return that afternoon. Laura supposed it helped to alleviate her aunt's pent-up emotions from days of worry.

"Well, thank goodness, you're safe. And for the second time, my gratitude goes to Grey Wolf." She pursed her lips thoughtfully. "Did Daniel tell you he went to Black Arrow's village the morning after your capture?"

"No, he didn't."

"Grey Wolf wasn't there, but he found out Black Arrow had sent a message to him. The chief told him he was sure Grey Wolf would find you if the army didn't. And Dan believed Black Arrow when he told him Yellow Dog and his followers had acted on their own."

"If it wasn't for Grey Wolf," Laura winced as the brush snagged in her hair, "I think Yellow Dog would have outdistanced the soldiers." She worked the brush through the tangle and after a couple final strokes, set it back on the table. "If he'd gotten away, I shudder to think where I'd be by now."

Sarah patted her arm. "Mercy, dear, don't give it another thought. It's over and done and that terrible man is dead." She squeezed her wrist. "And now the good Lord has rewarded Grey Wolf for what he did."

"Rewarded?" Laura queried.

"Why, by finding his brother, Captain Herrington." She smiled, sliding her fingertips underneath the cameo at Laura's throat. "It was awfully nice of Grey Wolf to give you their mother's cameo." She tilted her head wistfully. "Almost like the missing link that brought the brothers back together, isn't it?"

Laura smiled back. "Yes, I guess you could say that."

A light knock on the door brought Laura up from the bed and scrambling for her cotton wrapper. "Who is it?"

"It's me, Lucky."

Sarah waited until Laura had looped the sash around her waist before opening the door.

"Evening, Mrs. Osbourne. I, ah, was just wondering if—"

"Come in, Lucky," Laura said from the center of the room.

He removed his hat and strode inside the doorway, his spurs clinking across the plank floor. "That is, Dan was wondering if there was anything you or Mrs. Osbourne needed before we rode back to camp. He's going over a map of the mountain passes with the major, so I said I'd come over and see." His perusal swooped down the front of Laura's robe to her bare feet, then up again to settle on her face.

Laura noted her aunt's none-too-subtle grin as she held the door ajar. "I can't think of anything." She cocked her head inquiringly at her aunt. "Sarah?"

"No, don't need a thing." Sarah's amused grin mellowed as her brows drew together. "I suppose since Daniel said we're leaving tomorrow, that means first thing in the morning?"

He gave a quick nod. "Yes, ma'am, got all the folks geared up and ready to move out." His gaze returned to Laura. The lamplight reflected the animation in his blue eyes. "We'll have the buckboard here after reveille to load up your belongings." With another polite nod, he pivoted on his heels and hat in hand, strode out. The words, "I'll see you in the morning," trailed behind him.

Sarah closed the door. "Think Daniel really sent him to ask if we needed anything?"

"Of course, he did," Laura returned, but the glint in her eyes said otherwise.

Sarah folded her arms in front of her. "Lucky really thinks a lot of you, Laura. He was beside himself with worry. Almost as worked up as I was. He drove Dan crazy, threatening to strike out on his own to search for you. Had the major a bit annoyed, too, with remarks like probably the army soldiers couldn't track the noses in front of their faces."

Laura smiled. "That sounds like Lucky." She moved to the window again. The moon was rising steadily, spreading its silver light over the garrison. In the distance, a coyote let out a long, woeful howl.

Their ride back to the fort had been a long one, even though they'd made camp last night. She was surprised she slept as well as she did, considering Grey Wolf had lain only a short distance from her blanket.

She rode with Alex both days, Grey Wolf and Glen keeping well in front of the column of troopers, their pinto and bay trotting side by side. Thankfully, her brother had made a concerted effort not to ask about her harrowing experience, evidently sensing her wish not to relive it. They instead talked about her continuing on to California and reuniting with their father. She spoke of the reservations she had about seeing him again. Even though she would call him Papa, he could never take the place of Uncle James, who'd been like a father to her all these years. Alex understood, saying he felt much the same way.

Standing at the window, Laura looked to the barracks across the quadrangle. In some ways her situation was similar to Grey Wolf's. She could understand the challenge he faced reacquainting himself with a brother he hadn't seen in fifteen years. A person couldn't just turn back the clock and instantly reclaim the life he once had. Or his feelings, for that matter.

"Ahem … mind letting me in on what it is you're thinking about?" Sarah asked, nudging her shoulder against Laura's as she stepped up beside her.

"Oh, I don't know … why life has to be so complicated, I guess."

Sarah brushed back her side of the curtain and looked out. "Of all people, I should think you would know the answer to that. To make it more meaningful." She let the curtain drop. "You told me yourself that life ought to be an adventure, and it certainly looks like you're getting your wish."

Laura ignored the mocking tone in her aunt's voice and continued to stare out the window. "I wish we could stay longer. I'd like to see how Grey Wolf and Glen … well, how it works out for them."

Sarah leaned against the window frame. "I imagine it was quite a shock for Captain Herrington to discover his brother …" she hesitated, "what was the Christian name the captain called Grey Wolf when they were talking to the major this afternoon?"

"David," Laura answered quietly, the name tugging at her heart.

"To discover that David," her aunt continued, "has been living the life of an Indian all these years." She arched an eyebrow. "Surely now he won't be going back to that Cheyenne village, will he?"

Laura nodded, turning to face Sarah. "I think he will. He feels an allegiance to those people. Besides, I've talked with him enough to know he believes he's been away from the white man's world for so long, he couldn't adjust to it."

"Why, that's nonsense," Sarah declared. "Of course, he could. Granted, it would take some time. But he speaks perfect English. He's young, intelligent, with his whole life ahead of him."

"I've thought that, too." Laura shrugged. "Still, I know how much the Cheyenne mean to him."

The first notes of the bugler blowing taps filtered through the night air. Slowly, one by one, the lamps in the barracks flickered and died out. Stifling a yawn, Laura drew the curtains closed.

Sarah stepped back from the window. "I'm sorry. I didn't mean to stay so long." She leaned over and kissed Laura on the cheek. "It's just that I'm almost afraid to let you out of my sight. Of course," she conceded with a sigh, "if there's one place I know you're safe, it's here. Sweet dreams, dear."

Soon after Sarah left, Laura blew out the lamp and crawled between the sheets. As she laid her head on the pillow, a sudden breeze swirled through the window, parting the curtains. Annoyed, she threw back the sheet and swung her legs over the bed. But before her feet had touched the floor, a dark shadow filled the window, blocking the moonlight.

Instant fright knifed through her. For one heart-stopping second she thought of Yellow Dog. But, of course, it couldn't be him.

Then the form moved and took shape. And she knew. So familiar was the breadth of those shoulders, the length of that hair, and the cat-like stealth of those movements. He crawled over the window ledge and dropped inside.

"Grey Wolf! He straightened, his tall, masculine body silhouetted in front of the window. "What are you doing here?"

Without a sound, he crossed the room and sat beside her on the bed. His upper torso held a sheen of burnished gold in the moonlit room.

"Someone could have seen you. The sentries, they—"

"Shhh." The touch of his fingertips against her lips sent a shiver fluttering through her. "No one saw me. No one heard." His breath warmed her face as he leaned close. "As to why I am here ..." His gaze was on her mouth. He ran his forefinger across her bottom lip, tugging at it, then covered his mouth over hers and sucked lightly, rhythmically. "You know the answer to that," he murmured. He took her hands in his and smiled, the promise of passion in his eyes.

Laura was astonished by her physical need for him. One touch, one kiss, and she was his, always and every time. As he kissed her cheek, her temple, then reclaimed her lips, her insides melted like candle wax in a flame. She reached out for him, craving his fire, wanting to feel it against her. Hot, sultry, burning.

Every where he put his hands, up her arms, over her shoulders, across her back, she burned with desire. Her flesh ignited by degrees as he skimmed the nightgown to her waist and caressed her breasts with the titillating abrasion of those dark, calloused hands. Breathless, she clutched his sides while his thumbs circled the rosy aureole of her nipples.

"Grey Wolf, the curtains ..." air hissed between her teeth as her nipples changed from soft to hard, "shouldn't you close them?"

Another sensual moment passed before Grey Wolf's hands left her and he moved to the window. As he drew the curtains together, a breeze swept the bottom hem outward. Flickering moonbeams danced across the floor, emitting an ethereal light over Laura's nakedness.

"Maybe you should shut the window," she whispered.

He strode to the bed and pulled her into his arms. "Do not like to be closed in," he answered, his voice thick with desire.

The gown at Laura's waist floated down her legs, pooling around her feet. She sank against him, feeling his strength envelop her as he picked her up and laid her in the center of the bed. Now she was entering their world, where they could forget all memories of the past, all thoughts of the future. All that mattered was here, tonight, together in each other's arms.

Grey Wolf stepped out of his moccasins and shed his buckskin leggings and breechcloth. He stood before her naked, the lunar light playing over his well-muscled body. He looked as he always did, wild and free like the animal he was named after, wanting nothing or no one to tie him down.

And that was what made her loving him so bittersweet, she thought, as he stretched out beside her on the bed and gathered her close. Loving him meant leaving him.

"Laura?" He was frowning down at her. "Do I see sadness in your eyes?" With his fingers, he swept the hair from her face. "There is no time for sadness. Only time for this."

And with the sweet magic only he could perform, Grey Wolf made her feel like never before, touching her in new, erotic ways that took her to the edge and tasting her in secret places that sent her to heaven and back.

Instinctively, Laura not only took but gave—mimicking touch for touch, kiss for kiss, pleasure for pleasure. She discovered that satisfaction came with a sense of power. The power to make his body tremble beneath her lips and throb beneath her hands.

Before Grey Wolf had been the tutor, yet now it was she who taught him how to soar higher, burn hotter, plunge deeper. Laura knew he did not want her to forget this night, but she would make sure he, too, would never forget.

For a while, they slept. Bodies supple and satiated in the sweet afterglow of lovemaking, they laid under the sheet, arms and legs entwined.

Gradually awakening, Grey Wolf stirred at the same time Laura did. The room was darker now that the moon had risen higher in the sky. Lying on his side facing her, he waited for his eyes to become accustomed to the night.

"M-m-m," Laura murmured softly, tracing a finger up and down his arm exposed above the sheet. "It's wonderful lying with you in this bed."

Grey Wolf nestled his head closer to her side of the pillow. "I have not been in a bed like this since I was a boy."

Laura drew back. "You haven't?"

He smiled, finding her astonishment amusing.

"But what about when you stay with your friend, Jeremiah? Doesn't he have a bed for you to sleep in?"

"Yes, but I prefer to sleep outside."

Laura frowned. "Does that mean you'll sleep outside here at the fort?"

His smile thinned. "No, I did not refuse the room Glen offered. It is hard for him to accept my primitive ways as it is."

"Give him time. Once he gets to know you better and how you feel about the Cheyenne, he'll understand."

"I hope so." Grey Wolf withdrew his arm from around her waist and shifted onto his back. "Just as he does not judge all white men by the sins of a few, neither should he condemn all Indians for what the Pawnees did to our parents."

"Do you think he does?"

"Maybe not." He stared up at the rafters. "But many white men think Indians are all alike. They look at them as if they were animals. I have seen it in their faces and it angers me. It is the soldiers who often treat them the worst."

Laura pushed up and propped herself on an elbow. Concern etched a deep line between her brows. "I only met Glen a few days ago, but I can tell he's a lot like you. You're both headstrong and so proud of who and what you've become. But you can't turn your back on who you were ... and still are. Brothers. The same flesh and blood." The intensity in her voice made him turn his head and look at her. "Don't let your pride get in the way of your true feelings. Please ... don't forsake each other."

He lifted his hand to cup the side of her face. "My sweet Laura, you always speak from the heart. Don't worry. I would never forsake my brother. But neither will I forsake my other brother, Swift Eagle, nor any of Black Arrow's people. They mean too much to me."

Laura understood what he was telling her. Because Glen opened one door, did not mean Grey Wolf would close the other on the people he regarded as family, too. Like his pride, he had his loyalty, and for this, she admired him—and loved him even more.

Laura turned her face and brushed her lips inside the palm of his hand. Oh, God, how she loved him. Before she could stop herself, the words came out, whisper-soft into his hand. "I love you, Grey Wolf. I have since the first time you kissed me."

He threaded his fingers into her hair. "I know," he said gently. "I only wish I could make you understand why I—"

"Why you don't love me," Laura forced out, hurt and disappointment constricting her throat.

"I did not say that." He brought her closer. "But love is more than this ... more than wanting and needing each other. It is caring for each other, providing for each other. I know you could do those things for me, but I cannot do them for you. Not the way I would want to, the way I should." He pressed her tighter against him. "Not the way some one else could." His voice bespoke jealousy lurking beneath the surface.

Laura shook her head in protest. "But I don't want some one else. I'll never love another man the way I love you."

"Nor could I ever love another woman the way I love you. But no matter how we feel, it does not change who we are."

Laura bit her lower lip, a stinging heat clouding her eyes. Oh, God, he'd said he loved her. How could those words bring such feelings of happiness and sadness at the same time?

She swallowed hard, trying to force down her sadness and hold on to the happiness. She knew this was what he wanted her to do. To keep on denying the truth and logic of what he was telling her would only make tomorrow that much harder to face. At least this time when they said their good-byes, she would not take only memories with her. She would take his love.

She forced a smile. "Grey Wolf, I wish—"

Abruptly he pulled her to him, his mouth seizing hers, smothering her words. His lips were hard and persistent; their firmness telling her he wanted no more talk.

Like a flare from a single match, so quickly Grey Wolf's kiss reignited Laura's passion. And though neither thought it possible, because of their shared confessions of love, their union this time was the sweetest, the most meaningful, the most sensual they'd ever experienced.

Hours later, as dawn threatened to chase away the cloak of darkness, they stood at the window. Taking Laura's hand, he flattened the center of her palm over his chest. "Feel my heart beat," he said.

Beneath her hand, his heart drummed steadily.

He turned her palm and laid it over her own chest. "Feel yours."

Hers beat just as steady.

He wrapped her in his embrace, cushioning her head in the hollow of his shoulder. "No matter the distance between us, Bright Eyes, our hearts will always beat as one." Then he released her and swinging his leg over the window ledge, left as he had entered. A shadow in the night.

Departing the next morning was one of the hardest things Laura ever had to do. Leaving her home and friends behind in Pennsylvania had not been half as difficult.

While Dan and Lucky carried their valises to the buckboard, she and Sarah stood outside on the boardwalk expressing their thank-yous to Major Williams and Martha. Laura had been at the fort only a short time, yet the major and his wife seemed like old friends. Even Ed Fuller had endeared himself to her. His arm in a sling, he stood in the background behind the major, already having asked and received a good-bye kiss from "his red-haired angel."

As Sarah continued to talk to Martha, Laura stepped off the boardwalk where Glen and Alex stood. She was aware that a few feet away Grey Wolf watched her every move.

"Glen, Grey Wolf gave me his mother's cameo …" She hesitated, feeling the weight of Grey Wolf's gaze on her as her nervous fingers fumbled for the cameo at her throat. "But it's your mother's too, and I—"

Glen raised a hand to silence her. "If it hadn't been for you, Laura, David and I might never have found each other." He reached out and took her hand in his. "I'm glad he gave it to you. Please keep it."

For a second, his eyes softened significantly as he lightly squeezed her fingers. Laura sensed it was his way of assuring her that everything would work out between him and his brother.

"With Driscoll leading your wagon train," he said, "you should make California in good time." Letting go of her hand, he pulled his gloves from his waistband. "Now you must excuse me, Sergeant Avery is awaiting my orders." He inclined his head. "Say good-bye to your aunt for me."

"I will." Laura smiled warmly. "Good-bye, Glen."

Herrington put on his gloves and swung a departing glance at Grey Wolf. "I told the major we'd meet with him in his office at eight o'clock. I'll see you there."

Grey Wolf nodded. He turned back to Laura just as Alex whisked her into his arms.

"Good-bye, Sis. I'll write you often, I promise."

Try as she might, Laura couldn't keep the tears from spilling over. Batting at them with the back of her knuckles, she hugged Alex to her, hardly able to speak. "I'll … write, too." She looked into her brother's eyes and saw the tears behind his smile. "Oh, Alex," her voice cracked, "good-bye … and take care of yourself."

"You better keep that promise and write, young man," Sarah said, moving up beside Laura.

"I'll make it an official order," Major Williams quipped as he made his way past them toward his office.

Sarah laughed. "You do that, Major."

Stepping back so Alex could give her aunt a hug, Laura felt Grey Wolf's hand circle her waist. As he turned her toward him, everyone else faded into the distance.

"No good-byes," he whispered. His gaze upon her face was like a caress, gentle and warm. She could see her reflection in his eyes—eyes that always spoke more than words could say. She wanted to touch him one last time, but as she reached out her hand, he drew away.

Next to her, Sarah spoke up. "Grey Wolf …" The hesitation in her voice led Laura to wonder if she was contemplating whether to call him David instead, but she continued. "I will always be grateful for your rescuing Laura from that horrible Indian. And I'm so glad you and your brother are back together. Somewhere up in heaven your mother and father are smiling down upon you both."

"Yes, I know they are," he replied.

Dan stepped beside Sarah. "Darlin', I hate to be the one to break this up. I know how hard leaving is and all, but we need to be on our way."

"Come on, Laurie," Lucky yelled, standing next to the buckboard, "I'll give you a hand up." Not trusting herself to look back at Grey Wolf just yet, she stepped off the walkway and let Lucky lift her onto the seat. After Dan had bid everyone a last good-bye, he helped Sarah up and slid next to her.

As he flicked the reins and sent the wagon into a wide turn, Laura waved at Alex, and then returned her gaze to Grey Wolf. He stood with an arm crossed over his chest, his hand above his heart.

Smiling, she lifted her own hand and pressed it above her heart.

Steadily, never-ending, their hearts would always beat as one.

CHAPTER 28

Seated at a large roll-top desk near the hearth, Laura turned up the flame in the oil lamp, dipped her pen in the ink well and entered into her journal today's date, *October 26, 1860.* She hadn't planned to continue writing once she'd arrived in Placerville, but found the habit hard to break. Like an old friend listening quietly to what she had to say, her diary helped keep her life in perspective.

Since her arrival at her father's home two weeks ago, she'd had a difficult time making up her mind what the next step in her life should be. Papa, of course, hoped she'd continue to live with him and his wife, Elizabeth, whom he'd married in late July.

Their beautiful, two-story house located on the outskirts of town exemplified how well John's law practice had done over the years. His success had come from drawing up scores of legal documents for gold claims a decade ago and settling the disputes that often ensued between the miners. Last year he formed a partnership with another lawyer and acquired an influx of clients from the silver mines in Nevada. With the telegraph, pony express, and several stagecoach lines coming through Placerville, the increased commerce was a boon to his practice as well.

Laura liked Beth from the first day they'd met. She had an easy-going nature, and her energy was boundless. She managed the house, which included a Chinese servant and a gardener and often entertained guests, many of whom were government officials. Last night, the district judge and his wife came for dinner.

Setting her pen down, Laura leaned back in her chair. Doubtless, if she stayed, there wouldn't be a dull moment. Just today Papa had introduced her to Doctor Gordon, the county's only physician. He mentioned he had more patients than he knew what to do with and when informed of her medical training, spoke candidly that although the townsmen might balk at a woman assistant, he was willing to give her a try. He offered her a handsome wage to start whenever she wanted.

Laura's thumb fanned the pages of the journal as her thoughts turned to Sarah and Dan. Her aunt had expressed her wish for Laura to reside with them once Dan had built their ranch house in the Sacramento Valley. He, Lucky and Henry had already begun clearing the land. When the house was completed, Sarah and Dan would be married. She smiled. Everything was working out for them just as she had envisioned.

A hand touched her shoulder and snapped her out of her reverie. Her father stepped beside her.

"Papa, I didn't hear you come in."

John hooked a finger under her chin. "Do you know you have your mother's eyes and her smile," he said wistfully, his words more a statement than a question. "In fact, when you first walked into my office two weeks ago, I thought ..." his voice grew husky, "I thought I'd gone back in time and was looking at Lucy."

It wasn't only what he said that pulled at her heartstrings; it was how he said it. With so much love.

She'd never given much thought before to the pain he must have felt losing his wife. But now she could empathize with his loss. Grey Wolf hadn't died, but she'd lost him all the same.

John took a seat in a wing-backed leather chair in front of the hearth. The flickering flames from the fireplace reflected a warm glow over his ruddy complexion and lent a golden sheen to his rust-red hair.

A wave of nostalgia swept over Laura. "I wish I had been older and could remember more about her," she said. She positioned her chair at an angle facing him. "The one thing I do remember was her laugh. She had an infectious laugh, the kind that made you want to laugh along with her."

A reminiscent smile crossed John's face. "Beth laughs like that, too."

When Laura nodded without replying, her father looked away and an uncomfortable silence fell between them.

Several minutes passed before he met her eyes again. "Laura, I want you to know, Beth could never replace the feelings I had for your mother. No one could." His gaze dropped to his hands folded in his lap. "A mutual friend introduced Beth and I. She'd been a widow for a long time and, well ..." he shrugged, "we both realized that we had love still to give, so we—"

"Papa," Laura interrupted, "you don't have to explain. I understand. Beth's a wonderful person. I can see that she makes you happy. And you, her." She paused. "I know how much you loved Mother ... and how difficult it must have been for you when she died."

"Does that mean you forgive me?"

"Forgive you?" Laura repeated, surprised by the penitent look in his eyes.

"For leaving." He looked at her intently. "I meant to come back eventually. But from the sound of Sarah's letters and yours, I could tell she and James had made a good home for you and Alex and were doing a better job of caring for you than I could alone." His mouth flattened into a grim line. "And the truth is, the longer I stayed away, the harder it was to go back. I finally decided that my returning would disrupt your lives, do more harm than good."

Never in any of his letters had her father expressed the guilt he'd evidently been harboring all these years. It seemed he had suffered as much, if not more, by his leaving than she or Alex.

It was no surprise to find the bitterness she once felt toward her father had disappeared. In fact, she was happy for him. He'd found someone to share his life with and leave the past behind, just as Sarah had done with Dan.

"Papa, it's a mistake to let our past rule our future." She thought of Grey Wolf. Because of his past, he had been too stubborn and proud to let her be a part of his future.

"Those are some sage words coming from such a young lady."

"Yes, well, this young lady has done a lot of growing up in the last few months."

From the hallway, Sarah and Beth's voices filtered into the room. "Looks like you two have been having a cozy little chat," Beth said, entering through the alcove. She glanced from John to Laura. "I hope we're not interrupting?" Concern clouded her face.

"Of course not," Laura said with a quick smile. "What have you two been up to?"

"Beth has been showing me how she made the draperies in her bedroom." Sarah settled herself in an upholstered chair opposite John and shook her head. "Lord, I could never do as beautiful a job as she has."

"Balderdash!" Beth spouted. She leaned her hip aside John's chair and casually placed a hand on her husband's shoulder. "Don't sell your sewing short,

Sarah. I'll have John bring me down to the ranch and help you take measurements. Then we can order the material."

"Hey, whoa there, ladies," John said with a chuckle. "Dan doesn't even have a wall up yet and you're already talking about window curtains."

Beth grinned. "Never hurts to plan ahead."

From an adjacent room, their servant appeared. John acknowledged her with a nod. "Ah yes, Sung Lee, I bet you've come to tell us tea is ready."

The small woman gave a silent bow and retreated.

Standing, John eyed Beth and rubbed his mid-section. "Any more of that spice cake left, sweetheart?"

Beth linked her arm with his. "I'll see if I can scrape you up a crumb or two."

Rising to follow, Sarah glanced at Laura. "Coming, dear?"

Laura scooted her chair closer to the desk. "I'll be right there. Won't take me but a few more minutes to finish this."

As they left, she picked up her pen and with a flourish, hastily wrote of her meeting with the doctor. Then closing the journal, she placed it inside the small chest. The letter from Alex lay next to the wooden box. As she set it atop the journal, her eyes lingered on the envelope. He had posted it in August and her father had given it to her upon her arrival. She had read it so many times, she knew it backward and forward. God, how she missed him.

As she closed the lid, an image filtered through her mind, not of Alex, but of Grey Wolf. She missed him even more. Alex wrote that the major had hired him as their lead scout until Tucker returned from guiding a corps of government surveyors through the mountains. No doubt Glen had had a hand in persuading Grey Wolf to stay on at the fort.

Alex, however, had added a postscript, saying Swift Eagle had brought Grey Wolf an urgent message from a friend, and that he'd gone to Denver. She wondered if the friend was Jeremiah.

Laura frowned, suddenly irritated with herself for letting her mind wander. She was going to have to practice what she preached. Grey Wolf was a part of her past. If she was to get on with her life, she had to stop thinking about him.

She shoved back her chair and rose. And the only way to do that was to stay busy. She sighed, staring down at the chest. If she accepted the doctor's offer, her days would be occupied. She closed her eyes, allowing the image of Grey Wolf to resurface. But what about the nights? What was to keep her mind from dreaming and her body from yearning then?

David rode into the town of Placerville more tired than hungry and full of anxiety.

The collar of his jacket was furled high along the back of his neck, his hat pulled low to shade his eyes from the late afternoon sun. He scanned both sides of the street, scrutinizing the people who walked the boardwalks in front of the wood-framed, one-story buildings. Only a few were women, but he glanced at each one.

It had been four months since he'd seen Laura.

It seemed more like four years.

His stomach gave a jolt when a young woman wearing a blue coat and bonnet came out of a bank. He knew she wasn't Laura even before she turned his way, yet his hand tightened on the reins, the woman's slight resemblance intensifying his desperate longing for Laura.

As she stepped off the walkway and crossed the street, she smiled up at him. Glen had been right. What he wore made a difference in people's attitude toward him. Dressed in a jacket, trousers, hat and boots, he no longer resembled an Indian. That was the reason why the woman had greeted him with a friendly smile instead of a wary frown.

At the fort, Glen had convinced him to dress like the white man he was. In so doing, he would be accepted more readily by the soldiers. Of course, being the captain's brother had helped to gain their respect as well.

Ironically, Black Arrow had been pleased that he'd decided to take his rightful place among the whites. Perceptive and wise, he'd told his adoptive son that if the Cheyenne are to survive in the years to come, they will need people like David who understand their ways to represent them in the white world.

"You should not be forced to choose between us, my son," he said. "Keep an eye and ear in both worlds and we can all benefit. I will trust your vision and words to help keep peace with the white man."

Spotting a newly constructed building with a sign that read, *Eldorado Hotel*, he led Four Winds to the hitching rail in front of it. The muscles in his body screamed in rebellion as he swung out of the saddle and set his feet on the ground. He'd ridden the last leg of the trip hard and fast, fortunate to have crossed the high mountain pass with only a light snow at his back.

He looped the reins over the rail and gave the pinto a vigorous rub along his neck. The horse's ears pricked as he spoke soothingly in Cheyenne. He'd get a room first, and then look for a livery. Though Four Winds had taken to the army saddle well enough, it would be good to rid him of its restraints.

After untying the saddle bags, he swung them over his shoulder and stepped up to the door. About to open it, he stopped short, caught by the words on a sign nailed beside the entrance. NO CHINESE ALLOWED, and below it, NO INDIANS ALLOWED.

A flare of resentment bristled the hair on the back of his neck, but he quickly suppressed his anger, knowing he could not change the stubborn mind of a bigot.

He entered the small lobby where he saw a man dressed in a flashy green plaid coat and yellow vest standing behind a pinewood counter. This was only the second time he'd been inside a hotel. The first had been in Denver. Setting down his bags, he walked up to the clerk.

"Hello," the man said. "Here for the night or a meal in the dining room?"

"Both."

"Sign the register then." The clerk opened a ledger and after dipping a pen in an ink well, handed it to him.

As he wrote, he could feel the man studying him. After he handed back the pen, the clerk swung the ledger around and peered down his nose at the page.

"David Herrington ... hmmm, don't recall hearing the name before. Not from around these parts, are you?"

David could tell from the expectant look on the clerk's face, he waited to hear where he was from. He wondered what the man would say if he told him he'd come from his father's Cheyenne village.

"No," he answered tersely.

The clerk scratched his chin and shrugged. "Lodging is a dollar a night, paid in advance."

David pulled out a small pouch from the inside pocket of his jacket. He set it in front of the clerk. "Take it out of this."

The man opened the pouch, peered inside, then reached for a small scale at the end of the counter. After carefully weighing out the gold dust, he returned the pouch to David. "Down the hall, second door on the left. Meals are served from sun-up 'til sundown."

"Thank you." David retrieved his saddle bags. "Could you tell me where John Westbrook lives?"

The clerk's eyebrows lifted significantly. He looked out the front window of the lobby. "His law office is right across the street. If you hurry, you can catch him before he leaves."

David shook his head. "It is not about business. I would like to know where he lives."

"A personal matter, huh?"

"You could say that."

The clerk leaned an elbow on the counter. "His house is a little ways out of town, heading west. Can't miss it. The only fancy two-story between here and Sacramento."

David hefted the bags onto his shoulder and headed down the narrow hallway. Opening the door, he entered a room that looked much like the one in Denver, furnished with a bed, table, lamp, and a commode stand with a pitcher and bowl on top. Tossing his hat on the table, he dropped his bags at the foot of the bed and heaved a long sigh. He knew walking in here would bring back memories. Shrugging out of his jacket, he sat on the side of the bed.

A vision of Jeremiah on his deathbed and his last words floated through David's mind. *"I want you to know ol' J. T. Hornbuckle had the time of his life searching for that gold. Fact is, it was a hell of a lot more fun looking for it than mining it."* His attempt to laugh ended in a fit of coughing. Afterward, his breathing became more labored.

"… There's a time to live and a time to die, son" he continued. *"I don't mind leaving this earth, because I know what I have will go to the best friend I ever had. My will is legal and proper. All I ask is that you use it to make a better life for yourself."* He smiled and for an instant, his eyes brightened. *"If you play it right, you can have the best of both worlds … Indian and white."* Then his grip on David's hand slackened, and he was gone.

David learned from Jeremiah's partner, Charley that the placer diggings had been exhausted, and Charley was taking his share of gold and heading back to the states. Sadly, Jeremiah never got the chance to use any of his shares to build the store he'd talked about.

He lifted the flap of one of the bags and pulled out Jeremiah's will. Unfolding it, he stared at the printed words. Just paper, but it represented all his friend had owned.

And now it was his. The trading post, the land surrounding it and enough gold in a Denver bank for David, as Jeremiah had so aptly put, *"to make a better life for yourself."* He tucked the document back in the bag.

But it was a life that didn't mean a thing to him without Laura to share it. He raked a hand through his hair. He'd been such a fool to let her go. Because of her, he'd learned so much about himself. And when she left, he'd learned even more. He didn't want to live without her.

He was wrong when he said love couldn't change who they were. It had, only he'd been too blinded by pride to see it. Now he hoped it wasn't too late. He hoped their love was stronger than the distance that separated them.

CHAPTER 29

Sitting at her vanity, Laura turned to listen to the soft coo of a dove perched in a tree outside her bedroom window. She waited and was soon rewarded with a mimicking cry in the distance. Its mate, she was sure. Doves, she'd read, remained with the same mate for life.

A light tap at her door prompted her to swing back around. "Come in."

Sung Lee peeked in. "Good morning, Miss Laura. So sorry to bother, but a gentleman to see you."

"To see me?"

Sung Lee gave a short nod.

Who in the world? In the time she'd been here, she had not met the first gentleman—in fact, much to her chagrin, she hadn't *seen* the first gentleman she would want to have come calling. "Did he say who he was?"

"I in kitchen when Miss Beth answer door. She say, come tell you have visitor. She and Miss Sarah take man in drawing room."

"Thank you, Sung Lee. I'll be right down."

After the young woman bowed and pulled the door closed, Laura looked at her reflection in the mirror. Certainly what she wore was suitable for anyone who would come calling this time of day. Actually the dress was one of her favorites, an emerald green stripe, its bodice gathered in tiny pleats to the waist, the circular collar and puffed sleeves trimmed in white. It was so nice to dress in stylish clothes again. Most of the garments she'd worn on the wagon train had been relegated to the rag bag. She lifted a hand to the black velvet ribbon at her throat, making sure the cameo was centered. The medallion was always the perfect accent to whatever she wore.

"Well, I best not keep the gentleman waiting," she muttered, pushing away from the vanity.

Descending the stairs, she could hear her aunt's and Beth's voices. Maybe the caller was Doctor Gordon following up on his offer. She frowned. She wasn't sure if she wanted to accept. As she walked past the foyer, she spied the man's jacket and hat hanging from the coat rack. Mentally, she rehearsed some words to put the good doctor off before entering through the open double doors into the drawing room.

A low, resonant voice made her lurch to a stop. Her glance shot across the room to the man standing with his back to her, talking to Sarah and Beth. If she hadn't been near the back of a chair to brace herself when he slowly turned around, she surely would have dropped to the floor.

"Laura, dear," Sarah said with a lilt in her voice, "look who's here!"

Laura felt as though she'd stepped into a strange dream. The kind that mixed the familiar with the unfamiliar, the known with the unknown.

The man who stood on the other side of the room was Grey Wolf, yet he wasn't. The eyes, the face were his. But his golden brown hair had been trimmed to lie along the collar of a white linen shirt tucked into a pair of fitted beige trousers. He wore black leather boots over the pants and a black vest. He looked incredibly handsome.

She struggled to find her voice. "Grey Wolf, how did you … I mean, what are …" She couldn't find the words. Especially not now when he was walking toward her.

David stopped beside the chair. His gaze took in the way her dress draped her slender hips, accentuating her waist and the soft curvature of her breasts. An ache gripped him deep within when he lifted his gaze to the cameo on a thin, black ribbon circling her neck.

He cleared his throat. He wished they were alone. "Laura, I had to come. I had to see you." There was so much he wanted to say to her, yet he didn't know how or where to begin.

Sarah broke in. "I know you two have a lot to talk about." She smiled. "Beth and I will leave you for now. Maybe later we'll have tea." She gave Beth the eye, and both women disappeared out the double doors, closing them as they went.

That was all David needed. Now he knew how and where to begin. In one stride, he swept Laura into his arms and blazed his lips across hers. Hot and hungry, his kiss was much more than a greeting. It was sustenance for a starving man.

Drawing apart from her, he said, "For four long months, I have dreamt of doing that."

Laura dragged in a much needed breath. She slid her hands up the front of his shirt to where a patch of dark hair curled around the open vee of his collar. "Are you sure you're not dreaming now?" she asked weakly. "Because I think I am."

David threaded his fingers through her hair and pulled her head back, kissing her again, this time slower, deeper.

"Still dreaming?" he murmured.

Laura looked into his dazzling, crystal-grey eyes no dream could duplicate. "No," she answered. Fingering the collar of his shirt, she tried to calm the waves of excitement that rippled through her. "But you look so different."

He hitched one corner of his mouth into a half-smile. "The clothes felt strange at first, but I am used to them now." His hands glided down her back to settle lightly at her waist. "It took me long enough, but I have finally accepted who I am."

"And who is that?" She glanced at the bear fang hanging from the thong around his neck.

"A man who has the good fortune to walk two paths at the same time."

Laura inclined her head, loving the way he chose his words. "You mean, white and Indian?"

"Yes. I have taken back my white name. But to the Cheyenne people I will always be Grey Wolf."

"Your brother made you see, didn't he? Glen helped you understand that you shouldn't give up your heritage."

He nodded. "It seems when I found my brother, I found David."

"I'm so glad for you … and Glen, too."

"Laura, I want to hear you say it." He tilted her chin with his thumb and forefinger and looked at her lips. "Say my name."

She heard the urgency in his voice; saw the longing in his eyes and understood. "David," she whispered softly.

His hand curved her neck as he kissed her chin, her jaw line, and then the sensitive side of her throat above the velvet ribbon.

"Say it again," he urged, nipping at her ear lobe. "I want to hear it again."

Shivery sensations slithered down her neck as his warm breath fanned her ear. "David," she said, stronger this time.

"Ah, sounds good ..." he snaked his arms around her, "so right coming from you." Lifting her off the floor, he molded her lips to his, coaxing her mouth open, his tongue gliding inside to tease and taste.

Savoring the moment, Laura tried to ignore a light knock on the door. But the distinct sound of a door knob turning forced her to push from David's powerful embrace. Her feet alighted on the floor just as the door opened and Sung Lee entered with a silver tea service in her hands. Laura swept back strands of hair from the side of her face and hurriedly straightened her dress.

The woman lowered her eyes as she shuffled across the floor and set the tray on an oval table in front of the window. She took a moment to center the tea-cups in the saucers and fold napkins beside them. Only when she turned to go, did her dark eyes timidly glance their way. Then with a half bow, she shuffled back out the door, closing it behind her.

The brief interruption gave Laura's heart rate time to settle. Rather than feeling embarrassed by what Sung Lee had no doubt seen through those lowered lashes, Laura was amused.

"I wouldn't put it past Sarah and Beth to have sent Sung Lee to spy on us." She grinned up at David. "I'm sure when she reports what she saw as she entered, we won't be bothered again." She walked over to the table. "There are only two cups. Obviously they were planning to allow us our privacy a little while longer."

As she picked up the silver teapot, she realized she wasn't as calm as she thought. David's passionate kisses had left her shaken. And her mind was still reeling with the nagging question as to why he was here.

Holding a teacup in her other hand, she turned to him. "Want some?" she asked with forced lightness.

Impatience flared across David's face as he approached her. He whisked the cup and teapot from her hands and returned them to the tray. "I did not come all this way to have tea with you," he said, seizing her arms.

Laura met his gaze. "Why did you come? Surely not just to hear me say your name."

His eyes sharpened, regarding her for a long moment before he spoke. "No, I came to offer you my name."

Laura felt an odd flutter in her stomach. "To *offer* your name?" she repeated unsteadily.

His hands moved up her shoulders possessively. "I want you to be Missus David Herrington."

Now not only did her stomach flutter, but her whole insides did a flip-flop as well. She avoided his penetrating stare as the words rang inside her head ...

Missus David Herrington.

Too overwhelmed to speak, she took a step toward the chair, but his hands gripped her tighter, staying any further movement. His look told her he expected her answer that very second.

"David, seeing you was such a shock. Now you're asking me to marry you ..." She wavered, trying to take it all in.

"You still love me, do you not?"

Laura pressed her palms against his chest. "How could you ask such a question? You know I do." Her brows drew together in a deep frown. "But at the fort my love didn't seem to matter. You said—"

"I know what I said," he cut in. "I was wrong."

Reluctantly, David released her, allowing her to sink into the chair. He raked back a lock of hair that fell across his forehead. She wasn't going to make this easy. He wished he could pick her up and carry her out the door, no questions, no explanations. But deep inside, he could understand how she felt. He'd done a good job of convincing her that their love wasn't enough to make up for the differences in their lives. Well, it *was* enough; he just couldn't see it then.

God Above, not even his brother had made as much of an impact on his life as Laura had. He looked down to find her clutching the arms of the chair. And now he suddenly shows up as David Herrington wanting her to marry him. He couldn't blame her for being somewhat confused and reacting as she had.

He stepped to the large framed window. Outside a sudden wind sent a flurry of red and yellow leaves swirling to the ground. "After you left, I felt lost, my soul empty. For a time, I thought having my brother back in my life could fill that emptiness, but I realized you were the person I needed most by my side." He turned to face her. "Jeremiah once told me that it took the love of a good woman to temper a man and mold him into something better. How I wish he were alive today to meet such a woman."

Laura rose and walked over to him. She could see the grief shadowing his face and frowned. "David, are you saying Jeremiah is dead?"

Nodding, David looked out the window again. "I had suspected for a long time he was not well. But whenever I asked him, he denied anything was wrong. I found him in a hotel in Denver ..." his voice cracked, "so weak, he could hardly talk. The doctor could do no more for him. Said he was eaten up with consumption." He shook his head, his fists clenched at his sides. "He should have never worked that gold mine. If I had stopped him from packing up all his belongings and moving to that mine, he would still be alive."

Laura's lower lip trembled as she gazed up at him. "I doubt if it would have made any difference. With an illness like that, time was working against him."

It was easy for her to feel his sense of loss. Even though she'd never met the man, she knew how important his friendship had been to David. For so many years, Jeremiah was David's link between the Cheyenne and white civilization. She realized if it were not for that man's tutorage, David's transition into the white world would have been far more difficult.

Standing beside him, she watched the smattering of multi-colored oak leaves drift to the ground. "I didn't know he'd been digging for gold."

David braced a hand against the window case. "He found enough to make him comfortable in his old age, but he only lived long enough to make out a will and give it all to me." He bowed his head. "I would return every last nugget to the ground if I thought it would bring him back."

Laura pressed her fingers to the window pane, feeling the coldness from outside penetrating the glass. "I'm sure you would," she replied compassionately. "I know how much you'll miss him." Frowning with uncertainty, she looked up to find him watching her.

"Laura, I know what you're thinking. I'm here because of the gold ... because now I have something to offer you." He grasped her shoulders and turned her toward him. "I will admit I am grateful that I have money for you and me, but I would have come anyway. If Glen had not needed me to scout an expedition, I would have caught up with the wagon train before it reached here, and I would not have even known about Jeremiah."

He lifted a hand to the side of her face, his thumb tenderly stroking her cheek. "The Cheyenne believe a man's heart must lead him," he said softly. "Mine has led me to you." He combed his fingers into her hair, then bent his head and kissed her temple. "Only with you, Laura, am I truly myself, not Indian or white, but a man with hopes and dreams and the need for the woman he loves to be a part of them."

David's touch and words enveloped her like a warm, invisible blanket. She closed her eyes, finally letting herself slip into this dream-come-true.

"Say you will marry me." He cushioned her head against his chest and lowered his chin beside her hair. "Come back with me."

Laura never felt so wanted in all her life. She'd always known she belonged in this man's arms.

"Yes," she whispered, "I'll marry you."

"I want to build us a home," he was saying, seeming not to have heard her. He pressed her close, his strong fingers kneading her back. "Maybe a ranch like Dan said he was going to build. I can make a good living breeding and selling horses to the army and to the stagecoach and freight lines."

"Sounds wonderful."

David toyed with the ends of her hair hanging down her back. "Our brothers could be transferred any time, but for now we would be close to them … and I would be near Black Arrow's summer encampments."

She lifted her head and leaned back to peer up at him. "I would want a small ceremony here with my family first."

His brow creased, confusion and then wonderment flooding his eyes. "Are you saying? Does that mean—?"

Throwing her arms around his neck, she planted her smiling lips over his and gave him a resounding kiss. "It means, yes! And if you hadn't been talking so much, trying to persuade me, you would have heard me the first time. You, my darling, are looking at the future Missus David Herrington."

David belted out a hearty laugh. Sweeping her off the floor, he returned her kiss. Then putting her down, he took on that familiar look of a proud Indian with chin set and shoulders straight. "And," he emphasized, "I am looking at Grey Wolf's mate who will consummate her marriage to a Cheyenne warrior by sleeping in his tipi."

"We will go to Black Arrow's village?" Laura asked, feeling more enchanted by the minute.

"My father told me he will be watching for us when the summer moons return."

"But how did he know if I'd agree to come back with you?"

"At the fort, you remember, he said you controlled my destiny. He never wavered from that belief. He insisted I owed you my life, and that someday it would be yours."

"Oh, David, that's beautiful," she exclaimed, her voice filled with excitement. "And at the village, you will dress like a warrior, and I will call you Grey Wolf."

He nodded, pride continuing to dominate his features. "Just as you will wear my mother's white elk skin wedding dress, and all who see you will call you Bright Eyes."

And as those eyes welled up with tears of joy and happiness, Laura thought of the last lines of the poem she'd written the day she began her journal.

> *The future lays a path for me.*
> *Which one, my chosen destiny?*

Now she knew the answer. Her path was the same one David and Grey Wolf followed. She touched the cameo at her throat and smiled. Together, they'd found their destiny.

978-0-595-46934-5
0-595-46934-5

Printed in the United Kingdom
by Lightning Source UK Ltd.
133354UK00001B/108/A